D0950278

MIDNIGHT ROSE

"What do you want?" Diego asked.

"That is my question to you, *señor*. What do *you* want?
Why do you ask so many questions about La Rosa and her
hombres? Do you work for the sheriff, perhaps?"

Diego's vision began to clear a little, although the steady
pounding in his head continued. "No, I don't work for the
sheriff."

"No..." A slow smile curved her full mouth. Her low,
whiskey-coated voice grew softer. "But you are a stranger
to the Salinas, no? Why do you seek to know about La Rosa?
Perhaps it is the woman and not the *bandida* you wish to
know."

His body reacted instantly as she drew closer. He was
acutely aware of his nakedness beneath the blanket, even
more acutely aware of her feminine curves beneath the red
costume. A gentle fragrance of roses wafted on the night air,
filling his nostrils, making his head spin.

"You intrigue me, *Señor* Salazar," she whispered.
"Perhaps I will let you know La Rosa."

Robin Lee Hatcher

Midnight Rose

LEISURE BOOKS   NEW YORK CITY

A LEISURE BOOK®

November 1992

Published by

Dorchester Publishing Co., Inc.
276 Fifth Avenue
New York, NY 10001

To my editor, Alicia Condon,
for sharing my enthusiasm for *Midnight Rose* from the beginning,
when I said,
"...and La Rosa is a cross between Robin Hood and Zorro."
And
once again, to the *Thursday Night Gals*
—Lori Bright, Laurie Guhrke, Rachel Gibson,
Laurel Judy, Janet Mohr, and Sandy Oakes—
who have cheered La Rosa's exploits from first page to last
and helped make it such a fun book to write.
Viva la diferencia!

Midnight Rose

Preface

Portola and his Spanish explorers first laid eyes on the valley of the Salinas in 1769. The padres came next, establishing missions and bringing the white man's religion to the Indians who made their homes in the lush valley between the Gabilan and Santa Lucia Mountains. Spanish settlers soon followed, building their adobe haciendas on vast land grants bequeathed by the governor of Alta California. Later, the discovery of gold brought war and intrigue to the once peaceful valley.

After California was admitted to the Union in 1850, squatters (most of them disillusioned gold miners) moved into the Salinas Valley. They made constant trouble for the ranchers. Spanish and Mexican grants meant nothing to these desperate gringos. They saw vacant land and took it. Finally, a United States Land Commission was set up, before which every claimant under Spanish and

Mexican title had to present, within two years, his claim with documentary evidence. All lands for which claims were rejected were to be regarded as public domain.

Scheming lawyers, realizing the helplessness of these Spanish-speaking Californians, rushed in from all directions and prepared for a field day. Many of the ranchers went down in defeat, giving up their land and selling their cattle. Others willingly agreed to give up half of their land to lawyers in order to gain title and be free from squatters constantly declaring that the land was theirs.

In the midst of this troubled time, I have set my story. La Rosa is purely fictional, but I like to think there might have been such a woman to fight on the side of truth and justice. . . .

Prologue

"*¡Válgame Dios!*"

Startled from his sleep, Diego opened his eyes in time to see the horse rearing over him, front legs striking the air. He rolled away from the immediate danger even as he became aware of the thunder of hooves shaking the earth beneath him. It wasn't until he was on his feet that he realized the surprised cry had been a woman's.

"La Rosa, they come!" a man shouted.

The moon burst suddenly from behind a cloud, bathing Diego's campsite in a silvery-white glow. He had a brief glimpse of a red cape swirling through the air as the magnificent black horse spun on his hind legs to face the riders who had followed the woman up the hillside, skirting the boulders and deep ravines.

"There is no time, amigos," she called to them. "We must stand and fight."

13

The battle cry had scarcely left her lips when the first bullet whizzed past Diego's head. He dove for his rifle, once again rolling across the ground, this time toward the protection of a giant boulder.

Gun shots sounded all around him. Self-preservation demanded he return fire, but a glance at the masked faces of those closest to him made him hesitate.

"You'd best use your rifle, señor," a husky voice said. "If the gringos win the fight, they will not believe you innocent. They will kill you before you can tell them you are not La Rosa's hombre."

Diego turned his head to the right. Through the slits in the woman's red mask, he saw a pair of fervent dark eyes. Before he could form a reply or demand an explanation, another burst of gunfire exploded all around him. He decided he would choose to live and obtain explanations later.

He aimed his rifle high, hoping he could drive away those in pursuit without killing anyone. He pushed the red-masked bandolera—and the sultry sound of her voice—from his thoughts as he fired his weapon.

The battle didn't last long. Diego had chosen his campsite because it afforded him protection and a view of the surrounding area. No doubt, those were the same reasons his midnight visitors had chosen it. Those in pursuit had little hope of dislodging the woman and her band of outlaws.

At last, the gunfire died away, followed by the sounds of retreating horses. Silence fell like a heavy curtain around them. Finally, the woman stood and turned toward Diego, even as he did the same.

Her gaze moved slowly up the length of him, stopping when she was looking into his eyes. "You fought well, señor."

Before he replied, he gave her an equally careful perusal. Except for her black boots, she was clad entirely in red, from the snug hood that covered her hair, to the cape that draped over her shoulders and back, to the skirt—split for riding astride—that reached to a spot just below her knees. Beneath the cape, she wore a loose-fitting blouse. Her mask covered the upper portion of her face, from her forehead to the tip of her nose. Below the mask, he had a clear view of full lips and smooth, tanned skin.

She laughed, a throaty, seductive sound. "You do not know La Rosa? You are new to our valley, no?" She sobered. "I am sorry to have endangered you, señor. It is a poor welcome."

"Just what was this . . ." Diego began.

"La Rosa!" someone shouted. "Miguel is wounded."

She turned with a flourish of her red cape. She moved quickly, yet gracefully across the campsite. Curious and wanting answers, Diego followed her.

She knelt beside the victim and took hold of his hand. "Miguel?"

The masked man opened his eyes and looked up at her. "It is nothing. I can ride."

"We will have you to safety soon, amigo." She glanced up at the moonlit sky. "We must hurry."

Diego found himself ignored as the horses were quickly gathered. The woman bound the injured man's thigh, then assisted him to his feet. Another man joined her to help get Miguel onto his horse.

La Rosa paused as she took the reins of the big black gelding into her gloved hands, then turned to look over her shoulder. "Be careful, señor," she said to Diego. "It is often difficult these days to tell who is your friend and who is your foe. Things are not always as they seem." She swung up into the saddle and immediately spurred her horse forward.

Moments later, Diego's campsite stood empty and still. Soon he wondered if he'd merely dreamed the mysterious woman in red.

La Rosa.

If she were real, he would find her again.

Chapter One

Gardner Washington gazed out the window of his office across the sweeping plains and hills. From any window in the hacienda, he could look upon his land. Sixty thousand acres made up Rancho del Sol, sixty thousand acres of prime grassland covered with ten thousand cattle and four thousand horses.

"Things are very different now, *querida*," he said softly as he turned from the window, his eyes seeking the portrait of his wife above the mantel.

Francisca de la Guerra Washington smiled back at him serenely, forever young, forever beautiful.

He still missed her, even after twenty-two years.

A big man with a weathered face, his once sandy hair now turned steel-gray, Gardner Washington had lost little of his vitality or zest for life with the passing of time. He'd been blessed with a fine family and significant wealth, yet there were days, like this one, when he could think of little else but what he'd lost twenty-two years before.

He continued to stare at the portrait, his thoughts drifting back in time.

Gardner had spent most of his fifty-nine years in the saddle, the last thirty-four of them right here in the valley of the Salinas River, and he loved this land as fiercely as if he'd been born to it. Of course, it hadn't been a part of the United States when he'd come here. Alta California had belonged to Spain back then. Later, after it had passed into the hands of the Mexican government, he'd become a citizen of Mexico so that he could obtain a land grant for himself and his family.

"It is all very different," he whispered again. "I wonder what you would think of it." He waited, as if he expected her to answer.

Gardner would never forget the first time he'd seen Francisca de la Guerra. A girl of fifteen, she had come with her dueña to visit his employer's daughter. He'd lost his heart to her that very day and had wasted no time in petitioning her father for the right to court her. To his great joy, Francisca had returned his feelings. They'd married before the year was out. During their marriage, Francisca—his Spanish flower, he'd always called her—had given him nine sons and one daughter. She'd died right after giving birth to the twins, never reaching her twenty-seventh birthday.

So young . . . so long ago . . .

No, Gardner thought again as he gazed at the

painting, he'd never stopped missing her, not even after all these years.

He sat down on the chair behind his desk, glancing briefly at the letter that had arrived two weeks before from Texas. He hadn't time to reminisce about how things once were or what might have been. Today had needs of its own.

Once again, he lifted his eyes to Francisca's portrait. "What do I do about Leona ? How do I tell her?"

He closed his eyes as he rested his head in his hands, his elbows upon the smooth surface of the desk. He felt very old all of a sudden, and very alone. He needed Francisca's gentle wisdom. When it came to running the ranch or dealing with his nine sons, Gardner rarely felt uncertain. He was the head of Rancho del Sol, and his word was law. Through the years, he'd fought off all manner of disaster to build his ranch into the finest in the valley. He'd made the land his under Spain and then Mexico and now the United States. He was a man of influence and stature, a man listened to by his peers.

But Leona was another matter. For some reason, his daughter had always left him feeling out of his depth, even when she was just a baby. With the bat of an eyelash or the tiniest of smiles, she could twist his heart, making it almost impossible for him to be firm with her.

Perhaps it was because his youngest child, his only daughter, resembled her mother so much. Leona had inherited all of Francisca's beauty, including the thick, blue-black hair and the hint of violet in her wide, expressive black eyes. What she hadn't inherited, Gardner silently acknowledged, was her mother's compliant spirit.

Leona Desideria Washington had always been a headstrong child. She'd never understood why she couldn't—or at least, shouldn't—do everything her brothers could do. She'd chafed beneath the strictures which society—not to mention her father and brothers—placed upon a young lady. She was inquisitive and mischievous and intelligent and too often stubbornly independent, and she was definitely *not* going to like what her father had to tell her.

Gardner rose from his desk and strode across his office, stopping beneath Francisca's portrait and staring up at it for a long time. "What am I to do? It's been more than four years since Carlos died, and not a word. I thought the pledge was over, forgotten, a thing of the past. I wanted to keep her close to me." He sighed, feeling a great heaviness in his heart. "But it's a matter of honor, Francisca. I can't go back on my word. If it weren't for the Salazars, I would have died when I was still a boy. If I'd thought Dominguez would send another son in Carlos's place, I would have told Leona, but . . ."

He shook his head as he turned toward the door. He could talk to his wife's portrait forever, but it would change nothing. Dominguez *was* sending his son to California, and Gardner *would* have to speak to his daughter.

20

He would do it after the party. He could put it off no longer than that.

"Are your eyes closed?" Ricardo asked—for the fifth time in as many minutes—as he guided her out the back door of the hacienda.

"They're closed," Leona replied again, excitement and impatience mingling in her voice. "Where are you taking me?"

"I have a surprise for you. Don't peek."

She grinned. "I won't," she promised, knowing that it would be a difficult one to keep. She loved surprises, but curiosity was one of her worst traits.

Her twin brother's hands slipped over her eyes as they stopped walking. "I wanted to give you something special today. Are you ready?"

"Yes."

"Happy birthday, *gatita*."

As a child, she'd always hated it when her other brothers teased her, calling her *gatita*, a kitten, telling her she had a lot of growing up to do before she could be a lioness, as her name suggested. But she'd never minded the pet name from Ricardo. Perhaps it was because Ricardo understood her so well—sometimes almost better than she understood herself.

His hands slipped away from her eyes and she opened them, blinking against the bright sunlight. She gasped as she looked at the sleek golden mare with its flaxen mane and tail.

"She's yours," her brother announced proudly.

"Oh, Ricardo . . ."

"I knew you'd like her."

"She's beautiful." Leona stepped toward the mare and stroked her glossy coat. "Has she a name?"

"I've called her Glory. When she was born, I knew she was meant for you. Manuel has kept her at his place until now."

Leona turned to stare at her twin. "How old is she?"

"Three."

"You've kept her a secret from me for so long?"

Ricardo laughed. "You didn't think I could do it, did you? You think you can always read my mind. I'm glad to know you can't."

She returned his smile, knowing exactly what he meant. It was often disconcerting to find that Ricardo knew what she was thinking even before she told him.

"We'll go riding in the morning," he told her.

"I wish we could go now. Why don't we—"

"Father would never forgive us. We have guests coming for the *fiesta*. They'll be arriving soon, and you're the hostess. We'll go riding at first light."

Leona sighed. Her brother was right, as usual. Normally, if she wanted something badly enough, she could find a way around her father's objections, but he'd been acting a bit strangely for the past couple of weeks. There was an uneasiness, a sadness in his eyes that hadn't been there before.

"What is troubling *Papá*?" she asked her brother as they started back toward the hacienda. "Do you know, Ricardo?"

He scowled. "Why wouldn't he be troubled, with McCabe and the other *americanos* stealing so much land, driving so many people away?"

"It's more than that," she responded. "*Papá* has never been worried by a man like McCabe. Besides, *Papá* is an *americano*, too."

Ricardo was silent for a long while before his face broke into a bright grin, his dark eyes sparkling with mischief. "You're right. Perhaps he's more worried that his only daughter has become an old maid. Look at you, *gatita*. You are twenty-two today, and still you're not married. You aren't even betrothed."

She stopped, her look anything but amused. "You aren't betrothed, either, *mi hermano*, and yet no one feels there is shame in that. Why must I be in a hurry to be wed, just because I'm a woman? Is there nothing more important for me to do than keep a man's home and bear him children?" Her voice rose with increasing frustration. "Am I not just as able to help my father run the ranch as any of my brothers? Why should I have to live under another man's yoke? Do I not have my own father and enough brothers to tell me what I must do?"

Ricardo seemed to know he had gone too far. His smile vanished. "I'm sorry, Leona. I was only teasing."

She sighed deeply. "I know," she responded, forgiving him quickly. "I'm sorry I spoke sharply. I suppose it's because I'm tired. I slept little last night." She leaned over and kissed his cheek. "Thank you for Glory. She's the most beautiful

23

horse I've ever seen."

"You're welcome, *gatita.*"

"Now, I'd better hurry or I'll never be ready for the celebration." She walked toward the cool interior of the house.

The hacienda was aglow with lantern light and laughter. Gardner watched with pride as Leona moved through the large living area that bordered the open courtyard in the center of the house. She greeted their guests as they arrived, bestowing her lovely smile on one and all. She was equally charming to old curmudgeons and friendly young men, shy girls and weary matrons. He wondered sometimes how he could have sired anyone as beautiful as Leona.

Actually, he felt that way about all his children.

In his mind, he conjured up a picture of each of his sons. They were all handsome, each of them blessed with their mother's black hair and patrician features as well as their father's height. Strong and just men, unprejudiced in their views of others simply because of skin color or heritage, judging a man by his actions alone. He was more proud of his children than of anything else he'd accomplished in his life. They were his real legacy.

As Gardner stood musing, Tiago Cisneros approached Leona, his eyes filled with more than a fair amount of interest. Immediately, her oldest brother, Enrique, moved to stand behind her, his arms folded across his broad chest as he leaned against the wall at his back and scowled at the would-be suitor. Tiago exchanged only a few words before moving off to speak with another señorita.

Gardner suppressed a smile. His sons had inherited more than just their height from him. Like their father, they were all fiercely protective of Leona. Perhaps too protective.

Leona loved her brothers, but she'd always hated the way they'd tried to dominate her every move. They still did, even now that most of them were married and living in their own homes.

As soon as Tiago glanced nervously at something over her shoulder, she knew that one of her brothers was standing there, silently warning Tiago to be careful what he said and did to Leona. They'd been doing the same thing since she was eleven or twelve years old. That was when she'd first begun to show signs of developing into a woman. If any of them had ever listened to her, she could have told them they needn't worry about boys—or men—taking liberties. She was capable of handling such things herself. But, of course, they'd rarely listened when it came to their sister's friendships with young men. Not then, and not now.

When Tiago mumbled his apologies and moved away, she turned around. She didn't know it, but her scowl was almost identical to the one Enrique had given Tiago moments before. "Must you do that? Tiago is my friend. If he was bothering me, I would have sent him away."

"Feliz cumpleaños, niña." Grinning now, Enrique pushed off from the wall and stepped forward to give her a hug.

Despite herself, she grinned, too. She knew that Enrique would always think of her as a child. He'd been nearly ten years old when she was born, and he had always tried to take care of her, washing her skinned knees when she fell, wiping away her tears when she was hurt.

Enrique had known hurt, too. His wife had died in a riding accident several years before, leaving him with two small children to raise. For a time, Leona had feared that he would be like their father, quietly mourning the woman he'd loved and never again knowing the same happiness. But Enrique had recently begun courting a señorita from Monterey. Leona suspected that he might have found love again.

She was about to ask him about it when she heard loud laughter coming from the hall. She turned toward the sound as Manuel led his wife, Maria, into the courtyard.

"There she is," her second oldest brother said as he approached Leona, picking her up in his arms and twirling her around. "Happy birthday! Has Ricardo given you your gift?"

She nodded.

"And have you ridden her already?"

"No. I have to wait until tomorrow."

Manuel knew better than most how much she loved to ride. He'd been the one to first put her in the saddle and place the reins in her hand. He held a special place in her heart because of it.

Maria, large with the pregnancy of their fourth child, stepped up beside her husband. "Put her down, Manuel. You treat her as if she were still a little girl." She leaned forward and kissed Leona's cheek. "I never thought he would be able to keep silent about Glory. It has been a long three years."

"You'd best give your new horse to me to train," Alfonso said as he stepped into the gathering around Leona. "A *vaquera* needs a well-trained mount." He winked at her. "Or have you finally outgrown the desire to throw the *reata* at cows?"

"I'll train Glory myself, *mi hermano*." Leona returned the wink. "And I'll rope cows whenever I choose."

Alfonso, still a bachelor at twenty-nine, was the brother who had taught her how to twirl the *reata* above her head, then toss the loop over a cow's horns and pull it tight. He hadn't instructed her willingly at first. She had had to badger him into it. But she knew he felt a measure of pride in her skill.

Hearing more voices coming from the entryway, Leona lifted her eyes toward the door. Her smile grew as she moved away from her three oldest brothers.

"Mercedes," she called to her best friend. "When did you return from Vallejo?"

"Just this afternoon. You didn't think I would miss a *fiesta* for you and Ricardo, did you?"

Mercedes glanced quickly around her. "Where is Ricardo?"

"I'm not sure. I think he's showing someone my new horse. His birthday gift to me."

"Perhaps you would like to show *me* your new horse, pretty *señorita*?"

Leona turned around to meet Raul Hercasitas's appreciative gaze. She let out a tiny sigh. Dear Raul. He never seemed to understand that she was only interested in friendship with him. He hadn't even been dissuaded when he was told that she was promised to Carlos Salazar. He'd been even more persistent in the years since Carlos's death.

For a change, she was almost glad to see another of her brothers approaching, saving her from having to turn down another of Raul's offers.

José spoke a quick welcome to Raul, then took hold of Leona's arm. "Come say hello to Teresa. She has just managed to get the children to lie down for the night. They're always excited to stay over at their grandfather's house." He drew her away.

"*Gracias*," she whispered.

"*De nada*. You forget. I know Raul well. He is as tenacious as you." He grinned.

Leona elbowed him in the ribs but returned the smile.

José had learned just how tenacious his little sister could be when he'd begun teaching her to swim. She'd sunk like a rock more than once, and he'd had to haul her, coughing and sputtering, up onto the bank. Each time he'd suggested that she give up. She didn't need to know how to swim, he'd told her. She should be at home, learning to sew and bake bread. But Leona had been too stubborn. She'd wanted to learn how to swim, and eventually she had.

José's wife, Teresa, was seated in the living area just off the courtyard. She smiled serenely at Leona as she approached. The mother of four of Gardner's ten grandchildren, Teresa was everything Leona supposed *she* should be. Her sister-in-law thought of little beyond her home, her husband, and her children. Most important, she was happy just as she was, and she made her husband happy.

Before she could greet Teresa, she heard a giggle coming from an alcove shaded by tall green fronds. Her gaze quickly found her brother, Rafael, and his bride, Isabel, seated on a bench, obscured by deep shadows. The two had been wed four weeks before, and it was clear they were still caught in the throes of a grand passion and had eyes only for each other.

It was hard to believe that this lovesick man was once a boy who had taught his little sister to fence. They'd spent hours in practice—feint and attack, parry and thrust—until their foils seemed as heavy as broadswords, sweat ran down their backs, and their legs ached, neither of them willing to let the other win. Leona knew it had always slightly irritated Rafael to discover his pupil had become as proficient as her teacher.

"Eduardo will be acting the same way soon," Teresa said in a soft voice.

Leona looked at her sister-in-law, then followed Teresa's gaze across the room to where Eduardo was standing.

Just three years older than she, Eduardo had been the most likely to join in Leona's and Ricardo's escapades when they were little. It was this brother who had taught her how to shoot both a rifle and a pistol. It was Eduardo who had insisted that she be allowed to go hunting when several of the older boys had said she should be left at home. Eduardo was right beside her when she'd shot a bear as it attacked a herd of cattle.

It was plain to see that Eduardo was still interested in hunting, but bears were no longer his prey. His dark eyes were locked onto Jacinta Aguilar as she stood beside an imperious-looking dueña.

"I think you're right, Teresa," Leona said with a chuckle.

"And when are *you* going to fall in love, *mi hermana*?"

Leona smiled lightly and shook her head. Yet the question left her with a strange disquiet. Sometimes, even while she resisted the notion of marital bliss, she envied the love she saw so often when her brothers looked at their own wives. Sometimes she wished to be swept away by a grand passion, even though she knew she would never be satisfied to live the sedate life her sisters-in-law lived.

Not wanting Teresa to ask any more questions of that nature, Leona excused herself and wandered back into the center courtyard. She found another of her brothers just arriving.

Fernando guided his wife, Josefa, with a solicitous arm around her shoulders. Josefa, who at seventeen seemed hardly more than a child herself, was holding their first baby in her arms. Consuela, as pretty and as delicate as her mother, was just two months old and the apple of her father's eye.

"Buenas tardes," Fernando said as Leona walked up to the couple. "Come see our Consuela. See how bright her eyes are with interest. She notices everything."

Leona leaned close to Josefa's ear. "Has he started teaching her to read yet?" she whispered.

"No, Leona. Consuela is far too young for that," Josefa answered seriously, missing her sister-in-law's teasing tone.

"Well, don't be surprised if he manages it." Leona lifted her gaze to meet Fernando's and offered him a bright smile.

This brother was the quiet, studious one. It was Fernando who had taught her the joy to be found in their father's vast library. It was Fernando who had given her a real thirst for learning. He didn't care much for riding or shooting or roping but was happiest, instead, dealing with the business side of running Rancho del Sol or pondering matters of great importance to California or even the world.

Leona smiled to herself as another memory flitted through her mind. Even though she always mentally labeled him as the quiet one, it had been Fernando who'd beaten up the first boy who tried

31

to steal a kiss from Leona. Perhaps he wasn't so different from her other brothers at that.

"Our *gatita* gets older," a voice whispered in her ear, followed by a quick tug on her hair. "Has she still got her claws?"

"Gaspar!" She whirled to face him, her hands clenched at her sides as she glared into dark blue eyes so like their father's.

Of all her brothers, it was hardest for her to get along with this one. Just a year older than she and Ricardo, Gaspar had always enjoyed teasing her unmercifully. He'd delighted in pulling her braids and loved to turn creepy little bugs loose in her room and listen to her scream. Gaspar's contribution to her childhood education had been how to fight—or rather, how *not* to fight. Time and again, he'd pushed and teased and taunted her until she couldn't take it anymore. Then she'd lit into him, small fists flying. And, time and again, Gardner had pulled them apart and given her a lecture on the proper behavior of young ladies.

Still, she loved Gaspar and knew that he loved her equally.

"Happy birthday, Leona." He kissed her cheek. "We should do this more often. The *hacienda* never sees as many pretty *señoritas* as it does on your birthday." With another tug on her hair, he moved away, happily perusing every unmarried girl and woman in the room.

If Gaspar wasn't careful, Leona thought, they would find an enraged father on their doorstep one day, demanding that Gaspar do the honorable thing. She grinned. Perhaps it would serve him right.

Gardner looked over Padre Sanchez's head and saw Ricardo join Leona. Together, they walked to a bench in the center of the courtyard and sat down. Their heads nearly touched as they carried on a lively conversation. He knew Leona loved all her brothers, but she shared something special with her twin. They were very much alike, those two, despite being male and female. Perhaps that was why Leona had strained so hard against the rules society placed upon her, first as a girl, then as a woman. She'd always been determined to do whatever Ricardo did.

Again, Gardner smiled. None of society's rules—nor her father's, either, he conceded silently—had ever stopped Leona from doing what she was determined to do. Although she'd discontinued many of her tomboyish activities in recent years, at least when others were around, he knew very well what she was capable of doing if she had a mind to. Leona could ride as well as any man on the ranch, and she was more than just a fair marksman with a rifle. She excelled in fencing, wielding her foil deftly and with great precision. Who knew what other skills her brothers might have helped her learn behind their father's back. He shuddered, not even wanting to imagine the possibilities.

But tonight, she was every inch the proper señorita. Her full-skirted gown was a midnight-blue satin. A lace mantilla, the same color as her gown, covered her thick black hair, which she wore pulled back from her face. She looked much as her mother had looked when Gardner had first seen her.

Leona glanced up at that moment, and their eyes met across the room.

How shall I bear it if she leaves Rancho del Sol?

The question brought with it a physical pain to Gardner's heart. He knew, in many ways, that it would be like losing Francisca all over again.

He smiled at his daughter, then turned to circulate among their many guests, preferring not to dwell on such thoughts for the present. He'd already spent too many hours of this day lost in the past, remembering old heartaches. Tonight was a night for fun and celebration.

"Señor Washington?"

He looked at the young servant. "What is it, Anita?"

"There is a gentleman, a stranger, who wishes to speak with you. He said he is sorry to interrupt your celebration, but he has come a long way and it is important. He is waiting in your office."

Gardner felt a tightening in his chest. "Did this stranger give his name?" As he spoke, his gaze returned to Leona.

"*Sí, señor*. His name is Diego Salazar, from Texas."

34

Chapter Two

The adobe brick hacienda with its red-tiled roof and polished-wood floors had an unmistakable air of prosperity about it. It was obvious, from the size of the house and the fine furnishings which filled its rooms, that Gardner Washington had obtained great wealth in the years since he'd left the home of the Salazars.

Looking around the well-appointed office, Diego wondered why such a man could not find a husband for his daughter—no matter how homely she might be—without sending all the way to Texas.

You must do this, Diego, his father had told him. *It is fate that Señor McConnell is sending you to California, to the Salinas Valley. It is God's way of helping us honor our pledge. You will meet the señorita and see that I am right.*

He remembered how frail his father had looked, how weak his voice had sounded. Diego hadn't had the heart to argue with him any further, and so he had agreed to pay a visit to Rancho del Sol. But that didn't mean he had any intention of marrying this man's daughter, no matter what his father had promised. He would find some way to be released from the pledge, some way that would not bring Dominguez Salazar shame.

His gaze stopped upon the portrait of a woman above the mantel. There was an ethereal, almost other-worldly, beauty about the subject that defied explanation.

Now, if *that* were Señorita Washington, he might not be so quick to refuse her for his wife.

He shook his head in denial, discarding the thought as momentary insanity. Even if it were Leona—which he was certain it was not—artists were known for being more than a little generous to their subjects. If they always painted with complete honesty, no one would ever commission them to do portraits.

Unexpectedly, his mind conjured up another image. A masked woman, dressed all in red. A bandolera with an intriguing, sultry voice who rode astride a shiny black horse. He was certain no artist, no matter how talented, would be able to capture her beauty on canvas, a beauty Diego hadn't seen with his eyes but had felt in his soul.

La Rosa . . .

"Beautiful, wasn't she?"

Diego turned around, drawn suddenly back to the present, thoughts of La Rosa vanishing as quickly as they'd begun.

He needed no introduction to the man standing in the doorway. Except for the color of his hair, Gardner still fit Dominguez's description of him, even after more than forty years. He was tall, big-boned and broad-shouldered, with thick hair, now turned gray, and sharp blue eyes. His face was dark, weathered by years in the sun and wind.

"My wife," Gardner said, staring at the portrait behind Diego. "She died twenty-two years ago this night."

"I'm sorry, *señor*."

"Leona is a lot like her mother," he said softly. Then a curious smile curved his mouth. "And she is very different, too. Francisca would be surprised, I think, if she could see the daughter she gave to me."

Diego didn't even try to respond.

The older man's gaze dropped to his guest. "You look very much as I remember your father. How is Dominguez?"

"Not well."

Gardner nodded, his expression sad. "I suspected that must be the reason he was sending you now. After so many years, I thought . . ." He shrugged, then crossed the room and offered his hand. "Welcome to Rancho del Sol, Diego Salazar. It was always your father's greatest wish that our families would one day be united in marriage." He paused, then added, "Mine, too. Now that

37

Dominguez has sent you, the pledge will be fulfilled."

Diego frowned. Gardner made it sound as if Dominguez were the one who had insisted that the pledge be kept. Why didn't he admit that he could find no other man to marry his daughter and so had called on his boyhood friend to fulfill an ancient promise?

Gardner motioned toward the doorway behind him. "As you can hear, we have a house full of guests. The celebration is in honor of Leona and her brother's birthday. Come, you must join us. Later, when the guests have gone home, we can sit and talk in peace. I'm eager to hear about your family. Your father is a poor correspondent, and I an even poorer one."

Diego started to protest. He wanted to say that he had no intention of marrying Leona. He wasn't as honorable as his brother, Carlos, had been. He wasn't about to tie himself to a woman he didn't know just to satisfy some ridiculous oath. If he hadn't been coming to Monterey on business, he would have found some way to deny his father's request, no matter how ill Dominguez was.

Besides, Diego knew he would make a most unsuitable husband—for Gardner's daughter or any other woman. He wasn't ready to settle down. Not just yet. His work for Joseph McConnell's agency took him all over the country. His life was frequently at risk. What woman wanted a husband who was gone more often than he was home, a man who might never return if a job turned sour?

It wasn't as if he needed to marry to provide an heir for the Salazar ranch. His two older brothers were both married and had sired several sons between them.

When he *did* marry, Diego thought, it wouldn't be because two old men had long ago promised it would one day happen. He would choose whom and when he married. And it wouldn't be a señorita in California whom no other man wanted.

He tried to find the right words to explain things to Gardner. He felt certain that, once he had a chance to do so, he would be released from his father's pledge. Surely, this man wouldn't want such a reluctant bridegroom for his daughter.

But Diego was given no opportunity to speak before his host led the way out of his office and into the crowded house, filled with joyful guests.

Leona turned away from her brother, still laughing at something Ricardo had said to Mercedes. The laughter died in her throat as she lifted her eyes across the courtyard.

The man walking behind her father was above average height, although not as tall as Gardner. Lean and muscular, he was dressed like a vaquero. His black hair had been swept back from his face. His dark eyes were glancing at the people all around him as he drew closer to her.

It's him!

Her heart began to race in her chest, nearly taking her breath away. She felt as if she'd just run up a steep hillside, pursued by unknown forces.

He's come after me. Here, to Rancho del Sol. He found me.

Her eyes darted to her father's face. He was smiling at her, as if terribly pleased. How could that be?

She looked once again at the stranger.

Who are you? she wondered. *Where did you come from?*

Gardner reached out and drew her into the crook of his arm, kissing the top of her head as he turned around. "Are you enjoying your birthday, little rosebud?"

"*Sí, Papá,*" she whispered.

"Diego," he said, glancing at the man, "this is my daughter, Leona. Leona, this is Diego Salazar, the son of my dear friend, Dominguez."

Gardner's arm dropped from her back, and he stepped away, leaving her to face Diego alone. The blood was pounding so loudly in her ears she could scarcely hear her father's voice, let alone speak.

Diego reached out and took hold of her hand, bowing over it but not quite touching it with his lips. "Señorita Washington," he said as he straightened, "it is an honor."

His touch sent a shock down the length of her body, leaving her momentarily speechless.

It seemed impossible, but the young woman standing before him was even more beautiful than her mother's portrait.

Diego allowed his gaze to linger on her face, memorizing the finely sculpted features, from

40

the arched eyebrows to the round black eyes tinted with violet, from the petite nose to the high cheekbones, from the full, rose-shaded lips to the proud chin. Her thick hair gleamed with bluish highlights, fragile wisps curling around her face. The top of her head barely reached his chin. In fact, she appeared so diminutive that he wondered if a strong breeze couldn't carry her away. Her sun-kissed complexion was smooth and clear, and he had a deep urge to reach out and touch it with his fingertips, just to see if it were as soft as it appeared.

"Señor Salazar." Leona dipped her head and lowered her eyes. When she looked up again, she said, "Welcome to our home."

He felt like a tongue-tied schoolboy, staring at a girl at his first fancy dress ball. "Thank you," he managed to say, still unable to take his eyes from her.

"Carlos was your brother?"

He watched as she studied his face as intently as he'd studied hers seconds before. The assessment was thorough, and he knew she was trying to see beyond his looks to the man inside. This was no mere pretty face, he realized. He sensed her intelligence and discernment and was inexplicably pleased by the discovery.

"Was he, *señor?*" she asked, slightly louder this time. "Was Carlos your brother?"

"Yes. My oldest brother."

Suddenly, Leona glanced down at her hand, as if just realizing he still held it within his. A delicate blush colored the apples of her cheeks. "We were all sorry to hear of his death," she whispered, pulling her fingers free of his grasp as she spoke.

Why? he wondered. Why was she sorry? Because it had left her without a husband? A woman of her beauty must have plenty of suitors willing to make her a wife. She wouldn't need to send to Texas for a husband. Was it a matter of honor for her, too?

Or could it be she'd loved his brother?

No, she couldn't have loved Carlos. She'd only been a child of six when Carlos had visited the Washington family. His older brother had come to California to meet the girl his father wanted him to marry, then had gone back to Texas when he'd heard of the rebellion led by Sam Houston. Carlos had planned to return after Leona was of an age to marry, but he'd been killed during the war with Mexico and had never seen his betrothed again.

Poor Carlos. Had he known how beautiful his bride would be? Had he *wanted* to marry her?

"Will you be in California long?" Leona asked, meeting his gaze once more.

"I'm not sure, *señorita*." He was surprised—first by her question and then by his own reply. "We will have to see."

Gardner felt himself relaxing as he observed the exchange between the two. He'd never seen Leona react quite this way to a man before. It wasn't something she'd said or done or even the way she was looking at Diego. It was something intangible, but Gardner felt it nonetheless.

Perhaps Leona wouldn't object so strenuously to the idea of this marriage as she had to other offers when they'd been made. Maybe she would want it. Perhaps she'd actually been disappointed when there had been no wedding to unite the Washington and Salazar families.

Or maybe it was *this* man who would change her opinion of marriage. Perhaps she'd been waiting for him.

It would still be very difficult for Gardner to have his only daughter marry a Texan and leave California, but if she were to fall in love with Diego, it would make her leaving easier to bear.

Ricardo felt his sister's tension, a feeling mirrored in his own body, although he wasn't convinced it was for the same reason. It made him nervous to have this man watching Leona so closely. Did Diego see or hear things others did not? Had he somehow recognized her after such a brief meeting?

No, it wasn't possible. He was looking for problems where there were none. Still . . .

He stepped up to his sister's side, placing his left arm protectively around her shoulders and drawing Diego's gaze to him. "I am Ricardo, Leona's brother. Welcome to our *hacienda*, Diego Salazar. We've all heard the stories of your family's kindness to our father and of our father's love and respect for yours." Ricardo held out his hand toward Diego. "We hope we can return the hospitality, no matter how brief your visit must be."

The Texan took hold, and the two men exchanged an appraising gaze as their grips tightened in a silent test of wills.

I'll never allow you to harm Leona, Ricardo warned with his eyes. *Be careful what you say and do, or you will answer to me.*

Diego didn't so much as flinch beneath the warning glare of Leona's twin.

Gardner cleared his throat. "Ricardo, show Diego to one of the guest rooms. I'm sure he'd like to wash up after his long journey. Please forgive me, Diego. I was so eager to introduce you to my children, I forgot how tired you must be after such a long time on the trail. I'll have a servant bring in your things and put up your horse. You can meet the rest of the family later."

Diego let go of Ricardo's hand, a hint of a smile curving the corners of his mouth, as if he were somehow amused.

"Thank you, Señor Washington," he said as he glanced at Gardner. "I'd like to clean up. I'm not fit to mingle with your guests as I am."

"Think of my home as yours, Diego. If there is something you need, just ask for it. And, please, call me Gardner. After all, we're almost family."

Ricardo looked at his father, wondering at his words. He couldn't shake the feeling that there was more going on than just the visit of a family friend. He'd like to know what it was. He sensed that Diego's appearance at Rancho del Sol was going to have a profound effect on them all. Particularly on his sister.

"Come with me," he said to Diego, then began weaving his way through the crowd, trusting that their guest followed.

Leona stared after Diego and her brother. "Why is he here, *Papá*? Did he say?"

"What does it matter what brought him to California? It's good to have the son of my friend at Rancho del Sol. It will be good to hear about Dominguez and his family." His voice rose slightly. "Does a Salazar need an invitation to the home of Gardner Washington?"

She glanced at her father, surprised by the vehemence with which he'd responded to her simple question.

He cleared his throat. His face reddened. "Well . . ." He turned. "We have guests to see to, Leona." Abruptly, he strode away.

She stood alone for a long time after her father left her side. Her emotions were as tumbled as her thoughts. She didn't know which disturbed her more—her father's strange mood or finding Diego Salazar a guest in her own home.

Diego . . .

Even without a name, he hadn't been far from her thoughts—not since the moment Leona had ridden into his campsite at midnight, and he'd been forced to fight beside La Rosa.

Chapter Three

Mercedes watched the expression on her friend's face with interest. She was puzzled by the mixture of fear and excitement that brightened Leona's dark eyes. She felt a tingle along the back of her neck, a warning that Leona was headed for trouble.

She suppressed a grin, remembering how many times she'd felt that same little warning and ignored it, how many times she'd foolishly followed her friend into mischief.

Mercedes crossed the courtyard and stopped at Leona's side. "Who was that man?" she asked, glancing toward the empty doorway, then back at Leona. "I've never seen him before."

"Diego. Diego Salazar."

"Salazar?"

"From Texas." Leona met Mercedes's gaze.

"Carlos's brother?"

Leona nodded.

"Does it bother you that he's come, *amiga*?"

"No."

Mercedes wondered if Leona were telling her the truth. Even though she and Leona were closer than many sisters, Mercedes had never been sure how her friend had felt about her betrothal to Carlos Salazar or even how upset she had been by the news of his death. She'd secretly suspected that Leona was more disturbed by it than she'd ever let on. What other reason could there be for her remaining unmarried? Leona had certainly never been at any loss for suitors, yet she was still single at the ripe age of twenty-two.

Mercedes's mouth pressed into a flat line. She was in much the same position. She wasn't married or betrothed either, and she would turn twenty at the end of summer. If Ricardo didn't speak for her soon, she would have to decide on someone else or her father would choose a husband for her.

Unfortunately, Ricardo hardly knew she was alive—at least, not as a woman. He looked at her with the same affection that he felt for his sister—and that wasn't precisely the way Mercedes wanted him to feel when he was with her.

"You seem unhappy, Mercedes. What is it?"

She glanced at Leona and shook her head, not wanting to admit her true thoughts and yet unable to lie. "*Papá*. He is worried that I am not married, that I will have no one to care for me when he is gone."

47

"Señor Ramirez isn't ill, is he?"

"He is old. His heart is no longer strong." She shrugged, for the moment forgetting Ricardo. "But mostly, he is troubled. He must go before the Land Commission soon, and he fears he will be unable to prove his right to La Brisa. Twice now, Señor McCabe has come to our home, offering his help."

Leona grasped her friend's wrist. "Don't allow your father to trust Rance McCabe, Mercedes. He will lose his land if he does. That lawyer is no better than a thief. I fear he is even worse than most of us know."

"We will lose the land anyway, whether we accept McCabe's help or not."

"Please, Mercedes, ask your father to speak to mine again. There must be some way . . ."

Mercedes shook her head. "Even your *papá* cannot help if there are no papers to prove the Spanish grant. They are lost. We have searched everywhere."

"We'll find some way. Just don't allow McCabe to become involved in your father's affairs. He won't help you unless he also helps himself. Look what he did to the Perez family. He took half their land in payment—payment for nothing except to line his own pockets!" Leona's voice rose. "And what about the Estradas? They lost everything and have gone to Mexico. Their family has been in this valley for sixty years. It was their land, and McCabe stole it from them."

"Shh," Mercedes whispered, seeing heads turning in their direction. "Let's not spoil your birthday with such talk. This is a night to be happy, my friend."

Rance McCabe drove his buggy up to the front of the Washington hacienda. Bathed from without by the light of a full moon and from within by many lanterns, the house looked suitably festive.

McCabe grinned, thinking how surprised the ranchers and their wives would be when he walked into their midst. But he had heard that all of Gardner's friends and neighbors were invited to the party, and Rance McCabe was most definitely one of the man's neighbors. Bit by bit, he was acquiring land all around Rancho del Sol, driving the greasers back where they belonged— to Mexico. Soon he would wield more power in the district than Gardner Washington himself.

His jaw tightened. McCabe had been frustrated, upon coming to California, to learn that Gardner had already proven his claim to his land. This man was no uneducated fool who needed an interpreter to communicate with the U.S. Land Commission, like so many of the Spanish ranchers. This man was an American himself, an American who spoke Spanish as fluently as he did his native tongue, and he was literate in both languages as well. Even more troublesome, he was liked and trusted by the Spaniards in the area. Many of them had turned to him for help and advice about the Land Commission, and Gardner had taken it upon himself to warn them against McCabe.

Pasting a pleasant look on his face, McCabe climbed out of his buggy. He adjusted his suit coat, then headed for the door. He forced the tension from his shoulders as he waited. What had he to worry about, after all? Gardner had been only marginally successful in helping his neighbors. As a lawyer, McCabe knew a few more tricks and loopholes, not to mention having a friend or two on the Land Commission.

But that wasn't the reason he'd come here tonight. He'd come because he still wanted control of Rancho del Sol, and there were other ways besides the Land Commission to acquire it—or at least a part of it—and other ways to control Gardner's influence with his neighbors. The man had one very beautiful unmarried daughter, and her future husband would be certain to benefit by such a liaison.

The front door was opened by a petite servant girl. McCabe hardly gave her a glance as he handed her his hat and strode into the entry hall. "I'll find my own way," he said and moved toward the voices in the center of the house.

Upon reaching the doorway into the courtyard, he paused and swept the area with his gaze, not stopping until he found Leona. She was standing alone at the moment, a bemused look on her face, as if she were gnawing on a perplexing problem.

He felt a tightening in his loins just looking at her. Damned if she wasn't one of the prettiest women he'd ever laid eyes on. It would be a pleasure having her for his wife, even though she was half-Mexican. Of course, that wouldn't be a terrible handicap here in California. In fact, it might even give him more credibility among these people. If they trusted him, it would be all the easier to take their land from them.

Leona glanced in his direction. She looked away, as if she hadn't seen him, and then her eyes snapped back to meet his.

He felt her enmity clear across the courtyard. She hid it quickly, but not before he'd recognized it for what it was. He smiled, feeling the thrill of the unspoken challenge. He always enjoyed the sexual conquest of a difficult adversary. It was much more stimulating than taking a willing woman to his bed.

McCabe walked across the courtyard, feeling the hostile gazes as the other guests recognized him. In a matter of moments, silence had fallen all around him.

"Miss Washington, how very lovely you look." He took hold of her hand and raised it to his lips. "I trust that your birthday has been a pleasant one."

She withdrew her hand. "*Sí*, Señor McCabe," she replied with cool politeness. "It is always good to be with *amigos*. I did not expect you to be here." Her implication was clear.

McCabe offered a confident smile. "Who would not want to be counted as one of your friends, Miss Washington? Certainly it's my wish that we become friends. *Close* friends." He took a step backward. "However, I only stopped by this evening to pay my respects. Unfortunately, business demands my attention elsewhere." He bobbed his head in an abbreviated bow, then glanced around him quickly. "I don't see your father. Please tell him I was here and look forward to seeing him again soon."

Diego watched from a shaded corner of the courtyard as the auburn-haired gringo spoke to Leona. A handsome man in his late thirties, McCabe was dressed in the latest New York fashion, the cut of his coat almost concealing the slight paunch over his waistband. But his confident carriage demanded admiration and respect.

Leona appeared to feel neither of those two things for him.

After speaking a few more words, the man nodded once again, then turned and walked away from her. Diego could feel the tension in the air as everyone watched the man's departure—everyone except Diego. He kept his gaze on Leona.

Her delicate features changed. Where before he had witnessed a haughty politeness, he now saw only intense dislike, perhaps even hatred. He didn't need to look around him to know that other faces in the room would be revealing the same feeling. He wondered who the man was who had caused such a pall to descend on Leona and her guests.

Within moments, people began to stir. Voices rose as guests said their farewells. Gardner and

Ricardo appeared in the room opposite where Diego stood. He heard Gardner expressing his dismay that people were leaving so early, but it didn't stop the steady departures.

Ricardo stepped into the courtyard and approached his sister. "McCabe was here?"

Leona nodded.

"Why didn't you send for me?" His voice was angry. "I would have thrown him out."

"There wasn't time. Besides, it's best that we don't antagonize him intentionally."

"Why not? We—"

Leona placed her hand on her brother's arm. "The Washingtons can do more by working within the law, Ricardo. Let McCabe feel the sting of retribution from *others*." The look she gave him seemed to be saying even more than her words.

"I suppose you're right. It's only . . ." He let the words die unspoken, releasing a sigh filled with frustration.

"I know," she whispered, then turned as if to walk away. Her eyes collided with Diego's.

He stepped forward from the shadows. "Where have all your guests gone, *señorita*? I was on my way back to you, but it seems I am too late to join the celebration."

He knew she was wondering how long he'd been standing there. He even felt a bit guilty for his eavesdropping, but there hadn't seemed to be a good moment to reveal himself.

"Many have far to travel. It's better that they

journey together. Even on a moonlit night, the roads aren't always safe."

"I know. I had a run-in with some *bandidos* myself just last night."

Leona's eyes widened. "Where, *señor*? Were they close to Rancho del Sol?"

Her voice was as delicate as her features, and Diego felt a surge of protectiveness. He wanted to take her into his arms and offer her shelter from any danger, real or imagined.

Instead, he shook his head and answered, "No. It was nearly a day's ride south of here. I'm sure you have nothing to worry about. Besides, Rancho del Sol seems well-protected."

"It is." A tiny smile bowed her mouth. "Still, it's frightening to think that bandits ride so freely about the countryside. You are lucky they didn't slit your throat."

Diego merely nodded as his thoughts returned to the moment he'd first seen La Rosa. She remained clear in his memory, her red cape flying out behind her as her black horse reared on its hind legs. Her low, husky voice seemed to echo in his ears. *You do not know La Rosa?*

No, he didn't know the bandolera, but he wanted to. He wanted to know why a woman rode with a band of outlaws. He wanted to remove her mask and see the beauty that lay beneath it, the beauty he'd instinctively known was there.

"Is something wrong, *señor*?" Leona asked softly.

He glanced up, surprised by her question. And

disappointed, too. Disappointed that her voice hadn't sounded different—lower, more sultry. More like the mysterious bandida.

"No," he finally answered. "Nothing is wrong."

Her black eyes continued to study him, a tiny scowl drawing her finely arched brows close together in the middle of her forehead. She worried her lower lip with her teeth.

He quickly forgot his disappointment. *¡Dios!* She was beautiful even when she frowned.

Diego smiled. "I promise you, Señorita Washington. There is nothing amiss. Except that I am weary and could use a good night's sleep. If you'll pardon me, I will speak to your father before retiring."

"Of course." She lowered her gaze, allowing thick ebony lashes to brush against the golden skin of her cheeks. "Goodnight, *señor.*"

Could La Rosa be even half as lovely as this woman? he wondered briefly. Even at half, she would still be exquisite, for Leona Washington was beyond merely beautiful.

He would have to be careful, he realized, or he would fall under the spell of Leona's many charms. It would be better if he avoided such a pitfall since he had no intention of staying in California to marry the girl. It would be better for them both.

"Goodnight, *señorita*," he said, then moved quickly across the courtyard.

Chapter Four

Leona sat before the mirror in her bedroom, her fingers nimbly braiding her heavy blue-black hair into a single braid. Her eyes stared at her reflection without seeing it. Instead, she saw a tall stranger with intense brown eyes and a smile that revealed straight, white teeth.

Diego Salazar . . . Why had he come to Rancho del Sol? It was the same question that had troubled her throughout the long night.

Without Ricardo saying so, she knew her brother was worried that their unexpected visitor would somehow recognize that she was La Rosa, but Leona felt certain he wouldn't. She always disguised her voice whenever she donned her costume. It came naturally to her. She didn't even have to think about it. Not even La Rosa's men knew her true identity.

No, Diego Salazar would not guess that Leona

and La Rosa were the same person. But that still didn't explain why he'd come.

Her hands fell idle as she worried her lower lip with her teeth, her thoughts drifting to her father. She was suddenly quite sure that Diego's arrival at the Washington ranch was somehow connected to Gardner's strange mood. Perhaps she should have tried to find out what was troubling him before now. Guiltily, Leona realized that she should have been as concerned about her own father as La Rosa was about the ranchers along the Salinas.

A rap on her door interrupted her musings.

"*Sí?*" She twisted on the stool as her door opened.

Gardner's large frame filled the doorway. His dark blue eyes studied her for a moment before he stepped into the room, closing the door behind him. "Good morning, Leona."

"*Buenos días, Papá.*" She rose from her dressing table and crossed the room. Rising on tiptoe, her hands on his shoulders, she pulled him down to kiss his cheek. Then she gave him a thorough look. "You've seemed worried lately, *Papá*. Is something wrong?"

"No. I just wanted to talk to you before you go riding with Ricardo." He took hold of her arm and guided her back to the side of the bed. "Sit down, Leona."

"This sounds serious, *Papá*."

Gardner cleared his throat. "Well, yes, I suppose it is. It's about Diego."

Leona felt a sinking feeling in her stomach. She sat on the edge of the bed, her gaze locked on her father's face.

"I . . . I've known he was coming for about two weeks now. Dominguez wrote to me. I didn't expect him to arrive quite so soon, or I would have . . . I thought . . . well, I thought I had a little more time to tell you, to prepare you."

"Prepare me?" She frowned. "*Papá,* I don't understand. Why would you need to . . ."

Suddenly, she knew why. Without her father saying another word, she knew exactly why Diego had come to California.

Leona jumped to her feet. "Marriage?" she whispered.

Gardner nodded.

"But I don't know him."

"You will come to know him, just as you would have come to know Carlos if he'd lived long enough to return for you. You were a child when you met Carlos. You never knew him either, but you were betrothed to him."

"That was different, *Papá.* I *was* a child when the marriage was agreed upon. I grew up knowing I would one day marry Carlos. I accepted it without understanding it. Carlos was someone who lived far, far away, a dim face from my childhood. I don't think I really believed he would ever come to Rancho del Sol again. Besides, I didn't know what marriage meant."

Gardner let out a long sigh. "I know it's a surprise. It should have occurred to me that

Dominguez wouldn't let the promise of seeing our families united be forgotten just because Carlos died, but I . . ." He stopped speaking, then shrugged. "I gave my word, Leona."

"I don't want to marry Diego."

"You are my only daughter. Diego is Dominguez's only unmarried son. It is up to the two of you to keep the pledge. It is a matter of honor." He ran his fingers through his hair. "You are not the first couple to keep an arranged marriage, Leona. With time, you will come to care for him. I am certain of it."

Leona turned and walked to the window. Marriage. It sounded like a prison sentence to her. All her life, her choices had been made for her by her father and her brothers. Oh, she'd learned how to cajole and beguile them into stretching the rules. She knew how to ride astride and shoot and rope and do many other things which convention said she shouldn't, but what good did it do her? She couldn't allow others to see her skills. Propriety demanded that she ride sidesaddle now that she was grown. Except in the presence of her brothers and the Washington vaqueros, she couldn't rope or shoot. All that was expected of her—or would be tolerated by the outside world—was to look lovely, marry well, and produce children.

Marriage would mean nothing more than giving another man dominion over her life. She had enough masters already. She didn't want another. She wouldn't *have* another.

She turned to face her father. "I won't marry

him, *Papá*. I'm sorry. You will tell Señor Salazar that I must decline his offer of marriage."

"What?" Gardner's eyes widened.

"I'm sure he'll understand."

"Yes, but you don't seem to, Leona." Her father wore the darkest look she had ever seen on his face. "I owe everything to the Salazar family. They took me in when they could have left me to die like my father. Castillo and Elizabeth treated me like their own son. Dominguez became the brother I never had. We swore an oath before I left Texas that one day our children would marry. Now it will be done."

"But . . ."

Gardner's voice rose. "I'm a man of my word, Leona, and I am *still* your father. I have been lenient with you in the past. I've allowed you to do things of which your mother would never have approved. But it won't be so this time. If I say you will marry Diego Salazar, then you *will* marry him!"

"But, *Papá* . . ."

"No! We'll discuss it no more." He spun around and left her bedroom, closing the door hard behind him.

Leona couldn't believe it. He hadn't heard a word she'd said. He actually thought he could make her marry this man, this stranger, no matter what she wanted.

She felt herself grow cold. In truth, he *could* make her marry anyone of his choosing. Short of running away, she could not escape his decision.

But what if Diego didn't want to marry *her*? There could be no marriage without a bridegroom. Without Diego, her father wouldn't be so determined to see her married. Gardner loved her. She could even admit that he'd often spoiled her. He wanted her to be happy. She knew that. He would prefer her to marry someone she loved, the way he'd loved her mother.

So, she thought, all she needed was for Diego Salazar to refuse to marry her. Surely she could think of some way to make him do that. A tiny smile crept into the corners of her mouth as she returned to the dressing table, already mulling over the possibilities.

The compound at Rancho del Sol was much like a miniature fort. Besides the large main house, there were the quarters for the vaqueros, barns, stables, and corrals for the livestock, various outbuildings, a chapel, and a high, thick wall that protected everything within.

As Diego crossed the square that separated the house from the stables, he noticed how clean and well-run everything appeared. It didn't surprise him. Gardner had grown up under the iron hand of Diego's paternal grandmother, Elizabeth Salazar. A gringa from Massachusetts, Elizabeth was a no-nonsense sort of woman who'd run her home the way a general ran his army. Even today, at the age of seventy-nine, she could probably single-handedly defend her family's land against any intruder.

Still smiling as he thought of his grandmother, Diego stepped through the doorway of the stables. The air was filled with the sweet scent of new-mown hay. The hard-packed dirt floor was swept clean of debris. A fresh breeze flowed through the wide center of the building.

"It isn't fair!"

Diego stopped, surprised to hear the feminine voice, raised in anger, coming from the far end of the barn. He hadn't expected to find any of the Washington family up this early after last night's merry-making, especially not Leona.

"Why must I marry him, Ricardo? Why won't *Papá* listen to me? No one chose a wife for any of our brothers. They did that for themselves. Why must I be told whom to marry?"

"Because our father made a promise to Señor Salazar and now he must keep it."

Diego frowned.

"Well, I don't care what he says. I'm not going to marry Diego Salazar, no matter what *Papá* promised."

She didn't *want* to marry him? But . . .

A door swung open at the far end of the stables. Knowing he was about to be discovered eavesdropping for the second time in less than twelve hours, Diego started whistling. He meandered down the center of the barn, trying to look as if he'd just entered the building and had no idea anyone else was inside. He glanced into each stall, looking for his pinto stallion.

He stopped when he heard another stall door

open. Looking up, he saw Leona and Ricardo both staring at him.

"Good morning," he said, offering a nonchalant smile. "I didn't think I'd find anyone about so early after last night's festivities."

"Leona wanted to ride her new horse," Ricardo replied. "It was my birthday present to her. Would you care to join us, *señor*?"

Diego was ready to say no, but the hostile look Leona shot at her brother suddenly changed his mind. Although it shouldn't matter to him, he wanted to know why she disliked him so much after just one meeting. He hadn't done anything to make her feel this way. Why was she so dead set against marrying him? He'd known plenty of women who'd been more than willing, if only he'd been ready to settle down. With a little time, Leona would come to like him well enough. He didn't stop to think that her feelings about marriage mirrored his own.

"I'd like that," he said quickly. "I was just looking for my horse."

Ricardo pointed. "I think you'll find him in there."

"Thanks."

As he walked away from them, Diego heard Leona whispering something to Ricardo, but he couldn't make out what she was saying. Ridiculously, it made him grin, knowing she was angry at her brother for inviting him. This would probably prove to be an interesting ride.

* * *

Leona wanted to kick her brother in the shin, and it took a great deal of willpower to keep from doing so. "What did you do that for?" she hissed as soon as Diego's back was turned.

Ricardo only shrugged.

Silently cursing men in general and her twin in particular, she swung away from him, reentering Glory's stall. If she'd been able to settle in her mind just how she was going to make Diego leave Rancho del Sol without taking her as his bride, she might not have objected to his company, but so far, she didn't know how she was going to accomplish it.

She heard the whistling start up again. She glanced over the door and watched as Diego led his black and white pinto out of the stall. The stallion sidestepped, neck arched and tail held high, the whites of his eyes showing.

"Easy, Conquistador," Diego said softly. "Easy now."

The spirited animal snorted, shook his head, then quieted in response to his master's voice.

Leona watched as he saddled and bridled the stallion. She found she liked the way he moved around the horse. She sensed his strength, yet discerned a gentleness, too.

She felt a strange churning in her belly as she looked at the man's profile. The stables suddenly felt overly warm for this early in the day. Quickly, she turned back to Glory and lifted the sidesaddle into place, then tightened the cinch.

It really wasn't such a bad idea for Diego to join them on their ride, she told herself. It would give her a chance to study the man. Once she knew him better, she could more easily do the things which would most annoy him, thereby driving him back to Texas.

By the time she'd slipped the bit into the mare's mouth, Leona's confidence had returned, and she was feeling more herself. She was certain that, within a few days, Diego would leave Rancho del Sol, thankful that he had escaped a terrible destiny as Leona Washington's husband.

The moment Leona led her mare out of her stall, Diego strode across the breezeway. "Allow me, *señorita*," he offered.

As soon as she nodded, he placed his hands around her waist and lifted her onto the saddle. Even though he immediately released her, she would have sworn she could still feel his touch, even as he returned to his own horse and mounted up.

Mentally, she shook herself. What was wrong with her? She couldn't seem to keep a straight thought. She didn't care much for this disjointed feeling. It wasn't like her. She was normally very logical.

She drew in a deep breath. She needed this ride more than she'd known. It would clear the cobwebs from her head in no time.

Leona glanced at her brother as he joined her and Diego. He was riding the sleek bay gelding he'd named Raudo, which meant swift. It was an appropriate name. The horse had won countless races in the past few years.

As the threesome rode out of the stables, Leona found herself envying the men their freedom to ride astride. It made her angry, too. If every other female along the Salinas wasn't expected to ride sidesaddle—or worse, in a pony cart—she wouldn't have found it necessary to do likewise in order to appease her father.

She turned her head and found Diego watching her with intense brown eyes. It was the same way he'd looked at her two nights before after they'd fought off La Rosa's pursuers. Apprehension shot through her.

Would Ricardo's anxieties prove well-founded? Did Diego know the truth? Was it possible he'd recognized her as La Rosa?

She remembered the way she'd felt as she'd looked at him that night, his face bathed in moonlight. She'd thought him the most fascinating, most handsome man she'd ever seen. She'd wanted to know who he was. She'd even wished she could see him again.

Now he was here, and her greatest wish was to escape him.

The moment she passed through the gates of the compound, Leona kicked Glory into a gallop. She didn't care if Ricardo and Diego followed her or not. She needed to feel the wind on her face and see the earth flying away beneath her.

Chapter Five

"You heard?" Ricardo asked without preamble.

Diego turned his head and met Ricardo's direct gaze. He paused for only a moment before answering. "I heard."

"I thought so." He looked forward again, watching as his sister put more distance between herself and the two men.

There wasn't any reason for his feelings to have changed, but Ricardo found that his distrust for Diego had vanished overnight. In fact, he found himself liking the fellow a great deal. Perhaps it was because he sensed a strength of character in the Texan, a quality he found all too rare these days.

And there was something more besides. He sensed that Diego was a man capable of matching Ricardo's strong-minded, extraordinary sister. Diego Salazar was the first man Ricardo had ever felt that way about, and it pleased him.

Which didn't change the complications Diego's presence at Rancho del Sol presented. This man would not be as easily fooled as others. He would bear watching. Still, Ricardo couldn't deny the certainty that he and Diego were destined to be great friends.

"Is there another man she loves?" Diego asked, drawing Ricardo's thoughts up short.

"Leona?" He suppressed a smile, imagining his sister in love. "No. There is no one else. It's not marriage to *you*, señor, that's the trouble. It is marriage to *any* man that she wants to avoid. My sister wishes only to remain free to make her own choices."

Diego raised an eyebrow, as if he found Ricardo's statement slightly absurd.

"And what of you? It isn't love for my sister that's brought you here. Why have you come?"

The Texan's face became an expressionless mask. "Shouldn't we catch up with her? She might come upon some sort of danger, riding out there alone."

Ricardo stifled a laugh. It was on the tip of his tongue to say Leona could take care of herself as well as any vaquero, but he realized the folly of saying so just in time. Diego had seen La Rosa up close. He had talked to her, fought beside her. It would be better if he didn't know that Leona had the same strengths and abilities as the bandida.

"Sí. I think you are right," he replied instead. He pressed his heels against Raudo's sides, and the bay jumped forward in a burst of speed.

Within seconds, Diego's pinto had caught up to Ricardo's gelding. Neither man glanced at the other, and yet both were aware of the silent challenge. They leaned forward over the pommels of their saddles, communicating their desire for more speed to the animals. The ground thundered beneath the galloping hooves as a cloud of dust rose behind them, the horses matching each other stride for stride.

Leona heard their approach. She stopped Glory and turned, watching as the grinning men slowed their mounts, then trotted toward her. She felt a flash of betrayal as her gaze touched Ricardo's face. It was clear that a friendship had already begun between the two, and it made her feel excluded.

Quickly, she turned the golden mare around and urged her into a walk, allowing the young horse to cool off after the hard ride.

"Your stallion is a fine animal, Diego. He's the first I've found that could stay with Raudo. Perhaps while you're here you'll allow me to breed him with a few of my mares."

"Do you still have Raudo's dam? I wouldn't mind a foal by Conquistador out of her myself."

"*Sí*, we have her."

"Then we'll see what we can work out."

Leona's feelings changed to irritation as she listened to them. Normally, she would be as interested as Ricardo in crossing a fine stallion like Conquistador with one of their mares, but neither of them seemed to care about her opinion. They didn't seem remotely aware of her presence.

Why should they? she grumbled silently. *I'm only a woman.* The thought made her grind her teeth.

Ricardo trotted his horse up beside her. "You shouldn't have ridden off alone like that, Leona. Remember, there are *bandidos* in the area."

She didn't find him the least bit amusing and didn't deign to acknowledge his comment.

"Diego was worried that you might find yourself in danger."

"Was he?" she asked innocently. She turned her head as Diego approached her other side. "I assure you, *señor*. I am always safe on Rancho del Sol. The *bandoleros* wouldn't dare to come onto my father's land. Especially not during the day."

"I hope you're right, *señorita*. Still, I think you'd be wise not to ride so far from the *hacienda* without protection." Diego glanced past her, his gaze connecting with Ricardo's. "Why isn't something being done to catch these outlaws?"

Leona followed his gaze to her brother, waiting to see how he would reply.

Ricardo stared out at the rolling countryside for a long time. When he spoke, he made a broad sweep with his arm, indicating the vast expanse of land that spread like a green-gold sea before them.

"Our father could be considered a newcomer. He has been in California for only thirty-four years. Our mother's family, the de la Guerras, came to this valley many years before that. Our ancestors have lived by the Salinas for nearly seventy years. We have raised our cattle here. We have raised our children here. This is our home. The land is ours."

Ricardo turned his head, his jet-black eyes meeting Leona's. She knew he was warming to his topic and feared they were in for a zealous oration from her passionate brother.

Ricardo's gaze slipped to Diego. "The *californios* have always been a happy people. We raised our cattle for tallow and hides. We enjoyed our *fiestas* and *fandangos*. We shared our prosperity with those who had less. We welcomed newcomers into our midst. Their nationality did not matter. *Americano*, Irish, English. It did not matter. Men like our father were as much *californios* as any Spaniard because they loved the land and the people. Our allegiance was to California, not to Mexico or Spain. We cared little who claimed ownership as long as they left us in peace and allowed us to govern ourselves."

Leona felt her thoughts being pulled back in time to her idyllic childhood. It had been just as her brother described it. No, it had been even better than his words could express. She yearned for that time of peace and plenty when everything had seemed so much simpler. Such a time seemed far removed from the reality of today.

Ricardo's features hardened. "But now the government has allowed dishonest men to take everything away. The *americanos* do not understand our way of life. They think we are lazy, shiftless. They think we are stupid because so many cannot speak their language. They cheat our friends and our neighbors out of their land." He snorted. "When we cried unfair, the government set up the Land Commission to settle claims, but the stealing goes on. Lawyers like McCabe are the real outlaws, not the *bandidos*."

"Ah, yes, the *bandidos*. Tell me about their leader. Tell me about La Rosa," Diego prodded gently. "What do you know about her?"

Leona's breath caught in her throat as she looked at the Texan's face and saw the intense curiosity in his eyes. She wanted desperately to change the subject. She opened her mouth to speak but was interrupted by her brother.

"La Rosa is not a thief, *señor*. She is a champion of the people. She takes back what was already stolen. She worries McCabe and makes him yelp like a scalded dog."

"Ricardo, please," Leona said quickly when he paused to draw a breath. "May we talk of something more pleasant than outlaws?" She turned her eyes upon Diego. "I would like to hear about Texas. Please, tell us about your family."

Diego was struck again by the delicate beauty of the woman riding beside him. It didn't surprise him that she didn't want to hear about the exploits of roving bandits. This woman was the type who made men want to shelter her from the harsh realities of life. Yet, even as that thought crossed his mind, he recognized that there was a wealth of courage packed into her small frame. His grandmother would take a liking to her, he was sure.

"What makes you smile, *señor*?" she asked.

"I was thinking about my grandmother. Elizabeth Bartholomew Salazar, once of Boston, Massachusetts, but a Texan at heart. She and your father are a lot alike, I think."

"How is that?"

"She judges men by their actions, not their skin color."

"*Sí*," she said softly, "that is like my father."

"But unlike many others, she always wanted Texas to become part of the Union. There were many who disagreed with her, but she's a woman who makes up her own mind about things. She loved her husband and her family and was happy with her home on the frontier, but she never stopped being an American. I think if her son and grandsons hadn't fought against Mexico, she would have taken up a rifle herself."

Silently, he confessed that his grandfather, Castillo Salazar, wouldn't have felt the same. He'd been proud of the royal Spanish blood that had flowed in his veins. He'd never stopped grieving over Mexico's independence from Spain. It was just as well he'd died before Texas declared its own independence. It would have broken his heart.

"Our father was also proud to be an *americano*," Ricardo interjected. "He was glad to see California become a state. But the government has made no effort to protect those who were here first. We are too far away and too easily forgotten. My father only wants justice for those he has known for many years."

Diego was relieved by that bit of information. He didn't want to be on opposite sides of the fence with his father's dearest and oldest friend. "Isn't that what the Land Commission is supposed to be doing?"

Ricardo's black eyes became like granite, unable to conceal his anger. He opened his mouth, but before he could voice his reply, he was interrupted.

"Ricardo!"

The three riders pulled up their mounts in unison and turned. A rider was galloping toward them at breakneck speed.

"Ricardo!"

"It's Paco," Leona said to her brother. "What could have brought him here so early?"

Her brother shrugged, then moved his horse away from Leona and Diego, going forward to meet the man. When Paco stopped his horse, he spoke to Ricardo in an excited but low voice, gesturing dramatically with his hands. Diego strained to catch part of the conversation but failed.

Finally, Ricardo returned. "Paco needs my help," he said to Leona. "I must go with him."

"What . . ." she began.

He shook his head. "Continue your ride with Diego, *gatita*. It is nothing of importance."

Diego's gaze moved from Ricardo to Leona and back again. He sensed a taut undercurrent flowing between the siblings, yet had no explanation of why. It bothered him. Diego always preferred answers rather than questions.

That was one of the reasons he was so good at his job. He never let a question go unanswered. Never.

Leona stared into her brother's black eyes, trying to read what he was thinking. She knew without asking that Paco had brought word from the McCabe ranch. She knew that he wouldn't have come so early in the morning if it weren't urgent for La Rosa's band to act soon. What she didn't know was why. Was McCabe about to enact a bit of thievery of his own which needed to be stopped, or was it La Rosa's chance to take something away from him?

"Go on," she said, sounding much more serene and uninterested than she felt. "You were spoiling our ride anyway with all your talk of politics and lawyers."

Ricardo grinned at her, then glanced toward Diego. "We'll talk again, Diego Salazar."

A moment later, he was galloping away.

Leona let out a long sigh. "If I know Paco, he needs Ricardo to be his excuse for not returning home last night." She turned Glory around. "He was probably drunk, and now he wants my brother to lie and say he stayed at our ranch. I hope Paco's wife takes a broom to them both."

Diego's eyes widened, and then he laughed, a rich sound that rose from deep in his chest.

Her pulse jumped. Her stomach tightened. Her mouth felt suddenly dry.

"Do you always wish such things upon your brothers?" he asked, his voice filled with amusement.

She felt a little dizzy as she stared into his sparkling eyes, but she managed to respond sensibly. "With nine of them, there's always one who deserves it."

"I see your point, *señorita*."

Leona drew a deep breath, determined to restore her equilibrium, and she knew just the topic that would do it. Nothing stopped her colder than the thought of marriage. "Perhaps, Diego, since our fathers are so eager for us to marry, it would be all right for us to call each other by our given names."

The humor vanished from his face.

"And what about you, Diego? Is it *your* wish to marry me?"

"*Señorita*, I . . ."

"Do you want an unwilling bride?"

He didn't even try to respond this time. He simply stared at her with that unsettling, intense look of his.

"I wouldn't make you a good wife."

"Why not?"

An exasperated groan slipped through compressed lips as she dismounted and began to walk, leading her mare behind her. She was angry at herself for telling him she didn't want to marry him. She should have held her tongue and followed through with her plans. She should have found out what he wanted in a wife and then shown him what a poor one she would be.

His hand caught hold of her wrist. She stopped quickly, surprised to find him standing beside her.

"You didn't answer my question, Leona. Why wouldn't you make a good wife?"

"And you didn't answer mine," she countered, her voice quivering. "Do *you* wish to marry me?"

"It's the honorable thing to do. It would please our fathers and fulfill the pledge."

"So I'm told."

His grip loosened on her wrist, then his fingers slid down to take hold of her hand. He raised it toward his lips, his gaze never moving from her eyes. His mouth brushed her knuckles.

Dozens of men had done the same thing in recent years, but never had she felt a kiss all the way to her toes.

"You might find that you could grow to like me if you gave yourself the chance," he whispered.

She didn't say so, but that was exactly what she was beginning to fear the most.

Chapter Six

The Ramirez hacienda was small by many standards, but Mercedes had always thought it had a special charm. She especially liked the small patio in the center of the house with its many green plants. Even during the hottest days of summer, she could almost always find shade and a cool breeze here.

It was also here that she could sit and dream, undisturbed, about Ricardo Washington.

But she wasn't thinking about Ricardo this morning. She was thinking, instead, about escaping to her room—or anywhere away from Rance McCabe's lascivious gaze.

"There are ways that I can help you, Mr. Ramirez," McCabe said to her father, finally looking at him. "Without the documents to prove your grant, it will be difficult to run the squatters off your land, but it can be done. I can do it. If you do nothing, you'll lose it all anyway. This way, we can save something for you and your family."

He turned his apple-green eyes on Mercedes again. She shivered, hating the way he made her feel—unclean, stained, sullied.

"You have your wife and daughter to think about, Mr. Ramirez. Do you really want to force them to start all over again in Mexico? That's what will happen if you don't allow me to represent you before the Land Commission. You'll lose this ranch and everything on it. With gold miners and settlers pouring into California, it'll be hard for you to find a place to live. Don't put your family through that hardship."

Mercedes felt chilled to the bone. She would have sworn she could look into the lawyer's eyes and see only the blackness of his soul. It frightened her. Worse still, she saw a strange mixture of lust and hate in his expression. His gaze moved over her face and down to her breasts, then up again.

McCabe picked up his hat and rose to his feet. He nodded to Sebastiano Ramirez. "Well, you think about it. But don't wait too long. I'm a busy man. I've got my own ranch to run as well as my law work. I'll need some time to prepare your case if you're to have any hope of winning." Turning, he bowed slightly toward Mercedes. "Perhaps you could see me to the door, Miss Ramirez."

She glanced at her father and felt a sick tightening in her stomach. He seemed so much older than he had just a few months before. His dark hair was streaked with gray. Deep lines were carved in his forehead. His movements seemed slow, measured, even difficult. He was staring into space, as if he were now completely alone. She wanted to call out to him, to somehow bring back his vitality, his will to fight.

Instead, Mercedes rose from her chair and, with head held high, led the way out of the courtyard.

Pausing at the front door, McCabe took hold of her hand. "Talk to your father. He must be made to understand that he needs my help. Soon." His voice lowered. "If it's my fee he's worried about, perhaps you could help, Miss Ramirez."

"Me?" Her eyes widened.

"We might discuss other options of payment besides dollars or land." His fingers squeezed her hand. "You are a desirable young woman. I'm sure you could think of some way to compensate me for my help."

She thought she might be sick.

McCabe grinned. "You think about it. There is a great deal I can do for your father if I have your cooperation." He released her hand. "Without your help, who knows? I might not be able to save anything for him." He turned and left.

He was scarcely outside before Mercedes closed the door, then leaned her forehead against it, trying to quell the nausea that churned in her stomach. She was more frightened than she'd ever been in her life. To think that a man could say such things to her, and she was helpless to stop him. She didn't dare tell her father. Not now. Not with the way he looked.

Drawing a deep breath and swallowing hard, she finally found the strength to return to the patio. Sebastiano looked up at her as she stepped into the sunlight filtering through the greenery. Defeat and despair were written in every line of his face.

"*Papá*," Mercedes began, "please talk to Señor Washington. Leona says . . ."

"There is nothing Gardner can do for us, Mercedes. His lands were saved because he had papers to prove his right to them. Besides, he is a *gringo*, an *americano*. They would not take his lands, even if he could not prove ownership."

"That isn't fair of you," she chastised softly. "He has been your friend for many years."

Sebastiano nodded. "You are right, *hija*. It is not fair of me, and I am ashamed for thinking it. But *Señor* McCabe speaks the truth. Judging by the past, he is the only one who can help us save at least some of our land. Without him, we lose everything. Gardner Washington can't change that."

"Let me try, *Papá*. Let me speak to Leona's father again if you will not."

Sebastiano's gaze fell to the tiled floor of the courtyard. "If you wish to do so, Mercedes, you may."

"*Gracias, Papá*," she whispered, but his permission didn't quiet the fear in her heart.

Diego's thoughts were glum as he cantered his horse along the road to Monterey. He had cause to wonder if he'd taken leave of his senses. He'd spent the journey out to California coming up with all the logical reasons why he couldn't marry Gardner Washington's daughter, and within twenty-four hours, he'd found himself telling her that their marriage would be the honorable thing to do.

She didn't want to marry him. He didn't want to marry her. What on earth had possessed him to say what he had? He hadn't been so long without a woman that he was *that* susceptible to a pretty face.

He shook his head, trying to drive the woman's image from his mind. He had other things to think about now besides Leona.

He slowed his pinto as the waters of Monterey Bay came into view. Ships dotted the harbor, rocking gently with the tide. Nestled beside the sandy shores was the city of Monterey. For decades, it had been the provincial capital under Spain and Mexico. Now, with San Francisco drawing the gold miners and gamblers and the new state capital in Vallejo taking away the seat of government, Monterey seemed quiet and at peace. "The most pleasant and most civilized looking place in California when I was there in thirty-five," Joseph McConnell had said of it.

Joseph was the reason Diego had come to Monterey today. The man he worked for would be expecting a report from him soon, and he hoped Heath Curtis, their contact in Monterey, would be able to help provide a few answers.

He trotted Conquistador across a wooden bridge, his eyes ever watchful. He saw an old man driving a team of oxen down a dusty street. Outside the door of a small adobe house, he witnessed a vaquero stealing a kiss from a girl, who then giggled and rushed inside. Three soldiers leaned against the shaded side of a two-story building, their conversation dying as they watched Diego ride past them.

Joseph's instructions were easy to follow, and Diego found the Curtis Tavern without delay. The tavern was close to the water, the better to serve sailors off the ships. The single-story building was built against a sloping hillside, partially protecting it from the buffeting winds that blew in off the ocean.

Diego dismounted and wrapped Conquistador's reins around the hitching post. With another quick glance up and down the street, he stepped into the dimly lit tavern, then waited for his eyes to adjust.

"Buenos días, señor," a soft, feminine voice said from the recesses of the room.

His vision improved as the barmaid came toward him, swishing her bright red skirt from side to side with her right hand.

"Carmencita has not seen you in here before." She wore her white blouse pulled down from her shoulders, and her generous breasts barely kept from overflowing the low-cut neckline. She stopped a few feet away from him and gave him a slow perusal, starting at his boots and working up until her gaze met his. "Is there something Carmencita can do for you, *amigo*?"

"A beer."

The barmaid feigned a pout. "Only a beer, *señor*?" She winked at him and dropped one shoulder suggestively.

He grinned. "Only a beer."

Diego walked to a small table and sat with his back against the wall as Carmencita ordered the drink from the man behind the bar. Judging by Joseph's description, the bartender was Heath Curtis, but Diego wanted to be certain before he spoke to him.

One thing a man learned to do, when he was in Diego's line of work, was wait.

Leona turned expectantly when the knock sounded at her bedroom door. "Come in," she called.

Ricardo entered upon her command.

"What did you learn?" she asked the moment he'd closed the door behind him.

"McCabe has arranged to sell everything from the Estrada ranch to a dealer in Monterey." Her brother's reply was made in a low, confidential voice. "It will be taken to Monterey this afternoon and loaded aboard a ship in the harbor tomorrow. McCabe has spoken of the shipment to many people, hoping you will get wind of it. It's a trap, meant to catch you. He has many guards, but most will travel out of sight of the wagons. He's certain you won't be able to resist the challenge."

"Then he shall not be disappointed." Leona smiled tightly. "But the surprise shall be ours."

"*Gatita* . . . we cannot ride by day. It's too dangerous."

"Will Johnny be with McCabe's men?"

"*Sí.*"

"Then we won't ride by day. Johnny must find some way to delay the wagons. They must be forced to travel by night or stop along the way until dawn. Can he do it?"

Ricardo shook his head, then shrugged.

"Get word to the others. Tell them to meet by the bent oak an hour after dark. Tell them to be extra cautious. McCabe may have men watching the roads for any activity."

"Leona . . ." His tone was one of doubt and concern.

She met her brother's dark gaze with an unflinching one of her own. "We *will* do this, Ricardo. The Estradas were our friends. They had a rightful claim to their land, and McCabe cheated them out of it."

He drew closer to her, placing his hands on her shoulders. "You are only one, *gatita*. You cannot right every wrong."

"No," she agreed softly, "not every wrong. But I will do what I can when I can."

Ricardo shook his head again before turning away. "I will get word to Paco and the others." At the door, he stopped and glanced behind him. He stared at her in silence for a long time, then offered a slight bow. "Be careful, *mi hermana*."

"*Sí.* And you, *mi hermano.*"

*   *   *

Diego braced his elbows on the table. "Is there any truth to the complaints?" he asked the man across from him.

Heath nodded. "Yeah. Plenty of it. McCabe's as oily a snake charmer as I ever seen. I'm not sure about the men on the commission. They don't come into a place like this, so I haven't had a chance to meet 'em. McCabe may be payin' one or two t'see things his way, but I think it's more likely he's just good at what he does. Folks that don't do what he wants . . ." He shrugged. "He finds other ways to get rid of them."

Diego frowned. "Why hasn't something been done if it's so obvious?" he wondered aloud. "Why was the government forced to go to McConnell for help with this?"

"Obvious, sure. But provin' it's something else. You and I both know that. McCabe was a rich man before he come here, and he's even richer now. He's sly, and he's dangerous, too. People are afraid of him. It won't be easy to prove he's done anything wrong. 'Specially with how most white folks feel about Mexicans. Actually, sentiment's runnin' high against all foreigners." He paused a moment, his blue eyes direct. "I'm not sayin' that's how I feel. That's just how it is."

Diego nodded, not taking personal offense at Heath's words. He'd faced his share of bigots, and he'd already judged that Heath Curtis wasn't one of them. But knowing Heath was a fair-minded man didn't stop a flare of anger for those who weren't like-minded from heating his blood.

Just who were the *real* foreigners? he wondered. The Spanish Californians had been there long before the discovery of gold had brought Americans pouring in. He'd seen the same thing happen in Texas—the Anglos coming from the States, then trying to drive out those who'd been there first. It had happened to his own family, and he'd seen it with the Indians, too, tribe after tribe forced onto reservations because others wanted their land.

There was little he could do about such attitudes, but the prejudice, the stupidity, angered him nonetheless.

"McCabe isn't the only one tryin' to drive 'em out," Heath offered. "You know it as well as me."

"I know." Diego picked up his beer and drained the glass, then leaned back in his chair. "What about this La Rosa I've heard about?"

"Ah . . ." Heath chuckled. "It didn't take you long to hear of our Robin Hood of the Salinas, did it?"

"Robin Hood?"

"You've heard the English legend, haven't you? Robbin' from the rich to give to the poor?"

"Yes. Yes, I've heard the story."

Heath turned his head and motioned for Carmencita to bring two more beers. When he turned back toward Diego, he said, "Well, that's what the stories say she does. Except from what I hear, there's only one rich man she takes from."

"McCabe?" Diego finished for him.

"McCabe."

"A *señorita* with her own personal vendetta against McCabe. Sounds to me like La Rosa is swimming in dangerous waters."

Diego fell silent as he remembered the woman in red, astride her black steed. *¡Vive Dios!* He would like to see her again, if only to be sure she was as he remembered her.

"La Rosa does not fear danger, *señor*." Carmencita stopped beside him, holding the beer glasses in her hands. "Anyone can tell you that."

Diego looked up at the serving girl. He wasn't surprised that she had overheard his last comment. He'd seen her drawing close to the table. "What do you know of the *bandida*?" he asked.

"I know that she has helped many people. And not just her own kind, either, *señor*. She has seen that poor *americano* families have food and shelter, too."

Diego raised an eyebrow, allowing a note of sarcasm into his voice. "A literal paragon of virtue." He glanced at Heath. "Why hasn't the sheriff tried to capture the outlaws?"

Carmencita set the men's beers down with force, causing the frothy liquid to slosh over onto the table. "They will never catch La Rosa. No one would ever tell the sheriff anything about her." She spun around and marched away, disappearing into a back room behind the bar.

"I think I made her angry," Diego said as he picked up his glass.

Heath grinned. "But did you find out what you wanted to know?"

"I think so." He raised the drink toward his lips. "Yes, I think so."

Chapter Seven

"I have a bad feeling, *señorita*," Dulce whispered. "Do not go tonight."

Leona glanced over her shoulder at the maidservant. She couldn't see the girl's face in the darkened bedroom, but she could hear the tension in her voice. "You *always* have a bad feeling, Dulce Castro. It means nothing. I'll be all right."

Dulce laid her hand on Leona's arm. "*Vaya con Dios, amiga*. I will pray for your success and safe return." Stepping back, she held out the red rose toward Leona.

Leona took the bright flower, mindful of its thorns, and slid it into the deep pocket of her dress. Then, impulsively, she hugged the girl.

"*Gracias,*" she whispered.

As she released Dulce, she offered an encouraging smile before leaving the bedroom through the open window.

Hugging the shadows, she slipped through an opening in the wall that surrounded the hacienda and followed an arroyo away from the compound. It would take her about ten minutes to reach the hiding place where she would find Pesadilla, her black gelding. She knew Ricardo would have the horse already saddled and bridled for her.

As she jogged beside the stream bed, she thought of Dulce. Besides Ricardo, the girl was the only person who knew La Rosa's true identity. Leona had needed someone within her own household to help hide her absence whenever she was away. Someone she could trust. Who better than someone who had suffered at the hand of McCabe?

Dulce's brother, Victor, had been the first to lose his home to the gringo lawyer. Victor Castro hadn't been a wealthy rancher. His home and piece of land had been small by many standards. But they'd meant everything to him. With a little legal maneuvering, Rance McCabe had taken it all away.

Victor had protested to anyone who would listen, but to no avail. He'd sworn he wouldn't let McCabe get away with it, and finally he'd told his sister he was going to confront the lawyer about his thieving ways. It was the last time she'd seen him alive.

A few days later, Victor's body had been found. He'd been shot through the heart. The sheriff had blamed the murder on bandits and investigated no further.

It was then that Dulce had come to work at Rancho del Sol as Leona's personal maid. Seeing the girl's great sadness had stoked a fury in Leona's breast that couldn't be denied. She couldn't sit idly by and watch people suffer.

Not long after that, La Rosa made her first midnight ride.

The tall black horse nickered as Leona entered the narrow cove that obscured the corral and child-sized house. She and Ricardo had found this spot, sheltered by the hills, when they were little. It had become their own private hideaway. Later, after much pestering, their father had helped Ricardo build the adobe dwelling and put up a corral. The vaqueros knew of its existence, but it had always been understood that no one ever went there except for the twins. Even to this day, it remained their sacred ground.

Leona paused beside the gelding and stroked his muzzle. "You're ready for a good run, aren't you, Pesadilla?" she whispered. "I understand, muchacho, but you will not always be confined by this small corral. The time will come when you may be seen by day along the Salinas, and no one will wonder if you belong to La Rosa."

The horse shoved her with his nose.

She laughed softly. "It must be soon or you will grow fat on all the hay and grain Ricardo brings you, no?"

The black snorted and shook his head, as if in disagreement, then stomped his hoof impatiently.

"*Sí*, it is time we go. I'll only be a moment more."

Moving deftly by the light of the moon, she entered the adobe building where she'd spent so many hours as a child. She didn't bother to strike a match and light the lamp. She knew the interior of the small playhouse as well as she knew her own face.

She pulled the sofa away from the wall, then knelt and felt for the notch in the wooden flooring. Moments later, she reached into the secret place beneath it. Her fingers closed around the burlap bag hidden there and pulled it out.

Her heart began to beat faster as she changed out of her dress and petticoats and into the red costume. It was always the same. She felt like a different woman once she donned the attire of the bandolera. She felt free, even slightly exhilarated.

Quickly, she hid her other clothes beneath the floor, then pushed the sofa back into place. She picked up her sword and firearms, along with the red rose which came from the rose bushes that flowered year round in the special greenhouse Gardner had built for Francisca many years before.

Then, Leona hurried out to her waiting steed, a secret smile on her lips. Tonight, she would make Rance McCabe howl with rage.

McCabe swore loudly as he glared up at the sky. Heavy clouds, pushed by a steady wind, had rolled in from the ocean, obliterating the light of the full moon and casting his caravan into darkness.

"Orin!" he barked at his foreman.

"Yessir, Mr. McCabe."

"Bring the others in. I want these wagons surrounded."

"Yessir."

McCabe swore again. He couldn't believe that she-devil's luck. First one wagon fell into a rut and snapped its axle, then the other one had a draft horse go lame, and now it was darker than the souls of hell. Just the sort of night a witch like La Rosa would like.

She was out there, watching. He could feel it. She would have attacked before they reached Monterey if the wagons hadn't been forced to stop. And then the men he had in hiding would have ridden in and captured her.

Damn it! She should have been his prisoner by now.

But she was a sly one. Seeing them stopped, she'd waited until dark. The question was, how much longer would she wait before attacking?

"Come on, La Rosa," he whispered. "We're ready for you." Louder, he said, "Once the rest of the men get in here, be ready to shoot at anything that moves. Any man that lets those outlaws touch one thing on these wagons, I'll kill him myself. Same thing goes for anyone who falls asleep."

Diego stood at the window of his hotel room. The clouds had obscured the moon and seemed to blanket the town in silence. He felt restless, repressed, uneasy.

He hadn't been able to fall asleep, despite the lateness of the hour. His mind was too active. That wasn't unusual for him when he was working on a case. He'd been sent here to find out about irregularities with the U.S. Land Commission, and he'd already learned some interesting facts. However, that wasn't what he kept thinking about tonight.

As soon as he'd lain upon his bed and closed his eyes, she'd filled his head with her image. La Rosa. He'd seen her smile, heard her low, whiskey-coated voice. For a moment, he'd imagined her in this room. He'd have sworn the air crackled with danger. He'd envisioned himself taking her into his arms, kissing her, then reaching up to remove her mask.

Was she as beautiful beneath her disguise as he believed? Who was she? What sort of woman knew how to ride and shoot as he'd seen her do? Was she really a modern-day Robin Hood, trying to help the people of the Salinas? Or was she merely a clever thief, protecting her identity by endearing herself to those in need? And why was it only McCabe whom she attacked? What had he done to her?

Determinedly, Diego pushed the image in red from his mind as he turned away from the window. He wasn't being paid to investigate the bandida's activities.

He walked across the room and sat on the edge of his bed. Immediately, the memory of another woman came to him. Leona's face was no mystery to him. He could see her delicate beauty with great clarity. There were no secrets about Leona. In fact, she was unusually honest and forthright. She certainly hadn't minced words about not wanting to marry him.

Why did she think she would make him a poor wife? Why was she so determined not to marry? She was beautiful, desirable. Whenever she looked at him with those violet-black eyes . . .

Diego groaned as he fell back on the bed, staring up through the darkness at the ceiling. Being haunted by one woman was bad enough. Being haunted by two was unbearable. He'd better start looking for facts about the Land Commission and then get out of California before he completely lost his sanity.

Leona listened as Raul told her what he'd seen along the Monterey road. McCabe's wagons were stopped, and he and his men were camped around them, ready for a fight.

"He must have three dozen *hombres* with him. He is afraid of you, La Rosa."

She let out a throaty laugh, amused by Raul's information. It was just as she'd hoped. "Let us not waste time then."

"La Rosa . . ." Ricardo began.

Leona raised a red-gloved hand. "McCabe thinks I will fight him on his terms. He thinks I am a fool because I am a woman. He is wrong. He is the fool for leaving his *hacienda* unguarded for this night."

"We go to McCabe's ranch?"

"*Sí*, Ricardo. McCabe's ranch."

She heard the men's murmurs of approval as she pressed her heels against her gelding's sides. Her horse shot forward, quickly followed by the others as they sped south.

It was the middle of the night by the time La Rosa's band approached the home of Rance McCabe. The clouds had blown over, but the moon's glow seemed to have weakened as it dropped in the western sky. Still, it was enough light for Leona to motion to her men, giving them silent instructions.

McCabe's ranch house sat on a knoll. The construction of the large, two-story, wood-framed structure had been completed only a few months before. Dwarfed by the main house's size, a barn and bunkhouse stood behind it. There was no wall for protection, no visible signs of any guards. It seemed to Leona that McCabe was deliberately thumbing his nose at anyone who would dare threaten anything that belonged to him.

Stealthily, La Rosa's men dismounted and separated. Less than half an hour later, Leona stood inside the house. The few men whom McCabe had left behind would awaken with excruciating headaches and the embarrassment of being found gagged and bound but without lasting physical harm.

Leona turned up the lamp on McCabe's desk and looked around his office. There were costly paintings hanging on the walls, expensive sculptures on the mantel, tables, and floor. Despite whatever else she thought of the lawyer, she had to admit he had fine taste in the arts. It would be difficult to decide just what to take. She wished she knew what he prized the most. It couldn't be anything large, nor did it need to be anything of great monetary value.

"La Rosa?"

She turned toward the doorway.

Ricardo stepped into the room. "We have emptied the smoke house and pantry of food. Vincente found a safe in the upstairs bedroom. We've taken all the gold and paper money from it. It's time to go."

"*Un momento.*" Her gaze shifted back to the large oak desk. There, in a gilded frame, was a ferrotype of McCabe. He was grinning at the photographer with that self-assured, self-pleased look she'd seen him wear whenever they'd met. Instinctively, she knew that the photograph was important to him. She picked it up, and in its place, left the red rose. Then, wearing a smile herself, she turned toward her brother. "I'm ready."

La Rosa's hombres were all waiting for her outside the house. Tiago was holding Pesadilla's reins.

In a swift, graceful movement, Leona swung up onto the big gelding, then swept a gaze over the band of masked men surrounding her. She wondered, not for the first time, what these men would think if they knew the woman they followed was Leona Washington. Tiago Cisneros and Raul Hercasitas were two of Leona's most persistent suitors. Vincente Perez had visited Rancho del Sol often when Leona was a girl. Javier Aguilar worked with her brother, Manuel, on his ranch.

It had surprised her at first that no one guessed her identity. After all, it was Ricardo who organized each raid. When she'd asked her brother about it, he'd grinned and told her he'd led them to believe that La Rosa and he were lovers. Which explained why none of them had ever attempted to become more intimately acquainted with the bandida.

Pushing aside her musings, she spoke to the men in a low but commanding voice. "Give the gold you found in the safe to the Estradas and wish them well on their journey back to Mexico. Give the *americano* dollars to the family staying in the tent near the river. Distribute the food to those who need it most. You know who they are."

Heads nodded in agreement.

"*Vaya con Dios, amigos.*"

The words were repeated to her by several voices.

Ricardo backed his sorrel mare away from the others. "I will let you know when we need to ride again."

Leona spun her horse around and, side-by-side with her brother, galloped away from the McCabe ranch.

It was the wee hours of morning by the time Leona, garbed once again in a proper dress, crawled through the window of her bedroom.

Dulce, who was asleep in Leona's bed, awakened instantly.

"*Gracias a Dios*," she whispered. "You are safe. I had nearly given up hope, *señorita*."

Even as she talked, she began to help her mistress out of her clothes. Then she slipped a nightgown over Leona's head and guided her to her bed. She pulled the lightweight blanket up and tucked it beneath her chin, as if Leona were a child.

"We fooled him, Dulce." Leona yawned. "I wish I could see him when he sees that we've been there."

"Go to sleep, *señorita*. You can tell me all about it in the morning." Dulce tugged the blanket one more time before tiptoeing out of the room.

Leona heard the door close softly behind the maid. She let out a deep sigh as her eyes drifted shut. Oh, how she wished she could see McCabe's face when he found his cowboys tied up in the bunkhouse. Even more, she wished she could see him when he discovered the bandolera's rose on his desk.

She smiled sleepily. Yes, she was certain La Rosa's actions were going to make McCabe howl with rage.

Chapter Eight

"By gawd, Orin," McCabe shouted at his foreman, "I'll put the noose around her neck myself! I'll see she swings from the nearest tree. Nobody makes a fool of Rance McCabe. Nobody!"

He slammed his open palms down on his desk, his green eyes fastened on the wilting rose. How dare she? How dare she do this to him?

"Get out," he said, his voice controlled at last. "And see that no one bothers me."

"Yessir, Mr. McCabe." Orin backed out of the office, closing the door in his wake.

McCabe sank onto the leather-upholstered chair behind his desk, then reached forward and picked up the flower. He felt the prick of a thorn, then saw his own blood beading on the pad of his thumb.

He smiled grimly. Even he was able to appreciate the analogy of his wound. La Rosa was like a thorn, pricking him, making him bleed. She couldn't mortally wound him, but she could be a constant source of discomfort.

"Damn you," he whispered as he pulled open a desk drawer and dropped the rose into it. He stared down at it, the colors still vibrant compared to the dozen or more other dried roses that lay beneath it. "Damn you to hell."

He leaned his head against the high back of the chair and closed his eyes. He'd stayed awake all night, waiting alongside the road to Monterey with the wagons and all his men, certain that La Rosa would strike. But she never had, and he'd thought he'd frightened her away. This morning, he'd given his men orders to repair the wagon, replace the lame horse, and continue on. Then he'd ridden back to his ranch.

His hands knotted into fists against the armrests as he remembered discovering the rose on his desk. He could almost hear her laughter as she mocked him. She'd cleared out his larder, taken the money from his safe, and tied up his men, but at the moment, he only thought of the photograph she'd taken from his desk.

The ferrotype had been taken the day he'd become a full partner in Decker, Petre and McCabe, Attorneys at Law, New York City. It was a reminder to him of just how far he'd come from the boy of the slums he'd once been. It was a reminder of the power he wielded, the power he never meant to lose.

She'd known. The greaser slut had known what to take. How? How had she guessed what would matter to him most?

He drew in a sharp breath, causing his nostrils to narrow, then he opened his eyes. He *would* find her, and when he did, she would regret the things she'd done to him.

So help him, he would make her regret it all.

Leona sighed deeply as she turned her face toward the sky. The sun's warmth, drifting through the greenery that shaded the courtyard, felt good upon her skin.

"Leona?" Her father's hand fell upon her shoulder. "Are you ill?"

She looked up at him. "No, *Papá*. Why do you ask?"

"You seem pale to me, and there are circles beneath your eyes. You were nearly asleep during mass this morning."

"I'm sorry. I just didn't sleep well last night."

Gardner sat down beside her. "Is it because of Diego?"

"Diego? No, I . . ."

"I'm sorry if I went about it all wrong, Leona, but I've given the matter of this marriage a great deal of thought. It isn't just because of Dominguez and my promise that I want you to marry this man. You are restless, *hija*. I see it in your eyes. You need a husband. It's time you made a home for yourself. You're like your mother. You have so much love to give. I think you could love Diego Salazar, and he would be good to you. He will make you a fine husband."

She reached out, placing her hand over the top of his. "Oh, *Papá*, don't you see that I'm happy here? I don't want to leave you or my brothers and their families. My home is Rancho del Sol. I love *you*. Why isn't that enough?"

"It's not the same, Leona." He looked down at her, dark blue eyes filled with sadness. "One day you will come to understand the difference." Gardner leaned forward and kissed her cheek. "When Diego returns from Monterey, I will speak to him about setting a date for the wedding." Then he rose from the chair and left the courtyard.

As Leona watched him depart, panic filled her chest. She had to do something quickly or it would be too late. Once the engagement became official, once the date of the wedding was publicly announced, there wouldn't be anything she could do to stop it from taking place. Pride, if nothing else, would demand that she and Diego honor the pledge.

Restless now, her lassitude forgotten, she got up from the chair and wandered through the house, going from room to room as if in search of something she couldn't find. Finally, she entered the small greenhouse on the south side of the hacienda.

She paused just inside the door, next to a bush filled with blood-red roses. The bush beside it blossomed with roses the color of ripe strawberries. Leona touched a velvety bud, then leaned down and breathed in its delicate fragrance. As she straightened, she swept the greenhouse with her gaze.

According to her father, these roses had been one of her mother's greatest pleasures. Francisca had planted and watered and pruned them herself. There were dozens of bushes, each one of them producing a flower of just a slightly different shade of red or pink than all the rest. Whenever Leona felt overwhelmed by the men in her life, she came here. There was a serenity here that she couldn't find elsewhere. It made her feel close to her mother, even though she'd never known the woman who had given her life.

Francisca had loved making her home a place of peace and pleasure for her husband and children— or so Gardner had always said. Francisca's family had been the key focus of her life, each and every day. Leona suspected her father had told her this in the hope that she would develop the same desire for hearth and home and husband.

Gardner was destined to be greatly disappointed.

She sighed, feeling a bit disappointed herself. She wished she'd known her mother. Maybe then she could have been like Francisca. Maybe then she would have been happy with the way things were supposed to be. Maybe then her father wouldn't have to be disappointed.

Letting out another deep sigh, she left the greenhouse and headed toward her bedroom. Fatigue pressed down upon her shoulders, and she longed to lose herself in sleep.

Diego returned to Rancho del Sol after dusk. Gardner welcomed him back, asking if his visit to Monterey had proven fruitful. Diego replied in the affirmative.

Before leaving for Monterey, he'd told his host he was going to meet with the captain of one of the ships in the bay regarding an investment in a shipping venture. He hated deceiving his father's friend, but his work here in California demanded that no one know his true activities.

"The family has already had supper," Gardner said, "but I'll have Anita see that you get something to eat."

Diego stifled a yawn as he nodded. He was hungry, but mostly he was tired. Sleep had eluded him for most of the previous night. He wanted nothing more than to fill the empty cavern in his belly and then fall into bed.

"We have much we need to talk about, Diego, but I can see we should wait. You're still weary from your travels. We'll talk in the morning after you've rested."

He didn't have to ask to know that Gardner was referring to his marriage to Leona. He wondered what he was going to say when the time came. How was he going to tell Gardner that he didn't wish to marry his daughter?

But then he envisioned Leona, as he had throughout last night, and he wondered if it would be so terrible to take her for his wife. On the heels of that thought came another. . . .

He wondered if he'd gone stark raving mad!

Gardner summoned the maid. "Anita, see that Senor Salazar has something to eat."

"*Sí, señor.*" The girl hurried toward the back of the house.

"It won't take long. Our cook is used to whipping up something at short notice. With a family as large as ours, there's always someone coming in late." Gardner grinned. "I'll leave you to enjoy your meal in peace. See you in the morning." He walked away.

With a shake of his head, Diego wandered in the direction of the courtyard. He was surprised at how quiet the house was. He wasn't sure how many of Leona's brothers still lived in the main hacienda of Rancho del Sol, but he would have thought he'd have found someone still about.

"Señor Salazar?"

He turned to see the maid watching him from the doorway to the courtyard.

"I forgot, *señor*. This arrived for you yesterday." Anita handed an envelope to him, her eyes meeting his, then darting shyly away. "I will call you when your meal is ready." She scurried out of sight.

Diego turned into the first room off the courtyard. A lamp was burning low on a small table. He held the letter out to the light, expecting to see Joseph McConnell's handwriting. He found, instead, his grandmother's precise letters.

A coldness crept through him as he broke the seal. He knew, without reading it, what he would find there.

My dear Diego,

I pray that this letter will find you at Rancho del Sol. It is with a heavy heart that I must inform you of your father's death. He passed away in his sleep, only two days after you left his side. He knew the end was coming, and he told me he was glad. The pain had become nearly unbearable. But he said he was filled with joy, knowing you would soon marry Gardner's daughter, uniting the two families. You have honored your father in the way that mattered to him most. That knowledge should bring you some comfort, now in this time of sorrow.

Do not hasten back to Texas, for the rest of the family is well and there is nothing you can do here. Ramon and Pedro and their wives and children have surrounded me with their love and comfort. It is hard for a mother to see her only son die before her, Diego. Very hard.

I will await the news of your wedding. Please give my love to Gardner. He knows he was like a son to me in the years he was with us, and I have always been proud of all he has accomplished. I, too, will be glad to welcome Leona into the Salazar family.

Do not mourn your father's passing too greatly, my child, for he is free of pain and has gone on to paradise to be with our Lord and our Redeemer.

God be with you.

Your grandmother,

Elizabeth Bartholomew Salazar

Diego turned away from the lamp and walked out into the courtyard. He stared up at the sky, where stars twinkled beside a rising moon.

Two days. Only two days after he'd left the ranch, his father had died. Dominguez had been dead for weeks, his body long since laid to rest in the family graveyard.

His hand closed tightly over the letter, crinkling it into a ball. He felt a wave of guilt. His father's joy at the end of his life had been knowing his son would marry Gardner's daughter, and yet Diego had left Texas without any intention of keeping the pledge.

"Diego?"

He spun toward the sound of Leona's voice.

"I'm sorry. I didn't mean to startle you. It's just . . ." She stepped forward. "Is something wrong?"

He stared at her for a long time, aware of—and yet quite removed from—her delicate loveliness.

"Diego, what is it?"

He didn't talk easily about himself. He never had—even before he'd become an investigator for the Joseph McConnell Agency—but his profession had made it all the more difficult for him to do so. Still, there was something about the way she was looking at him with her wide, expressive eyes—eyes turned to ebony in the twilight of the courtyard—that made him want to answer truthfully.

"My father is dead."

She took a quick gasp of air. "Oh, Diego, I am sorry." She reached forward and touched his arm.

Later, he would wonder what made him do it, but at this moment, it seemed the most natural thing to do.

He gathered Leona to him, pulling her into his embrace and resting his cheek against her hair. He closed his eyes and allowed himself to feel the sharp pain of loss, barely mindful that, after a moment's hesitation, Leona's arms encircled him and her hands rubbed up and down his back in a gesture of compassion and comfort.

His thoughts traveled across time and distance, remembering his father as he'd once been—robust and intelligent, a man who'd savored every moment of life. He'd been a stern but just father to his sons. He'd been a faithful, though far from perfect, husband. He'd treated his own parents with respect.

Diego wished he'd been a better son. Now that it was too late, he wished he'd spent more time at the ranch in these past few years instead of traveling so much. He knew Dominguez had been proud of him, proud of what he'd accomplished during the war and since. Still, there was much he should have said, should have done.

Leona lifted her head from Diego's chest. "Does this mean you'll be returning to Texas soon?"

He looked down at her and stared into liquid dark eyes. "It was my father's dying wish that I should marry you," he answered softly. "I will stay."

She slipped free of his embrace and took a few steps backward.

It was surprising to Diego how empty his arms felt. Where moments before his chest had felt the warmth and comfort of her body against him, he now felt the cool touch of night air. Even in the shadows of night, he saw her face cloud over, felt her disquiet.

"It would be wrong for us to marry, Diego, even to honor our fathers." She turned quickly and fled the courtyard.

Would it? he wondered as she disappeared from sight. He wasn't so sure anymore.

Leona leaned against her bedroom door and forced her breathing to slow down. A myriad of emotions swirled in her chest while a confusion of thoughts spun in his head.

She'd wanted him to kiss her, she realized. She'd longed to turn her face up and have him capture her lips. Her heart spun out of control as she imagined what it would have been like to be kissed.

Kissed by Diego . . .

She pressed cool fingers against her hot cheeks, horrified by her thoughts. How could she be feeling this way? He'd lost his father. He'd been hurting. She'd seen it in his face. She'd wanted only to comfort him. Reaching out to touch him had been a spontaneous gesture, one of compassion and friendship, nothing more.

But when he'd held her . . .

She felt again the mad beating of her heart, felt a strange warmth spreading through her veins.

It was my father's dying wish that I should marry you. I will stay. . . .

I will stay. . . .

I will stay. . . .

"I don't want to marry him," she protested to the empty room.

But even she was beginning to wonder if she spoke the truth.

Chapter Nine

Leona strode into the kitchen early the following morning. "Good morning, Berta," she greeted the cook.

The squabbish woman, dressed in a brown dress and white apron, turned with a smile. "Miss Leona, I didn't expect to see you this time of day."

"I came to help you prepare breakfast."

Berta's dark eyebrows shot up on her forehead.

Leona raised a hand to silence the woman. "Not for everyone, Berta. Just for Señor Salazar. I'm sure it's no secret among the servants why he's here, so I needn't pretend with you." She tilted her head slightly and gave the cook a meaningful grin. "It's only fair that he should know what he'll be eating after we're married. Don't you think?"

"Oh, Miss Leona, I don't think that's such a good idea. You'd better let me—"

"Just hand me that apron," she interrupted. "And you're not to tell anyone that I did this. Particularly not my father. Do you hear me, Berta?"

"I hear you, Miss Leona, but I think it's a mistake. I do. I surely do."

Leona's grin widened. "But I don't."

Diego was surprised by the tapping. "Yes?"

"*Perdóneme, por favor,*" a female voice called to him through the door. "Are you decent? I have brought you your breakfast."

"My breakfast?"

"*Sí.*"

In his room? He sat up, then threw back the covers and rose from the bed, slipping quickly into his trousers and shirt. As he raked his fingers through unruly black hair, he called, "All right. You can bring it in."

The door opened, and Leona entered, carrying a tray. Behind her, a servant girl stood waiting in the hall.

"I thought you might not want to join the family this morning, so I made you your breakfast." She set the tray on the table beside the bed. "I hope it's edible. I'm afraid I'm a rather poor cook, Diego."

There was a spot of flour on the tip of her nose, and a pleasant flush in her cheeks. Diego found that he liked the combination. "I'm sure it will be very good."

"I cannot stay. *Papá* would never approve of my being alone with you in your room."

"Of course not. I understand."

Leona looked up at him. Her eyes widened a fraction, as if surprised by something she saw, then she ducked her head and hurried out of the bedroom, the door swinging closed behind her.

Feeling puzzled by the brief exchange, Diego rounded the bed and lifted the white towel which covered the tray. His gaze fell on a mess of runny eggs and cold tortillas. Any appetite he'd had disappeared instantly.

Madre de Dios! She hadn't really thought he would eat this, had she?

He sat down on the edge of the bed, still staring at the half-cooked breakfast. During the past decade, he had eaten in sumptuous restaurants in New York City and on sand-whipped battlefields in Texas. He'd acquired a taste for all kinds of cuisine, and he wasn't a difficult man to please when it came to food. But there was a limit to what even he was willing to put in his belly.

Why would she bring him . . . ?

Suddenly, he laughed. The little vixen! She was as transparent as glass. So she wanted him to despise her cooking, did she? Well, she was going to be disappointed. When the maid came to clear up the dishes, she was going to find them wiped clean—not so much as a speck remaining. Now all he needed was a way to dispose of the food before then.

Luckily, since he was hungry, he still had some dried beef in his saddle bags. That would hold him over until the midday meal.

*   *   *

"The *señor* is in his office," the maid said, then led the way down the hall. "He will see you now."

Mercedes followed Anita, feeling the nerves knotting her stomach.

Gardner was leaning over a sheaf of papers when she entered the room. He looked up, then rose from his chair and walked around his desk. "Mercedes, this is a pleasant surprise." He took hold of her hand.

"I hope I have not disturbed your work, Señor Washington."

"Of course not. You're welcome any time. You know that. In fact, we don't see you around here near often enough now that you're all grown up." Gardner guided her to a chair and motioned for her to sit down. "Does Leona know you're here? Did you send Anita for her?"

She shook her head. "It is you I came to see, *señor*. I have come to ask for your help."

"Your father's grant to La Brisa?" Gardner's smile faded. "It's about to come before the Land Commission, isn't it?"

"*Sí.*"

She could tell, even before he spoke, that her quest was futile. She heard him sigh, watched as he returned to his desk and sat once again in his chair.

When he looked up at her, his blue eyes were filled with regret. "I've talked to everyone I know, Mercedes, but I'll try again."

"Señor McCabe seems to think he can help my father keep half of the land, at least. Perhaps more." She shivered, thinking of the way Rance McCabe had looked at her, hearing again his vile proposition.

"He may be able to do it. The man seems to have a tremendous influence on the Commission's decisions." Gardner ran his fingers through thick, gray hair, the gesture revealing his own frustration. "Lord knows, I don't like the thought of McCabe taking any more land away from my friends."

Mercedes fought back the hot tears that welled in her eyes. Swallowing hard, she whispered, "Anything you can do, *señor*, will be appreciated. My father . . . I am afraid he has given up. He does not seem to have the will to fight any longer. I am afraid of what he might do."

"Tell Sebastiano that I'll come to see him tomorrow."

"*Gracias.*" This time, she couldn't stop the tears from falling.

Gardner rose and came over to her chair. He drew her up and into his embrace, patting her back as he'd done when she was a child. "Here now. Dry those tears, Mercedes. It may not be as bad as it seems. I'll talk to your father, and then I'll talk to the men on the Commission. We'll find a way to prove the Ramirez claim to Rancho La Brisa."

"*Gracias,*" she said again, choking back a sob.

Standing in the doorway to her father's study, Leona watched as Gardner comforted Mercedes.

She'd heard enough to know why her friend was here, and her anger immediately began to boil.

She knew that Gardner didn't believe he could help this time. She could sense her father's doubt. She could see his frustration. It made her own outrage increase.

He glanced up then, and their gazes met over the top of Mercedes's head. With his eyes, he cautioned Leona not to give voice to her ire. He knew as well as anyone her opinion of the American law that had come to the Salinas in the past year. She'd expressed it often enough to him and anyone else who would listen.

He stepped back from Mercedes, his hands on her arms as he looked down at her. "Dry your eyes and don't worry anymore, *niña*." Again he glanced toward the doorway. "Ah, here's Leona, come to steal you away from me."

Leona pasted a smile on her face as she entered the room. "Anita told me you were here. I was just about to have some coffee. Will you join me in the courtyard?"

Her friend nodded and tried to return the smile.

"Good." She hooked her arm through the other young woman's and led her from the study. "We hardly had time to visit the night of my birthday party. You can stay longer today, can't you?"

"*Sí.* I do not have to hurry back to La Brisa. Orlando is with me," she replied, referring to one of her father's vaqueros.

"Wonderful. We'll have a nice, long chat, and then you can have lunch with us before you go. Perhaps Ricardo will join us."

Her friend's smile was a little more earnest this time. "I thought he would be out with the *vaqueros*."

Leona was certain her brother *was* out tending to the cattle and horses, but she meant to send word for him to return to the hacienda. She knew that no one could brighten Mercedes's mood like Ricardo. She wished he would realize it, too.

An hour later, the two women were still seated in the courtyard, gossiping and laughing and reminiscing about the mischief they'd gotten into as children. It seemed that Mercedes—at least temporarily—had forgotten her family's troubles, and Leona was feeling quite satisfied with her successful diversions.

She would never have suspected that they would be so unpleasantly reminded of them.

Anita appeared in the doorway. "*Señorita*, you have . . ."

"No need for so much formality, girl," Rance McCabe said as he brushed past the maid. "After all, Miss Washington and I are well-acquainted."

Leona rose stiffly from her chair.

"I came to speak with your father, but your servant told me I just missed him. Gardner still likes to get out on the range, I take it. See what his men are doing. Makes good sense. Wouldn't want to let those greasers and Injuns start stealing right under his nose."

119

"We've never had a problem with *vaqueros* stealing at Rancho del Sol."

McCabe grinned in reply, then shifted his gaze to Mercedes. "A pleasant surprise to see you here, Miss Ramirez. I trust your father is well and not worrying himself too much over this land thing. I hope we'll *both* be able to help him out."

Mercedes didn't reply, didn't so much as bat an eyelash, yet Leona could feel her anxiety. She tilted her chin in a show of defiance as she stepped forward, placing herself between McCabe and Mercedes.

"I'm sorry you missed my father, Mr. McCabe. I will tell him you were here."

The man took no notice of her obvious dismissal. Instead, he crossed to an empty chair and sat down. "Warm for May, isn't it?" He allowed his gaze to move from her face, making a slow perusal of her down to her toes, then an equally slow journey back until their eyes met again. "I must say you look particularly lovely, my dear Miss Washington."

Leona allowed herself to think what she could do to him with her saber. With a few deft strokes, she could scar his face, perhaps remove that impudent look.

"Perhaps now isn't the time to say anything to you," McCabe continued, spoiling her fantasy, "but I've been hoping you would allow me to . . . well, shall we say, know you on a more personal basis."

"*Perdón?*"

"I think you understand me. I'm asking if I can call on you, Miss Washington. Perhaps with a goal of a more permanent relationship between us."

Leona's eyes widened, even as she heard Mercedes's startled gasp, but before she could speak, another voice answered for her.

"I'm afraid her *novio* would never approve." Diego stepped into the courtyard. He wore a pleasant-enough expression, yet Leona felt the hardness of his eyes as he looked at McCabe.

The lawyer rose to his feet. *"Novio?"*

"My fiancé," she translated.

Mercedes gasped again.

Diego came to stand beside Leona. His arm went around her shoulders, then drew her close against his side. She glanced at him just as he leaned down and dropped a kiss on her forehead.

"May I say, my dear Leona," he whispered near her ear, "that I never dreamed you would be such an accomplished cook in addition to being so beautiful. However was I so fortunate to find a woman like you?"

It took her awhile to realize he was speaking. From the instant his arm had encircled her shoulders and he'd kissed her, there had been a strange humming in her ears. She was just beginning to understand what he'd said when his arm dropped from her back and he stepped toward McCabe.

"Diego Salazar." He held out his hand. "And you, sir?"

"McCabe. Rance McCabe." He looked at the proffered hand with disdain.

Diego showed no irritation at the other man's rudeness. "Ah, the . . . lawyer. You're well-known, Mr. McCabe. I believe I heard of your firm when I was back east."

McCabe's lip lifted in an unconscious smirk. "*You've* been to New York?"

"I visited there a few times, when I was on holiday from college. I was educated at Harvard."

"You? At Harvard?"

"Yes. My great-grandfather was on the board of overseers many years ago, and my grandmother wouldn't hear of her grandsons going to school anywhere else. Three of us—my brothers and I—studied there."

Leona felt nearly as surprised as McCabe looked. She found herself staring at Diego's profile, as if for the first time, and realized there was little she *did* know about him. She'd reacted to him physically almost from the first moment they'd met. She'd always been aware of his handsome face and hard, muscular body. But suddenly she knew there was much more to Diego Salazar than his looks.

His brown eyes shifted to meet hers, and she felt a jolt in her stomach.

He flashed her a smile, then returned his gaze to the lawyer. "I'm afraid you must excuse us, Mr. McCabe. I promised I would take these delightful ladies for a ride this afternoon." He motioned toward the doorway, bowing his head slightly.

McCabe couldn't ignore this dismissal. His color high, his eyes sparking with contained fury, he rose from his chair. "Good day, Miss Washington, Miss Ramirez. I'll see you again soon, I hope." With that, he turned on his heel and left the courtyard.

For quite some time—or so it seemed to Leona—nobody moved.

Then, with a squeal of delight, Mercedes jumped to her feet. "Engaged!" she exclaimed. "Leona, why didn't you tell me?" She threw her arms around her friend and gave her an exuberant hug.

"It only just happened," Leona answered softly as her eyes met Diego's. The funny tickling sensation returned to her stomach. The humming returned to her ears. "It only just happened."

Mercedes declined to go for a ride with Leona and Diego but insisted that they do as they'd planned. "I'll wait here," she said. "Perhaps Ricardo will return early for lunch, and he can keep me company."

As they left the house, Diego could see that Leona's momentary surprise and subsequent speechlessness had worn off. Her eyes seemed more violet than usual. She carried her chin just a fraction higher as she briskly walked across the compound.

As soon as they passed through the wide doorway of the stables, she spun to face him. "How *dare* you tell such a story? Mercedes will have it spread up and down the valley before the week is over."

"It's no story, *señorita*. Your father and I discussed it this morning." He grinned. "Right after I'd eaten the delightful meal you prepared for me."

Her mouth opened a sliver, then pressed tightly closed again. She whirled and marched toward the stall holding her golden mare.

Diego decided he liked her show of temper. He didn't want a wife without any spirit. Of course, he would expect her to respect his wishes and obey him in all matters of importance. Still, he wanted a woman with a mind of her own and the ability to express it.

Quickly, he followed after Leona.

"I realize my timing wasn't perfect," he said, still smiling, as he stopped outside the stall.

She was standing beside her horse, running a brush over the mare's glossy coat. Her hand stopped in midair, and she turned her head to look at him. "No time would be perfect for such an announcement."

"Why are you so determined not to like me, Leona?" His smile faded, along with the teasing tone of his voice. "Your father approves of the union, and I think Ricardo will as well when he hears of it."

The anger seemed to drain from her. A sadness filled her wide, expressive eyes. "Tell me, Diego. Even though this marriage was your father's dying wish, would you have married me if you'd found me ugly or mad or—or stupid? Would you have bound yourself to a woman you didn't like, perhaps even despised, simply to please your father?"

"*Do* you despise me?" he asked in a low voice.

For a long time, she merely stared at him. Finally, she shook her head. "No." She looked away.

Diego opened the stall door and stepped inside.

"But that doesn't mean I want to marry you. And *you* didn't come here to marry me, did you? You thought you would find some way out of the marriage. If you'd been forced to, you simply would have refused and ridden away." She drew a deep breath. "Am I right?"

"Yes."

She faced him once again. "Then can't you see how unfair it is that I must marry you despite what *I* want? I can't just ride away as you can. Simply because I'm a woman, I must do as my father tells me."

She was so beautiful, and she looked so very sad. He wanted to bring a smile back to her lovely mouth. He wanted to see amusement sparkling in her expressive, dark eyes. He wanted to hear her light, delicate laughter. He'd known her only a few days, and yet her happiness had become very important to him.

He drew closer to her. He was tempted to take her in his arms but didn't try to do so. "I'll make you a deal, *señorita*."

"A deal?"

"Give us a month to get to know each other better. Perhaps you might come to like me, at least a little. At the end of the month, if you still don't care for me and want to break the engagement, I'll honor your wish. I'll tell your father that I can't marry you against your will."

Her head tilted slightly to one side. "Tell me one thing." She paused a moment, her eyes watching him intently. "When you spoke to my father this morning, did you agree to the marriage only because it was your father's dying wish?"

"No." The answer came quickly, and surprisingly, he realized he spoke the truth. He wasn't sure why he'd agreed to marry Leona Washington after being so determined not to wed, but it wasn't merely to honor his father. Nor was it because he found her so attractive, although that was certainly true, too. Perhaps the next month would reveal as much to him as it would to her.

Leona nodded. "Then I will accept your proposal, *señor*." She stuck out her right hand.

Diego took it within his but didn't shake it. Instead, he used it to draw her forward until their bodies were almost touching. Her eyes widened. Her mouth was slightly open. He felt a quiver run through her as his arms slipped around her back. His gaze never wavered from hers as he lowered his head. Only as their mouths touched did he close his eyes, the better to enjoy the sweetness he found there.

A strange weakness spread through Leona. If not for his arms around her, she knew she would have fallen to the floor of the stall. She'd often wondered what it would be like to be kissed on the lips, but never in her wildest imaginings had she come close to the truth. Diego's kiss had stolen her breath, as if she'd been running for a long while. She felt frightened and exhilarated at the same time. Totally out of control and yet totally aware of everything around her. She wanted it to stop. She wanted it to go on and on.

It was Diego who pulled back first. When she looked at him, she found his expression unnerving. His patrician features seemed suddenly harsh. His brown eyes swirled with emotions she couldn't understand.

He cleared his throat, then spoke in a very low voice. "I think we'd better go for that ride now."

She nodded, unable to speak.

For a moment, his eyes flickered to her mouth, and she thought he might kiss her again. She *hoped* he would kiss her again. But he didn't. He turned abruptly and left Glory's stall.

Leona placed a hand on the mare's back and forced herself to draw a deep breath of air as she tried to steady her quaking legs.

What, she wondered, had she gotten herself into?

Chapter Ten

Pesadilla sidestepped nervously, then bobbed his head, causing the silver on his bridle to jingle. Leona leaned forward and stroked the black gelding's neck to calm him, even as her own tension mounted.

By the light of the thin, last-quarter moon, she stared down at the house that was nestled against the hillside. It had once belonged to the Estradas. Now it belonged to Rance McCabe. And tonight, the lawyer himself was inside.

She turned her head, glancing at her brother through the slits in her mask. He too was staring down at the hacienda, his mouth set in a grim line. Ricardo had wanted the men to come without La Rosa tonight. He thought it was too dangerous for her. But Leona had rejected his suggestion. What irritated McCabe the most, she was certain, was that he was being harassed, not just by bandits but by a *woman*. This was her night to confirm her suspicions. This night she meant to meet her nemesis face-to-face.

A door opened at the back of the house and a man stepped outside. A moment later, a match flared. As he lit his cheroot, the man turned slowly in a circle. He paused a moment, then turned in the other direction, again making a full circle. After a few minutes, he dropped the cheroot and crushed it into the ground, then reentered the house.

"That's our signal," Leona said softly as she dismounted. "Let's go."

If everything went according to plan, Johnny Parker would be standing guard just inside the back entrance to the dining room. Hopefully, the strike on the back of his head she planned to administer would be hard enough to convince McCabe of its real intent without doing her gringo friend much damage.

Everyone knew that Johnny's signal meant there were only two guards stationed outside the house. Vincente and Tiago had already spotted them and were moving into place to make sure the men caused La Rosa's band no trouble.

Raul had been in hiding near the hacienda since early that morning. He'd counted only eight men as they'd arrived during the day. Discounting the two guards and Johnny, that left five others. McCabe and his two guests would be seated at the dinner table. At least one of the others had to be the cook. That meant there was one more unaccounted for.

Reaching the barn, Leona stopped—along with Ricardo, Javier, and Raul—and waited. Not even Leona could be certain that she heard anything. It could have been nothing more than the sigh of the wind. Or it could have been a surprised groan just before a man fell unconscious to the earth.

Finally, a soft chirping interrupted the silence of the night. It sounded like just another voice of nature, yet it caused Leona's muscles to tense in readiness. She saw two shadows sprinting toward the front of the hacienda. With a nod to the men nearby, Leona moved toward the back door, her pistol drawn and ready, her other hand resting on the hilt of her saber.

McCabe poured himself another drink of the excellent brandy. It cost him a small fortune to have it brought to California, but it was well worth it. Certainly his guests were impressed.

"More, Judge Hopkins?" he asked, holding up the decanter.

"I do believe I will." The man smiled at him. "I must say, Rance, I didn't expect to find things quite so comfortable and civilized here."

"We have done what we can to improve conditions. The Mexicans, of course, are a rather primitive people. Lazy, for the most part. It's difficult to get them to work."

"Yes, well, you've accomplished a lot in a short time." The judge sipped his brandy. "By the way, I appreciate your willingness to keep my visit confidential. I wouldn't want it generally known that my son"—he glanced at the younger man across from him—"and I are interested in acquiring land in this area. It could make it more difficult for us to get what we're after. You know, the locals might drive up their asking price for land and cattle. That sort of thing."

"I understand, sir." McCabe filled the judge's crystal goblet nearly to the brim. "That's why I suggested we meet here. Fewer people are apt to see you coming and going. The previous owners moved out a couple of weeks ago, and it's quite a distance to the next ranch. In the morning, you can leave by the same road you came in on, and no one will be the wiser."

Judge Hopkins—an enormous man with a flabby middle and triple chin—nodded, then sipped his brandy before returning his attention to the sumptuous meal on his plate. He cut himself a thick piece of beef and stuffed it into his mouth, chewing slowly and obviously savoring the flavor.

McCabe was pleased with how the evening was progressing. If the judge were to come to the Salinas Valley, he would be a valuable ally. Hopkins wielded a tremendous amount of power back east, and there was no reason to believe that the same power wouldn't follow him to California. The difficult members of the Land Commission wouldn't be able to ignore the judge as they'd sometimes ignored McCabe.

His gaze lowered to the brandy glass in his hand. He swirled the dark liquid inside the goblet, then took a long swallow, closing his eyes and enjoying the sensation as the brandy burned its way down his throat.

"Señor McCabe? I believe it is poor manners, even for *americanos*, for the host to begin eating before all his guests have arrived. Is it not so?"

McCabe choked, spraying a mist of brandy across the white tablecloth as his eyes collided with the vision in red standing just inside the doorway. One of his men lay unconscious at her feet. The other guard was being motioned from the dining room by one of her masked companions, who were clad all in black.

"Who are you?" he demanded as he rose to his feet, although he knew the answer to his own question.

"You do not recognize me, *señor*?" she asked in a deep, husky voice. "I am—how is it you say it?—wounded." She grinned at him as she stepped over Johnny Parker's inert body and approached the opposite end of the table, pulled out a chair, and sat down. "And after all the flowers I have given you, too. You did receive the one I brought to your *hacienda*, no?"

She was mocking him. The witch was actually mocking him in front of the judge and his son.

McCabe ground his teeth. "I got it."

"*Siéntese, por favor.* You need not stand on my account. Enjoy your *cena*." Her gaze flicked to the other men, seated on each side of the table, the judge on McCabe's right, his son on McCabe's left. "And you, *señores*. We have not had the pleasure of an introduction. I am called La Rosa."

The judge turned toward his host, his face a brilliant red. "Rance, what's the meaning of this? Is this some sort of joke?"

La Rosa laughed even as her smile faded. "Joke, *señor?* No. This is not a joke. You see, there are many needy people in the valley. So many who once owned *ranchos* and *haciendas*, *ganado* and *caballos*, but are now without. There was a time when the *rancheros* could share with any traveler because there was plenty to be had. But hard times have fallen. That is why I have come to the Salinas. To help *mis amigos*." She waved with her hand toward the masked men who stood around them. "We are most grateful for any donation from those who are more fortunate."

Leona pulled back a chair for herself and placed her feet up on the corner of the table. She was enjoying herself more than she'd ever dreamed. McCabe's impotence was nearly driving him insane. Even from her spot at the far end of the long table, she could see the vein pulsing in his temple.

"You're robbing us?" the corpulent man exclaimed. "Rance, do something!"

Leona allowed herself to smile again as she turned her gaze back on McCabe. *There's nothing you can do, is there? You know what I'm thinking, and it's killing you.*

She rose from the chair. "Your meal grows cold, *gringo*, and I can see you did not set a place for us. If you gentlemen will place your donations on the table, *por favor*, we will collect them and leave you to enjoy the remainder of your evening."

"I'm going to get even with you for this," McCabe said in a chilling voice.

"*Sí*. You will try, but you will fail." She waved her pistol at Ricardo. "*Amigo*, please accept the gentlemen's generous gifts."

Amongst grunts and exaggerated breathing, the three men emptied their pockets. Ricardo moved swiftly around the table, emptying their purses into a black bag.

"Now, *señores*, I am sorry to inconvenience you, but I'm afraid we must tie your hands. It should not be for long. Your *amigo* here"—Leona glanced down at Johnny—"should awaken soon, I think."

While she and Raul kept their weapons pointed at McCabe and his guests, Ricardo, Tiago, and Vincente quickly bound their wrists behind their backs and secured them to the chairs. Once it was done, Leona holstered her pistol, then pulled a red rose from the pocket of her skirt and laid it on the table.

"For you," she said, looking at McCabe. Then she swept a deep bow. "*Adiós. Nos vemos*. That means, I will be seeing you."

She backed out of the dining room, followed by her men. Before she was out the door, she heard McCabe's furious shout.

"You're damn right we'll meet again, and when we do, I'm going to see you swing. You hear me, La Rosa? I'll get even with you for this!"

She let out a throaty laugh, knowing it was loud enough for him to hear, then turned on her heel and sprinted toward the horses hidden on the hillside.

Ricardo was angry, but he held his temper in check until after the band of men had separated, each riding away into the night in a different direction. But after ten minutes of riding alone beside his sister at a break-neck speed, he shouted at her to rein in.

"Why did you do it?" he demanded as soon as they were stopped. "Why did you insist on tormenting and humiliating McCabe like that? You make him determined to catch you, Leona."

"He was already determined." She still spoke in the deep voice of the bandida.

"*Caramba!* You ridiculed him before others. You talked to him. Do you think he is a fool simply because he is a thief and liar? How many *californios* speak English as well as you do?"

There was no trace of La Rosa in Leona's reply. The heavy Spanish accent was gone as was the throaty resonance. "Not even La Rosa speaks English as well as I do."

"*Madre de Dios!*" He raised a hand in the air and looked up at the starry sky. "I must have been mad to let you talk me into any of this. It will get you killed."

"No, *mi hermano*. I won't die. I'm right to do this. McCabe has killed and robbed and humiliated. I only take back from him a little of what he owes to those he hurt first." She reached out and touched his cheek. "Don't be afraid for me."

"Justice doesn't always prevail, *gatita*," he replied gently.

"Then we must make sure it does this time."

Leona leaned forward and pressed her heels against Pesadilla's sides. The horse broke quickly into a full gallop. Ricardo could do little else than follow after her and pray that the saints would protect his mule-headed, kind-hearted sister.

Diego stepped outside. The compound was wrapped in the silence of darkness. Apparently, he was the only person at Rancho del Sol who couldn't sleep.

He took a deep breath of the cool night air, then strolled aimlessly away from the main house while a myriad of thoughts continued to churn in his head.

He'd written his preliminary report to Joseph McConnell this evening. From the information he'd been able to gather since his arrival, it appeared that the charges against members of the commission were true. It would be harder to prove McCabe's involvement. The lawyer was crafty. But Diego knew he would find the evidence he needed before he was through.

There appeared to be one commissioner who was on the take, deciding in favor of whoever could pay him the most. Which was the same as saying McCabe. Another commissioner was definitely prejudiced against the Spanish Californians, a prejudice that colored his decisions in favor of the American squatters. From what he could ascertain, Diego believed the rest of the commissioners were basically honest men trying to do a most difficult job.

It would take quite some time before he could expect a response from Joseph. In the meantime, he meant to gather what information he could about McCabe's other activities—those that didn't involve the Land Commission. It wasn't his job to do so, but he meant to do it just the same. It was clear to him that the local sheriff cared little what was happening in this valley.

His gaze moved over the compound of the Washington ranch. He couldn't help wondering what would have happened to this family if Gardner wasn't an American—a gringo. What would the commission have done? Would they have disregarded his claim to this land as they had others, despite his proof? Could Leona and her brothers have become homeless?

Leona . . .

Her name brought with it a feeling of contentment. He'd spent quite a bit of time in her company the past few days. He'd learned nearly as much in silent observation as he had in direct conversation with her. He found her a delightful contradiction in many ways.

Her appearance was that of a proper Spanish *señorita*—well-mannered, well-dressed, innocent of the harsh realities of the world, protected and sheltered by the many men in her life— and yet, Diego suspected there was much more to her than what was easily seen on the surface. There was no mistaking that her greatest passion was for the horses that were raised at Rancho del Sol. She was an expert rider with a keen eye for good horseflesh. On the other hand, she couldn't cook—as he'd learned first-hand—and she hated to sew or embroider. He knew she enjoyed reading and had an eclectic taste in books. Several times, he'd found her curled into a comfortable chair, a tiny frown creasing her forehead as she studied the book in her lap. She wasn't afraid to argue her point of view and did so on a fairly regular basis. She loved her brothers fiercely and yet fought against their protectiveness.

Diego paused and leaned against the compound wall, his thoughts lingering on Leona. She hadn't given him another chance to kiss her, and that he regretted a great deal. When he'd kissed her inside Glory's stall, he'd known that it was her first kiss. He'd tasted her innocence, felt her surprise of discovery. He'd also felt her response and had sensed there was great passion in her, just waiting for the right man to ignite it. And Diego was that right man.

He smiled as he considered the pleasures awaiting them both. He believed they could be happy together. Perhaps they could even learn to love each other. True, he had wanted to choose his own bride, but if he'd met Leona first, wouldn't he have chosen her himself? He was beginning to believe so.

He shook his head in self-deprecation. How could he have changed direction so completely in a week's time?

A sound caught his attention, and he was suddenly alert. Thoughts of Leona vanished as his eyes sought the darkness for trouble. He waited, listening. The sound grew clearer. Hoofbeats. Slow, unhurried. As if the rider were approaching with caution.

Why would someone be coming to Rancho del Sol in the middle of the night? If it were an emergency, the rider wouldn't walk his horse. Diego glanced toward the hacienda, wondering if he should alert someone or go after his gun.

He saw the horse and rider enter through the front gate. The pallid moonlight caused more shadows than illumination, yet Diego's keen eyes still recognized Ricardo.

What was he doing out so late? he wondered as he cautiously followed Ricardo toward the stables.

Once inside the barn, Leona's twin lit a lamp and set about unsaddling his mount. The horse had been ridden hard. Dried sweat matted its coat.

More questions flitted through Diego's head, more questions seeking answers, and a few suspicions as well. One suspicion in particular began to nag at him. He had no evidence, and yet, he was positive he was right. He decided to find out what Ricardo would tell him.

He stepped through the doorway. "Good evening, *amigo.*"

*   *   *

Leona had been ready to slip into her room through the open window when she'd seen someone step away from the wall and follow Ricardo to the stables. Quickly, she'd whispered to Dulce that she was back and for the maid to go to her own room, then she had hurried toward the stables. As she approached the open door, she heard Diego greet her brother.

"I didn't think to find you up so late," Ricardo replied.

"I couldn't sleep."

Leona peeked around the edge of the door. Diego was standing beside Ricardo's horse. While her brother removed the saddle and blanket, Diego's gaze ran over the animal. He touched the gelding's neck, then ran his hand over its chest and down its leg.

"You've ridden far tonight," he said thoughtfully. "To see a woman, Ricardo?"

Her brother turned and met the other man's gaze. For a moment, there was a flicker of doubt on his face. Then he smiled. "*Sí*, a woman."

"Ah . . ."

Ricardo grabbed a brush and began rubbing the horse's coat.

"I'm surprised you didn't take Raudo. Didn't you say he was the fastest horse on the ranch?" Diego reached out and laid his hand over the top of Ricardo's. "Or is it because he would be recognized too easily?"

"Recognized?"

"You've raced him too often. He's almost a legend. Someone would see him and know it was you. That wouldn't be good for La Rosa, would it?"

Leona caught her breath as she pulled away from the door. She pressed her back against the side of the barn, her heart hammering in her chest.

"I don't know what you mean," she heard her brother reply after a long silence.

"No?"

"No."

"You misunderstand me. I'm no danger to the *bandida*. But I *would* like to meet her. I'd like to talk to her. That's all."

"Why, Diego?"

"I'm not sure. Because I met her once and found her fascinating. I can't seem to forget her. Because maybe I'd like to help her somehow."

There was another lengthy pause. "I'm sorry, *amigo*. I am no use to you. I admire La Rosa for what she's trying to do for those in need, but I don't know her. I don't meet with her. I am not one of her *hombres*."

"Too bad. I'd hoped . . ." Diego's voice drifted into silence. Finally, he said, "Well, you'd probably like to finish up here and get to bed."

Leona didn't wait to hear him say goodnight. She hiked up her skirts almost to her knees and sprinted across the compound and around to the side of the house. She nearly dove through the open window in her haste to avoid discovery.

She sat on the floor, her head resting against the side of her bed, trying to control her rapid breathing. It had been a close call. Not that it would have mattered so much if she'd let Diego find her outside. She was certain she could have bluffed her way through that. After all, she could have said the same thing he had, that she couldn't sleep and had been taking a walk. No, she was more concerned that he'd guessed Ricardo rode with the bandida.

She pushed herself up and began to undress, her thoughts still in a turmoil.

Diego wanted to meet La Rosa. He found her fascinating.

More fascinating than he finds me? she wondered.

The question bothered her more than she cared to admit.

She tossed her gown and petticoats onto a chair, then slipped her nightgown over her head and crawled into bed. She rolled onto her side, closing her eyes as she waited for exhaustion to help her fall asleep.

I can't seem to forget her.... Diego's voice echoed in her memory. *I met her once and found her fascinating. I can't seem to forget her....*

But Diego was *Leona's* fiancé. He was going to be *her* husband. He had kissed her and made her feel things she'd never felt before. Shouldn't he be thinking of her instead of La Rosa?

You are *La Rosa!* Leona thought, and then didn't know whether to laugh or to cry.

She was actually jealous of herself.

Chapter Eleven

As the days passed, Leona began to doubt her own sanity. She was a woman torn in two, double-minded, wanting one thing one moment and another the next.

When she was with Diego, she often thought she could learn to love him. She admired many things she saw—his intelligence, his tenderness, his sense of humor. She couldn't deny that he was a pleasure to look at as well. She enjoyed hearing him talk about his family and the Salazar ranch. She listened with interest when he discussed the political climate in Texas, both before and after statehood. She wondered about his travels, what it had been like in Boston and New York and the many other cities he'd visited, and what had taken him there.

And all too often, she longed for him to kiss her again, if only to see if it was really as

143

wonderful as she remembered. She often found herself staring at his mouth, recalling the sensation of it pressed against hers, remembering the way it had made her feel hot and cold at the same time.

But when she was alone, she was certain marriage to Diego—or any other man—would be a terrible mistake. She was needed here, not in Texas. The people of the Salinas were counting on La Rosa for help. She didn't want to give control of her life to yet another man. If she married, her husband would expect her to behave as a proper wife, sitting at home and bearing his children while he did as he pleased.

No, marriage wasn't for her. She was perfectly happy the way things were. Perfectly happy.

Leona was thinking just such thoughts one afternoon as she watched Gaspar school a colt in a paddock behind the stables. Looking up, she saw Diego return from yet another overnight trip to Monterey. After taking care of his pinto stallion, he joined Leona at the fence.

"Beautiful," he said as his gaze swept over the two-year-old buckskin, then shifted to her. "Truly beautiful."

She felt a skip in her heart. "Your trip to Monterey was successful?" she asked, trying to conceal her sudden disquiet.

"I think so." He watched her a moment longer, then leaned his forearms on the top rail of the paddock as his gaze returned to her brother and the colt. "The town is full of talk about La Rosa again. Seems she paid another visit to Mr. McCabe. He's demanding that the sheriff do something to stop her and her men."

She studied his profile. Did he suspect that she was La Rosa? Was that why he was telling her this? A sixth sense told her no.

Perhaps he only spoke of it because of his fascination with the bandida, because he still couldn't seem to forget her. That possibility didn't make Leona feel any better.

"She is a foolish woman, this La Rosa," she said with a slight toss of her head. "They will catch and hang her. It's better to do as my father says. Better that we try to do things according to the law. Men like Señor McCabe can't always win." She pointed at the colt as Gaspar urged it into a canter at the end of the lunge line. "Look. See the way he carries himself. He's going to be as fine as his sire."

The thunder of galloping hooves and a wild whoop caused Leona and Diego to whirl around just as Eduardo rode into the compound. Her brother hurled himself from the saddle and entered the house without even tying his horse to the hitching post.

Leona glanced anxiously at Diego, behind her at Gaspar, then hurried toward the hacienda. She'd barely made it through the door before she was whisked up in a pair of strong arms and spun around.

"She said yes!" Eduardo exclaimed. "She said yes and so did her father!"

Her apprehension evaporated at the sound of joy in his voice. "Jacinta?" she asked as her feet touched the floor again.

"*Sí.*"

"Oh, Eduardo, I'm happy for you."

"Did you hear, Gaspar?" Eduardo asked as he glanced at the two men—his brother and Diego—standing in the doorway. "Jacinta and I are to be wed. There's to be a celebration at Las Estrellas to announce the engagement. Music. Dancing. Horse racing. A great *fandango.*" He turned to look at their father who was watching from the entrance to his study. "Like in the old days."

Gardner smiled. "Yes, like in the old days."

There was suddenly a cacophony of voices as more people filled the entrance hall. Dusty vaqueros congratulated Eduardo, slapping him on the back with their hats and complimenting him on his choice of bride. Her brother's happiness seemed to make the hall glow brighter than any lamp could have done. He was in love and eager to be married.

She wished she . . .

A slow heat spread through Leona as she realized what she'd been feeling, what she'd been thinking. Her gaze moved over the crowd until she found Diego. He was watching her with a penetrating gaze. Was it possible he'd been feeling and thinking the same thing as she?

Mumbling an inarticulate excuse, Leona fled to her room.

* * *

Gardner saw the look on his daughter's face just before she turned away. He experienced the strangest feeling in the pit of his stomach as he realized what her expression meant. She was falling—or had already fallen—in love with Diego.

It should have pleased him. It *did* please him. After all, he'd been the one to insist that the two should marry. Still, there was a small part of him that had hoped she wouldn't really ever leave Rancho del Sol. Or at least not California.

He sighed as he turned back to his office, closing the door behind him. His gaze immediately went to the portrait above the mantel.

"It has happened, my Spanish flower. Leona has fallen in love. And with Dominguez's son." Gardner crossed the room to stand beneath his wife's likeness. "I like him. He will be good to her. She will be happy, I think." Again, he sighed. "We must have our own *fandango* soon. To celebrate again."

Rance McCabe left the courthouse, carrying several briefs at his side. Today's victory helped ease, somewhat, the frustration that continued to churn inside him. He'd taken his fury at the incompetent sheriff out on his opponents in the courtroom. Now what he wanted was a drink.

He caught sight of the Ramirez buggy as it turned the corner and came down the street in his direction. The old man and his daughter kept their heads and eyes straight ahead as they passed by. It was obvious they'd seen him and chose not to offer a greeting.

They'd intentionally ignored him!

The fools! He'd offered to help them. He would have seen that they were left with something. He'd asked little for his services. Just some land and a few hours alone with Mercedes.

Now he would be merciless.

His anger began to rise in his chest again. Damn her! Did the Spanish whore think she was too good for him? Oh, these ranchers made a fine show of how protected and innocent their daughters were, but McCabe knew better. They were a hot-blooded, loose-moraled lot. Mercedes Ramirez had probably been tumbling in the hay since she was barely out of short skirts.

He thought of another beauty who had eluded him, and his mood grew even more foul. Leona Washington, engaged to that greaser from Texas. It was bad enough that Gardner had married one himself. Didn't the man have enough sense to make sure his own daughter married a white man? McCabe hated to think of the number of nights he'd lain awake, thinking about Leona and how much he would enjoy spreading her beneath him, making her cry out as he entered her.

Damn them! Damn them all!

McCabe spun around and headed toward a seedier establishment than the saloon that had been his earlier destination. He needed a woman even more than he needed a drink.

*   *   *

That evening, Diego sat outside with four of the Washington brothers and several of the rancho's vaqueros. There was a pleasant breeze blowing across the rolling plains. The air smelled of spring—green and full of promise. The night sky was studded with countless stars, white on black. Wine flowed from bottles to glasses, and the men's voices and laughter grew louder over the course of time.

Eduardo endured his fair share of good-natured, sometimes ribald ribbing over his impending nuptials. The bridegroom took it all in stride, oftentimes giving back as good as he got.

Diego's head had become a bit fuzzy from drink by the time he realized that the topic of conversation had changed from Eduardo's engagement to the bandolera, La Rosa.

"They say she is the most beautiful *señorita* in all of California," one of the vaqueros said.

"She is *very* beautiful," Diego agreed.

All heads turned in his direction.

"How would you know?" Gaspar demanded.

"I have seen her. Not without her mask, but I have seen her, and I know that she is beautiful."

A general murmur of disbelief erupted.

"No. It's true." Diego straightened in his chair. He stared at the men through wine-bleary eyes. "On my way here. She and her men took refuge at my campsite. I was nearly trampled underfoot. They fought off a posse hot on their trail."

"And what did you do?" Alfonso asked.

He imagined the fiery bandida, standing in the moonlight, her cape sweeping out behind her. He heard her sultry voice and envisioned her smile. "She told me I'd better shoot because the *gringos* would kill me if I didn't. So I did."

Another vaquero sat forward. "You fought with La Rosa?"

Diego nodded.

"*¡Caramba!* I would like to have been you, *amigo*. But I would have stayed with her. They say she is as great a lover as she is a fighter."

Ricardo socked the half-breed vaquero in the arm. "What do you know of La Rosa, Yurok?"

"I know I would like to take her to my bed if she is half the woman rumors say she is."

Vaguely, Diego was aware of Ricardo's sudden agitation, but he was too drunk with wine to give it much thought. Especially since Yurok's words had sent his own thoughts down the same path. He, too, wondered what it might be like to lie with the brave bandida, to feel her bare skin next to his, to make love to her beneath the stars and moon.

"Perhaps you are right, Yurok," Diego said as he poured himself more wine. "I should have stayed with the *bandida* a little longer."

Diego awoke, his head pounding, a reminder of the amount of wine he'd consumed before retiring to his bed. He groaned, placing his hands on the sides of his face and massaging his temples with his fingertips while he wondered what had awakened him.

"Wine." The throaty voice came out of the shadows. "She is a poor lover, no? She lures you with sweet-talk, then punishes you with the sharp tongue of a shrew."

He sat up quickly, paying for the sudden action with renewed pain. He felt as if his head was about to explode. He froze, unwilling to move again.

"You ask questions about La Rosa, *amigo*. Now it is my turn to ask a few of you."

A match flared. He heard glass clink against metal, then watched as a lamp came to life, casting its glow over the masked figure beside it.

Replacing the globe, the woman in red turned toward the bed. "We meet again, Señor Salazar." She swept a courtly bow in his direction.

He squinted against the light. "What do you want?"

"That is my question to you, *señor*. What do *you* want? Why do you ask so many questions about La Rosa and her *hombres*? Do you work for the sheriff, perhaps?"

Diego's vision began to clear a little, although the steady pounding in his head continued. "No, I don't work for the sheriff."

"No . . ." A slow smile curved her full mouth. Her low, whiskey-coated voice grew softer. "No, you do not." She stepped forward. "But you are a stranger to the Salinas, no? Why do you seek to know about La Rosa? Perhaps it is the woman and not the *bandida* you wish to know."

151

His body reacted instantly as she drew closer. He was acutely aware of his nakedness beneath the blanket, even more acutely aware of her feminine curves beneath the red costume. A gentle fragrance of roses wafted on the night air, filling his nostrils, making his head spin.

"You intrigue me, *Señor* Salazar," she whispered. "Perhaps I will let you know La Rosa."

The blood coursed hot through Leona's veins. She knew she danced with danger, like a moth with a flame, and yet she couldn't seem to stop herself. The light from the lamp fell across Diego's face, illuminating his desire. She felt it, too.

She reached forward with her left hand and raked her fingers through his hair as she leaned down to boldly kiss his lips. She wasn't surprised by the wild and furious emotions storming through her. She had felt them before, the day he'd kissed her in the barn.

But Leona had been cautious of the passions he'd aroused. La Rosa was not. As La Rosa, she could discover what she'd never known before. As La Rosa, she needn't fear anything. Not even her feelings for Diego.

Leona opened her mouth at the probing of his tongue even as she lowered herself to sit on the edge of the bed. She longed to get even closer to him but knew she could not.

And so she concentrated on what she could have. She breathed deeply, memorizing the smell of him. He'd bathed himself after returning from Monterey. He smelled faintly of soap—a clean, fresh scent. He tasted a little of wine. She nibbled his lower lip, then mimicked his earlier action, darting her tongue inside his mouth, running it over his teeth, then withdrawing. It amazed her how something so simple could become so provocative, so exciting. She wondered if he could hear the rapid beating of her heart.

She was so wrapped up in his kisses, she nearly didn't notice the movement of his hand in time. Just as his fingers touched her mask, she pressed the knife, which she held in her right hand, against his throat.

"No, *amigo*. It is better that you do not try to see my face. Much better for everyone. Even my trusted *hombres* do not know my true identity."

She rose and stepped backward, regretting that the kissing couldn't have continued a little longer.

Her gaze caressed his muscular cheat and arms; other than her brothers', she'd never seen a man's bare torso. But looking at him made her feel very differently from anything she'd ever felt when looking at her brothers. She longed to touch his skin, to feel it without her gloves. She longed to discover the answers to all the unspoken questions, all the mysteries that lingered between a man and a woman.

But her time with him was over. She couldn't risk remaining any longer. She was suddenly afraid. Afraid that she might lose her head to her growing desire.

"*Adiós, amigo*," she whispered, still breathless. "Perhaps we shall meet again."

With a sudden turn, she blew out the lamp and slipped through the open window. She disappeared into the night before he could get out of bed.

Chapter Twelve

It had been a mistake to visit Diego's room in the middle of the night. It had seemed an innocent enough prank to play when she'd overheard the men discussing La Rosa. She'd certainly enjoyed the passionate kisses she'd shared with Diego.

But those same kisses had somehow changed things.

Leona glanced at Diego. He was riding with her brothers and the other vaqueros, all of them dressed in their finest clothes for the day's festivities at the Aguilar ranch. Diego looked especially handsome in his silver-studded black jacket and black gaiters. His spurs had been cleaned and his boots polished. His dark hair was combed back from his face, and the brim of his hat shaded his eyes.

He'd acted very strangely ever since La Rosa visited his room. At first, she'd thought he suspected her, but later she'd begun to believe he was simply avoiding her. Perhaps avoiding her because he wanted La Rosa instead. Or perhaps because he simply didn't want her.

She turned her eyes back on the road before them, fighting a sudden urge to cry. She swallowed the lump in her throat and pasted a smile on her lips as she looked at her father who sat beside her in the buggy.

"I've never seen Eduardo so excited and happy," she said, pleased that her voice sounded normal.

"He's chosen well. Jacinta will make him a good wife." Gardner's eyes met hers briefly. "We must have a celebration for you and Diego soon."

"You agreed to give us a month," she replied softly as her gaze dropped to her folded hands, clenched within the folds of her dress.

Her father clicked his tongue at the horses, slapping their rumps gently with the reins. He was silent for a long time, so long she wondered if he'd heard her.

Finally, he said, "Diego explained to me that you wanted time to see if you might learn to like him. He stated that he would not marry you if you did not. I could do little *except* agree since there could be no marriage without a groom." His hand patted her knee. "But that isn't a barrier any longer. You *have* learned to like him, Leona. I know it's true. I've seen it in your eyes."

Again she found herself fighting tears. "I don't know that he wishes to marry me, *Papá*."

"Nonsense," Gardner replied gruffly. "Diego Salazar is a man of his word."

She didn't try to argue with him. She *couldn't* argue with him. But that didn't change what she feared in her heart. One day, Diego might ride away from Rancho del Sol—without her.

It was what she thought she'd wanted all along. So why did she feel so terrible now that it might happen that way?

Diego stared at Leona's lovely profile. He would have to be blind not to see the sadness written there, and he knew he was the cause of it. He felt a wave of shame for the way he'd treated her the past few days. It wasn't Leona's fault that La Rosa had come to his bedroom. It wasn't her fault that the bandida had kissed him and stirred his desires. But he'd avoided Leona as if these things *were* her fault.

Silently, he cursed. He'd allowed himself to become so intrigued by the mysterious bandida, so curious about her true identity, so determined to discover the truth, that he was risking something much more real and accessible. Leona Washington might not ride astride a black horse in the middle of the night or slip into a man's bedroom, brandishing a knife, but she was beautiful and intelligent. She had a kind heart and a quick wit. Remembering the kiss they'd shared in the barn, he also knew she was innocent, yet ready to be loved. And, most importantly, he knew he was falling in love with the pretty señorita.

Ah, that was the true problem. Even though he felt love growing for his betrothed, he couldn't seem to rid himself of thoughts of the bandolera. His own guilt was keeping him away from Leona.

Guilt? What had he done to feel guilty about? So he'd kissed La Rosa. What else could he have done? He'd been without a weapon. He'd been without clothes. She'd come to his room in the middle of the night when his brain was made soft with sleep and drink. No, he had no reason to feel guilty.

But that *was* what he felt, nonetheless.

Yet what could he do to change things? He knew himself too well to believe he wouldn't continue to try to learn La Rosa's identity. A woman so different, so unique, couldn't help but pique a man's imagination. The more he'd heard about her crusade against Rance McCabe and for the people of the Salinas, the more he wanted to know about her.

But that didn't mean he had to make Leona suffer because of it, he reasoned. Loving her would mean cherishing her, protecting her from all harm, both physical and emotional.

Leona must never know what had happened between Diego and the bandida, nor must she suspect his determination to discover who La Rosa was. She would only misunderstand and be hurt by it.

How could she help but misunderstand? He didn't understand it himself.

* * *

It looked to Ricardo as if every family within a hundred miles or more of Las Estrellas, the Aguilar ranch, had come to celebrate with the engaged couple. Certainly every young man with a horse to race was there.

Raudo danced nervously beneath him. Ricardo tightened his grip on the reins and spoke softly to the horse as he waited for the signal. With a wave of a colorful handkerchief, the race began. The six horsemen spurred their mounts away from the starting line.

For a few minutes, they ran as a tight unit, thundering along the road, a cloud of dust rising in their wake. Ricardo felt the bay pulling against the bit in his mouth.

"Not yet, *muchacho*. Not yet."

As they reached the marker and began the turn that would take them back to the finish line, Ricardo saw spaces appearing between several of his competitors. Now it was time to make his move. He let Raudo have his head. The gelding leapt into the front without any noticeable effort. He ran with a smooth, rhythmic gait, putting his big heart into each lengthy stride.

Ricardo shouted his victory as horse and rider sped across the finish. He slowed his mount, felt the horse's reluctance to stop. He laughed aloud.

"So, you would like to keep running, Raudo? Perhaps later. Now, we must collect our winnings, and I must find something to eat and drink. I am more easily tired than you."

As he turned the gelding around, his gaze fell upon Mercedes Ramirez, watching from the sidelines. She was dressed in a bright yellow dress with a flared skirt and tight waistline. Her long black hair fell in thick waves over her shoulders, framing her pretty face.

Pretty? No, more than pretty. She was beautiful. When had Mercedes become a beautiful young woman? he wondered as he stared at his sister's longtime playmate.

Suddenly, she disappeared into the crowd of milling guests. He forgot all about collecting his bets as he vaulted from Raudo's back and led the horse to the nearest hitching post, then set off toward the hacienda.

Long tables, set up beneath the shade of tall oaks, were covered with food. Musicians played gaily on their violins and guitars, drums and cymbals. People spilled out of the house and into the yard. Some of them clustered into small groups, laughing and talking. A few sang and danced to the music. Still others found entertainment with a cock fight behind the barn while the horse racing continued along the road.

It seemed to Ricardo that he looked everywhere, but he still couldn't find Mercedes.

Leona laughed as Diego spun her around in a circle, causing her midnight-blue dress to whirl about her legs. He held her arm up and danced around her, his heels stomping the hard-packed earth. He stared down, his dark eyes twinkling with merriment.

It had been one of the most wonderful days of her life, and it wasn't even half over.

She didn't know what had come over Diego, but she wasn't about to question the change. All the way over to the Aguilar rancho, she had been feeling about as low as a snail's belly, certain that Diego didn't want anything to do with her. But from the moment of their arrival, he had spent nearly every moment at her side. Only when he'd joined in a horse race had he left her, and then she'd found herself cheering him on to victory from the sidelines. She hadn't even minded not being able to race one of her own horses. At the time, it had been enough to watch Diego.

As she met his gaze, she was aware of a subtle change. She saw the smile leave his lips and his eyes, saw it replaced by something more intense. The music and laughter seemed to fade. The other dancers seemed to disappear. There were only the two of them, their hands entwined, their bodies almost touching, their gazes locked.

Her mouth went dry. She felt weak and feared her legs wouldn't support her much longer. Her skin began to tingle, starting with her lips, then moving down the length of her body.

"Have I told you, Leona, that you are the prettiest *señorita* here?" he asked.

She stared at his mouth. She liked the way it moved when he spoke. His lips were as smooth and pleasing to look at as they were to kiss.

"Leona?" One corner of that wonderful mouth turned up in a smile.

She smiled, too. "What?"

"Did I?"

She looked into his eyes again. "Did you what?"

Diego laughed. "Come with me. I think you need to get out of the sun for a while."

Still holding her hand, he pulled her off through a crowd of people, leading her away from the bustling hacienda and up into the chaparral and tall oaks that covered the flanks of the foothills. They walked in silence, climbing ever higher, until the noise from the celebration subsided into a gentle hum in the distance.

"This is better," Diego said at last, stopping beside a log. He took off his jacket and spread it over the bark, then motioned for her to sit. "Up here, I don't have to see your brothers frowning at me all the time."

"My brothers? But they like you."

He offered a wry grin. "Ricardo likes me. Perhaps Gaspar does, too. Enrique would rather I left California sooner than later, and Manuel looks like he wants to hit me every time I touch you."

Leona laughed. She'd known her brothers had done this with every other man who'd ever tried to court her, but she'd been oblivious to it with Diego. Perhaps it was because he hadn't let them scare him away as others had.

He sat down beside her. "You truly are the most beautiful *señorita* here," he said softly as his fingers touched her cheek.

She didn't feel like laughing any more. She shivered nervously.

"Don't be afraid of me, Leona."

"I'm not." She stared at his mouth again, waiting.

"I'd never hurt you."

"I know."

He kissed her with great gentleness. The touch sent a surge of wanting through her. She waited for his tongue to tease her lips as he'd done a few nights before in the darkness of his room. She waited for him to crush her body against his chest. She trembled with wanting and waited for him to steady her with his embrace. She waited in vain.

He drew back, his hands cradling her face. "Do you still think you will make such a terrible wife?"

She nodded, thinking of all the things he didn't know about her. Not just that she was La Rosa, but much more. He'd never seen her rope a steer or shoot a bear. He'd never seen her hike her skirts and climb a tree or strip to her undergarments and swim in a pond. He thought she was a lady, a proper *señorita*, delicate and shy and timid, but it was all an act she'd been playing to please her father. Diego didn't know who Leona really was.

If he knew, would he kiss me the way he kissed La Rosa? Or would he even kiss me at all?

Diego felt her tremble again, saw the simmering heat of undiscovered passion in her violet-black eyes as she stared up at him. He knew if she kept looking at him that way he would never be able to control himself again. It had

163

been hard enough the first time he'd kissed her.

He rose quickly from the log. "Come on. We'd better get back. We'll be missed. Engaged or not, I don't think your father or brothers would think it proper for us to be alone like this."

As soon as she stood, he grabbed his jacket, then took her hand and led her back to the hacienda. More than once, he was tempted to stop and sample her kisses again, but each time he resisted. He wasn't confident enough of his ability to refrain from taking more than she was ready to offer. He wanted to be certain of her feelings for him before he pressed for more.

They arrived just in time to see the betrothed couple standing on a platform. Two men, one of them leaning on a crutch, were standing on either side of them, glasses raised in a toast.

"To Jacinta and Eduardo," the one with the crutch shouted. "May God bless them with a long life and many children."

"My brother Miguel forgets the most important thing," the other man continued. "May Eduardo be blessed with great patience. He will need it with our little sister."

Laughter erupted as glasses were raised throughout the crowd, but Diego hardly noticed. His head was ringing with a voice from the past.

La Rosa! Miguel is wounded.

He stared at the man with the crutch. It had to be. This was one of La Rosa's hombres.

He watched as Miguel hugged his sister and kissed her cheek, then shook Eduardo's hand. A moment later, he hobbled down from the platform and became part of the crowd once again.

Diego's eyes scanned the gathering of people.

She was here. He was sure of it. One of these señoritas had to be La Rosa. But which one? Which one could she be?

He looked at Leona, quickly schooling his face into a mild expression. "Why don't you introduce me around? If I'm to become a part of your family, I'd like to know more of your friends and neighbors."

Chapter Thirteen

Mercedes could see why so many of the señoritas sought Gaspar Washington's attentions. He was tall and broad-shouldered like his father, with the dark coloring and striking looks of his Spanish mother. His sensuous smile was guaranteed to make a woman's heart flutter, and no one seemed as skilled at turning a señorita's head with a few well-chosen words as Gaspar.

But when his flirting eyes settled on Mercedes, her only thought was that she wished he were Ricardo.

"Dance with me, Mercedes," Gaspar said, sweeping a low bow before her.

She was ready to shake her head when she caught sight of Ricardo, making his way toward her through a crush of people. His black gaze locked onto her, and there was no mistaking that she was his destination.

At last! At last, Ricardo had noticed her.

"*Sí*, Gaspar, I will dance with you," she whispered quickly and offered her hand to him.

They were out amongst the dancers in a flash. Mercedes felt breathless from the very start. She swished the folds of her bright yellow skirt in time with the music, turning and spinning, her feet tapping a staccato beat against the hard-packed earth.

Gaspar shouted something flattering at her. She grinned in response, wondering if Ricardo might have heard but not daring to look for him. She was afraid he wouldn't be there after all.

Ricardo's eyes narrowed. No one knew Gaspar's love for the ladies better than he. His brother was in no hurry to settle down. He would rather sample as many women as possible before he found it necessary to marry. Gaspar had broken several young hearts before he'd even started to shave, and his lothario activities had grown worse with each passing year. Ricardo wasn't convinced that his brother was above stealing a girl's innocence without any intention of marrying her afterward.

Well, he wasn't going to allow that to happen to Mercedes.

The moment the music stopped, Ricardo pushed his way forward. With only a quick glance at his brother, he took hold of Mercedes's hand and looked into her eyes. "I think this is the dance you promised me, *señorita*."

Her eyes widened. She swallowed visibly. Finally, she nodded.

As the music began—a slow, almost mournful melody—he drew closer to her. "I wasn't sure you were here, Mercedes. I've had a hard time finding you."

"You were looking for me?"

"*Sí.*"

They turned to the music, their gazes locked.

She was even prettier than he'd thought. Her hair was as black as a raven's wing, thick and wavy and inviting. Her skin was smooth and without blemish. Her yellow dress revealed the womanly curves beneath it.

When had these changes in her occurred? Last time he'd looked, she'd still been wearing braids and following Leona wherever his sister led.

"When did you grow up, Mercedes?" he asked aloud.

The smile that bowed her heart-shaped mouth wasn't a girlish smile. It belonged to a woman, filled with secrets and intuition. "A long time ago, Ricardo."

"I must have been blind."

"I thought so."

He knew he was falling into a tender trap, but he had no desire to protect himself. He fell, a willing victim.

With the coming of nightfall, golden lanterns came to life everywhere around the Aguilar compound. The moonless sky glittered with stars, like diamonds upon a black velvet cloth. A few of the revelers departed for their own homes.

Most stayed to celebrate into the wee hours of the night.

For the first time today, Diego found himself alone. Not long before, Mercedes had appeared and dragged Leona away, whispering excitedly as they went. Now, Diego wandered into the house, once again seeking a man with a crutch.

He found Miguel, along with a dozen or so other men, in a sitting room off the center courtyard. Several men were smoking. When they spoke, voices were hushed but angry. Diego felt the tense mood of the men as soon as he paused in the doorway.

"They burned the shack to the ground and ran off the horses. They even smashed the ox-cart."

"I heard the squatter's boy was trampled by the scattering livestock. They have taken him to Monterey, but there's little anyone can do for him. He's not expected to live."

"I thought McCabe only did such things to the *californios* who own the land he wants."

Someone laughed harshly. "No, *amigo*. He will do it to anyone who gets in his way. I think he would drive his own mother into the ocean if it would make him more rich."

"Are they sure it was McCabe and his men?"

"*Sí*, they are sure. But they will find a way to blame the *rancheros*. Mark my words."

Ricardo noticed Diego standing in the doorway and motioned him into the room. There was a tense silence, as if some of the men were deciding whether or not to discuss the matter in front of a newcomer. He must have been judged worthy because it wasn't long before someone else spoke up.

"The sheriff was out to my *rancho* this week, asking questions about La Rosa. I wanted to tell him that I would ride with her myself if I knew who she was."

"Be careful, Cesar. Dinna let your temper get you into more trouble than you can handle."

Diego's gaze was drawn to the man who'd spoken with the heavy Scottish accent. He was much the same build as Gardner Washington—tall and brawny—but about twenty-five years younger. It was clear that the Scotsman was an accepted member of the group.

"What would you have me do, Ian?" Cesar queried.

"Just dinna give him any reason t'take your land, too. That's all I'm sayin'. 'Twould only serve McCabe's purpose to have you thrown in jail as a bandit."

Ricardo stood. "Ian's right. If we're going to stop McCabe and others like him, we can't be giving them any reason to take legal action against us. We've got to prove to the American government that the law is being improperly used against us. My father has written letters to men of influence in Washington. If we are patient and careful, we can stop McCabe before he takes any more."

Diego listened with interest. It was a nice, pat speech Ricardo had given, but something about it bothered him. Perhaps it was because it was so different from the one he'd spouted to Diego about La Rosa. It sounded more like Gardner speaking than Leona's passionate brother. The detective in him just couldn't let go of his suspicions. He was certain Ricardo knew the bandida, but he was equally certain he would have a hard time getting Ricardo to admit it.

Voices began to rise around him, several men speaking at once, drawing his attention back to the conversation. Listening to the stories of McCabe's atrocities against these people, it became more difficult for Diego to continue to feel like an outsider. The information he'd sent to Joseph McConnell could take weeks, perhaps months, to do any good. The legal system moved slowly at any time, but with so much distance between the nation's capital and its new state, it would be even more difficult for change to come soon.

Diego was filled with a terrible impatience. He wanted to do something to help these people. He wanted to do something now. But what? What could he do?

He glanced at Miguel Aguilar. La Rosa wasn't sitting idly by, waiting for help from Washington. She was doing something now. True, she was a bandit. True, she was breaking the law. But in all the conversations he'd listened to, no one had ever mentioned anyone being shot or killed by La Rosa or her men. She stole only from McCabe, and according to the rumors, she gave everything back to those less fortunate.

Somehow, he was going to find La Rosa. Somehow, he was going to help her in her crusade against Rance McCabe.

The music was louder. The dancing was more furious. Shouts of laughter permeated the night air.

Leona stood on the fringe and looked for Diego. She found him dancing with one of Ian MacDougal's young daughters. Her heart fluttered as she watched him, smiling down at the red-haired girl. With a sudden clarity, she realized she wasn't the only woman who was watching him with appreciation and longing. And many of them weren't satisfied with hanging back and just looking from behind their fans. They were staring at him boldly, invitingly.

One song led to another, and Diego continued to dance, this time with a pretty señorita whom Leona didn't know. Minutes later, he had yet another partner, followed by another and another. Judging by the look on his face, Diego was enjoying himself immensely. Too much, Leona realized peevishly.

When the music stopped again, she fought her way through the mass of people until she reached Diego's side. She lightly touched his arm with her fingertips. "May I speak with you a moment, Diego?" she asked softly. "Privately."

He smiled at her, much as he'd been smiling at all the women with whom he'd danced. "Of course." He bowed his head to his latest partner.

"Excuse me." Then he took Leona's elbow and escorted her away from the crowd of celebrants.

Leona had no idea what she intended to say to him. The possessive fury that had propelled her forward was foreign to her. She'd never felt jealous over a man before. She was out of her element now. She would much rather be wearing a mask and brandishing her sword than trying to explain her feelings.

"You seem upset, Leona. What's wrong?"

"Nothing. I . . ." She swallowed, then blurted out the truth. "I was afraid you'd forgotten me."

"Forgotten you?" Amusement curved his mouth. "No man could forget you."

Was he mocking her? A burst of anger stiffened her spine. "I'm quite sure all the *señoritas* you were dancing with didn't know you were thinking about me."

"No, I'm sure they didn't." His grin broadened. "Actually, they thought it was La Rosa I was thinking about."

Leona's eyes widened in surprise. "La Rosa?"

"Do *you* know who she is?"

"Why? Why would you want to know about her?"

Diego pulled her toward him. His voice lowered to a whisper. "Because I'd like to ride with her."

"You *what*?"

"I'd like to ride with her. I'd like to help her stop McCabe."

Her heart was hammering so hard she was certain he could hear it. There was a part of her that was pleased by Diego's wish to help. But another part feared that his interest in the bandolera went beyond that. She imagined his mouth upon hers, his tongue sliding intimately between her lips.

Leona averted her eyes. "Riding with La Rosa would be pure folly. No matter what my brother says, she is still an outlaw. You would only put yourself in danger."

"I'm not afraid of danger." His fingers tightened on her arms, drawing her gaze back to his.

"This isn't your fight," she whispered hoarsely, feeling afraid for him—and for herself.

"Perhaps not." He stared at her for a long time. "But perhaps it is." Another lengthy pause followed. "Do you know who she is?"

She shook her head, fighting tears, thankful she couldn't seem to speak around the lump in her throat because she wasn't sure she'd be able to lie to him.

Diego gathered her into his embrace, his arms sliding around her back. One hand stroked her head as he pressed her cheek against his chest. "I'm sorry. Of course, you wouldn't know. I don't know why I asked you." His lips brushed the top of her head. "Don't be afraid for me, Leona. I won't do anything foolish. I promise you."

In all her life, she'd never felt such confusion. She couldn't have explained to anyone why she was crying. Not even to herself. She didn't understand anything at this moment. Her own feelings—jealousy, envy, desire, fear—were foreign to her.

Fear?

Yes, she was afraid. Afraid of what would happen if Diego ever found out the truth. Afraid of what would happen if he tried to help La Rosa and got caught. Afraid of what was happening to this valley, to her friends and neighbors, to her own family.

And because she was afraid, she found great comfort within the safety of Diego's arms.

Chapter Fourteen

At breakfast the next morning, Gardner informed his daughter that he would host a party in two weeks to announce her engagement to Diego Salazar. Leona nodded meekly, too lost in her own thoughts to try to argue with him. In truth, she didn't *want* to argue with her father. There were still plenty of reasons why she knew she shouldn't marry Diego, but she could no longer say it was because she didn't know him or didn't want to be his wife.

She left the table after doing little more than pushing her food around on her plate. She scarcely gave her destination any thought as she headed for the barn, saddled and bridled Glory, then cantered away from the hacienda. She rode into the Santa Lucia Mountains, sometimes walking the mare, sometimes cantering, paying little attention to the passing of miles or time.

Her thoughts remained on Diego. Always Diego.

It shouldn't be like this. She should be thinking about what to do for the family of squatters whose boy had been so badly injured after McCabe's men drove them off his land. She should be planning her revenge against McCabe. She should be taking steps to protect those who couldn't protect themselves. There were those who counted on her now.

When Glory stopped, Leona looked around her as if awakening from a dream. She was surprised to find herself at the pond where José had taught her to swim.

The pool was small but fairly deep, the water crystal-clear. Fed by rain and, occasionally, melting snow from the highest peaks, a mountain stream spilled into the pond at its upper end. Another stream tumbled out the opposite side, carrying water down the eastern slope of the mountain, joining other creeks and brooks, growing wider and stronger on its way toward the Salinas River.

She dismounted, allowing Glory's reins to drag on the ground as she walked to the side of the pool, crouched beside it, and dipped her fingers into the water. It was icy cold. Still, it beckoned to her, inviting her in, promising a release from her building tensions.

"I will!" she exclaimed, as if accepting one of her brother's dares.

Glory started at the sound. The mare raised her head, turning large eyes on her mistress with a look that seemed to question Leona's sanity. Then she snorted and resumed her grazing.

"This is just what I need," Leona replied in a soft, confidential tone. A smile appeared in the corners of her mouth as she stood and began to unbutton her gown.

High up the mountainside, McCabe held his breath as he watched the young woman begin to disrobe. He wished he could move closer, but he didn't want any sound to give him away.

He licked his lips as she stripped down to her camisole and pantalettes, waiting to see if she intended to swim in the nude. He felt an uncomfortable throbbing in his loins and shifted in the saddle as he watched her step into the mountain pool. She squealed and hugged herself.

McCabe could imagined the nipples of her breasts puckering and pressing against the thin fabric of her camisole. He waited anxiously for her to wade farther into the water, wanting to see the pantalettes hugging her thighs and buttocks.

He could ride down and take her, of course. There wouldn't be anyone within miles to hear her scream. She would be powerless against him.

It was tempting. He was on fire with wanting. He'd wanted her since the first moment he'd laid eyes on her, a desire that had only grown the more he'd seen her dislike for him.

His fingernails bit into the pommel of his saddle. One day he would have her, but not today. Not this way. If he took her now, he would have to kill her afterward. Her father still had too much power in this valley to let McCabe get away with raping his daughter.

No, when he finally sampled the delectable joys of Leona Washington, it would be when he could do so at his leisure, returning time and again. He'd been wrong to want her for his wife, but she would make a suitable mistress. When the time was right, he'd find a way to make that happen. He had always been able to persuade people to come around to his way of thinking. He would eventually do the same with Leona.

She dove beneath the surface and swam the length of the pool. She came up, gasping for air. She didn't know if she'd ever felt anything so cold in her life, but it felt good, too. She gulped in several deep breaths, then plunged back into the pool, enjoying the feel of the water tugging on her hair and the tingling of her flesh.

Reaching the other end, she surfaced, teeth chattering. Once again hugging herself, she scrambled out of the water—and stepped into Diego's arms.

Leona's white undergarments clung to her, made almost transparent by the water, revealing her small, well-rounded breasts, the narrowness of her waist, the gentle rounding of her hips.

Diego stopped his gaze from traveling down any farther. He knew what he would see if he did, and he was already having a difficult time holding her at arm's length.

"What do you think you're doing?" he asked, desire making his voice sound gruff.

She looked at him with those wide, innocent, violet-black eyes of hers, beads of water glistening in her long eyelashes. "Swimming."

"*¡Válgame Dios!* I *know* you were swimming. Didn't you stop to think how dangerous this could be?"

She lifted a hand and pushed tangled strings of wet hair away from her face. Water trickled down the sides of her face and over her cheeks made rosy with the cold. "I'm a good swimmer." There was an impudent lift of her chin. "I wasn't in any danger." She tried to pull free from his grasp.

"That wasn't the sort of danger I meant. Look at yourself, Leona. I can see right through your clothes. What if someone else had come upon you up here? You were alone. You would have been defenseless."

Her gaze dropped to her camisole. A tiny gasp escaped her lips. Her arms rose to hide her breasts from his view as she stepped away from him.

This time he let her go and turned his back to her. "Get dressed, and I'll take you home."

What could she have been thinking to have done such a thing? Diego wondered as he stared at the blue sky, listening as she struggled into her clothes. She *hadn't* been thinking. That was the problem.

And, of course, she hadn't considered the dangers. She probably had no idea what her beauty could do to a man. Leona had been sheltered and protected by her father and brothers all her life. She didn't understand men's baser natures. She'd only been shown the best that life and marriage could offer.

"Why were you following me?" she asked, interrupting his thoughts.

He glanced over his shoulder. Seeing that she was dressed, he turned around. "I saw you riding away from the ranch and thought you might like some company. So I saddled up and came after you. It took me a while to find you. I didn't expect you to go so far. I thought you'd know better."

Her strong chin punctured the air again, and her eyes flashed with defiance. "I'm not as helpless as you think I am, Diego. I'm not afraid to be by myself in these mountains. I've been riding in them since I was a child."

Madre de Dios! She was beautiful. He remembered all too clearly how she'd looked, walking out of the water. He remembered the way his hands had ached to cup her breasts, how he'd longed to kiss the water droplets from the base of her throat, how he'd wanted to pull her hips tight against his own.

"You're not a child anymore," he said in a hoarse whisper.

Something about his voice caused a new kind of shiver to move up Leona's spine. She saw desire swirling in his eyes and felt a corresponding jolt of wanting. She almost wished he hadn't restrained himself. She almost wished . . .

"You're not ever to do this again." His words were more shocking than the icy pond had been.

"What?"

His eyes narrowed. "You heard me, Leona. You're not ever to do this again."

"You have no right to order me around."

"It's for your own protection."

She'd known it. She'd known that was how it would be. Just because he was a man, he was the one who would know what was best for her. She would simply be expected to follow his orders. If he thought it wasn't safe for her to swim, then she mustn't swim. It didn't matter what *she* wanted. It would only matter what *he* wanted.

Not trusting herself to speak, she brushed past him and headed for her horse.

"Leona . . ."

She took hold of Glory's reins.

"Leona!"

She turned to face him, fury loosening her tongue. "You'd better know just what sort of woman you're marrying, Diego Salazar. I am *not* a meek, simpering female, and I will *not* be ordered around like some simple-minded servant. I will *do* what I want, *when* I want."

"I didn't mean—"

"I *know* what you meant." She scrambled up onto the sidesaddle, hating it more at this moment than she ever had before. "You'd better be sure I'm the sort of woman you want to marry, Diego, because I fear I'll make you miserable."

With that, she spun her mare around and took off through the trees,

"I don't know what I did wrong," Diego lamented.

Ricardo squinted at his friend from beneath the wide brim of his hat as he leaned forward, resting his forearm on the pommel of the saddle. He suppressed an urge to grin. He probably shouldn't be enjoying the other man's confusion, but he couldn't seem to help himself.

"All I wanted to do was protect her," Diego muttered, his gaze locked on the rolling grasslands. "I don't understand her."

"No, *amigo*, there's a lot you don't understand about my sister." With his knuckles, Ricardo bumped his hat brim, pushing it up on his forehead. "There's a lot you need to learn about our *gatita*."

Diego turned his head to meet Ricardo's gaze. He lifted an eyebrow, a silent encouragement for Leona's brother to explain further.

Straightening in the saddle, Ricardo chuckled. "First of all, she doesn't want your protection. Oh, she may need it sometimes, but she won't want it." He shrugged and shook his head. "And mostly, she won't need it, either."

Diego looked both bemused and irritated—and well he should, Ricardo thought. Leona had been having that same effect on the men who loved her since she was a little girl. Ricardo saw no reason that it should be any different with her future husband.

He wondered just how much he should tell Diego and how much he should let the man discover for himself. He wondered just how understanding he would be, if the whole truth were known.

"Come on." Ricardo jerked his head. "We'll search that draw for strays." He nudged his horse with the heels of his boots and started down a gentle slope.

Of all Leona's brothers, Ricardo knew he was the only one who came close to understanding her. True, she had been a bit spoiled and pampered just because she was the only girl in the family, but she had also been frustrated as she got older by everyone telling her she couldn't do things her brothers could do, just because she was female. She had become adept at getting her way with the men in her family, from her father down to her twin and all the brothers in between. He wondered now how she would manage to get her way with Diego.

"She didn't have the usual childhood for a girl. Wherever my brothers went, I went, and wherever I went, Leona went, too." Ricardo shrugged. "She learned things that most girls don't."

He fell silent as his horse lunged up an incline. He stopped and waited for Diego to join him.

"It wasn't until she began to develop into a young woman that our father brought a dueña to Rancho del Sol to instruct and chaperon her." He grinned as he remembered the woman's horrified expression when she saw Leona—riding astride and wearing trousers—gallop her horse into the compound. "It was a difficult time for all of us. Señora Soberanes wanted to change Leona, and Leona didn't want to be changed. The *señora* was stubborn. So was my sister." He shrugged. "It was a stand-off."

Ricardo looked at Diego again. He liked this man. When he'd first met him, he'd been troubled by Leona's reaction to him. Now, he believed that Diego was the one man who could make his sister happy, the one man strong enough for his strong-willed sister. He hoped he was right.

"*Amigo*, if you want a meek wife who will blindly obey and look to you to do her thinking for her, don't marry Leona, I beg you. You'll only make her unhappy, and she'll make you miserable. She's learned to appear to be what people think she should be, but don't be fooled by appearances. Leona is Leona—and much more."

It seemed to Diego that there was as much Ricardo was *not* saying as he *was* saying. It was like a riddle of sorts. He wondered momentarily if his friend was playing a game with him, then decided not. He sensed that Ricardo was telling as much as he could without breaking a confidence.

Now it was up to Diego to learn all the facts.

He tried to imagine Leona as a child, growing up with so many brothers, tagging along wherever they went. Diego himself had been the youngest of four boys. He remembered the games they'd played, the scrapes they'd gotten into, the stunts they'd pulled on each other. He remembered the afternoons spent at the swimming hole, the wild rides across the Texas prairie, the laughter and the fights. He began to have an inkling of what Leona's girlhood must have been like, what had shaped the woman she was today.

He realized her twin was right. There was a lot Diego needed to learn about Leona, and he meant to begin learning it right away.

Ricardo removed his hat and drew a shirt sleeve across his forehead, wiping away the sweat that had gathered beneath the band. As he returned the hat to his head, he said with a half-jesting, half-serious expression, "And if you make Leona unhappy, Diego Salazar, she has nine brothers who will be unhappy, too. You wouldn't like that, *amigo*."

"I know," he replied solemnly. "I've thought of that before."

Ricardo chuckled. "It's not as bad as all that. If I didn't think you could make her happy, I wouldn't care if you understood her or not. I'd just see that you went back to Texas very soon."

Diego nodded silently, determined to follow Ricardo's advice. He had a riddle to solve. The riddle of Leona Washington.

* * *

It was Leona's intention to refuse to speak to Diego when next she saw him. She was prepared to show him the full extent of her anger. She intended to put the man firmly in his place.

Only he sabotaged her plans by apologizing to her just before supper that same day. He didn't mention the subject of her swimming in her undergarments, certainly not in front her father or brothers, nor did he bring it up privately to her. He was attentive without being overbearing. He asked questions without being nosy. He was his most charming, likeable self all evening long.

Leona was still pondering her fiancé's complexities when a rider brought a message for him. Diego read it while he stood not far from Leona, then told her that he had urgent business to attend to in San Francisco, and he didn't know how long he would be away. He left Rancho del Sol at sunrise the next morning.

Chapter Fifteen

Diego rode his pinto toward the Curtis Tavern. He was covered with dust from his days of travel. He was weary and thirsty, and it was still a long ride to the Washington ranch.

While he was in San Francisco, the weather had turned hot. Even here beside Monterey Bay, the air lay still and heavy. The sky, unmarred by clouds, stretched in an endless expanse of blue from horizon to horizon.

He paused inside the dim tavern to allow his eyes time to adjust to the sudden absence of bright light. He heard the barmaid's voice before he could see her.

"So, *señor*, you finally return. Carmencita has missed you."

He was almost too tired to grin. "You were mad at me the last time I saw you."

"I was wrong, *señor*. I was wrong about you."

She took hold of his arm and drew him to an empty table, set against the wall. "Sit down. I will bring you something to drink."

"Thanks."

As he waited, he looked around. The tavern was crowded today. Sailors, mostly. They filled the tables—smoking, drinking, laughing—and leaned against the bar. Behind that same bar, Heath Curtis was busy filling glasses with whiskey and beer. The bartender's gaze briefly met Diego's, just long enough to acknowledge his presence before Curtis returned to the job at hand.

Carmencita brought a beer back to Diego's table and set it in front of him. She leaned forward, giving him a generous view of her breasts, but there was nothing seductive about the look in her eyes. Her whole face softened as she spoke. "The doctor you sent, *señor*. He saved the *muchacho's* life. He will not lose his legs. The doctor thinks he will even be able to walk again."

Diego let out a long sigh. "I'm glad." He took a drink, then glanced back at the barmaid. "How did you know I sent the doctor?"

"Oh"— the coquettish smile returned to her mouth—"Carmencita knows many things." She straightened, one hand on her hip, the other tugging at the off-the-shoulder sleeve of her blouse, she winked at him suggestively. "You would be surprised what Carmencita knows."

He laughed. "I'll bet."

She flicked a strand of dark hair over her shoulder, then turned and walked back to the bar, her movements drawing the lustful gazes of nearly every man in the tavern.

Leaning back in his chair, Diego drained the glass of beer. He was glad to hear that the squatter's boy would not only live but probably be able to walk again. He'd known if anyone could help him, it would be Jeremy Adams. Jeremy had been the army doctor who'd ridden with Diego's regiment back in Texas, and Diego knew what a skilled physician he was. He was glad he'd kept track of Jeremy, glad he'd known the doctor was living and practicing in San Francisco, glad Jeremy had been willing to come down and take a look at the boy.

He wished the rest of his trip to San Francisco had been as successful. It seemed almost a certainty that Judge Emanuel Hopkins would soon be appointed to the Land Commission, and Diego knew that this wouldn't bode well for the californios.

Joseph's letter had instructed Diego to meet with another detective, Hiram Benjamin, in San Francisco and to confirm the judge's activities in the area. It hadn't taken the two men long to learn that Judge Hopkins had set his sights on the fertile lands of the Salinas Valley. A little more digging had revealed the judge's numerous contacts with a certain attorney named McCabe.

Diego's fingers tightened around his empty beer glass. If Hopkins and McCabe joined forces, they would soon drive every honest ranchero from the valley. Even a man like Gardner Washington wouldn't be safe.

Running his fingers over his hair to smooth it back from his forehead, Diego rose from the table. There was no point in rehashing things in his head. He'd left Hiram looking for anything they could use against the judge to stop his appointment. In the meantime, Diego meant to search even harder for evidence against McCabe—evidence that could be substantiated in a court of law, not mere rumor.

"You are leaving, *señor*?"

Diego set his hat back on his head, looking at Carmencita as she walked toward him. "Yes."

"But you must not leave until you have seen the *muchacho*. He and his father wish to thank you for what you have done." She hooked her hand through his elbow. "Come. I will take you to him. These *hombres* can manage without me for a little while."

Leona might as well have been invisible. Neither Ricardo nor Mercedes seemed the least bit aware that she was even with them in the carriage.

She smiled privately, amused by the sudden change in her brother. She had never expected her twin to become so befuddled by love. Certainly she hadn't expected him to fall so hard for Mercedes. She'd known, of course, how her best friend felt about Ricardo, and she'd truly hoped that two people she loved so much would find happiness with each other. But still, she hadn't been prepared for this . . . this . . .

Ricardo whispered something to Mercedes, who

then blushed and giggled. Leona sighed and rolled her eyes, setting her gaze on the passing landscape. She was glad it wouldn't be much longer before they reached Monterey. She wasn't sure how much more of this she could take.

Leona had two reasons for going to town today. First, she needed to choose some fabric for a new dress. She'd tried not to admit it to herself, but the truth was, she wanted something special to wear next week when her engagement to Diego was officially announced.

Her second reason was to visit the Hammond boy, the one who'd been hurt when McCabe drove that family of squatters off his land. The Hammonds had been given shelter by a widow woman in Monterey. Leona had heard that a doctor had come down from San Francisco to attend the boy and that it appeared he was going to live.

The news had cheered Leona as nothing else had since Diego left the ranch. The days since his departure had crept by at a snail's pace. There'd been no word from him, no sign of his returning. She'd spent the time vacillating between telling herself she was glad he was gone and missing him more than she'd known was possible.

Caramba! She was getting as bad as Ricardo.

It was all this inactivity, she decided. La Rosa and her hombres had not ridden for over two weeks. Neither Paco nor Johnny had brought any word from the McCabe ranch regarding the lawyer's activities. The silence was beginning to concern Leona, but Ricardo had persuaded her that, if there were trouble, they would have heard something.

Her brother stopped the carriage in front of a small adobe house on the outskirts of Monterey. There was a picket fence around a well-kept yard. Flowers bloomed on the south side of the house near the entrance.

"This is Señora Tremaine's *casa*," he said as he looped the ends of the reins over the dashboard. He hopped to the ground, then turned back to help Mercedes and his sister descend.

Just as they reached the front door, it opened. Leona's gaze flew up to meet a pair of familiar dark eyes. She felt a moment of shock, followed by a strange numbness as her gaze shifted to the pretty señorita at his side.

"Diego!" her brother exclaimed. "When did you return, *amigo*?"

"Just today," he answered. "I was on my way to the ranch now."

The woman beside Diego nodded knowingly as she returned Leona's stare. "So, this is your woman." A slow smile bowed her full mouth. "She is very pretty, *señor*. Very pretty." Her gaze moved to Diego. "Now, I must get back to the tavern. Señor Curtis, he will be very angry with me for being away so long."

"Thank you for bringing me, Carmencita."

"*De nada, amigo.*"

Carmencita slipped out the doorway and started down the street.

"You must be here to see Bobby," Diego said to Leona after a lengthy silence.

Her brain felt sluggish. Her heart still felt numb. "Bobby?"

"Bobby Hammond. The boy who was hurt. Isn't he why you're here?"

"Oh. *Sí.*" She mentally shook herself, trying to forget the terrible feeling that had washed over her when she'd seen Diego with that woman. She glanced toward her brother and Mercedes. "We came to see how he's getting along. We brought some things we thought the family might need."

Diego took Leona's arm and pulled her into the house. He introduced her to the Widow Tremaine, a plump woman with a friendly, round face and a tight cap of gray curls on her head. Then he led her into a cramped bedroom at the back of the house. Ricardo and Mercedes followed close behind.

A haggard-looking couple stood at the end of the bed. They were both thin to the point of gauntness, and Leona suspected they looked far older than their actual years.

"Bobby, you have more visitors," Diego said to the child lying on the bed, his legs covered with a light blanket.

Seeing the boy's pale, bruised face and pain-riddled eyes, Leona forgot all about herself and Diego and the señorita who had been with him just moments before. She knelt down beside the bed.

"Hello, Bobby. My name is Leona. Everyone is so sorry you got hurt. I wanted to come sooner, but you were too sick to have visitors. I brought some things I thought you might like."

Diego watched and listened as Leona began to charm the little boy, making him forget, if only briefly, the pain he was in.

She will be a good mother to our children.

The thought surprised him. Children? *Their* children?

He felt a pleasurable warmth. Yes, their children. His and Leona's.

A mental picture formed in his head, one of a house—no, a home—and Leona and children. And he was there, too.

Staring down at the back of Leona's head, he realized that he wasn't just falling in love with her. He *already* loved her. Completely. Totally.

And with that realization came a longing to settle in one place, to end the vagabond existence that had been his for so many years. He wanted a home of his own, land of his own, a family of his own.

The feelings were so unexpected that he turned around and slipped outside, afraid that others would be able to read his thoughts on his face before he had a chance to assimilate them himself.

Leona felt his absence, like a cold breeze against her back, but she didn't stop talking to Bobby as she emptied the basket she'd brought with her from the ranch. There were several toys and a couple of picture books and some clothes that one of her nephews had outgrown.

"Is there anything more that you need, Mr.

Hammond?" Ricardo asked the boy's father.

"No, sir, but thank ya kindly. 'Twixt Miz Tremaine's givin' us a place t'stay and Mr. Salazar sendin' Doc Adams down from Frisco, we figure we got everythin' worth havin'. The doc saved our boy's life and that's all we coulda asked fer."

Leona turned her head and lifted her gaze. "Señor Salazar sent a doctor to see your son?"

"Yes, ma'am, he did. All the way from San Francisco. 'Course, the doc here'd done all he could, but there weren't nobody thought Bobby'd live out the week. They wanted t'take his legs, but the missus, she wouldn't have it. She said if'n the good Lord saw fit t'take the boy home, she wanted him walkin' into glory on two legs." He put his arm around his wife's shoulders and squeezed her up against his side. "Then Doc Adams come. I don't know what he done. I just know we got us our boy back, an' the doc says there's a good chance Bobby's gonna be able t'walk agin."

"And Diego sent him?" she repeated, her eyes returning to the small boy on the bed.

"Yes, ma'am. The doc, he says they served together in Texas during the war. Spoke mighty highly of Mr. Salazar, too. I tell ya, ma'am, we feel mighty lucky. He don't know us from Adam. He didn't have t'go to all that trouble fer us or our son. Yes, ma'am. Mighty lucky."

Leona nodded as she brushed a stray lock of brown hair back from the boy's face. "It was nice to meet you, Bobby Hammond. When you get well, you come visit me at my father's ranch. I'll show you my horse and take you for a ride. Would you like that?"

Bobby nodded enthusiastically.

"Then you hurry and get well." Leona pushed herself up from the floor. Looking at his parents again, she added, "Please send word to Rancho del Sol if there's anything you need."

"That's right kind o' you, ma'am. Right kind. We never met so many good people as we've met since this happened. We're strangers here, but ya wouldn't know it by the way folks've taken us in and seen to us."

Leona felt a sudden sting of tears behind her eyes and her throat felt thick. Hard times had been etched into the Hammonds' faces. Poverty was clearly a fact they'd lived with for years. She didn't know what had brought them to the Salinas, only that they must have come here looking for a better life. McCabe's men had ruthlessly driven them from a small patch of land, maiming and nearly killing this child while they were at it. Yet Mr. Hammond had only spoken of the kindness of others and how grateful they were that their son had been spared.

"If it's all right, I'll come visit Bobby again soon," she said softly.

"We'd be pleased t'see ya, ma'am. Right pleased."

Leona quickly left the bedroom. She paused long enough to thank the widow for taking in the Hammond family and to offer whatever help might be needed. Then she went outside.

Diego was standing beside the Washington carriage.

Leona stopped suddenly as their gazes met. "Why did you do it?" she asked him. "You didn't know these people."

"Why did *you* come to see the boy?" he asked in return. "You didn't know them either."

"It's because of you he's going to live."

Diego shrugged. "I was lucky I knew that Jeremy was in San Francisco."

She thought of how angry she'd been at him the day he'd forbidden her to go swimming alone. She'd been so certain she would never forgive him. She'd even thought she might never speak to him again. She'd been more determined than ever to convince him that they were ill-suited for each other.

Now, it seemed as if those feelings had belonged to another woman.

"Leona . . . About Carmencita."

She blinked, then stared at him, not understanding.

"The woman who was here when you arrived."

"Oh." It felt like a giant hand was squeezing her chest.

"She wasn't *with* me, Leona. Not really. She'd heard that I'd sent the doctor from San Francisco. So she thought I ought to see how Bobby was doing. That's all."

"Oh." The heavy weight lifted from her chest, and she could breathe again.

He stepped toward her.

The weight returned with force. Her breathing grew shallow. Her heart beat erratically.

He raised a hand, stroking her cheek with his fingertips, then cupping her chin in his hand. "I missed you."

Her mouth went dry.

"I missed you very much."

His lips descended slowly, ever so slowly, until they covered hers. She sensed something new in this kiss, a deeper emotion. While she didn't understand what it was, she knew it would have a profound effect upon her, and it left her shaken to the very core.

Chapter Sixteen

This time when Diego awoke, his mind wasn't dulled by wine. He knew, even before he looked, that La Rosa was in his room.

He opened his eyes and turned his head. She was standing before the window, as still as if she were a statue made of stone, a dark silhouette against the white moonlight at her back. He knew she was staring at him, could feel the intensity of her gaze even though he couldn't see her eyes.

Slowly, he sat up, sliding his bare back up the cool wall. He bent his legs beneath the bed covers, then leaned his forearms on his knees. *"Buenas noches."*

She echoed the greeting softly.

He waved his hand toward the only chair in his room. "Please, La Rosa. Make yourself at home."

She didn't move. "You will marry this *señorita*? The one who lives here?"

"Leona?" He was surprised. Her question wasn't what he'd expected. "Yes, I'm going to marry her."

"Why?"

"Why?"

"Sí, *señor*. Why will you marry her?"

He stared at the bandida's shadowed form for a long time without answering.

La Rosa took a step forward. He caught a faint whiff of roses and wondered if the scent was really there or if it was just his imagination.

"Why, *señor*?" she repeated once again in that low, sultry voice that was so uniquely hers.

"Because . . ." He smiled as he pictured Leona in his mind. "Because I love her."

"You love her?"

He chuckled softly. "It surprised me, too," he admitted. "But it's true. I love Leona Washington."

La Rosa turned around and walked back to the window. As she looked outside, she asked, "Would you not rather have a woman like me, *señor*?"

If her previous question had caught him by surprise, this one left him speechless.

The bandida glanced over her shoulder. Apparently she didn't expect an answer, for she changed the subject quickly. "I hear you would like to ride with La Rosa. That you wish to help fight McCabe. Is that true?"

Diego straightened. "That's right. I would." Damn! He wished he could see her face. "Who told you? Ricardo? He rides with you, doesn't he?"

"You ask too many questions, Diego Salazar. Do not suppose you have the right to answers."

She looked out the window again, changing the subject as abruptly as before. "How do you know you love her?"

This time she waited for a response.

He wasn't sure how to answer. He wasn't sure he understood himself. It was simply something he knew, deep in his heart, without question. But how did he explain that to someone else? Only someone who had felt it could understand.

"I just know that I do, La Rosa."

"Tell me. What is she like, this Leona you love?"

The peculiarities of this moment were not lost on Diego. How strange to be sitting in his bed in the middle of the night, naked as a blue jay beneath the blanket, a masked bandida standing at his window, while he talked of the woman he planned to marry.

"She's beautiful, with skin as soft as rose petals and the sweetest smile. She's gentle and kind and . . ."

"So!" La Rosa laughed sharply. "She is pretty. She will make a nice ornament to hang on your arm. She will make an obedient wife, no? You will tell her what to do and she will do it."

The memory of Leona's fury by the pond flashed in his head. "I doubt it," he replied in a droll tone. "She's a bit more independent than that."

"And you will not learn to hate this independence?"

"It's part of what I love about her." As he spoke the words, he realized how true they were. "Leona is intelligent and not afraid to express her opinions. She's not going to let me or any other man tell her what to think or do." He paused, reflecting on the complexities of the woman he loved, more determined than ever to understand her better than he did now. Then he remembered her, kneeling beside Bobby's bed, her expression so tender and caring. "I think she must be a little like you, La Rosa. You both want to help the people of this valley. You just go about it differently."

La Rosa turned to face him once again. Her gaze seemed to bore into him from behind her mask. Finally, she spoke. "I will think about what you have said, *amigo*. Perhaps La Rosa needs you to ride beside her after all." She bowed slightly. "*Adiós.*"

With the agility of a cat, she moved through the open window.

Diego didn't bother to rise from the bed. He knew she would have disappeared before he could reach the window.

Leona's feet fairly flew across the ground, lightened by the soaring of her heart.

He loved her! Diego loved Leona!

When he'd kissed her outside Widow Tremaine's adobe house today, she'd dared to hope but hadn't believed it could really be true. She'd dared to think she'd read his feelings in his eyes, but the memory of the way he'd kissed La Rosa, his fascination with the bandida, had made her afraid.

That was why she'd gone to him tonight as La Rosa. She'd needed to know why he wanted to marry her, what he felt for her.

And now she knew. He loved her. He would be true to her. Even loving Leona, he could have lied to La Rosa. He could have kissed the bandida and made love to her, but he hadn't. He hadn't because he loved Leona.

She ran all the way to the hidden cove, yet she didn't feel tired when she got there. In fact, she was almost giddy with happiness. She felt as silly as if she'd had too much wine to drink. She wanted to laugh and to shout with joy.

It didn't take her long to change out of La Rosa's costume, returning it to its hiding place beneath the floor of the playhouse, wrapped in the burlap bag along with dried rose petals.

The walk back to the hacienda was completed at a much more leisurely pace, allowing her a sedate contemplation of her changing circumstances. She silently acknowledged that she had to delay the wedding as long as possible. Once they were married, La Rosa would be unable to ride, even if Diego didn't take her away to Texas at once. As much as she loved him—oh, how very much she *did* love him—and as much as it had pleased her to hear him say her independence was one of the things he loved about her, she wasn't fooled. Diego would never approve of her midnight activities.

She had only to remember how upset he had become when he'd found her swimming alone. She had only to remember the tone of his voice as he'd forbidden her to do so again. He would think the work she did as La Rosa was too dangerous. While she was ready to admit that it was risky, she was not ready to be forbidden to continue, and that was exactly what he would do. Because he loved her, because he was her husband, he would forbid it.

And *that* she could not allow.

She frowned a little, new doubts creeping in to spoil her joy.

Diego had said he loved her independence, but would he still feel that way if he knew how hard she would resist his efforts to control her? He saw her as sweet and kind and gentle. He thought her a properly raised señorita with no real understanding of the world around her. Would he still love her when he saw just how independent, how unladylike she could be? He was fascinated by La Rosa, but would he appreciate the same qualities in his bride?

Perhaps she had better find out before it was too late.

When Diego walked into the dining room early the next morning, Ricardo was just sitting down at the table, his plate filled high with food.

"Ah, good. You are up, *amigo*. I was hoping you would join me this morning, if you're not too weary from your trip. I'm riding south today. Our horses are wandering too close to McCabe's land. If we don't bring them north now, we won't see them again. They will simply disappear, I think."

"He steals your horses?"

"Not that we can prove."

Diego dished up some breakfast from the sideboard. "I'll go with you."

"Good."

The two men polished off their meal in a hurry, then walked out into the golden haze of dawn, long strides carrying them quickly toward the stables. Three horses were already saddled and waiting for them. Leona was mounted on one of them, sitting astride the saddle, her legs clad in trousers and high boots, her hair covered with a wide-brimmed hat. It was an outfit almost identical to the one her brother wore.

Diego stopped abruptly when he saw her, but Ricardo walked on, as if the sight were not unusual or unexpected.

"*Buenos días*," she greeted Diego in her light, sweet voice. "I knew you would come with us, so I saddled a horse for you. I hope you didn't mean to use Conquistador. After so long a trip, I thought you'd want to give him a rest. You'll like Chico. He's quick and well-trained."

Her brother took up his horse's reins and swung into the saddle, then looked at Diego. "Leona's a fine *vaquera*. She won't slow us down." He grinned, revealing a row of straight, white teeth.

"I'm sure she won't," Diego replied dryly, remembering how ably Leona rode sidesaddle at a mad gallop.

"Come on. It's a long ride to the boundary of our land." Ricardo nudged his horse forward.

Without another word, Diego mounted the remaining horse and followed after the twins.

He stared at Leona's back, irritated, feeling as if
he'd been set up but not understanding why just
yet. However, as time passed, he found himself
enjoying the view in front of him. He had to admit
that Leona did wondrous things for a pair of trousers, her thighs hugging the sides of the horse she
rode. Her derrière moved in a most delightful way
with each step of the horse.

He began to smile. Was he really surprised that
she would choose to ride like one of the vaqueros?
Or dress like one of them? Hadn't Ricardo hinted
at the same? For that matter, hadn't Leona warned
him that he didn't know her?

So that's what this was about. Leona was going
to let him know what he was in for if he married
her. She'd already shown him what kind of cook
she was. Now she meant to show him something
else.

He could have saved her the trouble, he supposed. He could have told her he loved her and
that, whatever she did, he would go on loving
her. He could have, but he didn't. He would
rather wait and see to what lengths she would
go to make him refuse her. After all, this could
be quite illuminating—and, perhaps, just a bit
amusing.

Diego nudged his horse into a trot, drawing up
beside Leona and her brother. When she glanced
his way, he nodded and offered an enigmatic grin,
then turned his gaze straight ahead.

"Nice outfit," he said. "Sensible. A skirt and petticoats would just get in the way when you're wrangling horses."

Ricardo made a strangled sound in his throat.

Diego ignored him as he squinted up at the sky. "Looks like it's going to be another hot day."

"*Sí,*" Ricardo answered, his voice unusually high-pitched. "A very hot day, *amigo*. Very hot."

Silence fell on the little group. After a few minutes had passed, they broke the horses into a canter, quickly leaving the hacienda behind them.

Diego had to admit it. He was impressed. She handled the reata almost as well as any man he'd ever worked with and better than many. She also rode the little cow pony with finesse and skill, guiding the gelding with the pressure of her thighs as she chased strays from ravines and arroyos.

As Diego watched Leona bunch a small herd of mares and foals into a tight band, he lifted his canteen and took a sip, rolling the water around in his mouth before swallowing. When she drew up her horse not far from him and looked his way, he held the canteen in her direction.

"*Gracias.*" She accepted it from him, holding the canteen in her hand while she pushed the hat from her hair. With the hat dangling against her back, held there by the string around her throat, she tipped her head and took a long drink.

Her face was covered with dust. Streaks of sweat had left muddy trails near her temples and ears. Her raven-black hair formed damp curls across her forehead. Her cheeks were flushed from the heat.

He thought she looked as enchanting as he'd ever seen her.

She met his gaze as she passed the canteen back to him. There was a question in her eyes that she couldn't seem to speak aloud. He thought it was time he answered it.

"Ricardo wasn't exaggerating when he said you were a fine *vaquera*. You're one of the best I've ever ridden with. Who taught you to throw the *reata*?"

There was a note of pride in her voice when she answered, "Alfonso."

"And to ride a horse like that?"

"Manuel."

He moved his horse forward, drawing up beside her, their boots nearly touching. "There is some advantage to having many brothers, I see."

Leona felt a bubble of happiness expanding inside her. "*Sí*. Sometimes there are advantages."

"I suspect there are other things they've taught you which I have yet to see." His tone was light and teasing.

"A few."

"I thought as much."

It was difficult to remember why she'd ridden out with him this morning, dressed as a vaquera. With him smiling at her that way, his brown eyes twinkling with mirth, it was harder still to remember the reasons why she must wait to marry him. But wait she must. "Diego?"

"Hmmm?"

"We needn't be in any hurry to marry after our engagement is announced. We have lots of time to get to know each other better."

His smile faded. With a swift, easy movement, he jumped to the ground. He walked over to her horse, clamped his hands around the waistband of her trousers, and lifted her out of the saddle, setting her on her feet before him.

"Are you still so certain you will make me a poor wife, Leona?" he asked as he leaned toward her.

She shook her head, nodded, shook her head again. She didn't know what she meant. She didn't even remember what the question had been.

He drew her up into his arms. The whole length of her body was touching his, and she felt a searing heat rush through her. When his lips met hers, her mouth parted instinctively. Her hands, once resting on his chest, slipped up to stroke the back of his neck, her fingers weaving through the shaggy length of his black hair.

She gave herself completely to the kiss, savoring every taste, every touch, every emotion. She felt as if she'd been born just for this moment. In fact, she thought perhaps she'd never even lived until this moment. It was glorious, and she never wanted it to stop. She wanted more. She wanted everything he had to give.

She wanted Diego.

His passion raged like a prairie fire. His tongue played over her parted lips, then darted into her mouth. Her small, firm breasts were pressed tightly against his chest, and her hips fit against his own. She wriggled, as if trying to get closer still, driving him nearly mad with desire.

He knew he had to stop soon, or he would find himself laying her in the grass and tasting more pleasures than were his right. He would forget that Ricardo was just over the next hill and could join them at any moment. He would forget everything except Leona.

His hands moved to her upper arms, and he set her slightly away from him. She opened her eyes. Emotions churned like a storm-tossed sea within their violet depths.

He'd suspected he would find passion in Leona, but he hadn't known how much. Nor had he known how he would respond to her. Only once before had a single kiss made him burn so quickly for a woman. Only when he'd kissed La Rosa.

His eyes widened a fraction as he looked down at Leona. Could it be?

No. It couldn't. He was crazy even to think it.

Still . . . the feel of her lips, the taste of her mouth . . .

No. He was imagining it. They were nothing alike. Even their voices were completely different.

He'd had too much to drink the night La Rosa had first come to his room. He was confusing his earlier kisses with Leona, remembering them as the bandida's.

Or was he?

La Rosa . . . No. It couldn't be.

Reason returned, and with it, enough insight to see what Diego was thinking. Leona had kissed him only once before with such abandon. That time she'd been in costume, her disguise making her reckless.

But this kiss had been the most dangerous of all. This kiss had left him wondering.

She could almost read his silent debate as he tried to decipher the truth. She would have to do something to end his conjecturing. She would have to do something very soon.

Chapter Seventeen

Gardner drew the horse to a halt in front of the dressmaker's tiny shop. "You're sure you don't want me to wait for you?"

"No, *Papá*. I'll join you when I'm finished." Leona alighted from the carriage, then turned to face her father.

She would have liked to go with him to the hearing, but Mercedes had asked that she not come. Señor Ramirez preferred to have as few of his neighbors witness the loss of his home as possible. He was an old and fiercely proud man, and this was a difficult time for him. To Sebastiano Ramirez, this was a day of personal humiliation and shame.

"Will you be able to help Señor Ramirez?" she asked softly, even though she knew what her father's answer would be.

Gardner shook his head. "I'll do what I can, but

I don't hold out much hope. The hearing's been delayed a couple of times while Sebastiano tried to find proof of the land grant. Without it . . ." He shook his head again.

Leona leaned forward and covered her father's hand with her own. "You've done all you could."

"But it wasn't enough. McCabe gains more influence with the commission every day."

"It isn't your fault, *Papá*."

"No."

She could tell he didn't believe his own denial. He felt he should have been able to do more. She understood his frustration because she'd felt it herself so often in her forays against McCabe.

Gardner gave her a half-hearted smile. "Get in there and try on that dress. You shouldn't be worrying yourself about anything except how pretty you're going to look for Diego at the *fandango*. Worrying isn't going to change a thing now. We'll just present the evidence as best we can and hope the commissioners will rule fairly. And Ramirez can always appeal the decision if he wants to."

Leona didn't even try to reply as she stepped back from the carriage and watched it pull away.

She felt anger rising in her chest. *The commission rule fairly?* Not as long as Rance McCabe helped pull the strings.

She'd started to turn toward the shop door when her gaze collided with the source of her enmity. McCabe was sauntering toward her, wearing a self-satisfied smirk. He was dressed in a finely tailored suit and carried a walking stick with a gold-inlaid handle. As he drew closer, he removed his top hat from his auburn hair, stopped and bowed.

"Good day to you, Miss Washington."

She acknowledged him with only the slightest incline of her head.

"I hear there are big festivities planned at Rancho del Sol for Saturday night."

Again, she remained silent.

McCabe stepped closer. "It's not too late for you to change your mind. Why marry a man so unworthy of you, my dear Miss Washington? You should have a man with wealth and power and influence. Why do you want to waste your life giving children to that . . . *Texan*?"

"The man I marry is no concern of yours, Señor McCabe." She started to turn away, but his hand on her arm stayed her.

"But it *is* my concern. Don't you know that I have come to care for you since we met? I could provide very handsomely for you. You would never want for anything." His fingers tightened on her arm. "I had harbored hopes that you might favor me."

Hatred roiled in her chest, snapping her resolve to remain cool and controlled. "I would as soon favor a rabid dog as you." She jerked her arm away from him. "Do you think I don't know what you do? Do you think I don't care what you're doing to my friends, my neighbors? You steal their land and their homes. You drive off their cattle and horses."

"Who says I do these things?" His eyes narrowed,

his voice became as hard as steel. "There's no truth to such rumors. I'm a lawyer, Miss Washington. I work within the law."

"You are a murdering coward."

McCabe reached for her again.

The moment his fingers closed around her left arm, her fury exploded. She slapped him with her right hand with all the strength she could muster. He released his hold, staring at her in surprise as a red mark formed on the side of his face. Slowly, the stunned look vanished, replaced by something much more sinister.

"You'll regret that, Leona," he warned softly. "I promise you. You *will* regret that."

"Never!" She spun away from him, quickly disappearing into the dressmaker's shop.

As she closed the door behind her, the tiny bell still jingling overhead, she felt a terrible dread wash over her, a premonition of great pain and suffering. She could taste the danger, thick on her tongue. For the first time since she'd donned the red costume, Leona wondered if La Rosa would prevail.

Diego had always had a knack for detective work. He knew how to watch and observe. He knew how to listen. He knew how to ask just the right questions in just the right way. For some reason, people seemed to open up to him when they wouldn't to others.

During the war with Mexico, his skills had served him well as a scout and a spy. Since then, he'd been considered one of Joseph McConnell's best agents. He was good at what he did, and he knew it, had always known it. That had been enough for him at one time.

But no longer. It wasn't enough because he cared too much. The issue had become personal. He cared about these people. They had become his friends, and he wanted to do something to help them.

Now, as Diego sat at the back of the hearing room, he was infuriated by his inability to stop what was happening. He'd gathered the necessary information about the commissioners and reported it to his superiors, but he couldn't be sure when, if ever, the government would appoint honest men to the commission as a result of his report. It certainly wasn't going to be in time to help the Ramirez family.

Out of the corner of his eye, he saw a movement. He turned and watched as the sheriff scratched his hairy chin. The man wore a bored expression.

Incompetent idiot, Diego thought as he stared at the man. He didn't protect the ranchers. He didn't protect the squatters. He didn't protect anyone but himself. While lawyers like McCabe stole from the ranchers in mock hearings such as this one, bandits roamed at will along the highways of the valley. Shootings and killings went uninvestigated while the sheriff sat on his fat behind and did nothing.

If Diego were the sheriff, if *he* had the power of the law behind him, he would find some way to stop McCabe. He would make it unnecessary for a woman to ride at night, fighting for justice, risking her life because the law had turned a blind eye upon the truth, and real bandits would find it was no longer safe to rob honest, hard-working people.

He rose from his chair and slipped out of the room, unable to listen to any more of the travesty. He knew it had already been decided that Sebastiano Ramirez would lose his land, long before he and his Californian lawyer had appeared before the commissioners. They would see no justice in that room this day.

His thoughts were dark as he left the building. He didn't pay much attention to where his steps were taking him. He was too angry, too frustrated to care.

What good was it, the work he had done, if the Ramirez family was still driven away? What had he accomplished? How slowly would the wheels of justice turn before McCabe was stopped?

Or would he ever be stopped?

Diego had to admit that the evidence against McCabe was circumstantial at best. His last communication with Joseph McConnell had suggested that the agency look into McCabe's activities in New York before he came to California. A sixth sense told him that the lawyer was far more dangerous, far more devious than most folks even imagined.

But the law wasn't guided by intuition. The powers that be might replace ineffectual or dishonest men on the Land Commission, based upon Diego's report, but that wouldn't mean McCabe would get what he deserved.

McCabe would still have all the land and cattle and horses he'd taken by less than honorable means. He would still be able to practice his own particular brand of law. He would still be wealthy and powerful. He might not be able to steal the land quite so easily from the ranchers, but he would still be able to take land in payment for his services. He would probably still be able to continue to bully and terrify the people of this valley.

Diego thought of little Bobby Hammond, trampled beneath the hooves of stampeding livestock. McCabe was responsible for the boy's crippled legs, and yet no one seemed able—or, as in the case of the sheriff, willing—to do anything about it.

Madre de Dios! McCabe had to be stopped. Somehow, he had to be stopped.

Diego looked up and found that he had arrived at the beach. Several ships rocked gently at anchor in the bay. Sea gulls circled overhead, their raucous cries puncturing the quiet of midday. He stared at the scene for a long time, allowing the lapping of the surf upon the sand to soothe his troubled soul. Finally, he turned his back on the ocean and swept his gaze over the peaceful town.

A strange possessiveness quickened in his chest. It was something he'd never felt before but had recognized in his father and brothers. It was something he'd wondered if he would ever feel. When he'd returned to Texas after his years at Harvard, he'd been restless. Even loving his family the way he did hadn't been enough to keep him at the Salazar ranch for long. He'd experienced plenty of guilt for not sharing the same feelings about Texas—and the ranch and all that went with it—that his father and brothers felt.

Now he knew why.

This was where he belonged. This town, this valley. When he pictured himself and Leona and their children, this was where he imagined them.

Vive Dios! Diego couldn't stand by and watch McCabe bring harm and heartache to so many in the place he was already thinking of as home. If the only way the lawyer could be stopped was by the harassment of a bandida, then Diego meant to help her do it. Tonight, he would convince Ricardo to take him to her. And if not, then he would have a talk with Miguel Aguilar. One way or another, Diego would see La Rosa again.

And in the meantime, he meant to find out more about Rance McCabe.

McCabe hadn't been required to attend the hearing, but he'd wanted to be there to see the old man's defeat. Sebastiano Ramirez had hired a different attorney, one who had lived in the area for two decades. A greaser like himself.

The old fool. Now Ramirez would have nothing. If he'd taken McCabe up on his offer, he could have kept at least half of his land.

McCabe walked out of the building. He should

have felt good about the way things were going. The commission would announce its decision by the first of the week. Ramirez and his family would be driven back to Mexico where they belonged, and the La Brisa ranch would be put up for sale. McCabe would buy it and sell off what he didn't want.

But at this exact moment, he wasn't thinking about the additional property he would soon own. Throughout the hearing, he'd continued to feel Leona Washington's hand as it struck his cheek. It was as if her fingerprints and palm had burned their impression into the side of his face. He wondered if others in the room could see the mark and guess what had happened.

To think he had once considered making her his wife. He must have been out of his mind. She was half-Mexican. No better than an Indian squaw or a Negro slave. Not even all her father's wealth would have made her worth marrying. She was good for only one thing, relieving a man's itch.

And no woman—not even Leona Washington— was so beautiful that he would tolerate an insult such as she'd paid him today.

McCabe climbed into his buggy and picked up the reins. He glanced toward the building that housed the U.S. Land Commission and saw Ramirez with that daughter of his coming out the door. Behind them was Gardner Washington.

Damn them! Damn them all! He was sick and tired of their superior attitudes. Why had he even tried to be helpful? They didn't deserve it. There was no reasoning with these people. If he were in charge of things, he would herd them up like cattle and drive them all back across the Mexican border. This country belonged to men like him, men of vision, men of power—*white* men.

By gawd, he would show them who this country belonged to!

Diego saw Leona step out of the shop. She was dressed in a lovely shade of lavender today, from her perky bonnet to her full-skirted gown to the tips of her slippers. As she pulled the door closed behind her, her skirts swirled and swayed in a delightful motion.

Mentally, he compared this vision of loveliness to the dusty girl clad in trousers he'd held in his arms. It was hard to believe she was one and the same.

Leona opened her parasol against the hot afternoon sun, then glanced down the street. When she turned her head in his direction, he doffed his hat and bowed.

"Hello." He grinned. Just seeing her had improved his spirits. She was like a pleasant breeze off the ocean, the kind that made a man feel that all would be set right. "Could this be the famous *vaquera* I've heard so much about?" he asked teasingly.

Her eyes searched his face a moment before she returned his smile. "I guess I do look a bit different today."

"Just a bit. And very pretty, I might add."

She thanked him, then glanced down the street a second time.

He stepped up beside her, his smile fading. "Are you on your way to the Land Commission?"

She nodded. "I didn't know you were coming to town today. You could have joined *Papá* and me."

"I decided to come after you left."

"Poor Mercedes," Leona whispered.

"Yes." He didn't try to argue with her or tell her things would be all right. He knew better and so did she.

"It's so unfair. That land belongs to the Ramirezes. It isn't right for it to be taken from them. Mercedes was born in that house. So was her father. How can they say it's not theirs simply because they have no paper to prove it?"

"I don't know."

"I wish there was something I could do." She looked up at him, her eyes awash with unshed tears. "Oh, Diego, I feel so helpless. It all seems so wrong, and there's nothing I can do about it."

Diego held her against his chest, offering what comfort he could while he felt his anger return. Leona's tears were one more thing for which McCabe would be held accountable.

Leona didn't know what had gotten into her lately. This was the second time in less than two weeks that she'd ended up weeping in Diego's arms.

She'd never been the crying sort. She couldn't afford to be. Not with nine brothers to keep up with. They never would have allowed her to tag along if she'd been a milksop, given to tears and whining. Instead, she'd learned to fight back, to give as good as she got.

It was something about Diego. He made her feel like leaning into him. He made her feel as if he could help her carry the heavy burden she felt resting upon her shoulders so much of the time. He made her feel that she could trust him.

Could she? Could she trust him?

That was something she was going to have to find out.

It was nearly noon of the following day when Diego rode toward McCabe's house. It looked strangely out of place in this country where almost everything was made of adobe bricks and roofed with red tiles. It was as if McCabe were saying, "I'm better, different from the rest of you."

As he drew up before the house, Diego felt himself being watched. From the corner of his eye, he saw several men pause in their work, but he didn't turn toward them or acknowledge their presence as he dismounted and wrapped his mount's reins around the post. Then he climbed the steps to the oversized front door. Before he could knock, it opened.

The servant who held the door—a young man of Spanish descent, which surprised Diego, knowing how McCabe felt about all of them—looked vaguely familiar to him, but before he had a chance to recall where he'd seen him before, McCabe appeared in a doorway off the entry hall.

"Good afternoon, Mr. McCabe," Diego said pleasantly as he removed his hat.

McCabe frowned, his only acknowledgment of Diego's greeting being a slight nod of his head.

"Perhaps you don't remember me. We met at Gardner Washington's. I am Diego Salazar." He took a step forward. "I wonder if I might have a few words with you?"

"Why not?" McCabe disappeared into the room behind him.

Diego glanced toward the servant who still held the door, then followed after McCabe.

The office was spacious, the main piece of furniture a large oak desk. Fine oil paintings hung on the walls. Expensive sculptures, both small and large, were a prominent part of the decor. Diego found it overwhelming and ostentatious and thought it said a great deal about the man whose office it was.

It took Diego only seconds to commit the room to memory. When his gaze returned to McCabe, the man had taken his seat behind the desk, an obvious ploy for a position of power. Diego didn't wait to be invited to sit down in the chair opposite him.

"I know you're a busy man, so I'll get right to the point." Diego leaned forward. "As you know, I'm engaged to marry Miss Washington. Although her father has settled a significant amount of land on each of his sons and will probably do so for Leona as well, I would prefer to choose a place of my own. Since you are active in representing a number of ranchers before the Land Commission, I thought you might be able to tell me what land might soon be available for purchase."

"You'd have the money to buy out one of them?" McCabe asked with obvious scorn and disbelief.

"Within reason, yes."

"You steal it?"

Diego reclined in his chair and crossed his ankle over his knee. The lazy smile on his face matched his careless posture, an attitude chosen to irritate the other man. "They taught me stealing was wrong when I was at Harvard. Even for someone of mixed race." He spoke with a trace of humor, belying the anger in his belly.

"What brought you here, Salazar?"

"I came to marry Leona. And apparently, I came just in time. When we first met, I recall you were seeking the lady's favors yourself."

A tic jerked at one corner of the lawyer's mouth.

"How about it, McCabe? If you don't want to help me, perhaps you can think of it as a favor for Leona."

The man leaned forward, his face darkening. "You're mistaken about my interest in Leona Washington. There's no reason I'd have to want to help her or any other Mexican in this valley, you included. I don't care where you went to school or how much money you've got. You don't belong here. Go back to Mexico, and let the white folks who deserve this land have it."

"I'm sorry you feel that way." Diego rose to his feet, all polite pretense vanishing. His voice was cool when he continued. "The land belongs to these people, and you'd better get used to having them around. They were here long before you or any other American. You can't drive them all out."

"Watch me." McCabe jumped up from his chair. "You'll see what I can do. They'll either go to Mexico or to hell. I'll get rid of every last one of the filthy bastards before I'm done. And that goes for you and that Washington bi—"

Diego wasn't even aware that he'd stepped forward, but McCabe stopped before he'd spoken the offensive word. If he hadn't, Diego knew he would have jumped over the desk and forced the expletive back down his throat, choking him on it.

For a moment, the two men just stared at each other in silence, mutual loathing thickening the air between them.

Finally, Diego placed his hat back on his head. He felt a small measure of satisfaction. He had learned what he'd come here for. McCabe was not a careful man when he lost his temper. It was something Diego might be able to use against him at the proper time. But he would ponder that later. Right now, his own temper was stretched to the limit.

Remarkably, his anger wasn't revealed in his voice when he spoke. "Think about what I said, McCabe. I want only to buy some land. If you have what I want for sale, I will buy it from you. If not, I will buy it from someone else. Either way, I will make my home along the Salinas."

He turned and left the house.

As he stepped into the saddle, he glanced toward the door and found the servant watching him with narrowed eyes. It was then that he remembered where he'd seen the man before. It was when he'd been riding with Leona and Ricardo. Ricardo had left with him, and Leona had said it was probably because the man's wife was angry about something.

Paco, Leona had called him.

Diego frowned thoughtfully as he turned his horse away and started down the road. He wasn't sure why yet, but it troubled him that this Paco knew Leona.

Chapter Eighteen

"Oh, *señorita*," Dulce said with a long sigh. "The *señor*, he will not be able to keep his eyes from you."

Leona turned once more in front of the mirror, slightly amazed by the woman she saw staring back at her. Her mass of black hair was worn swept up on her head in an intricate weaving of curls. Made of midnight-blue satin and velvet, her dress—copying the latest style from New York, the dressmaker had said—showed just enough bare shoulder to be acceptable without being scandalous. The tight-fitting bodice emphasized her narrow waist and high, firm breasts, and the wide-flaring skirt was generously decorated with lace, ribbons, and flounces.

Her heart skipped a beat. Would Diego truly like it? Should she have left her hair down? Was the neckline too low? Should she have stayed with a more traditional style? Were her cheeks too pale? Were her eyes too bright?

She took a deep breath, then let it out slowly.

She wasn't at all sure she cared for being in love. One moment she was giddy with joy and laughter, the next she was in tears. She found herself unable to sleep much of the time. No matter what she was doing or whom she was with, thoughts of Diego were always intruding. Whatever she did, she found herself wondering if Diego would like it, if he would approve.

Leona turned away from the mirror. "Are you sure you remember what you're supposed to do this evening?" she asked her maid.

"*Sí*. I remember." Dulce's hands clasped before her. "But I am not so sure that I . . ."

"You'll do just fine."

"I am not so good a rider as you, *señorita*. In truth, the horse terrifies me. What if I fall off just when I—"

"Dulce . . ." Leona touched the girl's shoulder. "You *will* do fine. I know you will."

She nodded and offered a weak smile. "I will try, but I am afraid. I do not want to fail you. You have been so kind to me. When I had nothing, you took me in and gave me hope." She shrugged her shoulders, looking helpless and small.

Leona spoke sternly this time, all signs of tender encouragement erased from her voice. "I wouldn't have chosen you if I didn't think you could do this, Dulce Castro. I'll be there at the appointed time. You'll be there, too."

Dulce's eyes widened a fraction, then she bobbed her head in affirmation. "*Sí*. I will be there."

"*Qué bien!*" She flashed a confident smile before turning toward her bedroom door, ignoring her own nervous butterflies that burst to life in her stomach.

Now that they knew Diego's intentions toward their sister were honorable, Leona's brothers treated him with more warmth than he'd felt from them in the past. He'd met a couple of them for the first time that afternoon, although he suspected that they had heard about him from their brothers long before now.

Facing the nine tall men, all in the same room at the same time, he could only be glad that he seemed to have passed muster.

Apparently, even though Ricardo had known Diego and Leona were to be engaged, he hadn't shared the knowledge with his older brothers, waiting instead for the official announcement. It made Diego wonder if Leona's twin had believed she would change her mind and refuse to be his bride, despite her father's wishes.

Strange, how such a supposition could cause him distress. From the moment it popped into his head, he found himself watching anxiously for Leona. The longer it took her to join the family gathering, the more nervous he felt.

"I know just how you feel," Eduardo said as he laid an arm around Diego's shoulders. "Now that she has you, she will keep you waiting. There is no reason for her to hurry now, no? Do not worry. She will be ready by the time the first guests arrive."

Of course, he thought, nodding in agreement. That's all it was. She was just taking her time to annoy him.

But he still didn't relax until she stepped into the courtyard.

The sight of her nearly took his breath away. He'd always known she was beautiful, but she'd never appeared more so than she did at this moment. The color of her gown was only a shade more blue than her raven-black hair. The long column of her slender throat, exposed so clearly by the tying up of her hair and the low neckline of her gown, seemed to beg for his kisses.

He turned away from the many brothers and their wives and children and crossed the flower-scented courtyard toward her. For a timeless moment, he stared down into her expressive eyes, feeling desire sweep through him. Finally, he took hold of her hand and lifted it to his lips, still meeting her gaze over the back of her wrist.

"You've taken my breath away," he said softly as he straightened. Truly, he did sound winded.

An attractive flush pinkened her complexion. Nervously, she moistened her splendid lips. The action sent another jolt of wanting through him as he imagined her lying in bed beneath him, her body naked, her face flushed, her lips moist and inviting.

Diego cleared his throat, trying to set his thoughts on something else before the desires she stirred in him became all too evident. Not just to her but to everyone else in the room. Especially to her brothers.

Yes, think of her brothers. That should cool your ardor.

"Your brothers are all here," he said as he offered his elbow. "I think they've decided to let me marry you rather than killing me."

Leona's laughter gurgled up like a mountain brook, light and carefree. Her eyes twinkled with merriment as she slipped her fingers into his arm.

Diego feigned indignation. "Oh, it's well for you to be amused, Señorita Washington, but I assure you, it is not a laughing matter." He glanced toward the gathering of men across the courtyard, all of them now looking their way. "I have never seen more than four of them together at one time. I never realized nine was so many."

She squeezed his arm against her. Through his coat sleeve, he could feel the softness of her breast. It was all too tempting to imagine touching much more.

Nine brothers. Nine large, overprotective brothers. And they're all watching me right this minute.

"They are mostly harmless," Leona whispered, still smiling, completely unaware of his inner turmoil.

"To you, perhaps."

She laughed again before leaning closer and saying in a conspiratorial tone, "Then I promise to stay very close to you, Diego, so they do not frighten you away."

He grew serious. "It would take more than your brothers to frighten me away from you, Leona. Only you can do that."

She stared at him, a look of surprise and wonder in her eyes. The amusement faded from her mouth. He waited, hoping she would tell him that all her reservations about their union had disappeared. He waited, hoping . . .

Before she could answer, there was a commotion in the entry hall as the first guests arrived. The spell was broken between them, and he knew that whatever she might have said was lost to him.

It wasn't long before the hacienda was filled to overflowing with laughing, talking people, all of them shaking his hand and congratulating him on his choice of brides and wishing them well for the future.

Leona slipped away from the crowd, taking refuge in her father's office. There was such a terrible crush of people, and the noise was deafening. She wanted a moment alone to savor the words that Diego had spoken to her nearly two hours before.

It would take more than your brothers to frighten me away from you, Leona. Only you can do that.

Her heart thrummed in response to the memory. That was the closest he'd come to making love to her with words. She'd wanted to say something equally beautiful to him, but her mind and voice had failed her. And then, her chance to speak had been stolen from her.

Leona crossed the spacious study and sat in a high-backed chair before the fireplace. Her gaze lifted to the portrait of her mother that hung above the mantel.

Did you feel this way about Papá? Before you were married, did you find yourself thinking about him all the time and mulling over all you wanted to say? But then, when you were together, did your tongue get all tied up? Oh, I wish you were here now. I wish I could ask you these things, Mamá.

She closed her eyes, trying to imagine what it would have been like, sitting with her mother, discussing her love for Diego.

The door opened, then closed. Leona felt a flash of irritation at the interruption. She'd only wanted a moment of solitude. Couldn't she even find it here?

And then she heard the soft, painful cry.

She leaned over the arm of the chair, twisting to look back at the door. "Mercedes?" She rose quickly, her displeasure forgotten at the sight of her friend's tear-streaked face. "Mercedes, what is it?" She hurried across the room.

"Ri . . . Ri . . . Ricardo," the young woman responded over choked sobs.

"Ricardo? But what has he done?" She took hold of Mercedes's arm and drew her toward the chairs.

"He wants me . . . wants me to . . . to marry . . . him."

Leona raised an eyebrow. "And that has made you so unhappy?"

Mercedes shook her head, then hid her face in her hands.

Leona waited patiently. She patted Mercedes on the back, offering what little comfort she could by her mere presence. She couldn't imagine why Ricardo's proposal would bring her friend to such a state. Mercedes had been in love with Leona's twin for years, only he'd been too blind to see it. He'd continued to think of her as a child long after she'd become a woman.

Finally, still sniffing, Mercedes dried her eyes with her handkerchief. Her eyes were puffy and her cheeks pale. "I am sorry. I should not have carried on so."

Leona gave her a small smile of encouragement but didn't speak.

"We must leave La Brisa soon. My father says we will go to live with his cousin in Mexico. He says he is too old to start over in this country."

"You're going away? But you and Ricardo . . ."

Mercedes swallowed hard. Her fingers twisted the handkerchief. "I cannot leave my mother and father. They will need me."

"Ricardo wants to marry you. He'll make a home for your parents."

"No." Mercedes glanced at the floor. "My father is a proud man. This is difficult enough for him. He does not want to take the charity of a neighbor."

Leona leaned forward, covering Mercedes's hand with her own. "Since when is it charity for a family to live together, to share what they have with each other? Ricardo would love your parents as if they were his own. His home would be their home."

"You do not understand, Leona." She looked up. Anger flashed in her eyes. "You cannot understand. Rancho del Sol still belongs to your family. The *americanos* have not been able to steal it away from you. It is good that your father is a *gringo*. That has protected you. All of you."

Leona was surprised by the bitterness that tinged her friend's voice. She felt condemned, guilty of something beyond her control. "My father is a *californio*, like yours."

Mercedes sighed. More tears welled and spilled over. "I know. Forgive me. I was wrong to say what I did. But it changes nothing. I must go with my family to Mexico. They will need me."

"Your father could appeal the decision."

"No. He hasn't the heart to fight anymore."

She wanted to tell Mercedes not to give up hope, that she would find some way to help. But what could she do? She couldn't get La Brisa back for the Ramirezes. She couldn't make the Land Commission see the error of its ways or change its decision.

Oh, but she *could* make sure McCabe didn't profit from Mercedes's loss. Damn his black soul to hell! She knew he'd used his influence upon the commissioners, swaying them to decide against Sebastiano Ramirez's claim to La Brisa. Well, she would make certain that he gained nothing from it. She wasn't sure how, but she knew she would think of something.

Mercedes stiffened her back, drawing Leona's gaze back to her face. "Look what I have done," she said. "I have spoiled your party. You should be out there with your other guests, with Diego, smiling and laughing. This is a joyous night. You should not be shut in here with me, wearing such a dark frown."

"And you must come with me." Leona rose to her feet, pulling Mercedes up, too. "Come along. We'll wash the tears from your face, and you'll find Ricardo and forget your problems for this one night. Tomorrow, things will not seem so grim. My brother will think of something. You'll see. Ricardo can be very resourceful."

She hoped she was telling Mercedes the truth.

Ricardo sat on top of the compound wall, staring over the rolling grasslands of Rancho del Sol. Behind him, sounds from the celebration rose and fell—music, shouts, laughter—but there was no happiness in his heart. Mercedes had refused his proposal of marriage. How could he rejoice when he was filled with despair?

He'd thought she loved him. From the moment he'd seen her at the Aguilar *fandango*, he'd thought of little besides Mercedes. He'd ridden to La Brisa every day. She had never turned him away. He'd even coaxed a few shy kisses from her. He'd had every reason to hope that they would marry one day.

How could he have been so wrong?

Perhaps he would have waited longer to propose, given her a little more time to get used to the idea of marriage, if it hadn't been for the Ramirez land hearing. Even though he hadn't heard the final decision of the commissioners, he knew what the result would be. The Ramirezes would lose La Brisa. And so he'd decided not to wait to propose to her. After all, he could give her and her family a new home. It would be the best solution for everyone.

He'd pulled Mercedes aside shortly after she'd arrived this evening. He'd told her of his love for her and had asked her to be his wife. He'd waited to see her smile. He'd waited to hear her own words of love.

But instead, she'd refused him.

Ricardo held his head in his hands as her rejection echoed in his ears. *No, Ricardo, I will not marry you.*

There'd been no explanation, no discussion. Just a simple, firm refusal. Then she'd turned and walked away from him without a backward glance.

He tried to come up with an explanation that would shield him from the pain he felt in his heart. But there was only one explanation. She didn't love him. She didn't want him. She'd never wanted him.

Caramba! What a fool he had been. She'd simply been toying with him, and he'd mistaken it for love. Gaspar must be having a good laugh by this time, seeing what a buffoon his younger brother had made of himself. Perhaps Gaspar had even kissed Mercedes himself. After all, his brother had worked his charms on many of the señoritas of the Salinas. He wouldn't have let a girl like Mercedes go untried.

No, Ricardo, I will not marry you.

He felt his anger welling even as his heart hardened. It was for the best, he told himself. He would get over his infatuation with Mercedes just as quickly as it had come upon him.

In truth, he was over it already.

Leona and Diego slipped away from the revelry, walking out of the compound onto the quiet plains, their way lit by a bright, full moon. They moved in silence. Words would have seemed an intrusion.

When at last they stopped, Diego slipped his arm around Leona's back. She rested her head against his shoulder. They stood like that, not moving, not speaking, for a long time.

Finally, Diego glanced down at her. "I'm glad you suggested we take this walk. There are some things I wanted to tell you."

She felt a twinge of anxiety.

"I meant to say something before tonight, but . . ." His gaze returned to the rolling panorama before them, a scene painted in silver and black. "I know you were unwilling to marry me when your father first told you of his wishes, but I think you've come to like me enough to believe we could live well together."

I more than like you, Diego. I love you.

"Yet even though you haven't objected to our engagement being made public, you still resist the marriage itself. Is it because you don't want to leave your family?" He glanced down at her but didn't give her a chance to reply. "You needn't fear that leave-taking any longer, Leona. I want us to live here, in this valley. I plan to buy some land and start our own *rancho*."

Her eyes widened. "We won't go to Texas?"

"Not to live. Only for a visit. I want you to meet my grandmother, and I want her to meet you."

"But I thought . . ."

He turned her toward him, cupping her face in his hands. "I've wandered for many years, searching for a place I could call home. I've found it here. Just as I've found you."

He kissed her, sweetly, gently, and she felt her heart melting. When he lifted his lips from hers, she stared up into his dark eyes and thought, *I can trust him with anything. He loves me, and I love him. When I tell him about La Rosa, he will understand. Surely, he will understand.*

The thunder of horse's hooves intruded upon their interlude. Diego turned toward the sound, placing his body between hers and the rider. Leona leaned to one side to peer around him, even though she already knew what she would see.

The woman in red reined in her black horse on the crest of a distant hill. Her head was turned toward the couple, apparently watching them, although she was too far away to see her masked face. Finally, she raised her hand in a silent salute. Then she turned the magnificent animal and disappeared into another valley.

Diego stepped away from Leona, staring across the moon-kissed hills and valleys. He didn't move or speak for what seemed a very long time.

Leona held her breath, almost regretting now that she had arranged for this moment. Dulce had pulled it off. She had sat the horse well. She hadn't fallen from the saddle as she'd feared. But now, should the time come when Diego knew the truth, he would also know that Leona had purposely deceived him.

He turned around. "I'm not sure," he said, a smile appearing in the corners of his mouth, "but I believe La Rosa came to wish us well."

Remembering her visits to his bedroom, Leona could only nod in agreement. That would be how it would seem to him. Why else would the bandida have appeared here tonight?

I should tell him the truth. I should . . .

Diego drew her back into his embrace. "I love you, Leona," he whispered and then kissed her again.

Words and explanations fled. Nothing else mattered for now.

Chapter Nineteen

Two nights later, Diego stood at the window of his bedroom, staring out at the moonlit compound. He frowned as he gnawed on troublesome thoughts.

Something was bothering Leona. She was jumpy and nervous and much too quiet. He'd thought that his confession of love would bring them closer together. He'd even half-expected that she would say the same words to him. She hadn't. Instead, she'd seemed to grow more distant. It was almost as if she were avoiding him.

And if Leona's mood was strange, her brother's was unbearable. The few times Diego had tried to speak to him, Ricardo had practically snarled at him in response. The man's anger was like a tangible presence. Everyone felt it and tried to avoid him as much as possible.

Diego thought back to the night of the engagement party. He wondered if something had happened between the twins of which he wasn't aware. Could it be that Ricardo didn't approve of her marriage to Diego after all?

No. Ricardo had already told Diego that he would have run him off if he didn't think Diego could make Leona happy.

So what had happened?

A moving shadow beneath the veranda caught his attention. He came alert, watching as the man stepped away from the house and into the silver light of the moon. It was Ricardo.

Where is he headed this time of night? Diego wondered as Leona's brother walked swiftly toward the stables.

He's on his way to join La Rosa, he answered himself.

He grabbed his rifle and pistol, then stepped through the window rather than taking the time to go through the house to the front door. By the time Diego entered the barn, Ricardo was already saddling a rangy sorrel mare.

"Take me with you," Diego said in a low voice.

Ricardo looked up in surprise.

"I know where you're going. Take me along."

Ricardo said nothing.

"I'll only follow if you refuse." He stepped up to the stall door. "I'm no danger to La Rosa. I want to help her. That's why I'm here."

"*Amigo* . . ."

"Let me help."

Ricardo stared at him in the dim light of the barn. Finally, he nodded. "Your stallion is too distinctive. Use the roan." He jerked his head, indicating another stall. "He's quick and hasn't been ridden for several days. He'll be fresh and eager to run."

"What about a mask?"

"I'll get one for you."

He moved quickly to saddle the horse Ricardo had suggested. When Diego led the gelding out of its stall, Ricardo was waiting for him, his hand outstretched, a length of black fabric hanging from his fingers.

"Wait to put it on until we are away from here." Ricardo swung up onto his horse. "Do you have your rifle?"

"Yes."

"Come on then. We must hurry. The others will be waiting."

Diego mounted the roan and followed Ricardo. They didn't speak as they walked their horses out of the stables and across the compound to the main gate. They were a good distance from the hacienda before they spurred their horses into a canter.

They rode at a steady pace for nearly half an hour before Ricardo reined in. When his horse was stopped, he pulled his mask from his shirt pocket and tied it around his head. Diego did likewise.

"We use first names only among the *hombres*. Tell them you are Diego and no more. Even if they guess who you are, it's safer for everyone if we don't confirm it." He paused a moment, then continued. "No one knows La Rosa's true identity. Don't try to find out. Follow her instructions. She's in charge. Don't question her decisions."

"How does everyone know when and where to meet? How do you communicate?"

"You don't need to know that, *amigo*."

Diego nodded. He understood. He couldn't be expected to be taken into confidence the first night out.

"Come. They'll be waiting for us."

Once again, they rode in silence, their way lit by the moon, a sort of eerie silence blanketing the rolling landscape. It was hard for Diego not to try to find out more. He wanted to ask what their destination was, what the plans were for the night. He was used to finding out everything he could in every situation. Not knowing left him feeling a strange anxiety.

At least, he hoped that was the reason for the disquiet in his soul.

Leona stiffened as her brother rode into the meeting place, a second man behind him. Although his identity was hidden behind a mask, she didn't have to ask to know who he was. She realized she'd been expecting this to happen. She'd known Diego would find a way to ride with La Rosa. It had only been a matter of time.

Tilting her chin for courage, she strode toward the two men. She glanced first at Diego, then at Ricardo. "Who is this you have brought

with you, *amigo*?" she asked, feigning ignorance.

"His name is Diego."

*I know that, mi hermano. But what is he doing
here?*

Diego dismounted. "I made him bring me, La
Rosa. I want to ride with you."

She turned on him with a flourish. "Why?" she
asked, a challenge in her voice.

"You know why. Because McCabe must be
stopped. Perhaps the law will try eventually,
but the wheels of justice move slowly. We can
do something now."

Leona nodded as she stepped toward him. She
placed her hands on her hips, knuckles down. Her
legs were braced as if against a strong wind. She
lowered her voice so only he could hear her. "You
should have waited for my summons, *señor*. I do
not like to be forced to accept a new *hombre*. Our
success depends upon secrecy, as does the safety of
my *amigos*."

His smile revealed a flash of white teeth below
the black mask. "I grew tired of waiting. I'm an
impatient man."

She couldn't help it. She was suddenly quite glad
to have him with her, even though she knew she
was risking much. There were already too many
lies and half-truths between them. This added one
more for her conscience to bear.

"You may stay, Diego."

She turned around and strode toward the other
men. They were wasting valuable time, standing

there talking. They still had a number of miles to cover.

McCabe felt his nerves stretching further with every passing minute. He'd love a smoke, but he couldn't risk it. He didn't want the red end of a cheroot to give them away. Not when they were this close.

Tonight was the night. He could taste it on his tongue, feel it in his gut. He was going to get La Rosa tonight. She wouldn't escape his trap. He had planned too carefully this time. He had outsmarted her at last.

He was convinced one of his own men was La Rosa's informant. He didn't know who, but he would find out eventually. It didn't matter for now. After all, this time it was going to work to his advantage. He'd been careful how he'd leaked the information. This time he'd set a trap from which she wouldn't escape.

"It's a shipment of gold being brought in from his mining claims," Leona told her companions. "He has not trusted any of his own men at his *rancho* with the information. He suspects there is someone who is telling us of his activities. It is only chance that we learned of it in time."

Her gaze swept from one man to the next. They were all listening carefully. She could feel their tension, their readiness.

"There will be two wagons. The first is a decoy. It will be traveling along Diablo Creek with many riders to protect it. The second wagon carries the real cargo. It has come up the main road from the south. There is only the driver and one other man, disguised as tinkers. Vincente has seen their campsite. They are only a few miles from here. McCabe has outwitted himself. He is certain we will attack the wrong wagon and has left his real cargo unprotected."

Again she looked from man to man. No one said anything.

"Then let us go," she said, turning to mount Pesadilla.

Diego's eyes remained on the bandolera's back. The big black horse she rode was high-spirited, but she was clearly always in control. She moved as one with the animal as it galloped across the countryside. Her cape billowed out behind her, giving her a winged appearance.

He thought of another woman who rode astride and wondered what Leona would think if she knew both her brother and her fiancé were among La Rosa's band of outlaws. Someday, he supposed he would tell her. Perhaps he might even tell her he'd briefly suspected that *she* was the bandida. Leona would probably be amused by that.

Actually, if he hadn't seen La Rosa with his own eyes while Leona stood at his side, he might still have wondered. He was glad his suspicions, fleeting though they were, had been proved wrong. He could never have permitted Leona to risk her life the way this woman risked hers.

Risk or no, he couldn't help but admire La Rosa. Perhaps he'd worked too many years undercover. Perhaps it had become too easy for him to live in the areas of gray. He saw few things as strictly black and white anymore. He recognized that La Rosa was an outlaw, and yet what she did was for good. What she took was given to others in need. And the man she took from deserved much worse than she had ever done to him, as far as Diego was concerned.

La Rosa slowed her mount, lifting her right hand as she did so. When she stopped, the men drew up beside her.

"The tinker's camp is over the next rise. Be careful. They are surely quick with a gun or McCabe would never have entrusted his gold shipment to just the two of them. If you must shoot, shoot to wound, not to kill." She glanced to her right. "Vincente, take Javier, Raul, and Tiago and circle to the right. Ricardo, you and Diego come with me." She turned the black horse to the left, whispering back over her shoulder, "*Vaya con Dios.*"

At her final words, Diego felt another sting of apprehension. His hand touched the butt of his gun, as if to reassure himself, but it didn't help.

The ominous feeling persisted.

The campfire had burned down to glowing coals. A faint odor of coffee wafted on the night breeze. The two men slept on bedrolls, one with his hat over his face to block out the bright moonlight, the other with his blanket pulled over his head. Two draft horses, their front legs hobbled, grazed not far from the wagon.

Leona's eyes took in the scene, then swept the surrounding area. The campsite was located in a valley between two low-lying hills. Trees and underbrush bordered a nearby stream. McCabe's men had not chosen the best of campsites. There were too many places for bandits to approach unseen, just as she was doing now.

It would also be an excellent place for an ambush.

She paused and listened. Was there a chance that Johnny was wrong? Could McCabe be waiting for them here instead of with the other wagon?

No, she decided. Johnny hadn't been wrong before. She was allowing herself to grow nervous without cause.

Leona drew her pistol, glanced quickly over her shoulder at Ricardo and Diego, then spurred Pesadilla forward as she fired her gun into the air.

The bogus tinkers were on their feet in seconds, but it was too late. La Rosa and her men had already surrounded them.

"We are sorry to disturb your sleep, *señores*." Leona moved her horse forward. "But we should like to look in your wagon."

The smaller of the two men spoke up in a whiny voice. "We are but poor tinkers. We have nothing of interest to *bandidos*."

"Perhaps not, but I think we shall look. If you are what you say, you have nothing to fear from La Rosa." She turned her head toward Raul, who waited closest to the wagon. "See what is inside, *amigo*."

Leona would forever wonder if she heard an explosion before she felt the impact or if the bullet struck in silence. At the time, she only knew that some terrible force plowed into her left shoulder, nearly unseating her. She groped for the saddle horn as Pesadilla reared and spun. She heard shouts and rapid gunfire and the pounding of horses' hooves.

The pain came in sharp, burning waves. Her vision blurred, and all she could see was the silvery-white light of the moon all around her. She could feel the mighty black gelding stretching into an all-out gallop. Instinct made her cling determinedly to the saddle, but it was only a matter of time before unconsciousness would overtake her.

She knew she was being followed. She knew it was McCabe. He would kill her. She knew that. But first he would humiliate her as she had humiliated him.

She didn't want him to have the pleasure. If she must die, she would prefer to die alone, not with him watching her.

She leaned forward and tangled her fingers in Pesadilla's long mane. "Faster, *muchacho*. Faster." She could only hope and pray that he wasn't carrying her back to Rancho del Sol.

She heard the splash of water, felt it spraying over her skin as the horse plunged into a stream. Pain ripped through her with each motion. Sheer will held her in the saddle.

When Pesadilla jumped onto the opposite bank, Leona knew they were not alone. Another horse and rider had drawn up beside them. She tried to urge more speed from the gelding, but she hadn't the strength. Through the blur of her pain-glazed vision, she saw an arm reaching for her.

So, this was how she was to die.

Leona slipped into a blessed black hole, escaping the pain and the fear.

Chapter Twenty

Diego could hear McCabe's men pass by no more than forty feet from their hiding place amongst the oaks and chaparral. He was grateful that the moon had finally slipped behind the mountain peaks, thankful for the dark shadows that blanketed the rugged hillside.

He held his revolver in his hand. La Rosa's pistol was beside his knee, as was his rifle. If he had to fire, he'd better make every shot count. There wouldn't be time to reload.

Miraculously, neither of the horses made a sound to give away their location. La Rosa was silent as well. Too silent. But there wasn't time to do anything for her now. He had to get her away from here first.

He waited a long while after the sounds of the search party had faded before he moved. Finally, when he felt it was safe, he turned his attention on the bandida. He knew that a large portion of her red costume had been darkened by her own blood. The night was too black to evaluate how badly she was wounded, but he could try to stop the bleeding.

Diego worked quickly to bind the wound as best he could, then lifted La Rosa and laid her on her belly over the saddle of her horse. Then he mounted the roan and started up the hillside. If they were to find safety anywhere, it would be among the sharp ridges and high peaks of the Santa Lucias.

They rode through the night, climbing ever higher, the horses picking their way carefully in the darkness. It wasn't until the first hint of day lightened the sky to pewter that Diego reined in. He whispered a prayer of thanks when he saw the small cabin, its door hanging open on only one hinge. He hadn't been certain he would be able to find it again, especially in the dark.

Drawing his pistol, he led La Rosa's horse toward the building. He dismounted and quickly looked inside. It was clear that no one had been here since he'd chanced upon it several weeks before during a few days of exploration of the area. He'd guessed then that the log cabin had been deserted for many months. The room smelled musty. The dirt floor was covered with leaves and needles and the droppings of tiny animals. But against one wall, there was a rope bed covered with a worn tick mattress; on a nearby shelf were a couple of blankets. There was even a stone fireplace, a wooden bucket, and some cooking utensils.

Diego stepped inside and moved across the small space to the bed. He picked up the tick mattress and shook it free of debris and dust, then flipped it over. He tested the rope springs to make sure they were sturdy. Satisfied that the bed would support the woman, he returned to the black gelding and lifted La Rosa's unconscious body from the saddle.

Once he'd carried her inside and laid her on the bed, he worked quickly to unbind her shoulder, then cut away her blood-stained blouse. Thankfully, the bleeding seemed to have stopped. Closer inspection, however, revealed what he'd feared most. The bullet was still lodged inside. He would have to cut it out or it would cause a fatal infection.

"You must be strong, La Rosa," he whispered, his gaze moving to her mask. "This will be very painful."

He stared at her only a few seconds before making his decision. Then he reached forward and removed the mask.

"*Madre de Dios!* It *is* you!"

He tortured her, the beast. He took hot brands and pressed them against her shoulder, driving them into her flesh, keeping them there until she screamed in agony. She tried to push him away, but her arms wouldn't move. She was paralyzed. She was at his mercy.

But he was merciless.

The pain seemed endless . . . endless . . . endless. . . .

For three days, Diego stayed close by her bedside. He wiped her fevered forehead with damp cloths. He forced trickles of cool water into her mouth. He bathed the wound, keeping it clean, and prayed to God that there was no infection growing inside. He spent hours staring at her pale face, feeling her increasing weakness as if it were his own.

He was no surgeon, but he wasn't a stranger to gunshot wounds either. He'd been able to remove the bullet without too much trouble, although he'd known she was in terrible pain because of it. Her screams had made him want to die himself. But once the bullet had been removed and the wound dressed, there'd been little for him to do but wait.

And so he waited—hour upon hour upon hour— all the while blaming himself for not knowing it was a trap, for not stopping La Rosa from riding into it, for discarding his suspicions that Leona might be the bandida, for not protecting the woman he loved from danger.

How could he have been so easily misled? He should have known the truth long before their passionate kisses had caused him to wonder if the two women could be one. He should have known from the very start. Why hadn't he? And why hadn't he done something to protect her? If she died . . .

He closed his mind to the possibility. He couldn't think about it. *Wouldn't* think about it.

Diego rose from the rickety stool beside the bed. "I'll be back," he told her softly, though he knew she didn't hear him.

Stepping to the doorway, he looked outside. Keen eyes studied the terrain, alert for any sign of danger. At last satisfied that no one had discovered their hiding place, he picked up the wooden bucket and carried it to the stream. He dumped the contents of the bucket onto the ground, then refilled it with fresh, cool water.

Before he went back inside, he checked on the horses, making certain they were still secure within the dilapidated corral behind the cabin. Later today, he would stake them out to graze.

A soft moan reached his ears, driving all other thoughts from his head as he hurried back inside.

"Leona?" He sat down on the stool and took hold of her hand. "Leona?"

She moaned again.

He felt her forehead with his other hand. Her skin was cool and clammy. The fever had broken.

Diego closed his eyes and silently thanked God for sparing her, ending his prayer with a promise. *I give my word. I won't let her risk her life like this again.*

A delicious smell permeated the air. It made Leona's mouth water. She ran her tongue over her lips and found them cracked and dry. She tried to lift her fingers to her mouth, but they felt as if they were weighted down. Likewise, she couldn't seem to open her eyes.

She tossed restlessly and felt a stab of pain shoot through her, starting at her shoulder and ending in her left foot. She groaned.

"Leona. Wake up, Leona."

It was Diego, calling to her. Oh, how wonderful it was to hear his voice. She'd been so lonely for him.

"Por favor, querida," he whispered near her ear. "Look at me. Let me see your eyes."

The effort was almost too much, but finally she succeeded. His face swam in a blur above her. The light made her eyes sting.

"Ah, you are back."

"Diego . . ." His name sounded more like a croak.

"Here." He slid an arm beneath her shoulders and lifted her slightly. "Drink this."

She felt the rim of a cup against her lips. She sipped at the cool water. It felt good on her scratchy, parched throat. With effort, she raised her right arm and covered his hand with her own as she drained the cup.

"More?" he asked.

She nodded.

After she'd finished the second cup, she lay back on the bed with a sigh. Her vision had cleared by this time, even as the pain in her shoulder had intensified. She glanced down and to her left. She was covered with a couple of old blankets, and she knew without looking that—except for some sort of bandage that was wrapped around her upper torso and shoulder—she was naked beneath them.

She frowned. "Where are we?"

"In the Santa Lucia Mountains."

She closed her eyes again, trying to remember how they'd gotten there. She had no memory of it. She was obviously hurt, but what had . . .

It came back to her in a flash, everything about that night, right up to the moment the pain had ripped through her and she'd thought she was going to die.

"What about the others?" She kept her eyes closed. She didn't want to look at Diego when he answered her.

"I don't know. I only had time to take care of you."

Ricardo . . . Raul . . . Vincente . . . Javier . . . Tiago. What had happened to them? Had they been shot, too? Had they been captured?

"I think they must have escaped, Leona. McCabe and his men were most concerned with capturing you. They knew you were wounded and came after you at once."

She looked at him then. "How long have we been here?"

"Four days now."

"Four days?"

"Yes." Diego rose to his feet and moved across the cabin.

Leona turned her head so she could see him. She watched as he hunkered down near the fireplace and dipped a cup into a black pot hanging on a tripod over the fire.

"I snared a rabbit yesterday and made a stew. It's not very good. We haven't any salt to season it with, but I think you should try to eat some. At least drink the broth. You'll need to get your strength back before we can ride out of here."

He straightened and faced her, holding the cup in his hand, a ribbon of steam rising from inside. She saw the weariness in his eyes. She saw the tension in the corners of his mouth. It occurred to her then that it had been Diego who had removed the bullet from her shoulder, Diego who had cleansed and bandaged the wound, Diego who had tended to her around the clock for the past four days.

She felt herself growing warm with embarrassment as she realized that he had removed her clothes, had seen her naked as no one but her maid had seen her since she was a small child, had tended to her most personal needs while she lay helpless and unconscious.

And then, she realized something else. He had called her Leona.

She lifted her hand and touched her face where her mask had been. It was gone!

Of course it was gone. Diego would have removed it while he was caring for her. Did she think he would remove the rest of her clothing and yet leave her masked?

She stared at him, wondering when he would speak of the lies she'd told.

He approached the bed. "Drink this broth. You'll feel better when you get something into your stomach. We can talk later."

Yes, later. They would talk later. Much later, if it was up to her.

For the first time in days, Diego fell into a deep sleep. The moment he lay down on his bedroll, spread on the floor beside the bed, and closed his eyes, he felt his body relax. Knowing Leona was on the road to recovery drained the last bit of tension from him, and he drifted into slumber.

Sometime during the night, he heard her cry out in terror and pain. He sat up, instantly alert for danger, only to find Leona wrestling with a nightmare. He tried to calm her with words, then he held her in his embrace. Even after she'd quieted, she wouldn't let go of him.

Finally, not knowing what else to do and unable to keep his own eyes open any longer, he joined her on the bed. Holding her against him, he glided back to sleep.

Chapter Twenty-One

Ricardo searched the mountains for some clue to his sister's and Diego's whereabouts but found none. It had been easy enough to find signs of McCabe's search party. There had been many horses, many riders. They'd fanned out from the narrow animal trails, combing the mountainsides, trampling the forest underbrush. Their tracks would have been clear to even the most untrained eye.

He suspected that Diego had been more careful in his passing. He also thought it likely that his friend had doubled back and wiped clean what tracks he'd left behind as soon as he'd been able to do so.

He hoped he was right. If McCabe had found them . . .

Ricardo wouldn't let himself think about Leona's gunshot wound. He told himself that

Diego would be able to care for her. Worrying about it would do her no good.

He had known there was always a possibility that something like this would happen. In fact, Leona and he had planned for just such an occurrence. If ever one of them was unable to make it home after a raid, the other was to explain their absence by saying they'd gone for a visit to Manuel's ranch.

Ricardo had done just that. He'd told Gardner that Leona had wanted some time to herself, that she was feeling anxious about marrying Diego and leaving California, and that she'd thought some time with her sister-in-law Maria and her children would calm her. Then he'd told his father that Diego had chosen to return to San Francisco to conclude his business while Leona was away from Rancho del Sol.

Now all that was left for him to do was wait. Ricardo hated the waiting most of all.

In her sleep, Leona sought refuge from the pain by drawing closer to a place of warmth. As she slowly made her way back to consciousness, she wondered about the source of that warmth. She never guessed that, when she opened her eyes, she would find herself snuggled against Diego's body, his arms wrapped around her.

She stared at him for a long time without moving. His jaw was covered with black stubble, sprinkled with just a smattering of gray. His hair was rumpled and badly in need of a trim. Even in sleep, he looked weary to the point of exhaustion, and she knew it was because of her.

She shifted slightly, still seeking a way to ease the throbbing and burning in her shoulder. The movement sent a sliver of cool air along her skin. Sudden awareness caused her to look down.

Her naked breasts seemed very pale beside the dark skin of his bare chest. She knew she should have been shocked by the sight, but for some reason, she wasn't. It seemed right for them to be together like this. She felt safe, protected, secure. Though the pain persisted, she drew strength from his nearness.

Leona sighed, snuggling into the shelter of his arms as she was lured back into the healing bonds of sleep.

Later that afternoon, when Diego had returned from a few hours of hunting, he found Leona sitting up in bed. She had wrapped one of the, blankets around her torso, tucking its corners in to secure it under her arms. With the fingers of her right hand, she was trying to work the snarls from her long hair.

He dropped the quail he'd shot onto the floor near the door, then leaned his rifle against the log wall. As his gaze returned to Leona, he said, "You shouldn't be up yet."

She was incredibly pale. Her violet-black eyes were dulled by pain. Her already slender figure had grown alarmingly thin. She'd lost a lot of blood and had fought off a persistent fever. And yet, she had just enough strength left to try to defy him.

"I needed to move around. I can't stand to lie still for so long." She let out an exhausted sigh. "I wish I had a brush and a change of clothes."

"We're lucky to have what we do," he answered, trying to sound stern. But in his heart, he knew a moment of joy. If she was well enough to start fussing about her appearance, she was surely on her way to full recovery.

"*Sí.* I guess we are." She dropped her hand to her lap, suddenly looking defeated and overwhelmed.

Diego crossed the room and settled onto the bed behind her, his legs straddling her narrow hips. "Here. Let me try."

Slowly, he worked his fingers through the thick tresses. After nearly a week without attention, her hair was in a hopeless tangle. Still, he kept trying, gently tugging whenever his fingers encountered another knot. It was more than just wanting to please her that kept him beside her. He found the action pleasing to himself as well.

"Diego?"

"Yes?"

"You've said nothing about it."

He didn't have to ask what she meant. "We'll talk when you're stronger."

"I'm sorry I had to deceive you."

He leaned forward, laying his cheek against her hair, closing his eyes even as he closed his mind to thoughts of losing her.

"You understand why I had to do it?"

His lips brushed her head. "We'll talk of it later, Leona. When you're well."

She reclined against him, resting her back on his chest, her head in the curve of his neck and shoulder. His right arm circled her as her temple brushed his cheek. His left arm, avoiding her wound, lay on her upper thigh. He felt a tremor run through her as she exhaled a lengthy sigh.

"*Gracias,*" she whispered.

Diego wasn't sure just what she was thanking him for, but it didn't matter. He continued to hold her against him, long after her even breathing told him she'd fallen to sleep, exhausted by her efforts to sit up and tidy her hair.

He smiled gently. "*De nada, mi tesoro. De nada.*"

When Leona awakened, she found herself once again sleeping in Diego's embrace. Shadows danced against the walls of the cabin, cast there by the flickering red and yellow lights of a fire on the hearth, and she knew it was night. The odor of roasted quail lingered in the air. She was ravenously hungry. She wondered how she could have slept so hard and so long while Diego had prepared supper.

She moved, as if to rise, then caught her breath as a stab of pain knifed her shoulder. For just a moment, she'd forgotten about her injury, but she'd been reminded of it quickly enough.

Diego laid a gentle hand on her side. "What is it, Leona?"

"I'm hungry." It embarrassed her to say so, but she had another need as well. "And I . . . I need a few minutes alone," she added in a whisper, feeling a flush heat her cheeks. She was reminded that he'd cared for *all* her needs while she'd been gripped by fever and weakened by blood loss; yet her embarrassment remained keen at the mention of such personal needs now. "Would you . . . would you help me outside?"

He sat up, dropping his long legs over the side of the bed. "You're too weak to go outside."

She closed her eyes before he stood up. She knew he was wearing underdrawers. She'd felt the fabric against her skin while they were lying together. Still, at the moment, his state of undress only added to her embarrassment.

She heard him moving about the cabin, listened as his footsteps brought him back to the bed.

"This isn't much of a chamber pot, but it will have to do."

Leona forced herself to open her eyes. He was holding a small black kettle in his hand. He set it on the floor next to the bed, then took a step backward. His eyes studied her face for a moment before he turned away.

"I'll step outside."

He'd been right, of course. She never would have made it outside. She had to fight off waves of dizziness just to get up from the bed. But she was determined to do this without calling for help.

By the time she was back beneath the shelter of her blankets, she'd forgotten her hunger. She lay on the bed, closed her eyes, and tried to ignore the pain and weakness. She hated the helplessness more than just about anything.

Diego wasn't surprised to find her back in bed, fast asleep. He'd known that her efforts to get up would drain what little reserves she had. Nonetheless, it was another step on the road to recovery, and he was encouraged by it.

He sat on the stool at the bedside and watched her sleep. A tiny frown had drawn a crease between her eyebrows. He reached forward and smoothed it with his thumb.

His thoughts drifted, filled with scenes of Leona. He saw her brandishing a pistol. He saw her, masked and dressed in red, slipping out the window of his bedroom. He saw her on horseback, riding like the wind, at one with the night around her. He saw her swimming in a mountain pond, her white undergarments clinging to her like a second skin. He saw her dancing, eyes flashing with laughter. He saw her wearing trousers and hurling a reata after a wild colt. He saw her face flushed with anger and stubbornness as she argued a point with one of her brothers.

"You're a fighter, *querida*," he said in a low voice. "You won't remain weak for long. Be patient."

He felt a sudden, sick tightness in his belly as he recalled how close she'd come to being killed, how many times she could have taken a turn for the worse instead of getting steadily better. Such thoughts brought a swell of agony to his heart. He would rather die himself than lose Leona.

"Never again," he whispered.

Never again would he allow her to ride as La Rosa. She would realize the danger of it now. She would have to acknowledge that she and her hombres could ride no more. McCabe would have to be stopped some other way. Diego would do whatever had to be done, but Leona must be protected.

Strange, even after he'd known he was in love with Leona, he had continued to be intrigued and fascinated by the bandida. He hadn't given more than a passing thought to the perils La Rosa had faced whenever she rode against McCabe. He had only recognized her courage and determination and admired her for it.

But everything had changed when he'd removed her mask and found the woman he loved beneath it.

"Never again," he repeated, then leaned forward and kissed her forehead.

Ricardo had no premonition of impending disaster as he rode through the gates at Rancho del Sol.

In fact, he'd met with Johnny Parker this afternoon and was feeling somewhat encouraged by his report. Johnny had told Ricardo that McCabe had returned to his ranch a week ago in a fury. With each passing day, he'd grown more sullen. Ricardo could only take that to mean that Leona and Diego had escaped, despite all the lawyer's searching. In his heart, he believed that Diego was even now nursing his sister back to health. Before long, they would both return, and all would be well.

Only, she hadn't returned soon enough.

Ricardo recognized Manuel's carriage standing near the entrance to the hacienda and knew that his lies about his sister's whereabouts had been found out. He tried to think what he would say to his father. He hadn't long to mull it over in his head.

The front door opened, and Gardner, followed by Manuel, Eduardo, and Gaspar, stepped outside.

Schooling his face into a welcoming expression, Ricardo turned his mount toward his father and brothers. "*Buenos días*, Manuel!" he called as he swung down from the saddle. "I didn't think we would see you at Rancho del Sol again so soon. How is Maria?"

"She's fine. She and the children are inside."

Ricardo had feared as much. He plunged ahead, hoping his efforts at deception weren't revealed on his face. "Then Leona has returned. Good. I need to speak with her about . . ."

"Leona isn't here," Gardner interrupted, a scowl hardening his features.

"She isn't?" Ricardo glanced toward his oldest brother. "But why not?"

Gardner answered, "We were hoping you could tell us. You're certain she told you she was going to Manuel's?"

Ricardo turned toward his father, looking him straight in the eyes. Was it worse, he wondered, to cause his father to worry by lying about Leona's whereabouts or to cause his father to worry by telling him the truth?

He decided it would be better to stick to his story for now. He hoped he wasn't making a mistake. "I'm certain that's what she said."

"Gaspar"—Gardner glanced away from Ricardo— "go to La Brisa and ask if Mercedes has seen or heard from her. Eduardo, go with your brother. If Leona is not there, ride to the other *ranchos* and see if anyone has seen her today. Be discreet. We don't want gossip to start before we're sure what's happened. Gaspar, you bring word back to me after you've talked to Mercedes." He returned his gaze to his youngest son. "Ricardo, I want you to find out what business Diego had in San Francisco. If you have to go there yourself, do so. I want to know where he is. If you find him, bring him back at once."

Gaspar took an angry step forward. "You don't believe Diego has had something to do with her disappearance, do you?"

"I don't know," his father answered. "I only know my daughter has been missing for a week. Go, all of you, and send word to me as quickly as you can."

Grimly, Ricardo nodded. As he turned toward his horse, he sent up a silent prayer that Leona would have a speedy recovery and return soon. Otherwise, Ricardo would be forced to tell their father the truth. He could only feign ignorance so long before his conscience would demand that he tell what he knew.

Chapter Twenty-Two

Her improvement could be measured almost by the hour rather than by days. Leona sat up for long periods of time. Her appetite returned. She walked unassisted. The color came back to her cheeks, and her eyes regained some of their sparkle.

Just ten days after the ambush, Diego found her sitting in the sun, her back resting against the cabin wall, her eyes closed. She was wearing her split riding skirt and Diego's extra shirt that had been in his bedroll. Her own blouse had been ruined the night she was shot. What had been left of it, he had torn up and used for bandages. She had braided her hair into two thick ropes that hung over her shoulders, the ends brushing against the gentle swell of her breasts.

That was the moment when Diego knew they must leave the mountain cabin soon. Very soon. Perhaps immediately.

Looking at her, he was gripped by an overwhelming desire to possess her. For many days, he had bathed her body and changed her bandages and slept with his chest pressed against her naked breasts, sharing his warmth against the cool mountain air that invaded the cabin at night. His only consideration had been to see her well. Never once had he been affected by the perfection of her body or thought of the pleasures he could find there.

Now, he did.

When she tentatively lifted her left arm, testing her shoulder, the shirt pulled tight against her breasts, as if to tease him. He longed to cross the ground between them, to draw her up to her feet and into his arms, to press her against him, to kiss her as he hadn't kissed her in a very long time.

He turned away, reminding himself of how sick she had been. She wasn't interested in his kisses, let alone in satisfying his other desires.

He grabbed his rifle. "I'll see what I can find for our supper," he said gruffly. "Don't do too much while I'm gone." He marched quickly away.

Leona watched him leave as disappointment washed through her. She'd hoped he would come and sit beside her. Now that she was stronger, she'd even hoped that they could talk about what had happened the night she'd been shot. She wanted him to know what it meant to her that he had been with her all this time. She wanted to be able to tell him that she loved him, too. She'd never told him so, and it was time that she did. She wanted to talk about their future.

She didn't understand the sudden change in him. She'd thought her returning strength would make him glad. Instead, he'd distanced himself from her, as if she had the plague.

Leona rose quickly to her feet, then steadied herself from the momentary dizziness with a hand against the cabin wall.

She supposed she should spend some time thinking about their return to Rancho del Sol, instead of trying to figure out Diego's strange moods. After all, they had been gone for over a week now.

Ricardo, if he hadn't fallen into McCabe's trap, would have explained her absence to the family by telling them she'd gone for a visit to Manuel's. Because of the distance and the size of his growing family, Manuel came to the main ranch infrequently. That story had always seemed a fairly safe alibi. Of course, when she and Ricardo had chosen it, they hadn't thought either of them would be gone for such a long time. Actually, neither of them had truly believed they would ever be hurt.

Leona walked slowly toward the creek, then knelt beside it and scooped a palm full of water up to her lips.

Of more concern, she thought now, was how Ricardo had explained Diego's absence. Surely he wouldn't have said Diego had gone to Manuel's, too. They would have to return to the ranch at different times from different directions. Hopefully, she would be able to learn from Ricardo what he'd said and then be able to warn Diego.

A glance down at her attire revealed another worry. She couldn't very well return to Rancho del Sol wearing Diego's shirt and La Rosa's stained and tattered skirt. She would have to change her clothes at the play house first, which meant she would have to go there by night, yet she couldn't just slip back into the house as she usually did.

Her head began to ache. She sat back on her heels, closed her eyes, and lifted her face toward the sun. She was frustrated by her inability to think straight. It shouldn't have been so hard for her.

"Leona."

She opened her eyes to find Diego standing close by. "I thought you were going hunting," she said, not unaware of the pleasure she felt at his return.

His expression was grim. "It's time to leave."

"I know. I was just thinking the same thing." She rose to her feet. "But I can't go back dressed like this."

His gaze swept over her. Finally, he nodded. "You're right. You can't go back like that."

"I hid my clothes outside the hacienda. If I can get to them . . ."

"Tell me where they are."

She raised an eyebrow. "It would be simpler for me to show you, Diego."

"No. You'll stay here while I go for them."

"But . . ."

"Don't argue with me, Leona. If someone were to see you in that skirt, they would guess you were La Rosa. Especially if they can tell you're injured. We don't know who might know that the bandida was shot. The story may be over the whole valley by this time. We've got to get you back to Rancho del Sol with as little risk as possible—preferably without being seen by anyone." He walked past her toward the corral. "Tell me where to find your clothes. If I ride hard by night, I can get them and be back by sunrise."

Leona opened her mouth to object, then closed it. She supposed he was right. No, she *knew* he was right. But she hated not having any say in the matter. Once they were safely back at Rancho del Sol, she would have to tell him how she felt, but she hadn't the strength to argue with him now.

By the time Diego returned to the cabin the next morning, he thought he'd come up with a plan that might work—with a little luck. On their way down the mountain a few hours later, he detailed it for Leona.

"You'll take the roan and ride to Manuel's at sunset. You'll tell him that we had a fight, and you went to a friend's without telling anyone where you were so that you could think about things. I was angry, too, so I also went off to be alone. In the morning, you can return home. I'll come back in a couple of days."

"Why must I take the roan?"

"Because any woman on a black horse these days is going to cause people to wonder. I won't draw as much attention with him." He glanced over his shoulder. Leona's expression already revealed strain. He knew that the jerking gait of the horses as they descended the mountain had to be painful for her, but she hadn't uttered a word of complaint.

As their eyes met, she nodded. "All right. As long as you understand that Pesadilla is still La Rosa's horse. She rides no other."

"Since La Rosa won't be riding again, that really doesn't make any difference to—"

Leona stopped the black gelding suddenly, and the animal snorted and tossed his head in protest. "What do you mean, La Rosa won't be riding again? My wound isn't that serious. In another week or two, I'll be as good as new."

"No." Diego turned his horse toward her. "The risk is too great. McCabe is determined to capture the *bandida*. I won't have you putting yourself in danger again."

"*You* won't?" She stopped speaking, groping for the right words and coming up empty. "*You* won't?"

Her anger was white hot. He would have sworn he could feel the waves of heat upon his own skin. He nudged the roan forward. "Leona, you could have been killed. I can't take the chance that it will happen again."

"The people need La Rosa," she replied in a low voice that warned of the fury behind it.

"The people need someone to stop McCabe and those like him. It doesn't have to be La Rosa. It could as easily be me—or Ricardo or a competent sheriff."

"You have no right to tell me I can't ride. I gave life to La Rosa. I organized my *hombres*. They're loyal to me and to the cause. If I choose to ride as La Rosa, I will."

Diego's own anger was sparked by her defiant tone. "I have the right of a husband to protect his wife."

"You forget, Senor Salazar. We are *not* married."

"We will be."

Leona slapped the ends of the braided reins against Pesadilla's rump, causing the gelding to jump forward. "Not if I refuse," she called back to him.

Diego had learned long ago to swallow his anger, to hold back hastily spoken words, and to wait for a better time for a counterattack or gentle persuasion, whichever was called for. Years of training forced him to keep silent, but it was one of the hardest things he'd ever had to do. He wanted to make sure she understood that they *would* be married and she *would* give up her midnight rides as La Rosa.

Leona silently cursed a blue streak. She'd known it would be like this. She'd known he would be just another overbearing, domineering male. She'd dared to hope that Diego would be different, that he would understand her, that he would accept her as she was. But her hopes had been cruelly shattered.

She was so angry that she didn't see the rider appear from the chaparral until he called her name.

"Leona!"

She stopped as Ricardo galloped toward them.

"Gracias a Dios!" he exclaimed as he drew up before her. "I've been looking everywhere for you. I was afraid—"

"I'm fine, *mi hermano*. What of the others? Was anyone else hurt? Were any of them taken prisoner by McCabe?"

"No, they are well, but there *is* trouble, Leona. Our father knows you haven't been at Manuel's. He's searching for you now." He glanced toward Diego. "And you, *amigo*."

She felt a stab of alarm but pushed it aside, forcing herself to remain calm. "Don't worry, Ricardo. We have a plan. I need only to get to Manuel's for tonight. Tomorrow, I'll be able to explain my absence. *Papá* may be angry with me, but he'll believe me."

She might have been right. She just might have been able to convince her father that she'd merely gone away to think—if only he hadn't followed Ricardo to the mountains without her brother's being aware of it.

When Gardner came into sight, followed by Gaspar and Eduardo, Leona felt her heart sink.

Her mind went numb as she gazed into blue eyes filled with disappointment. She saw no remnant of her gentle, tolerant father in the rigid expression of the man riding toward her.

No one spoke for a long while after the three men reached the others. Leona felt their condemnatory looks like hot brands on her skin. She wanted to say something, but her throat had closed up and she couldn't seem to speak.

"You've been with him all this time in the mountains," Gardner said at last, not in question but as a statement of fact. A verdict.

"*Papá*, I can explain."

"You could not wait until you were married? Is this how I have raised you?"

"No, *Papá*, it isn't like that. We . . ."

Gardner turned his horse away. "You'll be married at once. We'll send for the priest."

"But I don't want to marry Diego."

Her father looked back at her, his voice so low she nearly couldn't hear him. "Then you should have thought of that before spending more than a week with him in these mountains." He turned straight ahead. "We'll speak of it no more."

Leona looked at Diego, but she found no help there. She felt that this was his fault, even though she knew it wasn't. After all, what could he say or do? Unless they told Gardner that Leona had been shot while trying to rob McCabe of a shipment of gold, nothing would change what appeared to be true.

Which was worse? she wondered. To let her father think she'd been sleeping with Diego, living as his woman, or to tell him that she was the bandida, La Rosa?

"Señor Washington." Diego spurred his horse past Leona.

Gardner glared at him.

"I'm prepared to marry your daughter immediately. In fact, I welcome your decision. But I want you to know that she is innocent of wrongdoing. Things are not as they appear. Whatever wrong was done was my fault, not hers."

"I said, we'll speak of it no more," her father repeated, but a little of his disapproval seemed to have faded from his gaze as he turned it back on Leona.

For just a moment, she forgot how angry she was at Diego and was grateful for what he'd said to Gardner.

Her father's gaze moved to Eduardo. "Take word to Padre Sanchez that we'll require his services tomorrow afternoon. Gaspar, you let the family know to be at the ranch before noon. Ricardo can take word to the Ramirez family. I'm sure Leona will want Mercedes with her for her wedding." He looked at his daughter once again. "Come, Leona. There's much to be done and little time to do it."

"*Papá*, please listen to me."

But he turned a deaf ear as he rode down the hillside, once again followed by Eduardo and Gaspar.

Leona turned to her twin. "Ricardo, what can I do?" she whispered.

"*Nada*," he replied. Then he, too, started down the mountain, leaving her alone with Diego.

"It's for the best, Leona," he said. "You know that I care for you, that I love you."

She didn't look at him. "You will not oppose me when I ride as La Rosa?"

"You know I can't let you do that. Not after what happened."

"Then this marriage is not for the best." She turned a rebellious glance in his direction. "And if you don't know it now, Diego, you will learn it with time."

With those words, she cantered Pesadilla away from Diego.

Chapter Twenty-Three

Rance McCabe doubled his fists at his sides as he stared out the window of his office. His eyes narrowed in anger.

Damn Gardner Washington! What right had he to poke his nose into other folk's business? He had his land. Why did he have to try to keep McCabe from getting what *he* wanted?

He hadn't believed it when he'd heard the news. Gardner had actually convinced Sebastiano Ramirez to appeal the Land Commission's decision to the federal courts rather than leave for Mexico where he belonged. The old fool! Ramirez had already sold almost everything of value to pay his attorney's fees. A lengthy litigation would strip him of what little he had left. Why didn't he just leave now?

McCabe turned away from the window and crossed to a table holding the decanter of brandy. He poured himself a generous portion, then carried the glass to his desk and sat on the chair behind it. After a lengthy swallow, he reclined in the chair, forcing himself to relax.

Ramirez stood little chance of proving his claim, he reasoned. Emanuel Hopkins was expected in Monterey soon. The judge would see to it that La Brisa fell into the proper hands.

McCabe's thoughts wandered to Ramirez's pretty daughter. Perhaps he should offer his services to her once again. Perhaps this time she would be more receptive to his suggestions. After all, her father had lost their case before the commission. She'd been there to see it for herself.

Ah, he thought, he would love to teach the haughty señorita a thing or two. If he had her in his bed, he would prove how wrong she'd been to scorn his attentions. In fact, she owed it to him.

Damn her! She owed him at least that.

McCabe ground his teeth as lust hardened in his loins. Lord, he needed a woman in a bad way.

Mercedes felt her heart skip painfully as Ricardo was shown into the sitting room. Ever since her father had decided to appeal the commission's decision, she'd been hoping she would see Ricardo, but there'd been no opportunity. She'd wanted to explain to him why she'd so abruptly turned down his proposal of marriage. Now that there was some hope that her family wouldn't be forced to leave, perhaps . . .

One look at his face told her he wasn't in the mood to listen to her explanations.

"Buenos días." Holding his hat in his hand, he bowed formally, never looking into her eyes. "I've brought news from Leona. She and Diego are to be married tomorrow, and she would like you with her."

"Tomorrow?"

"Sí."

"But why so soon? She said nothing . . ."

"It was decided suddenly."

Mercedes wondered what he wasn't telling her.

"Your parents are invited, too."

"They aren't here. They've gone to San Francisco to consult another attorney."

At last, Ricardo looked at her.

"My father has decided not to go to Mexico yet. He's going to appeal to the federal courts." She leaned forward in her chair. *Please hear what I'm telling you, Ricardo*, she thought. *Please understand why I did what I did.*

"I am glad, Mercedes. I hope he will be successful." He returned his hat to his head.

She rose from her chair, sensing that he was reluctant to remain in her company longer than necessary. She was filled with a sense of panic and despair. She'd waited so very long for him to notice her, to see that she was a woman ready to love and be loved. She'd wanted to be his wife and the mother of his children. She hadn't meant to hurt him, but she'd had no choice except to refuse. If he would only give her a chance to explain, surely he would see . . .

But she understood that his anger went too deep for explanations.

"I must go," he said stiffly. "We'll send a carriage for you in the morning."

Don't go, Ricardo. Please. "I'll be ready." *Ask me why. Just ask, and I'll tell you.*

He turned away. She followed him to the door.

As he stepped across the threshold, he said, "The hacienda is quiet today."

Just as her upbringing would not allow her to pour out her heart to Ricardo without some sign that he still cared, neither would her pride allow her to tell him that her father had been forced to let most of the servants and vaqueros go. She wanted his love, not his pity.

"*Sí,* it is quiet."

For just a moment, she thought he might turn and look at her again. She thought he might gaze into her eyes and see how much she loved him. If only . . .

"*Adiós,* Mercedes. Until tomorrow."

"Until tomorrow."

Slowly, she closed the door, not wanting to see him climb on his horse and ride away.

It had been painful for Ricardo to come to La Brisa, painful for him to see Mercedes. He didn't like admitting it, even silently. For two weeks, he'd been able to fool himself into believing he was over her, that he no longer felt anything, not even anger. But as he rode away, he knew he was lying to himself.

He still felt, and it still hurt.

At least when he'd heard the Ramirez family was going to Mexico, he'd found some comfort in knowing he wouldn't have to see Mercedes again. Now they had decided to stay. He *would* see her again.

And again and again and again.

If Sebastiano won his appeal, he and his wife and daughter would never leave this valley. Ricardo would see Mercedes at weddings and christenings and *fandangos*. He would run into her in Monterey and at mass. He would visit Leona and she would be there, too. He would probably even be invited to her wedding when one was arranged for her.

He cursed. He was letting his heart run away with his head. It hadn't been even a month since he'd spied Mercedes at the Aguilar *fandango* and realized she had blossomed into a woman. If he had lost himself to her so quickly, he could get over her just as quickly.

Unable to stop himself, he glanced behind him, almost wishing that he would find her watching from her doorway and knowing, if she had been, that he would have returned and professed his love for her once again.

Evening settled over Rancho del Sol with an uneasy silence.

In her room, Leona walked from window to

door, from door to window, from window to door. Her wound throbbed and she felt bone-weary, but still she couldn't stop her pacing.

Dulce stood helplessly by, watching her mistress. "*Señorita*, you must rest. Come and sit down."

"No one cares what I think or what I want," Leona muttered. "My father says I shall marry Diego. Diego says I shall not ride against McCabe. It's as if I have no voice. They don't even hear me."

"*Señorita . . .*"

"Am I not worthy of being heard, just because I'm a woman?"

Dulce sighed. "It is the way of things."

Leona whirled on the maid, her dark eyes snapping with fury. "*Why* is it the way of things? I can think and reason and feel as much as they do. I can ride any horse on this ranch. I can rope the cattle. I can shoot a gun and brandish a sword." She sniffed derisively. "Yet, because I was born a woman, I have no say in my future."

"*Por favor, señorita.*" Dulce placed her hands on Leona's arms and guided her toward the bed. "Haven't you taken on enough, trying to fight McCabe? Will you fight the ways of the world as well? You must rest. You are hurt. If you don't wish your father to learn of your injury, you need to lie down and rest."

Defeat, dark and heavy, swept down on Leona as she sat on the edge of the bed. "I love him, Dulce," she whispered.

"I know."

"But I can't stop being La Rosa. Not until McCabe is defeated."

"I know that, too, *señorita*." Dulce eased Leona back on the mattress, then covered her with a light blanket. "So does Señor Salazar."

"He's forbidden me to ride again."

Dulce just shook her head.

"We'll make each other suffer until we destroy our love." She turned her face to the wall as she closed her eyes. "I don't want it destroyed, Dulce," she added faintly.

The maid's hand stroked Leona's brow, then brushed her hair back from her face. "I know, *señorita*. I know. Do not worry. It will all come out right. You will see. La Rosa, she will triumph."

With Dulce's words echoing in her ears, Leona drifted into a troubled sleep, filled with dreams of black horses and red capes, campfires and gun fire, Diego and McCabe, weddings and kisses.

Diego's kisses . . .

Diego was in the barn when Ricardo returned to the ranch. Leona's brother was wearing the same gloomy look that everyone in the hacienda had worn throughout the day, Diego included.

Ricardo glanced at him as he stopped Raudo. The bay tossed his head impatiently as his rider dismounted.

"Mercedes will be here tomorrow?" Diego asked as he walked across the barn.

"She'll be here."

"Good. Maybe that will help Leona."

Ricardo started to loosen the girth on the saddle, then paused as he turned his head to look at Diego. "I'm sorry, *amigo*. I should have known I was being followed. I'd searched for you twice before without success, but I was certain you were hiding in the mountains. I knew McCabe hadn't found you, so where else could you be? But once my father knew Leona wasn't at Manuel's, I knew I'd have to tell him something soon. Today was my last chance to find you."

"It's all right." Diego laid a hand on his friend's shoulder. "We were to be married anyway. I'm just sorry Gardner thinks your sister went willingly with me to the mountains. I'm sorry he thinks I would misuse his trust in that way."

"Well, we can't tell him what really happened." Ricardo stared hard into Diego's eyes as he lowered his voice. "How badly was she hurt? Is she out of danger?"

"Yes, she's out of danger."

Her brother nodded, then continued to unsaddle his horse. Neither of the two men spoke again until Raudo was groomed, watered, and fed.

Finally, as Ricardo turned away from the gelding's stall, he let out a long sigh. "I suppose I must go inside and speak to him."

"Gardner's been waiting."

"He's going to want to know how I knew where to find you."

"You didn't know. It was just a guess."

Ricardo nodded. "I know, but I'm not sure he's in the mood to believe me—or anyone else—just now." He shrugged in resignation, then headed for the barn door.

"Good luck, *amigo*," Diego called after him.

"*Gracias*. I'm going to need it."

Remembering Leona's anger, Diego thought they were all going to need some luck to make it through the next day.

Diego wasn't really surprised when he awoke in the middle of the night and found her in his room. Except this time, she hadn't bothered with a red mask or any other form of disguise.

A candle flickered on the table beside her. He supposed it was the light that had awakened him. Or perhaps he'd simply felt her presence.

He sat up. "You shouldn't be here."

"You must stop the wedding, Diego."

"There isn't anything I can do. Gardner is determined that I do right by you."

"Nothing happened between us. There's nothing to put right."

"No, but are you willing to tell him what *did* happen?"

She stepped closer to his bed. "There must be another way to stop it."

Diego's gaze lingered on her face, her beauty still clear to him, even in the dim candlelight. "I don't want to stop it."

He could see that she wrestled with confusion, could feel it in the very air around them.

"Diego . . ." Earnest pleading filled her soft

voice. "Do you remember the night you told La Rosa that you loved me . . . Leona?"

"Yes. I remember."

"You said that my independence was part of what you loved about me."

"I remember that, too."

A final step brought her to his bedside. The flickering light of the candle danced over black hair that hung unbound over her shoulders. It revealed the roundness of her breasts beneath the thin fabric of her nightgown. He could smell the freshness of her clean skin, caught the light fragrance of her perfumed soap.

"Diego, listen to me, please. I can't stop being who I am. If you ask it of me, I will fight you."

He took hold of her hand and drew her down onto the bed beside him. He touched the side of her face, pushing her hair away so he could see her more clearly. "I don't want to change you, *querida*. I don't want to fight with you. I want to love you, to protect you." His arms encircled her, and he drew her close to him.

He felt only a momentary resistance as their lips touched before she seemed to melt into his embrace. Her mouth parted willingly at the urging of his tongue. He caressed her back, then drew his hand along her side, across her ribs, until he could cup her breast.

She inhaled but didn't try to pull away. Her own hand stroked the length of his bare arm with a feather-soft touch, a touch that would drive him mad if he didn't stop it soon.

Diego broke the kiss and drew back from her. "I think this had best wait until after the wedding," he said hoarsely, desire robbing the air from his lungs.

Leona felt the same breathlessness. The wild longings that coursed through her didn't stop just because the kissing did. She wanted nothing more than to throw herself back into his arms and feel his lips upon hers again. She wanted his hand upon her breast.

But loving him wasn't why she'd come to his room. She'd come to warn him. She *had* warned him, but she didn't think he'd listened to her.

"You cannot conquer me with sweet words and promises, Diego."

"You're wrong. *Amor conquista todo*," he responded, his voice soft, his gaze tender. "Even me."

Leona shook her head, knowing she'd failed to make him understand. "You can't protect me from being who I am. I won't give up what freedom I've found. I can't. I must remain true to myself." The lump in her throat caused her words to come out in a whisper as she rose from the bed. "Remember what I've told you."

She turned, walked across the room, then paused beside the table to stoop and blow out the candle. Darkness blanketed the room once again.

"I pray you will not be sorry, Diego Salazar."

With those words, she left through the open window as she had done twice before.

Chapter Twenty-Four

Gardner stood beneath his wife's portrait, staring up at it as he spoke. "The old hacienda is much smaller than this one. There were just the two of us, Francisca and me, when I built the house. I set it near the mountains because Francisca liked to go walking in them in the evenings." After a moment's silence, he turned to look at Diego. "It's yours now, yours and Leona's, for as long as you wish to stay there. I hope you'll be as happy as we were."

"Thank you, Señor Washington. I'll do my best to make your daughter happy."

Gardner struggled with his conflicting emotions. He liked Diego, had liked him from the first day he'd arrived at Rancho del Sol. He knew that the Texan had won Leona's heart. But no matter how hard he tried, he couldn't understand what had possessed them to go into the mountains together. He suspected there was something he wasn't being told, but neither Leona nor Diego had offered any sort of explanation. Even Ricardo had played dumb when Gardner had grilled him last night.

He sighed. It didn't matter what the reason for their indiscretion had been. The fact remained that Leona had spent more than a week alone with this man. His daughter. His beautiful, innocent, headstrong daughter. He could understand her wanting Diego. Her mother had been a passionate woman as well. But Leona should have waited until after the wedding.

And now she said she didn't want to marry Diego after all.

Gardner shook his head, feeling very tired. A man worked all his life, building his empire, for only one reason. For his children. But what was most important was not that they have the land and the wealth. It was that they were happy. More than anything, he wanted Leona to be happy.

As if he'd read the older man's mind, Diego repeated, "I'll make her happy, Senor Washington. I love her."

"I hope so, Diego." He shook his head once more, then squared his shoulders. "I hear voices. Our guests must be arriving. Come with me, and we'll greet them together."

Leona didn't know how Anita and Dulce had done it. Overnight, they had managed to alter one of her best gowns—adding lace and flounces to the full skirt and modifying the neckline—and produced an elegant wedding gown.

While Dulce fussed with Leona's hair, weaving it with ribbons, Leona stared at her image in the dressing table mirror. It was a melancholy face that stared back at her.

Dulce's hands stopped in midair. "You must not look so sad, *señorita*. It is not good that you go to your husband without a smile. You love him. He loves you. That is what is important."

Leona nodded. She knew her maid was right. In truth, she wanted to smile. She wanted to be happy. There wasn't another man in the world she would rather marry than Diego. He had long since won her heart. But he wanted too much from her. He wanted far more than she could give. He wanted to change her, to make her into something she was not.

"*Señorita,*" Dulce said, bending down so that her face was next to Leona's; their gazes met in the mirror, "you are La Rosa. You have brought hope to many people. You have never run from a fight. You have taken your sword and your *pistola*, and you have challenged the devil himself. Will you run now?"

Leona was silent as she considered the question. Then she sat a little straighter on her chair. "No," she whispered. "No, I won't run." She looked at her own reflection and felt a sudden surge of hope. "No, I won't run," she repeated as a smile curved the corners of her mouth.

"Good. That is better. Now I begin to see the bride."

The hacienda at Rancho del Sol had its own chapel, and it was there that the large Washington family, Mercedes Ramirez, and the priest gathered for the marriage of Leona and Diego.

The bridegroom stood at the front of the chapel and stared over the heads of Leona's brothers, looking into space. He didn't dare look directly at them. He'd felt their hostility as they'd arrived for the wedding, and he'd known that Eduardo and Gaspar had told the others just where they'd found Leona. It was a good thing he wanted to marry her, for he wouldn't have had another choice.

When the door opened, Diego's gaze refocused. The opening was empty for a moment, and then she stepped into view.

His heart nearly stopped at the sight.

It wasn't that there was anything so unusual about what she wore. The gown of royal purple had a modest neckline and long, puffy sleeves. The fitted bodice accented the gentle rounding of her breasts and the narrowness of her waist, and the full skirt swayed as she stepped into the chapel, revealing matching slippers on her feet. An attractive gown, yes, but it was the woman who made it beautiful.

Their gazes met across the length of the chapel, and he felt a surge of love for her the like of which he'd never felt before. He knew, beyond any doubt, that this was the woman with whom he was destined to spend the rest of his life. He silently thanked his father for making that pledge so many years ago. And though he wished Carlos hadn't died in the war, Diego couldn't be sorry that it was he who was standing in this chapel in his brother's place.

Unexpectedly, Leona smiled at him. He felt his mouth go dry and his heart quicken. He'd been so afraid she would find some way to defy her father. He'd been so sure she would refuse him. She'd never said she loved him. She'd always said she was afraid that she would make him unhappy, that she would make him a poor wife.

He remembered the kiss they'd shared last night in his room. He remembered the feel of her body next to his. No, she wouldn't make him unhappy. She could never make him unhappy.

He prayed that the priest would not be long-winded.

Leona scarcely heard Padre Sanchez as he spoke the words that would bind her forever to the man at her side. The discomfort in her shoulder seemed insignificant beside the overwhelming joy and love that filled her heart.

Was it like this for all brides? she wondered. Did they notice only the groom while everything else around them was merely a blur?

Diego's eyes were such a rich shade of brown, like fertile soil kissed by sunlight. His hair was as black as ink. His face was filled with sharp angles—a long, straight nose, a firm jaw.

And he had a wonderful mouth.

She felt a familiar tingle in her belly as she stared at his lips, thinking of his kisses. The tingle turned to fire as she thought of his lean torso, his muscular arms, the feel of his skin against hers.

Tonight, he would hold her in his arms again, not just to share his warmth as he sought to make her well but to make her his wife. This night there would be nothing chaste about their embrace. She didn't understand all that awaited her, but she wasn't afraid.

After the words were spoken, Leona hugged her father and kissed his cheek. As she looked into his eyes, she wished she could remove the disappointment she saw there. She wished she could explain what had really happened in the Santa Lucias, but she couldn't. It would not help matters for him to know that she was La Rosa or that she had been shot.

"Diego will be a good husband to you," Gardner said, his voice sounding strained.

"I know, *Papá*."

"He loves you."

"I know, *Papá*."

Gardner placed his hands on her upper arms and squeezed. His grip caused a spasm of pain to shoot out from her shoulder, but it was the way he continued to look at her that brought the tears to her eyes.

"I love you, too, Leona," he said softly.

"I know, *Papá*." She sniffed. "I'm sorry I disappointed you. I wish I could explain. . . ."

Gardner cleared his throat as he looked up at the sky, blinking quickly. "Yes. Well. Here's Diego with the buggy. You'd best be on your way if you're to reach your new home before nightfall."

She nodded, her throat suddenly thick with emotions.

She turned toward Mercedes, who stood close by. Quickly, she hugged her friend. "Thank you for coming."

"I'm glad I could be here, *amiga*. You are a beautiful bride."

Leona squeezed Mercedes's hand. "Don't give up hope. Tell him how you feel. He'll listen."

"No." Mercedes shook her head. "He doesn't want to hear anything I have to say. He no longer cares."

"His pride is hurt. Be patient, Mercedes. He will come around."

The girl nodded. "I hope so." She put on a brave smile. "But you shouldn't be thinking of me now. Look. Diego is waiting for you. Go on." She kissed Leona's cheek. "And be happy."

Leona turned her head, her gaze meeting Diego's. She felt the now-familiar tumble in her belly. "I will be," she replied quickly, then stepped toward her husband and the waiting buggy.

* * *

Mercedes was silent throughout the drive home, despite Gasper's attempts to make light conversation. She'd hoped, of course, that it would be Ricardo who drove her back to La Brisa, but he'd made himself scarce as soon as the bride and groom had left the hacienda.

"You should have stayed at Rancho del Sol," Gaspar said as they pulled up before the ranch house.

She smiled sadly at him. "No, it's better that I'm at home. La Brisa is where I belong."

"Would you like me to come in?" he offered. "We could talk for a while."

She shook her head and quickly got out of the carriage. "No, Gaspar. I'm fine."

He leaned forward. "You needn't fear me. I can see where your heart lies. My little brother won't be blind forever. I'll try to knock some sense into him."

"No!" she exclaimed, then added more softly, "*Gracias*, Gaspar, but it's better that you say nothing. The fault is mine."

He shrugged. "If that's what you want."

"It's what I want."

Mercedes stood outside and watched as the Washington carriage drove away. As it grew smaller in the distance, she felt the solitude closing in on her. Suddenly, she wished she had stayed overnight at Rancho del Sol. La Brisa was far too quiet tonight.

She shivered as she turned to go inside. Even though afternoon was beginning to fade, the air was still warm. Yet she felt a terrible chill. She longed for nothing more than something warm to drink and then to crawl into her bed and seek solace in sleep.

Chapter Twenty-Five

The small house, built on the slope of the mountains, had been cleaned and aired. New curtains framed the windows. There was food in the pantry and plenty of wood stacked beside the cast-iron stove. Through the open bedroom door, Leona could see the bed with the blankets and sheets turned down in invitation.

Blushing as she envisioned Diego in bed beside her, Leona wondered which of her sisters-in-law had done this for them. More than likely several had had a hand in it. That they had accomplished so much in so little time was ample proof of their devotion.

"Would you like me to bring in some water from the well?" Diego asked as he closed the door.

She twirled to face him. After a moment's silence, she shook her head. "I'm not thirsty."

Even as she spoke, she felt a strange heat moving through her, leaving her flushed, almost feverish. Perhaps she did need some water with which to cool herself.

"Something to eat?" He stepped closer.

She swallowed. "I'm not hungry," she replied in a small voice.

"Nor am I. At least, not for food." Diego reached forward, touching her cheek with his fingertips. "You are so beautiful. The first time I saw you, I knew I'd never seen anyone more beautiful than you." He paused, a slow smile spreading from his mouth to his eyes. "Señora Salazar . . ."

His touch moved to her hair. Deftly, he removed the lace mantilla, then freed the ribbons, dropping them one at a time on the floor near their feet. The hairpins followed, allowing her heavy hair to fall freely about her shoulders and down her back.

A shiver of anticipation shot through her, leaving her skin tingling. Despite all her misgivings about their union, she couldn't deny that she longed for him to hold her, kiss her, possess her. She was eager to learn just what it meant to become one with this man.

Suddenly, Diego's arm swept beneath her knees, and he lifted her into his embrace. With quick, purposeful strides, he carried her into the bedroom. He didn't lay her on the bed as she'd expected, but instead held her in his arms, simply staring into her eyes.

The intense look left her feeling dizzy and breathless.

Muted sunlight from the dying day filtered through the curtains that covered the windows, casting a golden aura over the two lovers. Leona felt the luminous radiance caressing her skin, seeping into her pores, flooding her veins. There was something unreal about this moment, as if it were happening in a dream. Time had ceased to exist within the walls of this room.

Finally, he set her feet on the floor. His hands cradled her head as he bent to kiss her lips. It was a tender kiss with the lightest touch, and yet it started a storm inside her of enormous proportions. If not for his hands to hold her steady, she knew she would have collapsed.

"I've wanted you for a long time, *mi tesoro*," Diego whispered as his fingers began to loosen the ties and buttons of her gown.

"As I have wanted you," Leona answered with honesty.

One by one, her wedding garments fell away, forming a pool of colorful silks and satins and lace on the floor. She felt a strange combination of fear and impatience as she waited for the moment she would stand naked before him.

The soft fabric of her camisole slid over her breasts. She sucked in a tiny breath as cool air caressed her flesh. Her nipples hardened and dimpled.

"Ah, *querida*, you are more beautiful than I remembered."

As Diego's hands gently fondled her breasts, he kissed the curve of her neck. Again she felt the weakness in her knees, and with it came a feeling akin to pain in her loins. She closed her eyes as she took hold of his arms to steady herself. A groan escaped her lips.

Beyond the rushing sound that filled her ears, she heard his corresponding groan. With more haste than he'd shown before, he freed the tie of her pantalettes, allowing them to fall to her ankles. Then he lifted her and laid her on the bed.

For a moment, Leona kept her eyes closed, waiting for the spinning sensations to cease. Finally, missing his touch, she opened her eyes to see what delayed him from joining her.

With dusk settling over the bedroom, she saw Diego as she'd never seen a man before—naked and aroused. Even as she felt herself blushing, she didn't look away, couldn't look away. She was intrigued and fascinated by the sight of him—his broad chest, his muscled arms, his narrow waist, his long legs, his tumescence. She was not so innocent that she didn't understand his readiness for her. Again, she felt a mixture of anxiety and anticipation.

Diego lay on the bed beside her. His mouth possessed hers, leaving her breathless once more, then broke away to begin a slow pattern of kisses over her body. His lips moved to her cheeks and eyes and forehead. They nibbled on the tender lobes of her ears. They brushed against the sensitive skin in the curve of her throat. When they closed over the tip of one breast and began to suckle, Leona's hands flew to his head, her fingers tangling in his dark hair. She wasn't sure whether she sought to push him away or draw him closer.

"Diego . . ." she whispered.

His response was to move to her other breast and tease it with the same tender torture, playing with the nipple with his tongue, then sucking lightly. As he did so, his hand alighted on her stomach and began a gentle stroking of her flesh, moving in slow circles, each one growing larger until his fingers touched the small thatch of hair between her thighs. There, his hand lingered.

Leona gasped and stiffened.

She'd thought, from the things Maria had told her, that she was ready for this night. She'd thought she understood what was expected of her. But suddenly, she felt ignorant and unsure of herself. The feelings he had loosed within her were startling, strange and foreign to her. She didn't know how to react.

Diego moved away from her breast, drawing his body up alongside hers, braced on one elbow. "Don't be afraid of me, Leona. I promise to go slowly. If you feel pain, it will only be for a moment."

She opened her eyes to look up at him.

He kissed her, gently, slowly, completely, then drew back to gaze into her eyes.

She felt the uncertainty drain away as quickly as it had come. "I'm not afraid of you, Diego," she answered, a slight quiver in her voice despite her trust.

He smiled, a look so sensual it left her even weaker than his kisses. He continued to stare down at her as his hand slid lower, his fingers finding and caressing the sensitive bud.

Her eyes rounded in surprise even as her body responded to the touch, moving against him, with him. She hadn't expected . . . it seemed so . . . she didn't know . . .

Then he kissed her again, and she was sent spiraling into a whirlpool of new and exciting emotions.

By the time Diego moved above her, she was on fire with a nameless need. She wasn't afraid. There was no room for fear in her heart. Somehow, she knew that only when he was inside her would she find a release for the building tensions that filled her, making every nerve ending in her body scream for fulfillment.

As he entered her, she felt her own body resisting the intrusion, followed by a sharp, unanticipated pain. Her eyes flew open, widened in surprise as a tiny gasp escaped her lips. He paused at the sound and met her gaze. She could sense his fight for control and knew that he was trying not to hurt her, forcing himself to wait until she was ready.

The moment of pain passed, and still he didn't move. Still he only watched her. Frustration began to build inside her. It mounted to a fevered pitch. She needed him to do something, but she didn't know what. With her eyes, she pleaded with him to help her. Her breathing came in little gasps as she waited . . . waited.

Diego withdrew ever so slightly, then pressed deeper within. His careful, precise movements were more than she could bear. Instinctively, Leona grabbed his hips and pulled him deeply into her, arching her body to meet his. She groaned, but not with torment, only with delight.

Together, they began to move, finding the rhythm of a dance as old as time. Pleasure filled her body, a pleasure such as she'd never known, such as she'd never suspected could exist. With every movement, she sought to become more a part of him.

The pulsing blood inside her head seemed to quicken, and she rushed to keep pace with it. She wrapped her arms and legs around Diego, as if not to do so would send her hurtling out into space. Tiny sounds filled the room, but she was unaware that they belonged to her as, together, they climbed toward an explosion of passions.

As Leona teetered on the brink of discovery, she cried his name, then plummeted over the edge, Diego's own cry of release a faint echo in her ears.

She wasn't sure how long she lay there, Diego above her, her body still joined with his. She couldn't even be sure that she hadn't fainted or drifted off to sleep. Her mind seemed sluggish, reluctant to work.

She was aware that he supported his weight on his forearms. She felt the sheen of sweat on her skin. Her heart slowed to a steadier beat, and her breathing returned to normal.

When Diego began to withdraw, her body automatically tightened around him. "No," she whispered, reluctant to be separated from him. "Not yet."

She opened her eyes to find him watching her, that sensuous, knowing smile once more on his lips. She marveled at the sense of freedom that coursed through her. She felt beautiful and unashamed beneath his gaze. She knew she belonged here in his arms as she'd never belonged anywhere before. At this moment, she thought she would willingly die now rather than be separated from him.

"The *gatita* is truly a *leona*." He chuckled, a warm sound coming from deep in his throat. "You are as wild as the great cats, *querida*. I'm thankful for your sheathed claws."

Her body flexed again in response to his words, to the satisfaction she heard in his voice. The spontaneous reaction brought her a burst of pleasure where their bodies were still joined and, with it, the memory of the intimate delights they had so recently shared.

Diego turned onto his side, taking her with him. She felt a wave of lassitude sweep over her as she nestled close against him. His lips brushed her forehead. His hand stroked her hair, then slipped to her neck and down to her arm. His caresses ceased as his fingers touched the bandage around her shoulder.

"Your wound . . . Does it hurt you?"

"No, it doesn't hurt. I have forgotten it."

He pulled her more tightly against him, his mouth near her ear. "I won't ever allow anything to hurt you again, Leona. You have my promise."

Her heart tripped. How she hoped and prayed that he meant what he said. But did he know that no hurt would be greater than if he tried to make her become someone or something she was not? She still feared he didn't understand.

His embrace relaxed. His breathing slowed. *"Mi tesoro . . . mi gatita . . . mi leona . . ."*

She longed to return the words of affection, to tell him how much she loved him, but she couldn't. She sensed that her silence was her last wall of defense against losing herself completely. Once Diego knew that he held her heart captive, she would be helpless against any demand he made upon her. Once he knew Leona loved him, La Rosa would be defeated as never before.

With a sigh on her lips, she wondered if it was so terrible that he wished to protect her. Was it wrong for him to cherish her, to want to keep her safe from harm?

No, that wasn't wrong, but asking her to change would be. She had to think of her friends and neighbors over her own safety. She owed her allegiance to her hombres, to the poor and the dispossessed. As La Rosa, she had promised them aid. She had to keep her word to them. If Diego demanded that she stop fighting against McCabe, she would find herself fighting Diego as well. La Rosa had to keep riding until Rance McCabe was driven from this valley for good. Diego would have to accept that.

I can't change, Diego. I can't be less than what I am. Don't ask it of me. Please, my love. Don't ask it of me.

She lay awake long after his even breathing told her he slept, wondering what the future held in store for them.

Chapter Twenty-Six

McCabe gripped the saddle horn as he lifted the bottle to his lips and gulped down the last swallows of brandy. Discovering that the bottle was now empty, he tossed it aside. He heard the shattering of glass as it struck a rock. The sound was a sharp contrast to the silence of the night.

The anger that had been building in him for two days burned in his belly more hotly than the alcohol he'd consumed. When he'd set out from his ranch house this evening, he'd known there was only one cure for the rage he felt. He wanted a fair measure of payment, and he knew just where he would find it.

La Brisa Ranch lay before him. A soft glow glimmered through the curtains of one room. The rest of the place lay in darkness.

McCabe grinned. Sebastiano and his wife had yet to return from San Francisco, and Mercedes was home alone. Or as good as alone. Lack of funds had forced the old ranchero to dismiss most of his employees. There would be no one to object to McCabe's impromptu visit.

Yes, he meant to be compensated this night for all the trouble he'd had of late. Nothing had gone right. He'd been harassed and made a fool of by that masked witch who called herself La Rosa. Even after he'd laid such a clever trap for her and she'd been shot, the stupid idiots who worked for him couldn't find her and bring her to him. To add insult to injury, Gardner Washington had prevailed upon the Ramirezes to fight the commission's decision, keeping McCabe from acquiring the land and cattle he craved so desperately.

Well, he was through playing the gentleman with these greasers. He would show them who their better was, and he would begin with the girl who'd first scorned his offer of help. He would show Mercedes Ramirez how much better it was to have a white man between her thighs than some dark-skinned Mexican. He would teach her to respect him. When he was through with her, she would be pleading with him not to leave her.

Grinning, he guided his horse toward the hacienda.

Leona awakened suddenly, her heart racing, the memory of the nightmarish scream still echoing in her ears. She sat up, uncertain of her surroundings, the room as black as ink.

"Leona?"

She gasped and drew away from the voice in the dark.

Fingers closed around her arm. "Leona, what is it?"

With a cry of relief, she pressed herself into the safety of Diego's embrace.

He stroked her hair. "What's frightened you, *querida*?"

"I . . . I don't know. I thought . . . I thought I heard someone scream. It was so real, Diego. Someone is in trouble. I can feel it in my heart. Someone is in terrible trouble."

"It was only a bad dream." He kissed her temple. "Only a bad dream."

She snuggled closer to him, trying to still the rapid beating of her heart. She shuddered as another wave of panic sliced through her.

"Do you want to tell me about it?"

She tried to remember what she'd been dreaming, but all that remained was the echo of terror. "I don't recall anything but the scream. It was a woman, a terrified woman. And I could feel something evil close by."

"It was probably a mountain lion. They can sound like a woman screaming, especially in the night." He stroked her back in a gesture of comfort.

She felt the tension begin to ease from her body. Of course. He was right. That's all she'd heard. There hadn't been a dream. It hadn't been a premonition of danger. There was nothing evil lurking in the darkness. She'd merely heard the cry of a mountain lion as it hunted by night.

The longer Leona lay in his arms, his hands caressing and rubbing her back, the more relaxed she became. There was a rightness to this moment, and there was no cause for her to be afraid.

"You hurt my feelings," he whispered near her ear, his tone light and teasing. "I'd hoped to leave you with more pleasant dreams."

The last dregs of her fear were replaced by the memory of Diego's lovemaking. A different and very pleasant kind of tension filled her body.

"You did." She kissed his chin, feeling the roughness of the stubble growing there.

It wasn't long before the bad dream was completely forgotten, not to be remembered again that night.

Late the following morning, it was Diego's turn to wonder if he was the one having a bad dream.

He stared grimly at the plate set before him. When he glanced up, he leveled a droll look at his bride. "You weren't doing it just to avoid marrying me, were you?"

"What?"

"The breakfast you made for me when I first came to Rancho del Sol. It wasn't just to frighten me away." He returned his gaze to the charred remains of his breakfast. "You really can't cook."

Any look of apology that had been on her face when she'd set the plate on the table vanished at his words. Leona's chin shot up defiantly and her eyes glittered in warning. "I never claimed I could."

"No." Diego couldn't repress a chuckle. "You never did." Before her anger could get entirely out of hand, he jumped up from his chair and pulled her into his embrace. "I suppose I shall have to find my sustenance in other ways and other places." He laughed again, low in his throat this time. "Come here, my little morsel, and let me nibble on you."

It pleased him that she didn't resist. It pleased him even more that she wasn't afraid or ashamed to unleash her own passions.

He was considering doing far more than nibbling on his delectable wife when a knock on the door interrupted the pleasant interlude. Leona stepped back from him, her eyes wide with surprise as she tried to straighten her dressing gown, a blush coloring her cheeks.

"If that's one of your brothers," Diego grumbled, "I'll skin him alive."

Leona grinned, her momentary embarrassment already forgotten. "Only if I don't get to him first."

Quick strides carried Diego across the room. He lifted the latch and opened the door a few inches. "Heath!" He opened it wide.

The tavern owner nodded, his gaze darting to Leona, then returning to Diego. "Sorry t'bother you, Diego, but I've got some information which I think might be important. Mr. Washington told me where I could find you. Can I speak with you. . . . privately?"

"Of course." Diego turned to look at Leona. She was watching him with questioning eyes. "Heath Curtis, this is my wife, Leona Salazar."

"Pleasure t'meet you, ma'am." Heath touched the brim of his hat. "I apologize for disturbin' you."

With the fingers of one hand, Leona pushed her rumpled hair back from her face. "It's quite all right," she replied.

Again she looked at Diego, her expression seeking answers to her silent questions, but he provided none as he stepped outside.

"I won't be long," he said over his shoulder, then closed the door behind him. He led Heath Curtis a few steps away from the door and windows.

"I really am sorry t'barge in on you this way, Diego. I didn't know you was gettin' married."

"We decided rather quickly."

Heath grinned. "I can see why. Wouldn't want to risk a pretty filly like her gettin' away." His expression sobered as he withdrew an envelope from his shirt pocket. "It's from Hiram Benjamin. Says he wants you to come to San Francisco as quick as you can. Seems he's got a lead about Judge Hopkins that just might keep him off the commission, but he needs your help."

Diego took the missive from Heath and opened it, quickly scanning the letter. From what he could see, Hiram's information, if it could be corroborated, was just what they needed to bring about some badly needed changes. But time was of the essence.

He glanced toward the house. He hadn't yet told Leona what had brought him to California. He'd let her go on believing it was just to honor their fathers' pledge. And according to his agreement with the Joseph McConnell Agency, he had to leave it that way for now. The government required absolute secrecy on this mission. Until McCabe and Hopkins were stopped, Diego couldn't tell her the truth.

He slapped the palm of his hand several times with the letter, a frown furrowing his forehead. Just what *was* he going to tell Leona? He could take her with him to San Francisco, tell her it was their wedding trip. But once they got there, how would he explain his absences? He would probably be required to be away from her most of the time. And there was always the element of danger that went with his undercover work. If the wrong people found out what Diego was doing, they just might try to use Leona to get to him.

He drew in a deep breath, silently acknowledging that he'd be better off to leave her here. She would be safer, here with her family. He knew she was going to be angry with him, but he'd just have to find some way to make it up to her later.

"What're you goin' to tell her?" Heath asked.

"That I've been called away on business."

"Not a very good thing t'have t'do on your honeymoon."

"No, but it can't be helped." Diego raked his

fingers through his unruly hair. "I guess I'd better go in and tell her."

Heath tugged on the brim of his hat, pulling it down further on his forehead. "Well, you don't need me hangin' around. Good luck."

His voice was resigned. "Thanks."

Diego watched as Heath mounted his horse and cantered away from the small adobe house. Then he turned around and went to face the music.

It had taken all of Leona's willpower not to tiptoe over to the door and try to eavesdrop on the men's conversation. She couldn't imagine what would have brought anyone out this way this time of day. The man must have started out very early to have gone first to Rancho del Sol and then here. What could be so urgent? And just what was the man's connection to Diego?

The door opened suddenly, drawing her gaze as Diego stepped inside. Leona rose from the chair where she'd forced herself to sit and wait. She hoped her anxiety didn't show on her face.

"Your friend isn't going to join us for coffee?" she asked when she saw that her husband was alone.

"No. He needed to return to Monterey."

"What's wrong, Diego?"

"Nothing, I hope, but I'm going to have to take a quick trip to San Francisco to check on my shipping investments. There might be some problems brewing. If I move quickly, I'll be able to save things."

Relief flooded Leona. "I'll begin to pack at once. How long do you think we'll be gone?"

"I'll have to go alone this time, Leona." He crossed the room, stopping before her. His fingers closed lightly around her arms. "Please understand. There's no point in dragging you along when I wouldn't have any time to spend with you. I don't know how long it will take or where exactly I'll be."

She stared into his eyes and felt a flash of alarm. His expression was so sincere. His voice sounded normal. And yet she had a sudden and unshakable feeling that he was lying to her, that his trip had nothing to do with shipping investments.

Diego drew her closer to him. "Please, *querida*, try to understand. If I lose my investments, we'll have a difficult time starting our ranch here in the Salinas. I want to give you a good home and all of the fine things your father has given you."

"But . . ."

"Don't argue with me. It's hard enough that I must leave you now." He kissed her, pulling her tight against him.

Leona forgot all her questions, all her suspicions. They were drowned in a stormy sea of emotions that left her clinging to him for support.

"I'll come back to you before you know I'm gone," he whispered, his breath warm against her cheek. "And I'll miss you every moment I'm away."

She felt a terrible ache in her breast and knew that she would miss him, too. Much more than any words could express. How had he done this to her? In one night, he'd become her life, her very existence. She knew that when they were apart, each second would seem an eternity.

She looked up once more into his brown eyes, eyes alight with love. Despite her initial doubts about what was taking him away, she didn't doubt his feelings for her.

Nor hers for him.

Taking his hand, she silently led him into the bedroom. If he would leave her, he would leave knowing what he was missing while he was away. If he would go, then she would make him regret every moment they were apart so that he would hasten back to her arms.

"I'll help you pack later," she said softly as her dressing gown fell to the floor.

He didn't argue with her.

Chapter Twenty-Seven

The small house beside the mountains seemed much too empty now that Diego was gone. Leona sat on the bed, wrapped in the tangled blankets, and listened to the silence, wondering what she would do with herself until he returned.

Diego had suggested that she go to Rancho del Sol, but she'd refused. She didn't want to spend the first week of her marriage under her father's roof, especially if she had to spend it without Diego. She supposed it was wounded pride. She didn't want to tell Gardner that, less than twenty-four hours after their wedding, her husband had felt it more important to tend to business than to her.

She closed her eyes as the memory of his touch caused fluttery sensations to fill her chest. To think she had once believed herself immune to such feelings! And now here she was, only minutes without Diego and already breathless for his return.

With a sound of frustration, Leona tossed aside the blankets and rose from the bed. She bathed and dressed quickly, reminding herself throughout her ablutions that she had never been one to wait for a man's directions and she wasn't about to begin doing so now.

Since her return to Rancho del Sol two days before, Leona's thoughts had been centered upon Diego and her marriage to him. It was time that she found out what Rance McCabe had done during her absence. Without the threat of La Rosa hanging over his head, there was no telling what she might find.

But how did she learn what she wanted to know?

She didn't want to seek out Ricardo for the same reason she didn't want to see her father. She had no wish to explain Diego's absence.

She could pay a visit to McCabe, but she doubted she would learn anything valuable from him. He was too careful in the words he spoke. He wouldn't reveal himself so easily. Besides, what plausible reason could she give for her visit when she'd made it clear what she thought of him?

If she could get word to Paco or Johnny Parker . . . But they would have no reason to tell her anything. They reported only to Ricardo or La Rosa, not to Leona Washington.

Leona Salazar, she amended, and felt a corresponding emptiness now that the man whose name she shared was gone from her side.

Well, she couldn't just wait here, counting the minutes, or she would go mad.

Mercedes! Mercedes would want to see her. She was alone while her parents were in San Francisco, and she could probably use someone to talk to. She'd looked so sad and dejected yesterday during the wedding ceremony.

Perhaps Leona would be able to be of some help. Perhaps she would even be able to think of a way to mend things between her brother and her dearest friend.

It didn't take long for Leona to saddle her palomino and set off for La Brisa.

Diego had a strong urge to turn around and ride back. Something told him he should have taken Leona to Rancho del Sol before leaving. She'd promised she would send for Dulce so that she wouldn't be alone at the old hacienda, and she'd explained why she didn't want to return to her father's house. He'd been swayed by her dark eyes and the sad turn of her lovely mouth. Besides, he wasn't exactly pleased that he'd been forced to leave his bride of one day. It was highly probable that Gardner Washington wasn't going to like it either.

But Leona wouldn't be alone more than a few hours. Her maid would be with her. Besides, the little house was located well within the borders of

Rancho del Sol. No one would dare to bother her there.

Still, he kept hearing her defiant tone as she'd refused to quit riding as La Rosa. *I can't stop being who I am. If you ask it of me, I will fight you.*

But that was before they'd married. That was before she'd come to him with such sweet abandon. He'd promised to care for and protect her. She'd seen how much he loved her. She wouldn't do anything foolish while he was gone. A few days. Only a week or so. What mischief could she get into in such a short time?

Turn around . . . Go back . . .

But time was short. This could be their only chance to legally put an end to McCabe's activities along the Salinas. Diego had to act quickly if he and Hiram Benjamin were to get the information they needed.

His spurs asked Conquistador for more speed. He would work quickly and return to his bride, and he would find that he had worried for nothing.

For some reason, as Glory cantered toward the Ramirez hacienda, Leona recalled the terrified scream she'd thought she'd heard in the night. Her pulse quickened as a chill settled in the pit of her stomach.

It was only a bad dream, she reminded herself. *Or a mountain lion.*

Still, she couldn't shake the ominous feeling, a feeling that grew stronger with each stride of the golden mare. By the time Leona reined in her mount, her mouth had gone dry with fear.

Whatever is wrong with me?

She hopped to the ground, then wound Glory's reins around the hitching post and stepped toward the door. She noticed the quiver in her hand as she raised it to knock. Quickly, she drew a deep breath, once again silently berating herself for her foolish behavior.

She had to rap twice more before the door was finally opened by an aging servant woman. One look at the woman's crinkled face, and Leona's fears returned.

"Ines, what's wrong?" She spoke loudly, almost shouting, for she knew the servant was nearly deaf.

"It is the young mistress, *señora*. She has locked her door and will not open it to me. She ate nothing when she returned from your father's *rancho* yesterday. When I tried to take her food this morning, she told me to go away."

Leona took a quick breath of air, then let it out, almost as a sigh of relief. "She's unhappy. That's all. Things aren't going well for her and my brother."

"It is more than that, *señora*." Ines shook her head. "I have been with the *señorita* since she was born. I know her voice. I am frightened for her."

Leona patted the old woman's arm. "I'll talk to her. It will be all right. You'll see."

She turned and hurried toward the bedroom at the back of the house. She tried not to let Ines's words bring back her own feelings of trepidation, yet she found herself looking into all the dimly lit corners, as if expecting something evil to pounce upon her before she could reach her destination.

"Mercedes," she called softly as she tried to open the door. It was locked. "Mercedes, it's Leona. I've come for a visit."

All was silent.

She rapped on the door, once, then again, louder this time. "Mercedes, open the door."

Still no answer.

Leona glanced behind her at Ines. "Could she have left the house?"

The woman shook her head.

"Mercedes!" This time she pounded on the door with her fist. "Ines is worried about you. So am I. Please, open the door."

She heard a small sound from inside the room, then nothing.

Again Leona looked behind her. "Ines, get one of the *vaqueros* to come inside. We'll break down the door if we must."

"There are no *vaqueros, señora*. The *señor* has let them go."

"All of them?"

Ines shrugged. "All but a few, and those I have not seen for several days. They are with the cattle."

"What of the other house servants?"

"There is only me."

"Madre de Dios!"

She'd had no idea that it had come to this. Why hadn't Señor Ramirez come to her father for help? Gardner would have lent the man money to see him through until all was settled with the commission. How much more hadn't Mercedes told her?

Leona struck the door with her fist again. "Mercedes—get up this instant and let me in."

She only waited a brief time before she turned away with a cry of exasperation. She hurried toward the front door, her footsteps then carrying her outside and around to the back of the house. If she had to, she would break a window, but she would get into that room.

But she didn't have to. The window was ajar, as if waiting for her. Leona gathered her skirts above her knees and scrambled through the high opening.

She could see Mercedes's outline beneath the bed coverings. The girl was curled into a tight ball, her head drawn beneath the blankets like a turtle into its shell.

"Mercy," Leona called softly, using an old childhood nickname, "what's wrong? Why wouldn't you get up and open the door?" She stepped closer to the bed.

"Go away, Leona." The voice was muffled, barely audible. "Please go away."

"Nothing can be so bad, *mi amiga,* that you must hide from the world. If it's Ricardo, I'll talk to him for you. I'll send him to you."

"No! I don't want to see him. Just go and leave me."

There was something so painful, so unbearable about the tone of her voice that Leona was tempted to obey, lest she hurt her even further. But she couldn't leave Mercedes alone like this.

Taking another step, she reached out to take hold of the bed covering. She drew in a deep breath, knowing she was about to make Mercedes mad for not heeding her request. She hoped it *would* make her friend angry. Anger would draw her out of the black hole of depression.

With a quick jerk, she pulled back the blanket.

Mercedes made a helpless squeak in her throat and rolled away, covering her head with her arm.

"*Valgame Dios!* Mercedes, what—"

She was naked. The shredded remnants of her nightgown lay on the bed beside her. The sheets beneath her were darkened with blood stains. There were pale bruises on her arms and wrists, even her thighs. Her cheeks and chin were red, as if they'd been rubbed with a rough brush.

Leona felt a sickness rise in her stomach as she realized what had happened.

"Oh, *mi amiga,* no. No . . ."

She wanted to deny what her mind told her was true, but she couldn't escape it.

Hastily, she pulled the blanket back over Mercedes, then knelt down beside the bed and reached for her friend's hand. Mercedes flinched at the touch, but Leona clung to her.

"Who did this to you?" she asked in a hoarse voice.

Mercedes shook her head.

"Who did this to you?" she demanded, louder this time. "Look at me. You must tell me. If you know who did this, you must tell me."

"I can't. No one must know. No one must ever know." Mercedes opened her eyes, eyes that were puffy and reddened from the tears she'd spent in the night. Her fingers tightened around Leona's hand. "You must swear you will tell no one. No one, Leona."

"But, Mercy . . ."

"No one!" Her voice was filled with panic. "It would kill my father to know of this. He is not well. He is not strong. His heart . . . The shame . . ." She groaned and turned her head away as she bit her lip before continuing. "*Por favor*, Leona. If you love me, you will give me your promise you will never tell anyone what has happened here."

She wasn't sure what to do. It was difficult to think past her own shock and the rage that was beginning to roil in her chest. After a moment's pause, she nodded. "All right, Mercedes. I'll give you my word. But only if you tell me who it was and how he came to be here."

Mercedes rolled her head back toward Leona. Her face looked so pale, her eyes so lost. A whimper escaped her throat.

Leona rose from her knees and sat on the bed. She pushed the tangled snarls of her friend's dark hair back from her face. "Tell me."

"It was . . . it was . . . Rance McCabe."

In her heart she had known it. Somehow she had known it. She'd heard it in her dreams last night. She'd felt it as she'd ridden over here today. *Something evil . . .*

McCabe. Damn McCabe! How dare he defile Mercedes? How dare he destroy something so gentle and beautiful?

Mercedes's grip tightened. "You promised. You will tell no one."

"Until you release me from my vow, I will tell no one," she replied softly.

And then Leona made a second promise, a silent one. She would make Rance McCabe rue this night. Before she was finished with him, he would wish he'd never set eyes on the Salinas Valley.

In response to Leona's persistent but gentle prodding, Mercedes, in softly spoken, broken sentences, revealed a horrifying glimpse of what had taken place in her room during the night.

Mercedes didn't know how McCabe had gained entrance to the house. She only knew that she'd been awakened by the sound of the lock sliding in her bedroom door. When she'd realized it was an intruder, she'd tried to scream but there had been no one to hear her, even if he hadn't covered her mouth with his hand, nearly suffocating her.

Spewing vile words about her and her family, McCabe had torn her nightgown from her body and brutally assaulted her. Not just once, but again and again. He'd laughed when she'd said he would be caught and punished. He'd told her no one would believe her, surely not the sheriff. And then he'd threatened her family if ever she told anyone.

When Mercedes fell silent, Leona held her in her arms and allowed her to weep. Leona's own cheeks were streaked with tears. Her heart felt as bruised and battered as Mercedes's tender flesh. She longed to be able to take away the hurt and humiliation. She was frustrated by her inability to do more than utter useless words of comfort.

Unbidden, she remembered how beautifully Diego had introduced her to the special intimacies shared between a man and a woman, and the unavoidable comparison with Mercedes's night of terror made her want to keen and wail for what her friend had lost.

"He must pay for what he has done to you," she said at last, outrage returning to replace her anguish.

Mercedes opened her eyes and stared up at Leona. The pain revealed in those eyes was almost more than she could bear.

"You promised you would tell no one."

Leona nodded. "I won't, but McCabe will still pay."

"There is nothing to be done." She hid her face again. "It will be better if we go to Mexico. My shame is too great to remain here. What if someone should hear of it?"

"It isn't your fault, Mercedes. The shame isn't yours. It's McCabe's. He raped you. If Ricardo knew, he would—"

Mercedes clutched Leona's arm, her fingernails biting into her skin. "Ricardo must not hear of this! *Madre de Dios*, I would rather die than have him know." She drew in a ragged breath. As she let it out, she whispered, "I shall never be clean again. I am not fit for anyone now."

It was useless to argue with her, Leona realized. It wasn't the time. Later, when Mercedes could think a little more clearly, when she could listen to reason again, but not now.

Stifling her own urge to scream and rail, Leona did what she could to bring Mercedes comfort. She had Ines heat water for a bath and told her to prepare something for her mistress to eat. She explained that the young woman was distraught over her broken romance with Ricardo and wished to see no one, not even the old servant.

It was Leona who carried the hot water to the bedroom and filled the tub. It was Leona who helped Mercedes out of bed and into the water scented with bath oils. It was Leona who washed away the evidence of McCabe's cruelty. Afterward, it was Leona who helped Mercedes don a fresh nightgown, then led her to a bed now spread with clean sheets.

And all the while, Leona's hatred grew. Again she swore an oath that McCabe would pay for what he had done. He would pay slowly and painfully. To thrust a sword into his belly and rend him in two would be too easy. He must suffer as Mercedes had suffered, as Mercedes would suffer for a long time to come. His agony could not be just one night but must last.

It must last until the moment he was dispatched to hell for all eternity.

Chapter Twenty-Eight

She rode alone under a moonless sky. Although she carried a red rose in her pocket, this night she was not dressed as La Rosa. She wore all black, from the hat on her head and the mask that disguised her face, to the loose-fitting shirt and the trousers that clung to her hips and thighs. She moved as one with the swift black horse that galloped across the grassy plains in the bleak hours of the night.

Leona felt herself wrapped in a cocoon of icy control. She didn't allow her thoughts to dwell on the atrocity that had befallen her dearest friend. She concentrated only upon the task ahead of her.

While still out of sight of her destination, she tied Pesadilla in a shelter of trees, then continued to the McCabe ranch on foot. She moved with the stealth of a cat, all her senses attuned to any sign which would warn her that danger awaited. But all lay in silence. There was no one to stop her.

McCabe was a fool.

There were no guards about. He thought himself impervious. He still thought no one would dare defy him. Even though the bandida had invaded his house once before, he still thought no one would dare attack him on his own land. She knew that his bunkhouse was filled with men who would come running at the first sign of trouble, but no one bothered to keep watch in the midnight hours.

Caramba! McCabe was a careless fool.

She smiled grimly. He probably thought the threat of La Rosa had ended when she'd been shot during his ambush. He was too sure of himself, this gringo lawyer.

Yes, McCabe was a fool, and she was about to prove it to him.

Leona slipped into the house, pausing just inside to listen. Silence was as thick as the darkness.

Stealthily, she moved toward the stairs, guided by a keen memory and a sixth sense. Her face was turned up to the second floor of the house. She knew where his bedroom was. She knew he was there, in his bed, sleeping, oblivious to danger. Like a hound after the fox, she pursued her prey, though he didn't know it yet.

As she drew closer to the master's bedroom, her heart began to hammer in her chest. Adrenaline flowed through her veins, and every nerve in her body was tingling with awareness.

McCabe . . . I am here, McCabe.

All day, she had thought of this moment. From the time she'd ridden away from La Brisa, she'd been laying plans for this night. She'd known she had to come alone. She had to face McCabe by herself. She wanted him to know that it was a woman who dared to defy him, a woman who demanded justice and retribution.

Slipping inside the bedroom, she paused, listening. She could hear his snores. That he should sleep while Mercedes lay in torment caused hate to rise like bile in her throat. For a moment, she longed to kill him while he slept.

No, death would be too easy for him. She had other plans for Rance McCabe.

She took the vial and cloth from the bag she'd carried with her from the hacienda. She worked quickly, yet with great care, keeping the chloroform far from her own face as she poured it onto the cloth. Then, with deliberate, silent steps, she moved toward the bed.

Leona waited impatiently for McCabe to regain consciousness. She felt a strange detachment as she gazed at the man in the flickering light of a candle.

After his initial struggle, he had succumbed quickly to the anesthesia. It hadn't been easy to work with his inert body. McCabe was a large man, weighing a good eighty or ninety pounds more than she did. But somehow she'd managed to accomplish what she'd set out to do.

She'd gagged him so that he couldn't speak or shout for help when he came to. Then she'd stripped him of his nightshirt and tied him—spread-eagled and stark naked—on the bed, his hands bound to the headboard, his ankles secured with ropes to the footboard. She could have settled for merely tying his hands behind his back, but that wouldn't have been enough. She wanted him to have at least a taste of humiliation. It wouldn't change what he'd done to Mercedes, but she hoped it would be something he wouldn't soon forget.

When she heard him groan, she rose from the chair and approached the bed. It took several minutes for his eyes to open, even longer for them to clear. When they did, she watched as he tried to sit up, then struggled against the ropes that held him. Satisfaction warmed her when she recognized the sudden fear in his eyes as he met her gaze.

"So, Señor McCabe, you awaken. I was afraid I would be forced to leave before we could have our little talk. That would have disappointed me. I have looked forward to this meeting. More than you know."

She slowly drew her sword from its sheath. She touched the edge, as if testing the sharpness of the blade, and watched as beads of sweat formed on his forehead.

"You wonder why I am here, no? I can see that you do. *Sí, gringo*, it is La Rosa. I am alive. I am here in your house. You do not like that I come uninvited? *Perdóneme*. I could not wait any longer."

Leona turned her head and looked around the room, allowing the time to tick away in tense silence. She realized that she could actually smell his fear. Without his men or his gun, he was a coward. He was only brave enough to hurt helpless women.

She glanced back at him. "You wonder also why I am dressed in black, do you not? I will tell you. I am in mourning. I am in mourning for one who was innocent and now bears much pain. Do you know for whom, *gringo?* Do you know for whom I mourn? Can you guess?"

He tried to spit the cloth from his mouth, to no avail.

Leona sighed dramatically and shook her head. "It is difficult to carry on a conversation when only one can speak, but I'm afraid I cannot trust you to speak softly. You can understand my concern, no? Besides, I think it better that you listen, *gringo*. You would do well to hear me and obey."

She walked around the bed to the other side, then back to her original place. Her eyes raked over his body, and she emitted a disparaging noise. She could see that her disdain enraged him, and it gladdened her.

And then her control snapped. With a sudden movement, she swung her sword in a wide arc, stopping it a mere inch above his abdomen.

A frightened cry was muffled in his throat. His head jerked up from the bed. His gaze darted to the tip of the sword. Then his eyes widened, and she knew he had only just realized that he was naked.

When he looked at her again, she laughed wickedly.

"You have let yourself go to fat, *gringo*." She allowed the sword to touch his skin. "If I were to skewer you, it would be like sticking a pig."

His face reddened as he wrestled against the ropes, jerking his arms and legs with great force. Leona brought the sword up to his throat. He stilled instantly.

There was no trace of laughter remaining in her voice. "You are a pig, and one day I shall see that you are roasted over a pit of your own making." She leaned forward, lowering her voice. "I could kill you now, *gringo*. I could do it quietly, with just my sword. One swipe and I could slit your throat. You would lie there helplessly while your life's blood flowed out onto the bed. They would find you in the morning, your fat body white, your lips blue, your eyes lifeless." She flicked the blade and nicked him. "It would be so easy for me, no?"

The man's flesh had turned the color of paste, a sharp contrast with the red trickle that ran down his neck and dripped onto the sheets. He swallowed, and his Adam's apple bobbed in his throat. Beads of sweat rolled down the sides of his face.

Suddenly, there was no holding back her hatred and contempt for the man. Her voice shook with rage as she leaned toward him. "Do you want to know why I don't do it? It is because you must suffer first. You must suffer as you made the *señorita* suffer. And all the *californios* and *americanos* will know that La Rosa is the one who makes you suffer. They will laugh at your helplessness. They will know that you are not man enough to stop me."

McCabe made a guttural sound in his throat, half-protest, half-whimper.

With intentional slowness, she dragged the sword point down the length of his torso, not stopping until the saber touched the limp sex organ that lay between his legs. She heard his intake of breath, watched as his stomach muscles tightened. She felt no embarrassment at the sight of him. Only revulsion.

"Know this, McCabe," she warned harshly, her gaze meeting his. "If you rape another woman, I will cut off the part of you that offends me most and feed it to the dogs."

Suddenly, she couldn't bear being so close to him. There was a stench in her nostrils. She felt suffocated by it. She stepped backward and resheathed her weapon. Then she removed the red rose from her pocket and tossed it onto his chest.

"When they find you in the morning, *gringo*, trussed up like the pig you are, they will know that La Rosa has returned. They will know that a woman did this to you. You did not kill La Rosa when you laid your trap. You failed as you will always fail. I will return. You cannot stop me."

She blew out the candle, dashing the room back into utter darkness.

Robin Lee Hatcher

"I will be like the thorns of that rose, *gringo*. I will prick you and leave you bleeding. This I promise you."

Under the cover of night, Leona slipped as silently from the house as she had entered.

Chapter Twenty-Nine

Diego should have felt at least some satisfaction. Judge Hopkins was already on his way back to the nation's capital to answer the charges leveled against him. He wouldn't be causing the people of the state of California any trouble. In addition, some strongly worded instructions to the commissioners overseeing the Mexican and Spanish land grant claims were likely to help curb some of the worst abuses. The word from Joseph McConnell was that the information Diego and the other investigators had provided had made a difference.

But neither of these things was enough for him. It was McCabe he wanted stopped, and the hard evidence he'd sought against the man had eluded him once again. The informant had disappeared before Diego had even reached San Francisco.

Diego guided Conquistador along the dusty streets of Monterey, headed toward the Curtis

Tavern. He would have preferred to bypass the town and get right home to Leona, but Hiram Benjamin had asked him to deliver a message to Heath as soon as possible. He wasn't going to do any more than drop it off and have something to wet his parched throat before moving on. With luck, he would be lying in Leona's arms before nightfall.

He tethered his horse to a post outside the tavern and stepped through the doorway into the dusky barroom. He paused, giving his eyes a moment to adjust to the change of light.

"I don't know what the hell he wants me to do about it. He's the one with all the money. Why don't McCabe just hire himself a few more men t'do the job if'n he don't like the way I handle things around here? There's only me and my deputy and a lot more ground than we can cover."

Diego turned his head, recognizing the sheriff's voice at once. He felt his usual disdain as he looked at the miserable excuse for a lawman.

"It ain't my fault, I'm tellin' you," Sheriff Kincaid said to the two men with him, waving his arm for emphasis. "Hell, he's got plenty o' men workin' his place. Why ain't they doin' somethin' to stop those outlaws if they're such an all-fired danger to folks? I ain't never heard anybody else complainin'." He took a long swallow of beer, then lowered his voice as he leaned forward. "Shoot, maybe she's just in his head. Nobody else's been bothered by her that I've heard tell of. I'm beginnin' t'think McCabe's not all right up here." He tapped his forehead with his index finger.

Diego felt a twinge of suspicion. A quick glance toward the bar found Heath Curtis, and Diego walked toward him. Jerking his head toward the sheriff, he asked, "What's that about?"

"Seems La Rosa is angry with McCabe. His cattle've been scattered from here to the Estrella River. The old Estrada hacienda burned to the ground two days ago. Now I hear there've been several attacks on McCabe's supply wagons on their way up to his mines. McCabe's madder than a hornet, an' he's been givin' the sheriff an earful."

He should have known. Damn it! He should have known she would do something like this the moment he turned his back. What did she think she was doing? He'd told her he didn't want her attacking McCabe anymore. He'd told her it was too dangerous. Was she intentionally trying to get caught by provoking McCabe further?

"How 'bout you?" Heath asked in a low voice, drawing a beer as he spoke. "What'd you find up north?"

Diego took a drink before answering. "Not enough." He pulled the message from Hiram Benjamin out of his pocket. "This is for you. From Hiram." He drained the beer from the glass. "I've got to move on. I'll come back to town in a few days and fill you in. Right now, I want to get home to my wife."

And when he got there, they were going to come to an understanding about La Rosa, once and for all.

Ricardo sat astride his bay gelding, his body leaning forward, his forearm resting on the saddle horn, watching the young colts and fillies romping amongst the grazing mares. It was a good crop of foals this year. They would bring a good price in a couple of years.

Several mares lifted their heads in unison, large dark eyes staring in the same direction, announcing the approach of another rider. Ricardo turned his head to see who was disturbing his solitude.

"Buenas tardes, hermano." Leona brought her golden mare to a stop beside him.

He acknowledged the greeting with a nod, then returned his gaze to the herd. He assumed she had decided to make another raid of some kind on McCabe. He hoped he would be able to dissuade her. They had ridden nearly every night for the past week. They were all tired. The men needed a rest, and so did she.

He wondered if her renewed zeal against McCabe had anything to do with Diego's absence. Was Leona just trying to fill up her nights because her husband had left her so soon after the wedding? Had the marriage been a terrible mistake? Or was there another reason for her obsession with destroying Rance McCabe?

Something was troubling his sister. That was for certain. He could feel her disquiet whenever they were together, just as he felt it now. When he looked at her, he saw the strain, the sadness, on her face.

"I have been to see Mercedes."

His jaw tensed. He hadn't been expecting this.

"Go to see her, Ricardo. She needs you. Far more than you'll ever know."

"You're wrong." Bitterness stung his throat. "She doesn't need me."

Leona leaned sideways in her saddle and touched his arm, forcing him to look at her. "*Mi hermano*, we have always understood each other too well to try to pretend, to try to hide our feelings from the other. I know that you love her. I also know that she loves you. Your pride was wounded when she turned down your offer of marriage. But she had her reasons for doing so, and it wasn't for lack of love. If you would only try to talk with her . . ."

He pulled away, nudging Raudo forward. Leona followed on Glory as they moved through the mares and foals, scattering them over the grassy hillside.

Mercedes was never far from Ricardo's thoughts, but he didn't want to see her. It had been hard enough on him at Leona's wedding. He didn't need to put himself through that again. It tore down too many of his carefully constructed defenses.

His sister reached for him again. "Ricardo, you must listen to me," she demanded, her tone forceful.

He glared at her without reply. He'd had enough of her interference. He didn't want to talk about Mercedes, now or any other time. He wanted to rid her from his thoughts altogether, and he couldn't do it with Leona's reminders.

"Mercedes is sick," she continued, her voice softening. "I fear . . . I'm afraid . . ."

His heart faltered. "What? What's wrong with her?"

"I can't tell you." Leona turned her face away from him. Her voice fell almost to a whisper. "I don't think she wants to live. I can't help her. Her parents can't help her. I don't know what else to do. I think you are her only hope."

With a sharp jerk on the reins, Ricardo spun his horse around, ready to gallop toward La Brisa.

"Wait!"

There was something in Leona's cry that caused him to obey. He pulled up and waited for her to join him.

"*Mi hermano*, you must be careful. Don't press her to tell you what is wrong. Just let her know you love her." Leona's eyes met his with assurance. "You do still love her. Now you must help her."

There was much she wasn't telling him. He wanted to make her reveal what it was, but he knew it would be useless to try. If she had made up her mind to keep it a secret, she would do just that, no matter what he said to her.

"*Sí,*" he replied, feeling another sharp pain in his chest as he admitted what he'd been denying for weeks now, "I still love her. I will do what I can to help her."

"*Vaya con Dios.*"

"*Gracias.*"

Leona watched her brother until he was a mere blur in the distance, then she turned Glory toward home. She felt a great weariness. Her shoulder had been throbbing all day. She wanted nothing more than a cool bath and to crawl into bed early for a change.

It would be daylight for several hours yet, and the summer heat would linger even longer. Perhaps tomorrow she and Dulce would take the buggy and go into Monterey. They could picnic on the beach and let the sea breezes bring them a breath of cool air off the ocean.

It wasn't just because she was tired that the idea occurred to her. Seeing Mercedes today had fueled her desire for revenge, and she hadn't changed her resolve to make McCabe suffer. But she needed to know what people were thinking and saying about La Rosa. She needed to know what the sheriff was doing. McCabe wasn't going to draw her into another trap as easily as he'd done the last time. La Rosa would prove herself too smart for him.

Leona brushed damp tendrils of black hair back from her forehead and temples as her thoughts strayed to Diego. It seemed he'd been gone an awfully long time. Even though she and La Rosa's hombres had ridden almost every night for the past week, she hadn't been too busy to miss him.

Sometimes, after she'd returned in the wee hours of the morning, she had lain in bed, staring at the ceiling and remembering the way he'd made love to her. She would feel again the touch of his hands as they stroked her body. She could taste his kisses on her mouth. She could hear the deep timbre of his voice as he spoke words of love. She could see the heated look in his eyes as he watched her.

Rather than allow her thoughts to dwell on Diego's absence, she forced herself to think about Mercedes's pain. She made herself recall the hate in her heart for McCabe and all the harm he'd done to people Leona loved. For at least a short time, she knew these thoughts would keep her loneliness for Diego at bay.

"Ricardo," Mercedes's mother whispered as Ines brought him into the room.

"*Buenas tardes, señora,*" he replied, offering a slight bow to Ofelia Ramirez. "I have come to see Mercedes."

The woman wore an expression of quiet desperation as she shook her head. "She will not see you. She will see no one. No one except Leona. She doesn't come out of her room. She eats nothing. And sometimes I hear her crying. She has been like this ever since her father and I returned from San Francisco. I don't know what to do for her, Ricardo. I don't know what to do."

"*Señora,* I respectfully ask that you let me see Mercedes, whether she wants it or not." Ricardo slid the brim of his hat between forefingers and thumbs as he held it in front of him.

He could see the woman wavering as she weighed the propriety of allowing him into her daughter's bedroom against the hope that he might help Mercedes overcome whatever malaise had taken hold of her. He pressed his advantage.

"*Perdóneme, señora,* but I *must* see her."

"*Sí.* You must." Ofelia's eyes pleaded with him. "Help her, for I cannot."

He turned on his heel and headed toward the bedrooms. When he and Leona were children, they had played with Mercedes in her room when they visited La Brisa. He hadn't been in the back of the house for many years now, but he hadn't forgotten which room was hers.

He didn't bother to knock. He simply opened the door and walked in.

The shutters had been closed and locked over all the windows. The air was thick with the heat of afternoon. No lantern or candle burned to relieve the darkness, and the room seemed fraught with fear.

"Go away."

The voice he heard was lifeless and empty sounding. It sounded nothing like Mercedes. Her voice was usually carefree and melodic.

After closing the door behind him, Ricardo moved forward. Just enough light filtered through the shutters for him to see the slender form beneath the sheet. Her back was to him, and she was curled into a ball.

When he reached the bedside, he spoke. "Mercedes, it's me. I've come to talk to you."

There was a tiny gasp beneath the sheet. "Ricardo . . ." A lengthy silence followed. "I don't want to see you."

"I'm not going away, Mercedes." He walked to the opposite side and sat on the edge of the bed. "We must talk." He felt a rising impatience. "I love you, Mercedes, and I'm not leaving until you talk to me."

"Did . . . did Leona . . . tell you?" The pain in her voice was unbearable.

Ricardo's chest ached at the sound of it, and his own voice softened in response. "Leona told me nothing. I came to see you because I love you, Mercedes. I can't stand being without you. I've been miserable ever since the night you refused to marry me. *Por favor, muchacha.* Look at me." He reached out and drew back the sheet.

Her hair had been plaited in a single thick braid. Stray wisps had pulled free to curl near her cheeks—pale cheeks in a thin face. There were dark circles beneath her eyes.

"Mercy . . ." he whispered.

She looked at him, and his heart caught.

"I beg you, Ricardo. Go away and leave me in peace."

He wished he could. Looking at her was almost too painful to bear. But instead of leaving, he gathered her into his arms as a father would an injured child. Wordlessly, he began to rock, his embrace holding her close against him, his cheek rubbing the top of her head.

Whatever has happened, I'll make it all right. I swear it. I swear it to you, Mercedes.

He felt more than heard the tiny whimper that slipped through her lips. A moment later, it was followed by another, and then another, until finally a torrent was loosened. Great, racking sobs shook her body. She clung to him as if she were drowning in her own tears, her fingers biting into his arms as she buried her face in his chest.

He gathered her as close as he possibly could. "Don't be afraid," he whispered. "I won't let you go. I'll never let you go, Mercedes. Don't be afraid anymore."

Chapter Thirty

As she rode toward the house, Leona's heart leaped with joy at the sight of Diego's pinto stallion.

He was home! He was home at last!

She kicked Glory, and the horse fairly flew across the final distance. Leona jumped down from the saddle before the dust had settled, not bothering to tether the mare before running toward the front door.

"Diego!" she cried as she entered the house.

He was standing in the doorway to the bedroom, La Rosa's cape draped over his arm. Wringing her hands, Dulce watched helplessly from a corner of the parlor.

Leona's smile vanished as her husband turned a thunderous gaze in her direction. Her heart rose in her throat. "Diego . . ."

"Why did you do it, Leona?" His voice was as hard as steel.

"I had to."

He took a step forward. "Do my wishes mean nothing to you?"

"Diego, you don't understand."

"You're right. I don't understand. You were shot. You could have died. I told you you weren't to do this again. The risks are too great."

She lifted her chin as her own anger flared. "I had no choice."

"No choice?" he bellowed, tossing the cape onto the floor. "Of course you had a choice. You could have chosen to obey me. I told you not to ride. What was Ricardo thinking of to let you do this? Is he as mad as you? You can't attack McCabe every night without someone getting hurt."

Leona's hands closed into fists at her sides. Her voice rose in answer to his. "I don't ask my brother for permission to do what I must. Nor do I mean to ask you. I told you. I told you before we married that you could not change me. La Rosa must ride. McCabe must be stopped."

"*Vive Dios!* There are others who can stop McCabe. La Rosa is not the only one."

"Who?" she demanded. "Who has stepped forward to do it? Have you?" She pushed the hat from her head. "No, even *you* came to La Rosa. Even *you* wanted to ride with the *bandida*."

His face darkened, but he said nothing.

What could he say? she wondered. She spoke the truth. Those who would resist and fight McCabe all came to La Rosa. They didn't fight him on their own. They wanted La Rosa's help.

"The law will stop him," Diego said finally. "It might take time, but the law will stop him. I'll see that they—"

"When?" Her rage was as much over her own ineffectual efforts as it was in response to his demands. "After how many more innocent people are murdered? Must someone else lose a brother like Dulce did? Must another boy be trampled and crippled for life? How many families must lose their homes and their cattle and their lands before he is stopped? How many women must be—" She cut off her question before she revealed what she'd promised she wouldn't. She whirled around, turning her back on him. "You might be willing to wait, but I'm not."

Leona hurried back to Glory, intent on riding away, but Diego caught her before she could pick up the horse's reins.

He spun her around to face him. His hands closed over her upper arms as he pulled her close to his chest, forcing her head to drop back so that she gazed steadily up at him.

"Don't you understand?" he asked in a low voice. "Don't you understand that it's for your safety I demand this? I won't risk losing you, Leona. I won't risk your life."

Her anger dissipated as she stared into his pleading dark brown eyes. Her own voice softened in response to his. "Diego, it's you who doesn't understand. It isn't your place to decide if I will or won't risk my life. It's my choice. It's my right."

He looked at her for what seemed a very long time, not speaking, not moving. Then, with a groan of frustration, his arms embraced her and his mouth possessed hers.

She returned the kiss with all the pent-up passion she'd been feeling for days. When he swept her legs from the ground and carried her back into the house, she gave no thought to La Rosa or McCabe. She didn't want to think about the very real problem that still stood between her and Diego. For at least a short while, she would think only of him and their love.

Later, she would try to find some way to make him understand.

Twilight blanketed the bedroom. Diego stared up at the ceiling, Leona nestled against his side, her head resting on his shoulder, her raven-black hair spilling over his arm. She slept, exhausted by their passionate, almost furious lovemaking.

Diego smiled lazily, remembering her cries of ecstasy. *Madre de Dios,* how he loved her! He was consumed by his love for her. It made it difficult for him to think of anything else.

It didn't even matter that she had yet to tell him she loved him. He could see her feelings so clearly in her violet-black eyes. He even thought he understood why she refused to speak the words, but he didn't know how to ease her fears about what he expected of her. He didn't want to change her, only to love and cherish and care for her. Once she learned that, she would tell him what he longed to hear.

His smile faded. Simply because she'd made love to him didn't mean she had capitulated to his demands. She hadn't agreed to stop riding as La Rosa just because she'd allowed his return to her bed. She would continue to fight him on this. She would continue to defy him. Short of tying her up or locking her in the bedroom, she would find a way to continue her attacks on McCabe until he was driven out of the valley, once and for all.

Diego turned his head and buried his face in her hair. He closed his eyes, breathing deeply. He could ride with her, of course, but that wouldn't guarantee her safety. It hadn't helped her before. He hadn't kept her from being shot.

His arm tightened in a reflex response to his thoughts. He could have lost her then. He'd come all too close to losing her.

Frustration welled in his chest. Damn! He should have had something on McCabe by this time. Something that would hold up in a court of law. Something that would put him behind bars where he belonged. Everyone seemed to know what McCabe did—the lying, the cheating, the killing, the stealing—but the man was careful always to have an alibi.

And it didn't help that La Rosa and her hombres were considered bandits. The people might call her the Robin Hood of the Salinas, but the law wouldn't be as generous. If McCabe did capture La Rosa, the law would be on his side.

Caramba! He had to think of some way to protect Leona without causing her to hate him for it.

His men were laughing at him behind his back. None of them had the guts to do it to his face, but McCabe knew they were doing it just the same. Poking fun at him. Making him the butt of their jokes. There wasn't a man on the place that hadn't heard how McCabe had been found last week, naked and tied up in his own bedroom, a rose lying on his chest.

McCabe strode to the window of his office and stared outside as dusk settled over the yard. He could see several guards at their posts. There were others that he couldn't see.

Laughing at him, he thought again, and clenched his hands into fists as he turned away.

If the laughter weren't bad enough, his inability to stop the bandolera's raids on his property had McCabe seething with a white-hot rage. She and her men seemed to be everywhere, from one end of this infernal valley to the other. They seemed to know just when and where to hit, just exactly where he would be the most vulnerable. It had been bad enough in the weeks before, but La Rosa's assaults in the last eight days had cost him dearly, more dearly than he cared to admit to anyone.

Damn the bitch! She wasn't going to get away with it. He was going to catch her, and when he did, she would wish she'd killed him when she had the chance. Before he turned her over to the law to be hanged, he was going to do things to her that would make her regret her own birth. She would be pleading with him for mercy before he was through.

McCabe sat down behind his desk and leaned back in his chair. He pressed his fingers together, his eyebrows nearly touching as he frowned in concentration.

He'd been going about things all wrong up to this point. He'd been trying to catch the bandida when she attacked him. Well, no more. McCabe was the one going on the attack.

He pulled a sheet of paper from his desk drawer, then dipped his pen into the ink. Methodically, he began listing the names of the families of Spanish blood from Monterey to the southernmost ranch in the valley. He didn't know them all, of course, but he could fill in the blank spots later. Beneath the family names, he noted the names of daughters and wives who he imagined would be the right age.

He guessed La Rosa was in her twenties. She had a woman's figure, but she had the agility of youth. Although he was loath to admit it, she was intelligent, or she would never have escaped the traps he'd laid for her.

And what of her looks? He tried to envision her without her mask but failed. Yet something told him that, when he at last unmasked her, he wouldn't be surprised. He would know her.

His fingers tightened on the pen as he remembered the way she had poked him with her sword, the way she had toyed with him, threatened him. He heard her sultry voice, filled with disdain, as she called him a pig.

She would pay for mocking him. Whoever the greaser whore was, he would find her and she would pay!

Sometime in the middle of the night, Leona came slowly awake, reluctant to give up the pleasant dream that had left her feeling warm and eager for Diego's touch. It was a moment or two before she realized that she hadn't just been dreaming about Diego being with her. She was nestled against him, her head cradled in the curve of his arm and shoulder.

She tried not to think about the heated words they'd exchanged upon his return. She knew that their lovemaking had changed nothing between them. He was still determined to protect her, and she was still determined to have her revenge against McCabe.

If she could tell him about Mercedes, perhaps he would better understand, but she had given her word and would not break it, not even to make things easier between her and Diego. Besides, the basic problem would still exist. The real issue was whether or not he had the right to tell her what she could or could not do.

Ah, Diego, mi corazón, *I warned you, but you wouldn't hear me. I don't ask to always have my way. I only ask to be given a say in my life. Is that so very much?*

She sighed as she closed her eyes.

If only I did not love you . . . but I do.

Like others that same night, Ricardo found himself sleepless. He'd given up his futile attempts to find rest over an hour ago, and now he sat in a chair outside the house, smoking a cheroot and staring up at the starry sky.

No matter how hard he tried, he couldn't rid himself of Mercedes's image, couldn't rid his ears of the sounds of her pitiful sobs. Except to tell him to go away when he'd first entered her bedroom, she hadn't spoken anything beyond his name for the rest of the afternoon. She'd simply cried, and in her tears, he'd heard the depths of a pain that left him feeling lacerated and mangled.

What had happened to cause her such despair?

Leona knew, but his sister wouldn't tell him. Apparently, she had given her word not to tell him or anyone else, and his sister always kept her word, not matter how difficult it might make things for her.

The Ramirezes certainly didn't know what had happened. All he'd learned from them before leaving La Brisa was that Mercedes had been like this since their return from San Francisco. They'd come back, filled with hope after meeting for several days with an attorney, but their joy had been overshadowed by their daughter's nameless grief.

Someone had hurt her, but who? And how?

Ricardo tossed away his cheroot as he rose from his chair. He ground the smoking tobacco into the dust beneath the heel of his boot, then sauntered toward the corral. Once there, he leaned his arms on the top railing and stared, unseeing, at the yearling colts inside.

One thing had been made clear to him during the hours he'd spent with Mercedes. He could no longer even try to fool himself into thinking he didn't love her. He'd never stopped loving her.

His anger and hurt had vanished as well. This was no time for him to hold himself aloof, bemoaning his wounded pride.

Most importantly, she loved him. He knew it, if only by the way she'd clung to him in her grief. She needed him, and he would be there for her, for however long it took.

Somehow, he swore silently, he would make things right.

Chapter Thirty-One

Warily, they faced each other across the table, each of them remembering the passion they'd shared, each of them remembering what was as yet unresolved between them. Dulce, sensing the tension, served their breakfast in silence, her eyes averted. When she finished, she skittered away like a scared rabbit.

Leona was the first to gather her courage and speak. "Was your journey successful? Are your investments more secure?"

"Yes."

His eyes were such a rich brown, like the fine chocolate bonbons her father had bought her when she was a child. The way he used them to caress her skin, to speak to her heart . . .

"I won't have to go away again, Leona. I'll be here with you. Every day . . . and every night."

In response to the deep resonance of his voice,

she felt a tiny shiver of delight skip along her spine. It reminded her of the way he whispered to her when they were making love. She could almost feel his breath on her skin.

"I think we should ride over to Rancho del Sol today. I want to talk to your father regarding property in the valley. I'm eager for us to have a place of our own, and I'd like his guidance when the time comes for us to buy some land."

A place of their own. A home with lots of bedrooms, enough for all of their children. Sons, just like their father. They would grow up tall and handsome and strong. And daughters, too. Daughters who weren't afraid to face the world on their own terms, who didn't need a man to tell them what to think or what to do.

"Then I'm going to have a few words with Ricardo." His announcement was like a cold bucket of water thrown over her pleasant daydreams.

She didn't have to ask him what he meant. He was going to tell Ricardo that La Rosa wouldn't be riding again. He was going to demand that her twin not help her anymore.

She gave her hair a little toss of defiance. "It won't do you any good, Diego. Ricardo isn't the one who decides what I do." She jabbed her fork at the food on her plate. "I decide that for myself."

"Leona . . ." he said softly. "Listen to reason. I'm only trying to do what's best for you."

She stubbornly refused to look at him as she ate her breakfast without tasting a single bite, her angry thoughts churning in her head. She wouldn't let him do this. She wouldn't allow it. If Ricardo refused to continue helping her, she would summon her hombres herself. And if she had to, she would ride alone. She'd done it once. She could do it again. But she would not be stopped. Not until McCabe was destroyed.

She placed her napkin beside her plate, then rose from her chair.

"I'll change into my riding clothes and be ready to leave whenever you are."

She heard his exasperated sigh as she swept past him on her way to their bedroom.

"Well," Diego muttered as the door closed behind her, "I didn't handle that very well."

"No, *señor*, you did not."

He had forgotten that the maid was there.

Dulce stepped toward the table. Her hands were clenched together so tightly that her knuckles were white. Her dark eyes were as wide as saucers, and her chin quivered as she met his gaze. "She does not do this for herself."

"I know that, Dulce."

"Do you, *señor*? Did you know that this McCabe stole my home and murdered my brother? But the sheriff, he did nothing. That is when La Rosa rode for the first time. She rides not for herself but for others who are helpless. Because she is strong and others—like me—are weak."

Diego ran his palms over his hair. "She was nearly killed."

"*Sí*. I have been afraid for her every time. I have prayed for her safety. I have pleaded with her not to go. But it is a part of her. She cannot help herself. She *is* La Rosa, *señor*. She cannot stand by and do nothing. She must fight."

He knew Dulce was right. Leona and La Rosa were one and the same. Only how did he protect her? How did he keep the woman he loved from harm?

Dulce's nervousness seemed to depart. Her voice when she spoke was clear and strong. "If someone you loved had been killed or raped by McCabe, would you stand by and do nothing, *señor*? Would you let someone else do the fighting for you?"

"Of course not."

"Then why do you expect less of your wife?" she asked gently.

Diego opened his mouth, as if to argue with her, then closed it. He had no argument. She was right again.

With her eyes averted, her momentary courage depleted, Dulce busied herself with clearing the table of the breakfast dishes.

Diego watched her for a moment or two before rising from his chair and turning toward the bedroom. He didn't know yet what he was going to say to Leona. He just knew he didn't want this wall to continue to stand between them. They had to find some way to knock it down.

Leona was sitting on the edge of the bed when the door opened. She knew it was Diego and refused to look up.

"Leona . . . I was wrong."

His words caught her entirely off-guard. She

turned her head, meeting his gaze, and waited for him to continue, certain that she must have misunderstood him.

"I was wrong," he repeated.

"About what?"

"About forbidding you to do what you feel you must."

He crossed the room and stopped in front of her. He held out his hands, and when she took hold of them, he pulled her to her feet.

"Do you think we can reach some sort of compromise?" he asked, his eyes searching her face.

Her pulse was rapid. She could feel it beating in her chest and wondered if he could hear it, too. "A compromise?"

The palm of his hand cupped her chin, tipping her head slightly backward. "Leona, I love you. If I could, I would protect you from the world. I would build you a paradise with high walls, and I would keep out all things unpleasant, anything that might cause you a moment's worry or unhappiness." He leaned down and brushed her lips with his. "But I don't think you would be happy, locked up like that, no matter how beautiful the paradise."

She shook her head, but at the moment, she wasn't so sure. Maybe she would be happy if he was there with her.

"I won't try to stop La Rosa. But I ask you to promise me something."

Her throat felt tight. "What?"

"I, too, need to do what I feel I must. I need to watch over you. Promise me that La Rosa won't ride without me at her side. Promise me that you'll let me protect you as best I can."

"Oh, Diego . . ."

She threw her arms around his neck and kissed him hard. She knew that it hadn't been easy for him to give in to her on this. She understood that he only wanted to keep her from harm. That he cared enough to relinquish his control of her life said more than a thousand words of love could ever say.

"I promise," she told him, her lips brushing against his as she spoke. "I promise."

Then words became unnecessary as they found other ways to express their love.

McCabe reined in his horse and sat staring at the adobe house set against the slope of the mountain. It was small and unimpressive. A bitter taste burned his tongue, as he thought of how Leona Washington—no, Leona Salazar—had spurned him and all his wealth to marry another greaser. McCabe could have given her respectability, along with almost anything else her heart desired.

He uttered a string of vile oaths, angered that he still lusted after Gardner's daughter even now.

As he'd sat up late into the night, making his list, he'd come back to Leona again and again. He'd pictured her in his mind, seen her in her lovely gowns, her thick black hair cascading around her shoulders. He'd heard her light, expressive voice, imagined her melodic laughter. She might be half-Mexican, but she knew how to act like a lady. Even though she'd been unable to completely disguise her dislike of him, she'd always treated him with proper courtesy. The idea that she could be the infamous bandida who wielded a gun or a saber with an expertise most men would envy was preposterous.

And yet he couldn't shake the growing conviction that Leona was the bandolera La Rosa.

It had first occurred to him when he'd written the name of the Ramirez wench on his list. He'd known immediately that Mercedes couldn't be La Rosa. When he'd bedded the girl, she'd done nothing but cry and whimper. She hadn't even fought him for long, not after he'd hit her a few times. She'd been too paralyzed by fear. That was probably why he'd let her live. Because she'd been so afraid he'd known she would stay silent.

Whoever La Rosa was, she would be a fighter. She would scratch and claw and scream. She would buck and bolt. If he hit her, she would try to hit back.

No, Mercedes Ramirez couldn't possibly be the bandida.

And then he'd thought of how close Mercedes and Leona had always appeared. Like the best of friends. If Mercedes had told anyone what McCabe had done to her, it would have been Leona.

If Leona was La Rosa . . .

I am in mourning for one who was innocent and now bears much pain.

Yes, it made sense to him. Now he just had to

make her slip up just once. When he knew for certain that she was the bandida, he was going to enjoy making her regret her midnight visit to his room.

Jaw clenched tightly, McCabe spurred his horse forward. His eyes studied the corral and outbuildings. Nothing special or out of the ordinary there. No dogs ran out to bark at him as he approached the house. No chickens cackled noisily. If not for the lone horse standing in the corral, he might have thought he'd heard wrong about where the new Mrs. Salazar was living. Dismounting, he brushed the dust from his clothes as he approached the door. He rapped briskly and waited.

But it wasn't Leona he saw when his knock was answered.

The woman—obviously a servant—grew pale at the sight of him; her eyes rounded.

"I've come to see your mistress. Is she at home?"

She shook her head.

"Where is she?"

"Señora Salazar and her husband have gone to Rancho del Sol." She swallowed quickly, then added, "But they shall return soon, I am sure."

He didn't believe her. He had the feeling they had left not long ago. She had said it to make herself feel less alone.

He smiled.

She was like a frightened little bird. He could almost taste her fear. He liked that. He liked women to be afraid of him. He remembered the Ramirez girl's terror and felt lust heating his loins. Briefly, he toyed with the idea of forcing his way inside the house and using this woman to relieve the tension that had been building inside him throughout the night. No one was around for miles. No one would ever know. He could make sure she remained silent—permanently. He wouldn't make the same mistake again that he'd made when he was finished with Mercedes.

Know this, McCabe. If you rape another woman, I will cut off the part of you that offends me most and feed it to the dogs.

The lust he'd felt vanished as the unwelcome memory echoed in his head. He ground his teeth and turned abruptly away, not bothering to say another word to the young woman in the doorway.

He let out a string of curses as he swung into the saddle, damning La Rosa and all her supporters to hell and swearing again that he would find and punish her. He wouldn't rest until he'd learned La Rosa's true identity. He wouldn't rest until he'd made her suffer for all she'd done to him.

Chapter Thirty-Two

Diego caught Ricardo just as he was ready to leave Rancho del Sol.

"May I talk to you a moment?" he asked as his brother-in-law led his gelding out of its stall.

"I'm on my way to La Brisa."

It was easy to see that Ricardo was impatient to be on his way. There was an unusual tension around the man's mouth, and his eyes were anxious.

"This won't take long," Diego persisted. "Why don't I just ride with you part of the way?"

Ricardo nodded as he mounted his horse. He scarcely looked at Diego as he rode past him and out of the barn. Diego hurried back to Conquistador and swung onto his back, then cantered after his friend.

"Is there something wrong at La Brisa?" he asked as soon as he'd caught up with him.

"Leona hasn't told you?"

"No."

"Mercedes is ill."

"I'm sorry, *amigo*. I didn't know."

Ricardo gave a little shrug, as if it was painful for him to talk about it. His face revealed his fear and confusion. Diego remembered the way he'd felt when he'd been nursing Leona and felt a wave of sympathy for his friend. He wished he had some words of comfort to share.

"What is it you needed to tell me, Diego?"

He nodded grimly. It was probably just as well that they speak of something besides Mercedes. "It's about La Rosa."

Ricardo's eyes widened a fraction, but he didn't say anything.

"She seems to have become more obsessed about her attacks on McCabe."

"*Sí.*"

"Do you know why?"

Her brother shook his head, a tiny scowl creasing his forehead. "No."

"She's going to get careless if she keeps this up. She can't go on attacking him almost nightly. Next time he lays a trap for her, she might not be as lucky."

They rode in silence for a while, the two horses walking at a steady pace. Diego let his gaze roam over the countryside, noting the cattle dotting the land, the gentle breeze that stirred the grasses, browning now beneath the summer sun.

A man would do a lot to protect a place like this. A woman, too, he admitted to himself. A woman like Leona would fight hard to hold on to what was hers. She would fight beside him if he let her, or she would fight alone if she had to, but she *would* fight.

He turned his eyes on Ricardo. "She's promised she won't ride without me again. I want to make sure she keeps that promise. I can't risk losing her."

"I understand, *amigo*. I won't let her ride alone."

He pulled back on the reins, stopping Conquistador. "Thanks, Ricardo." As the other man rode on without him, he added, "I hope Mercedes is well soon."

Diego's question gnawed at Ricardo as he cantered toward La Brisa Rancho. Why *had* his sister become more obsessed about harming McCabe? It was almost as if he'd done something to her personally. Could McCabe have harmed or threatened her while Diego was away? Had something happened at the old hacienda that she hadn't told him about?

He remembered the gleam in her eye, the slightly different tone of her voice on those night raids. Something had changed. Her hatred for the lawyer had become a tangible presence that rode with them.

Why? he wondered again.

It was a question that dogged him all the way to the Ramirez ranch. It wasn't until the house came into sight that his concern for Mercedes shoved his troubled thoughts to another corner of his brain. He would have to think more on it later. For now, Mercedes needed his full attention.

He understood Diego's desire to protect Leona all too well. He knew he couldn't bear for anything to happen to the woman he loved. Even if she still refused to marry him once she'd recovered from this malaise, he would gladly accept it as long as she was well and strong.

He was greeted at the door by Sebastiano and Ofelia. When he asked them if there'd been any change, they could only shake their heads and tell him that they'd summoned the physician from Monterey, but their daughter had refused to see him.

"She asked for you in the night," Ofelia said. "When she slept, I sat beside her bed, and I heard her whisper your name." She took hold of his hand. "You must help her, Ricardo."

"I will do what I can, *señora.*"

Without another word, he headed for the bedroom, hoping against hope that he could perform the miracle her parents were asking of him.

"Berta?"

The plump woman turned away from the stove. "Miss Leona! Lord-a-mercy, I wasn't expectin' to see you! Come in here and let me have a look at you."

Leona stepped into the kitchen.

"My, my. I can see that marriage agrees with you, child, just by the twinkle in your eyes."

Leona felt a warm blush rising in her cheeks.

Berta laughed when she saw it. "When I seen that man, I just knew he was the right one for you. I just knew it. He's keepin' you happy, ain't he?" She chuckled suggestively. "I'm surprised you got enough energy to come see us, if'n I'm any judge of men."

Leona had withstood her share of Berta's teasing through the years, but today, the cook's humor was a bit more risque than usual. It occurred to her that she was viewed as a woman now, not a naive girl. While she liked the way that made her feel, she was still a tad uncomfortable with the older woman's ribald jesting.

"Berta . . ." She willed the blush from her cheeks. "I want to ask you a favor."

"Anything, Miss Leona. You know that."

"I'd like to learn how to cook."

The woman's eyebrows shot up on her forehead, her eyes wide with surprise. A second later, a loud guffaw filled the kitchen.

"Berta, I'm serious."

The cook tried to stifle her laughter. "I can see you are, child, but you forget who's tried to teach you before. Landsakes, you want to kill that good lookin' man o' yours before you've even been married a month?"

"That's not funny."

Berta wiped the grin from her face even as she wiped her hands on her apron. "No, I don't suppose you think it is." She drew in a deep breath, then let it out slowly. "Just what is it you want to know how to make?"

Leona's temper cooled a fraction. Berta had a right to be skeptical. Every time she had tried her hand at cooking, she'd ended up burning something or serving it half-raw. Once she'd even set the kitchen on fire. If not for Berta's quick thinking, the whole hacienda might have gone up in flames and smoke.

But this wasn't something to be joked about. She wanted to surprise Diego. She wanted to give him something he wouldn't expect. He had seen how important it was to let her make her own choices. Now she wanted to give him something special in return.

"I don't know." Leona shrugged, answering Berta's question at last. "Something easy. I tried fixing his breakfast, and it turned out just awful."

Berta turned back to the stove and checked whatever was simmering in the pot. "I remember when you did that. But I thought you made it awful on purpose."

"Not *that* time." Leona grimaced at the memory. "I tried to cook breakfast the day after we were married, before Dulce came to stay with us. It was a disaster." She moved over to the table and pulled out a chair to sit on.

"Well, I'll be . . ." Berta faced her once again, a knowing smile curving the corners of her mouth. "You love that man o' yours a lot, don't you, Miss Leona?"

She nodded, swallowing around the lump in her throat.

The cook came over and sat down opposite her, her expression serious as she gazed into her eyes. "There's no shame in being who and what you are, Miss Leona. There's nothing that says you ain't a right fine woman, just 'cause you can't cook like some fancy chef in some Frisco restaurant. There's a lot more than that what goes into makin' a man a good wife."

"I know, but I . . ."

"You forget, I watched you growin' up. Landsakes, child, you can do ten times anything most women ever could do."

"But . . ."

"You got Dulce. Why don't you just leave the cookin' t'her, and you concentrate on makin' Diego happy in other ways."

Leona blushed again. She stared down at her hands, folded on top of the table. "Just teach me how to make *one* thing."

"All right. If it means that much to you."

"It does."

Berta rose from her chair. She jerked her head toward the pantry. "You'll find an apron hangin' on a hook just inside the door. Put it on, and we'll see what you can learn."

Leona jumped up. Skirting the table, she threw her arms around the squat woman's broad shoulders and gave her a tight hug. "Thank you, Berta."

"Don't go thankin' me 'til we see what happens."

* * *

Ricardo sat beside Mercedes for several hours. Often, he talked about when they were children, remembering the many escapades they'd been through together. Sometimes, he talked about the night of the Aguilar *fandango*, the night he'd realized she wasn't still a little girl with pigtails and short skirts. Other times, he sat in silence, simply holding her hand.

Never once did she reply. Nor did she cry as she had the previous day. She simply stared into space, pulled so far inside herself that he was afraid he might never reach her. He found her current behavior far more alarming than her wrenching sobs and the buckets of tears she'd shed.

"What happened, Mercy?" he whispered as he leaned closer to her, staring into blank eyes.

"*Señor*, I have brought you some coffee."

He didn't turn his eyes from Mercedes. "*Gracias*, Ines."

A wrinkled hand settled on his shoulder. "She is still the same?"

He nodded.

"Something evil happened to her that night. The *señora*, your sister, she knows what it was. I saw it in her face when she left here. I felt her rage."

Dios . . . No!

He was scarcely aware that Ines had removed her hand and walked from the bedroom, closing the door behind her. An icy chill spread over him as awareness pushed its way into his brain.

Not that. Dios, por favor, *not that. Not to Mercedes.*

As much as he tried to deny it, as much as he prayed that it wasn't true, he knew in his heart it was. It became so clear to him—Mercedes's horror, her withdrawal into herself, along with Leona's new obsession, her unrelenting determination to totally destroy McCabe.

He slipped onto the bed beside Mercedes and pulled her into his arms. She stiffened, resisted. He felt her rising panic.

"It's me, Mercedes. I won't hurt you. I won't ever hurt you. No one will ever hurt you again."

She turned her head away from him, her voice little more than a whimper. "Don't touch me. I'm not . . . fit to touch."

Her words were like a knife in his belly. They twisted, ripping and tearing, leaving him bleeding and torn. He tried to shut out the images, but once they had begun, they couldn't be stopped. Almost as if he'd been there, he imagined McCabe forcing himself on Mercedes, a girl innocent of the act of love, an act now made evil and ugly.

"You're wrong," he replied hoarsely. "Oh, Mercedes, you're wrong. You're good and clean and sweet." He gently turned her face toward him with his fingertips. "I love you. It will be all right. I'll make it right. Trust me, Mercedes."

A confusion of feelings was revealed in her eyes as she looked up at him for the first time that day. The pain in his gut became almost unbearable, but he wouldn't look away, wouldn't release her.

Somehow he had to make her understand that his love wouldn't waver again.

Later, when he kissed her forehead and tucked the sheet close around her shoulders and tiptoed out of the room, then he would allow himself to feel the rage, then he would allow the sickness to erupt. But not yet. Not just yet.

Chapter Thirty-Three

Ricardo was waiting for Leona when she and Diego returned to the old hacienda. "I need to speak with you," he said to her as she dismounted, not bothering with a greeting. "Alone."

Leona glanced at her husband, then back at her brother. "All right."

Ricardo took hold of her arm and led her up the slope of the mountain behind the house. His strides were long and purposeful, and she had to run to keep up with him. When he'd put plenty of distance between them and the house, he stopped abruptly and turned to face her.

"Why didn't you tell me?" His voice was filled with bitterness.

"Tell you what?"

"You *know* what."

She was afraid she did, but she couldn't be sure.

"No, I don't," she said quietly. "Not unless you tell me."

"McCabe raped her."

Leona let out a lengthy sigh, her gaze dropping to the ground near her feet. "So . . . Mercedes told you. I didn't think she would."

The groan that came from his chest was like nothing she'd ever heard before. She glanced up quickly, realizing her mistake. Mercedes hadn't told him. He'd been guessing, and now Leona had confirmed his suspicions.

She reached out to touch his arm. "Ricardo . . ."

He jerked away.

"She made me promise I would tell no one. She feared the news would kill her father. She thought his heart wouldn't stand it. She is ashamed and frightened, Ricardo. She thinks you will despise her if you learn of it."

He didn't act as if he'd heard her. "I'll kill him for this." With that, he brushed past her and started down the mountain.

"*Mi hermano,* wait!" Leona rushed after him, catching him by the arm. "You're not using your head. Let La Rosa and her hombres take care of him. He won't get away with it. He'll be punished."

He shook free of her grasp. "I have no patience for running off cattle or stealing gold or burning empty haciendas. I want to cut out his heart."

She knew her twin perhaps better than she knew herself. Ricardo was not easy to stir to anger, but when it was ignited, his fury was all-consuming. This was one way that she and her brother were diametrically different. Leona was usually able to bridle her anger, using it to sharpen her wits, forcing herself to act in a cool, precise, and controlled manner. Ricardo, on the other hand, exploded with rage, reacting with recklessness, never thinking beyond the immediate need for action.

She knew there would be no reasoning with him now. She understood his temper. She'd felt it herself. She still did. But she couldn't let him go charging into certain disaster. She had to at least try to stop him.

"Ricardo, please listen to me. I have sworn that McCabe will suffer. And his suffering must be long and tormenting. Give La Rosa a chance."

He scowled at her.

"Give me two days to come up with a plan. We meet the others by the bent oak on Friday night. Give me that long." She stretched out a hand toward him in supplication. "*Por favor.* I promise you, McCabe will not escape La Rosa's wrath—or yours either."

He stared at her for a long time, his black eyes unblinking. She felt his pain and outrage and understood it because it matched her own. Finally, he gave her an abrupt nod of his head before continuing down the hillside.

Leona watched as he untethered his horse, mounted up, and rode away. She wondered if she shouldn't have tried to make him stay with her.

Wisps of clouds scudded across the quarter moon, causing silver and gray apparitions to dance and whirl over the earth. Leona hugged herself as she stared out the window at the ghostly dervish. She felt a strange chill in her bones.

"Tell me what troubles you."

She turned at the sound of Diego's voice. She could barely make out his form as he sat up in their bed. She shrugged, not certain she could put her foreboding into words, not sure she even wanted to try.

"It's Ricardo, isn't it?"

"*Sí.*"

He rose and came to stand beside her. His arm moved protectively around her shoulders. "Tell me."

"I'm afraid for him."

"Why?"

Again she shook her head.

He turned her to face the window. Then, folding her into his embrace, her back against his chest, he rested his chin on the top of her head. His fingers gently stroked her arms. He didn't pressure her with questions. He was simply there for her, and she was glad.

In all the weeks she had led her band of hombres against McCabe, she had never truly been afraid. She had thought out each attack, plotting with great care. Her plan had been a simple one, to harass and pester McCabe until he left the Salinas Valley. She had instructed her men to shoot to injure, not to kill. They had kept none of the lawyer's misbegotten spoils for themselves but had given them away to others in need.

Things had changed now. Her desire for revenge had become much more personal. She wouldn't be satisfied with just driving McCabe out. She wanted him to suffer. Perhaps she even wanted him to die.

Another shiver ran through her, leaving her almost numb with cold.

Even on the night she'd gone to McCabe's ranch alone, she hadn't known fear. Instead, she had felt a great sense of power. In the nightly raids that had followed, she had led her men with confidence, always in control, always cool under fire.

But tonight she was afraid. She couldn't shake the premonition that something terrible was about to happen. Like the night she'd heard the scream in her sleep, she felt the presence of evil, and she knew there was no escaping it. It had to be faced and conquered.

Diego felt the shiver run through her, and he tightened his hold. He'd seen his bride in sorrow and he'd seen her in anger. He thought he'd learned to deal with those emotions, at least with a small measure of success. But he didn't know how to help her now. It caused his own heart to tighten with trepidation.

It didn't help to know that McCabe had come to see Leona while the newlyweds were away. Dulce had told Diego about the lawyer's visit while Leona and her brother had been arguing up on the hillside.

What could he have wanted to see her about? Diego wondered. Why had he come here?

He didn't like it. It was too coincidental.

If only he knew what she was withholding from him. If only he knew why the sudden obsession with totally destroying McCabe. She'd always despised the man, but this was something more. If only he knew what . . .

"Get in there!"

McCabe looked up just as his foreman shoved a figure, dressed entirely in black, into his office.

"I found this fella skulkin' around outside, boss," Orin said as he stationed himself in front of the doorway. "He was wearin' this." He held up a black mask.

McCabe leaned back in his chair. He hid the leap of excitement he felt as he stared at the man's face. "Ricardo Washington. Whatever brings you to my ranch so late at night?"

Ricardo remained silent, his black eyes flashing with hatred.

"Come now, Mr. Washington. Surely you must have a reason for wandering around my ranch in the middle of the night, dressed like a thief. In that get-up, you might even be mistaken for one of La Rosa's band. You could be shot before anyone asked any questions."

Ricardo glanced toward Orin, as if trying to assess his chance for escape.

"My patience grows short," McCabe said, louder this time. He leaned forward. "Tell me what you're doing here."

The response was spoken in a deadly calm voice. "I came to kill you."

McCabe raised an eyebrow as a low chuckle escaped his throat.

With an angry cry, Ricardo hurled himself over the desk, his hands reaching out to close around McCabe's throat. The lawyer clawed at his assailant's fingers as his chair tipped over backward, carrying the two men crashing to the floor. He heard his foreman's shout but could make no sound of his own.

His eyes swam with splotches of black, and just as he feared he would lose consciousness, he heard a thud. The hands around his neck loosened as Ricardo toppled sideways to the floor.

McCabe dragged in a raspy breath.

"You all right, boss?" Orin grabbed hold of his elbow and helped haul him to his feet. "Mr. McCabe?"

"I . . . I'm fine." He glanced at Ricardo's still form. He could see a red stain on the side of his head, clotting his black hair. "Tie him up and lock him in the cellar. When he comes to, let me know. I may want to have a talk with him."

"Yessir, Mr. McCabe." The foreman grabbed Ricardo by the arm and dragged him across the floor of the office.

"Orin!"

The man glanced back at his boss.

"How many of the others know he's here?"

"Just me, Cluff, Anderson, and Parker."

McCabe stroked his neck. "I want two men guarding him all the time. Don't trust anybody. I still think we've got a spy here who's been passing on information to that bunch of thieves and cut-throats. Somebody just might try to set him free when we're not looking."

"This one's not gonna get loose, boss."

"See that he doesn't."

When the door closed again, McCabe righted his chair and sat down. His heart was still pounding rapidly in his chest. It was partly from his close call, but mostly, it was because of the man's identity.

Ricardo Washington was one of La Rosa's masked bandits. Surely that confirmed his suspicions about Leona Salazar. She had to be the bandida. She just had to be!

Were all the bandolera's men her brothers? he wondered, then quickly dispensed with that notion. The Washington men were unusually tall. The masked outlaws he'd seen with La Rosa were mostly average in height. No, even if Leona was La Rosa, the rest of the bandits weren't all her brothers.

Of course, Ricardo could belong to the band without the leader being his sister. It was possible the bandida wasn't even from the Salinas. It was possible . . .

No, he was sure of it. There were just some things a man knew, even when he didn't have the evidence to prove it. Every time he thought of the way Leona had slapped him the day of the Ramirez hearing, every time he thought of the disdain in her wide, violet-black eyes, he knew that she was the one.

And now he had his chance to prove his theory. Her twin was locked up in his cellar. La Rosa would have to try to free him, and when she did, McCabe would be waiting for her.

Chapter Thirty-Four

"No arguments, Leona. We're going into Monterey. I've already got Dulce packing us a picnic lunch."

Leona's hand, holding the hairbrush, stilled over her head as she met Diego's gaze in the mirror. Her breath caught in her throat. He was so incredibly handsome, and his love for her shone brightly in his dark brown eyes.

She shouldn't go, of course. She needed to talk to Ricardo. She needed to get a message to Johnny Parker at the McCabe Ranch. She needed to find out just what the lawyer had been up to lately. She had to devise a plan to put an end to his influence and destruction in this valley, once and for all.

But Diego looked so hopeful, she didn't want to disappoint him. They had been married less than two weeks, and already he had come to mean the world to her.

Several times, she'd come close to telling him so, yet she hadn't been able to do it. Each time, she'd remembered his stern commands as he'd tried to tell her she couldn't ride as La Rosa any longer. It didn't matter that, in the end, they'd reached a compromise. She was all too aware that he could change his mind on a whim. Once she told him how very much she loved him, he would hold all the power over her, and he would know it. She would be helpless to resist him. She couldn't do that.

"I thought we would go over to Rancho del Sol again. I need to talk to Ricardo."

"You can see your brother tomorrow. Today is for you and me."

She looked away from his reflection. Tilting her head to the side, she resumed brushing her hair. "Berta is expecting me."

"Berta? The cook?"

She ignored the question in his voice.

"Cooking lessons?"

She waited to hear his laughter.

Diego crossed the room to stand behind her at the dressing table. He took the brush from her hand. Then he leaned over and kissed her temple. "You don't have to know how to cook. I love you just the way you are."

Gooseflesh rose on her arms as he whispered the words near her ear. She closed her eyes and let her head fall back slightly. Seizing the opportunity, he kissed the exposed column of her throat. Leona moaned softly, delighting in the warm sensations that coursed through her in response to his gentle loving.

"However"—He straightened and started running the brush, with brisk strokes, through her hair—"we can talk about that some other time. Today, we're going to enjoy ourselves. We're going to go shopping for things you don't need. We're going to walk barefoot in the sand and gather seashells. We're going to eat Dulce's picnic lunch and lie on the blanket and stare at the sea gulls and listen to the water lapping against the sides of the ships in the harbor and feel the sun on our faces." He leaned down again, placing his cheek next to hers and looking at her in the mirror. His smile was filled with devilish delight. "And then we're going to come home beneath a star-studded sky and we're going to make love until dawn."

Her cheeks grew warm. "Diego . . ."

"It's what we should have been doing ever since our wedding day. I should have said to hell with my investments and stayed here with you. And you should have forgotten all about McCabe."

She twisted toward him. "I can't forget about . . ."

He silenced her with a solid kiss on the mouth, a kiss that lingered until she felt limp with desire. When he pulled away, he stared deeply into her eyes. "Today we forget everything except each other. We deserve this one day."

Leona's heart fluttered in response to his words and the look in his eyes. He was right. They deserved this one day. "All right," she answered softly. "I'll be ready in just a little while."

Ricardo's head pounded like a big bass drum. When he tried to lift his hand to touch the spot that throbbed the worst, he found he couldn't. His hands were tied behind his back.

Carefully, he opened his eyes. The room was inky black and smelled dank. He closed his eyes again and rolled onto his back.

Dios, what a fool he'd been! Johnny had warned him last week that McCabe had started posting sentries right after he'd been found, naked and bound, last week. He shouldn't have tried to come after the lawyer without some sort of diversion. But he'd been so angry!

Ricardo took a deep breath, then let it out, trying all the while to ignore the pulsating torment in his head.

When Johnny had first told him what La Rosa had done to McCabe, Ricardo should have known that something terrible had happened. He should have put two and two together long before he did. When he'd asked Leona about it, she'd merely said she'd grown tired of waiting and had wanted to humiliate McCabe so that he wouldn't forget it. He should have known better.

He thought of Mercedes, and his anger returned, the same blinding anger that had brought him here and made him McCabe's captive. Damn! McCabe was no fool—as much as Ricardo would like to believe he was. The man would know how to use his prisoner to his advantage.

Well, at least Johnny Parker knew he was here. He'd caught a glimpse of him as he was being shoved at gun point toward the house last night. Johnny would . . .

Johnny would what? Ricardo was his only contact. He didn't know who La Rosa really was. He didn't know the identity of any of the other hombres. Johnny couldn't do anything except try to free Ricardo, and that would be plenty risky now that McCabe was so wary of everyone.

He was forgetting Paco. Between Paco and Johnny, maybe there was some hope of escape.

Dry hinges creaked, causing a shaft of pain to lightning down the back of his skull. He opened his eyes to see the sliver of pale light spilling over a rickety stairway. He heard the footsteps before he could see the boots, legs, and body of the man to whom they belonged.

"So you're awake. I was beginnin' to wonder if you was ever gonna come to." It was the same man who'd taken him to McCabe's office last night. "Sit up and let me have a look at your head."

He put a hand over Ricardo's arm and hauled him upright. Ricardo cringed beneath the increased throbbing in his head, and an involuntary moan slipped up from his throat.

"Stopped bleedin'. I'd say you ain't hurt all that bad. The boss'll be glad to hear it." He turned away.

"I'll have somebody bring you somethin' to eat and drink."

"What does McCabe mean to do with me?" Ricardo asked, giving himself a little more time to look around the room that made up his jail cell.

It appeared that he was in some sort of cellar. The walls were made of earth and stone. The floor was hard-packed dirt. His cot, covered with a thin mattress and one inadequate blanket, was set near the wall. A barrel of some kind was in the opposite corner. Otherwise, the room was barren. Certainly there was nothing he could use for a weapon.

"All depends," the man answered. "If you're useful to him, he'll keep you alive. If you're not, I'd say you're gonna have some sort of unfortunate accident." He chuckled. "Yessir, an accident. They happen all the time."

He disappeared up the stairs. The door closed, and Ricardo was plunged back into total darkness.

Despite her doubts, Leona found that she'd been able to put her worries aside and enjoy herself. Diego had bought her a new bonnet and taken her to the dressmaker's, where he'd ordered her several new gowns, ignoring her protests that she didn't need them. They'd played with a litter of brown and white puppies which they'd discovered at the Widow Tremaine's house, and Diego had told Leona to choose one. Despite the woman's protests that he could have the puppy for free, he'd paid the Widow Tremaine and told her he'd come for the dog as soon as it was weaned. Finally, they'd walked along the beach, leading their horses behind them, until they'd found a secluded stretch of sand.

Lying on the blanket they'd brought from home, Leona stared up at the clear blue sky. She felt a pleasant lassitude, as if all her cares had suddenly and completely vanished. A breeze blew across the bay, bringing with it a salty spray off the ocean.

"Hungry?" Diego asked as he rolled onto his side and tossed an arm over her belly.

"Not really."

"I am." He nibbled on her neck.

"I thought you meant for lunch."

"So did I." His kisses trailed to the gentle swell of her breasts above her bodice.

"Mmmm."

"Ah, *querida* . . . "

She lifted her head and looked down at him just as he glanced up. She saw the now familiar look of desire sparking in his eyes and felt a corresponding need flare in her loins. Bracing himself on one arm, he brought his body alongside hers and claimed her mouth in a searing, breath-stealing kiss.

She opened her mouth, allowing his tongue access. She caught it lightly between her teeth and gently sucked, then released it. She delighted in the taste of him.

Her body strained toward his. She pressed her breasts against his chest, matched her hips to his, felt the swell of his desire against her softness. She ached to have him inside her. Her mind tormented her with images of the pleasures that awaited them when they had more privacy.

His lips, hot and demanding, continued to plunder her mouth while his hand slid between them to cup her breast. He caressed her through the fabric of her bodice, teasing the nipple until it grew taut.

Leona moaned into his mouth. Her head was spinning and her skin tingled.

"Perhaps," he whispered when their lips parted, "we'd better see what Dulce packed us for lunch before we forget ourselves."

"I think you're right," she replied breathlessly, yet she wasn't able to pull herself away from him. She had no desire for food, only for Diego.

He swallowed. "We forget how far one can see along the bay," he said, his voice breaking. "It's not as private as it looks." He sat up.

Leona closed her eyes as she sought to steady her reeling world.

She heard Diego rummaging through the bag that carried their lunch.

"Chicken. Bread. Dried fruit."

"Diego?"

There was a moment of silence. She imagined him looking at her. "*Sí?*"

"I don't want to eat. Can't we just go home?"

Again, her question was followed by silence.

She opened her eyes and met his gaze. Desire flared in her belly again, even more furious than before, a desire that she saw reflected and matched in his eyes.

"*Sí, mi corazón,* let's go home."

All in all, it had been a perfect day. Now she was looking forward to the night.

Chapter Thirty-Five

Diego recognized the boy who delivered the letter the next morning as the one who swept up at the Curtis Tavern. He gave him a few coins for his trouble, then opened the envelope, his eyes darting first to the signature at the bottom. It was from Heath, as he'd surmised.

Hiram will arrive today along with Joseph McConnell. Former commissioner has confessed to accepting bribes and McCabe has been implicated. Expect him to be arrested within days. Urgent that you meet with Joseph and Hiram today. Meet us at the tavern. Heath Curtis

At last!

Diego glanced toward the house. After today, he'd be able to tell Leona about his own work to stop McCabe and others like him. She wouldn't have to risk her life any longer, riding as La Rosa. They could put all this unpleasantness behind them. They could concentrate on building their own ranch and living their own lives.

He reentered the house, pausing just inside the doorway when his eyes found her. She was working beside Dulce in the kitchen. Her thick, black hair was tied at the nape with a ribbon. Her face was flushed from the heat of the stove. When she turned her head, he saw her tiny frown of concentration, and he couldn't stifle the laugh that rose in his chest.

"What are you snickering at?" she demanded, just a bit peevishly.

"You."

Her eyes narrowed.

He crossed the room in several swift strides, picked her up from the floor, and spun her around in his arms.

She slapped his arm. "Put me down, Diego."

Instead, he kissed her. When his mouth broke away from hers, he said, "I've got to go into Monterey again today. On business. Do you want to come along?" His voice lowered. "Perhaps we can find a more private stretch of beach."

Her eyes widened and fresh color brightened her cheeks.

"It's more fun than learning to cook."

She was tempted. He could tell by the way she was looking at him.

"I promise," he added, his arms tightened around her.

She let out a disappointed sigh and shook her head as she pressed her hands against his chest.

"I can't, Diego, no matter how much I'd like to. There is so much to do here, and I really must visit Mercedes this afternoon. I haven't been to see her for three days. She'll be wondering why I don't come."

"Has the doctor said what's wrong with her?"

Leona dropped her gaze, not looking at him when she answered. "No one seems to know what's wrong with her." She stepped back from him. "You go on to Monterey without me. You can take care of your business, and I'll see Mercedes. I'll be back here waiting for you by the time you return."

He cupped her chin with his fingertips. "You're not in any danger, being with her? She isn't contagious, is she? I don't want you risking your health."

"No, Diego, I'm in no danger."

He heard a catch in her voice when she answered, but when she looked up at him, her eyes were clear and guileless.

He thought again how happy she would be when he could share his news with her. He was tempted to do so now, but years of training and his oath of secrecy kept him from it. He supposed it didn't matter when he was able to tell her, just as long as McCabe was stopped. That was all that really mattered.

He placed a kiss on the tip of her nose. "I'll try to be back before nightfall."

"I'll be waiting for you."

It wasn't until after Diego had ridden away from the hacienda that Leona remembered it was Friday. This was the night she would meet with her hombres. This was the night she had to tell Ricardo her plan to stop McCabe once and for all.

Except she had no plan.

It had been easy enough in the past. La Rosa had simply been a source of irritation to the lawyer, like a burr caught in his pant leg. Now things were different. He had to be destroyed, and she had to come up with a way to accomplish McCabe's destruction before Ricardo did something foolish.

The promise of nightfall had cast a gray light over the valley, and still Leona didn't have a solution. The same frown she had been wearing throughout the day still creased her forehead as she laid her red costume across the bed and prepared to change her clothes.

"*Señorita?*"

"What is it, Dulce?"

"Someone is coming. It isn't the *señor*."

Out of habit, Leona glanced quickly out the bedroom window, confirming that Pesadilla was out of sight. She'd brought the black gelding from his secret corral earlier in the afternoon and had tied him behind the tack shed to await their rendezvous at the bent oak.

Turning from the window, she picked up her costume and shoved it beneath the bed, then proceeded to the front door. When she opened it, she encountered the last person she wanted to see.

"Good evening, Leona," McCabe said smoothly as he removed his hat and bowed slightly.

She hated the way he said it, resented his assumption of friendship by the use of her given name.

"*Buenas noches,* Señor McCabe."

"Sorry for dropping by so late, but I didn't want to put off this visit. I was hoping to give you and your husband my congratulations and best wishes."

"That is kind of you, *señor*, but unnecessary."

"I also wanted to apologize for what I said to you the day of the Ramirez hearing."

She stepped outside and closed the door. "I accept your apology," she replied stiffly.

"Would it be possible for me to speak to Mr. Salazar?"

"He's in Monterey on business."

Her stomach felt tight, her mouth dry. She didn't like being alone with him, not without her saber and her pistol. She didn't trust him. She thought of what he'd done to Mercedes and bile burned her throat. If she'd had her riding crop in her hand, she would have struck him with it.

"Leona . . ." He cleared his throat. "Apologizing wasn't the only reason for my visit. I'm afraid I have some bad news for you."

"Bad news? For me?"

"Your brother, Ricardo . . . He's one of La Rosa's band of outlaws."

She looked at him, wide-eyed. "Ricardo? Don't be ridiculous!"

"I'm not. I assure you. He tried to attack me the other night. He's a prisoner at my ranch at this very moment. He refuses to talk, but eventually I'll get him to tell me who this La Rosa is and how to find her. When he does, then I suppose I'll turn him over to the sheriff and let the law deal with him."

"The sheriff doesn't know you've captured him?" she asked, trying not to let her apprehension show in her voice.

"Sheriff Kincaid is an idiot. Everyone knows that. I'm not turning your brother over to him until I have the information I need." McCabe grinned. "It isn't him I want. It's La Rosa. For all I care, Ricardo could go free as long as I get the *bandida*."

He suspects I'm La Rosa.

The thought didn't surprise her. She knew he was toying with her, daring her to try to save her brother, hoping to prove he was right, hoping to capture the bandida. How like McCabe to think he could outwit her.

"I'm only telling you this because of the affection I still hold for you, Leona, my dear."

She thought of him as he'd been the night she had visited his ranch alone. She pictured him, fat and naked, lying on his bed, whimpering like the coward he was. She wouldn't let him win this round. She would beat him in this as in all other things.

"Would you allow me to visit my brother, to talk to him? Perhaps I can help you learn the truth. I'm sure Ricardo was at your ranch for some other reason than to cause you harm." She offered a wheedling expression. "Please, allow me to talk to him."

"Well, I suppose it couldn't hurt anything. Why don't you come with me now?"

"Now?"

He nodded, his green eyes daring her once again. "I realize it's late, but I'm sure you're worried about him. I'll see you safely home myself."

If she didn't go, he would wonder at her lack of concern for her brother. If she did go, she would be going without her usual weapons or disguise, without any of her hombres.

But she really hadn't any choice. There would be no plausible reason for her to refuse to go with him if she and Ricardo were innocent.

No, she hadn't any other choice.

"Of course. I'll come with you at once." She turned back toward the house. "Just give me a few moments to get my wrap. There's a chill in the air tonight."

Leona tucked her pistol into her reticule. "If we are to help Ricardo, someone must get inside the house. Without me, my brother could be killed before we reach him. McCabe doesn't know it, but he's done us a favor." She turned toward Dulce. "Do you remember what you must do?"

"*Sí*. I am to wait for Señor Salazar and tell him all you have told me. If he does not return in time, I am to leave him your note and ride to the bent oak to tell your *hombres* your plan."

"Good." Leona reached out and clasped Dulce's hand. "I'm counting on you."

"I will not fail you, *señora*."

"I know you won't, Dulce." She turned away from the maid and picked up a small knife in its leather sheath. Then she slipped it into the garter on her thigh.

She was taking a risk. She knew that. The cards were stacked against her as never before. McCabe had decided the rules of this game, and she would be forced to play by them. There were many things that could go wrong. Many more than she cared to think about.

Diego, I wish you were with me.

She took a deep breath as she straightened, letting her skirt fall back in place. "Dulce . . ."

"*Sí, señora?*"

"If anything goes wrong—if I don't return—tell Diego that I loved him more than life itself."

She hurried out of the room and out of the house before Dulce had a chance to reply.

Chapter Thirty-Six

The dankness of the cellar was beginning to get to him. Ricardo felt the cold in his bones, a chill that he was certain would never go away, even when he got out of here—*if* he ever got out of here.

Worse yet, his thinking was being numbed by the total darkness. It was as if the world had ceased to exist. Only when someone brought him his food and water—twice yesterday, twice today—had he caught a glimpse of light. Then it had been so brief, he'd been left to wonder if he'd actually seen it or only imagined it.

How long had he been here? Was it just two days? Yes, they'd only come down twice yesterday and twice today. Or had he been unconscious longer than he thought? It certainly felt longer, and without the coming and going of the sun, he couldn't be sure. Had he lost track of time?

Could it have been longer? He was beginning to wonder.

Ricardo rose from the cot and stretched his arms overhead, thankful at least that they had exchanged the tight ropes for a pair of manacles. He could at least feed himself now.

He hadn't seen McCabe since the night he'd been taken captive. Nor had he seen Johnny or Paco. He wondered if McCabe suspected them of being spies for La Rosa. If so, their lives were in as much danger as his own. Perhaps he'd already locked them up, too—or worse, perhaps they were already dead.

He cursed angrily, as he'd done so often since he'd awakened in this stinking hole in the ground. After all, this was his own fault. He'd acted like a fool, coming here as he had. He'd known McCabe was taking more precautions, that his men were guarding the ranch house with diligence these days. Johnny had warned them, and still he'd barged in, intent on murder, blinded by his own rage.

He sat down on the cot, an overwhelming wave of despair threatening to sink him. Mercedes needed him, and he couldn't go to her. That was the worst part of all.

"Don't worry, Diego," Joseph McConnell had told him several hours ago. "I'll make certain that La Rosa and her men are cleared of any and all charges. There'll be no repercussions as long as their activities cease. After all, from what you've told me, Rance McCabe has been their only target. With him in prison, there'll be no one to speak against them."

Diego smiled grimly to himself. It was over. By tomorrow, McCabe would be in the custody of federal officers. Diego had been surprised by what had turned up. The lawyer wasn't only guilty of bribing members of the commission. He had also been charged with the murder of his former law partner in New York.

As he cantered his pinto toward home, his way lit by a nearly full moon resting above the Gabilan Mountains, he imagined what it would be like when he told Leona what had happened. Not only would he be able to tell her about McCabe, but he was free to explain his part in all of this. He would also be able to tell her that he'd resigned from the agency. He wouldn't have to worry anymore about messages being delivered at odd hours, calling him away from her.

And they wouldn't ever need to argue over La Rosa again, he thought with satisfaction. The bandida would take her place among the other heroes and heroines of myths and legends, while Leona remained safely within the circle of Diego's arms. They could live in peace from now on.

Diego smiled as he approached the old hacienda, but the look of pleasure disappeared when he saw the woman in red cantering her black horse in the opposite direction.

Caramba! What was she up to now?

He shouted for her to stop, to wait, and then angrily rode after her.

With McCabe riding beside her, Leona trotted Glory up to the front of the lawyer's two-story wooden house. She felt as if eyes were staring at her from every direction, but she didn't look about her or try to find the positions of the guards as she dismounted and tied her mare to the post.

It was Paco who opened the door for them. His expression revealed nothing, not even surprise at seeing her there. She wondered if he knew where Ricardo was being held. She wondered if he might have guessed that she was La Rosa. If only she had a moment to talk to him, to take him into her confidence . . .

"Come inside, Leona," McCabe said as he led the way. "I'll have Paco here bring us some refreshments. I'm sure you're thirsty after the dusty ride." Over his shoulder, he said, "Paco, bring some coffee for Mrs. Salazar and be quick about it." With a wave of his hand, he motioned her into the parlor.

Leona did her best not to brush against him as she stepped through the narrow doorway. This room, like the lawyer's office, was filled with priceless paintings and sculptures. She let her eyes linger on an exquisite oil painting over the fireplace.

"You have quite a collection, Señor McCabe."

"Thank you. I'm proud of it. It took me many years to get some of my most coveted pieces."

She couldn't help wondering how he'd acquired these objects. No doubt they were stolen by one means or another.

"Do sit down, my dear. That worthless Mexican should be back soon. He's slow-witted, but he doesn't cause me any trouble and his wages are cheap."

She clenched her teeth, choking off an angry rejoinder. Schooling her face into a neutral expression, she turned around. "I'm not concerned about your servant situation, Señor McCabe, or chatting over a cup of coffee. I would much rather get to the matter that brought me here. Where is my brother?"

"Of course." His smile was forced. "Do sit down, and I'll have him brought to you."

"Oh, *señor*, I am so glad you have come."

"Dulce?"

The maid servant pulled off the red mask, revealing worried eyes. "*Sí*, it is I."

"What are you doing dressed as La Rosa? Why are you riding Pesadilla?"

"There is no time to waste, *señor*. I will explain on the way to the bent oak."

It was easy for Diego to see how nervous Dulce was. She was gripping the saddle horn with one hand, and her other hand shook as she turned the big black. He knew without asking that Leona was in trouble. That was the only reason Dulce—

who was terrified of horses—would be riding the spirited gelding.

"Where is she?" he asked as he guided his pinto alongside Pesadilla.

"She has gone to Señor McCabe's. He has taken the *señora's* brother prisoner."

"Ricardo?"

"*Sí.*"

He felt a cold dread seep through his veins. Leona had gone to McCabe's alone. She had gone without her disguise or her weapons or any help. Why hadn't she waited for him? Hadn't she promised she wouldn't ride without him at her side?

He glanced at Dulce, clad in the red costume. His mouth thinned. Well, Leona had kept her word. She hadn't ridden as La Rosa without him. She'd gone as Leona.

Vive Dios! She'd known what he meant!

"The *señora* had no choice. McCabe came to the hacienda to tell her he had captured Señor Ricardo. He said she must go with him if she would prove her brother's innocence. The *señora* told me she must get inside to help her brother when La Rosa's *hombres* ride tonight."

"Just exactly what is her plan?"

"You and the *hombres* will stampede McCabe's livestock and cause whatever diversion you must to draw away his guards. While McCabe and his men are fighting, she will help her brother escape."

Diego motioned at her costume. "And what's your part in all this?"

"This was my own idea, *señor*. If McCabe sees La Rosa riding with the others, he will think he is wrong about the *señora*. He will not be watching her, and she will have a better chance."

Diego considered everything the woman had said. It wasn't a flawless plan, but considering the options, he supposed Leona had done what she had to do. They would proceed as she'd wanted— with one exception. Diego was going to be inside with her when the shooting started. He wasn't leaving her to face McCabe alone.

"We'd better ride for the bent oak," he said, spinning his pinto around. "It's getting late."

Leona rose from her chair when she heard the rattle of chains. She turned around just as Ricardo stepped through the doorway.

"*Válgame Dios!*" she whispered as their eyes met across the room.

Her brother's black clothing was wrinkled and stained, and even from this distance, she could see the congealed blood that matted his hair to the side of his head. His jaw was covered with several days' stubble of beard. But it was the hollow, haunted look in his eyes that caused her the greatest concern.

"*Mi hermano*, you're hurt," she said, hurrying toward him.

He shook his head. "It's nothing."

She clasped his hand between hers.

"You shouldn't be here," he told her.

Even though she couldn't see him, she knew that McCabe was listening from the foyer. She had to be careful. She had to keep Ricardo with her for as long as possible. Even if everything were on schedule, Dulce would only just now be meeting the others. Leona could only hope that Diego had returned in time.

With a quick motion of her finger in front of her lips, Leona indicated to Ricardo that he should remain silent. She pleaded with her eyes for him to understand. Then she led him to a chair and pressed him down onto it, her hands on his shoulders, before turning toward the door.

"Señor McCabe?" she called.

He appeared quickly.

"I must have some warm water and a cloth to tend my brother's injury."

He didn't move.

"If you want my help in finding the *bandolera*, then you must do this. You can't expect my brother to answer questions when he is in need of care."

He frowned, then turned away. "Paco, bring some water and bandages."

She wasn't fooled by his quick disappearance. She knew the lawyer was still within hearing distance. She knelt beside her brother's chair and grabbed his hands with hers. "Trust me," she mouthed silently.

Ricardo nodded.

Aloud, she said, "You must tell me why you came here, dressed like that. Surely it is not true that you are one of La Rosa's men?" She shook her head.

"No," he answered, following her lead, "but I thought the disguise might be useful after I killed McCabe."

Leona sucked in a quick breath.

"If I hadn't been caught, no one would have known it was me beneath the mask. They would have blamed the *bandidos,* not me."

"Ricardo . . ."

"He deserves to die for what he did to Mercedes."

Her heart sank in her chest. Even if she were to convince the lawyer that her brother was not one of La Rosa's men, McCabe would never let Ricardo go now. He couldn't risk being accused of rape.

Looking into her brother's eyes, she wondered if he understood what she was trying to do. She prayed that he wouldn't say anything more about McCabe and his feelings about the man. The lawyer was ruthless, of that she had no doubt.

She decided to pretend she hadn't heard—or didn't understand—what Ricardo had said. "*Mi hermano,* if you know who the *bandida* is, you must tell me. Señor McCabe says he doesn't want you. He just wants La Rosa. Do you know? For my sake, tell him. Then he will let you go."

"I don't know who she is, and I don't care."

Leona glanced toward the window. Moonlight had spread a white frosting over the earth outside McCabe's house. Inky shadows reigned wherever the moon's glow couldn't reach.

How soon would La Rosa's hombres come? she wondered. Would it be soon enough?

It might work, Diego told himself as the riders galloped across the moonlit countryside. *With luck, it just might work.*

He glanced toward Dulce. She was wearing the mask again, but it was easy to tell from the set of her mouth that she was petrified. Only her love for Leona was keeping her in the saddle. He wished, for her sake, that she were a better horsewoman. He worried about her keeping her seat if she and Pesadilla were pursued.

He also wished he knew for certain how many men McCabe had at his ranch. A lot would depend upon the numbers. They would be six, not counting Dulce, against how many? Ten? Fifteen? Twenty? And how many of them would be inside the house itself?

Dulce had said Leona had her knife and a pistol. But what if . . .

A knot twisted in his stomach.

While they were still out of sight of the McCabe ranch house, the small band slowed, then stopped their mounts. Diego's gaze slid from one man to another. The air seemed to crackle with tension. They all knew that Leona's and Ricardo's lives depended upon them this night. They were no longer fighting for a woman whose identity remained a mystery. They were fighting for their friends.

"Vaya con Dios, muchachos," Diego said aloud, then he sent up a more fervent silent prayer that God would keep them all safe.

"Vaya con Dios," someone else responded.

Diego turned Conquistador and cantered toward the McCabe ranch house.

Chapter Thirty-Seven

"Come on, Washington." McCabe grabbed hold of Ricardo's arm and yanked him up from the chair. "If you don't want to talk to your sister, you can just go back to the cellar until you find your tongue."

"Señor McCabe . . ." Leona started to protest.

He shoved her brother into the hallway. She started after him, but the lawyer's frame filled the doorway, blocking her exit. "We'll just let him think about it awhile."

"But you must have heard what he said. He doesn't know anything about La Rosa."

"I heard what he said." His voice was harsh. "Sit down."

She didn't care for the way he was looking at her. The glint in his eyes held a strange mixture of hate and lust. What was he going to do now? she wondered. Was he going to try to make her his captive, too? Or had he a worse fate in mind?

"Why do we keep up this pretense, Leona? We both know who La Rosa is."

She tilted her chin. "You are wrong, *señor*. I don't—"

"Damn it!" He took a threatening step toward her. "Don't call me *señor*. I'm not one of your damn Mexican friends."

She moved away from him, hiding her apprehension as best she could.

"Admit it, and I swear I'll go easy on your brother."

"I think it's time I went home," she said as she reached for her reticule.

But he was faster than she was. He snatched it from the arm of the chair, and before she could stop him, he'd opened it and pulled out the pistol. He pointed the weapon at her.

"Sit down, Leona, and let's have a talk."

She didn't doubt that he would kill her if she provoked him. And if he did, Ricardo would die, too. She stepped sideways and settled onto a chair.

"That's better." He sat down across from her, the gun still aimed in her direction.

A man stepped into the doorway. "Got us another visitor, boss."

"Who is it?" McCabe snapped.

"Said his name is Salazar."

She felt a flash of relief. Diego had come back from Monterey in time. He hadn't stayed with the others. He was here to help her.

McCabe grinned. "Show him in but remove his gun first."

"Yessir."

"Orin!"

"Yessir?"

"Tie up Paco and put him in with Ricardo."

The foreman paused only a second before responding. "Yessir."

McCabe shrugged at Leona. "Paco's not bright enough to be in cahoots with you, but I'd rather not take any chances. As far as I'm concerned, you can't trust any greaser, even a stupid one."

"I'm not interested in what you do with your servants, Señor McCabe," she replied, using her haughtiest tone of voice, "but I would like to know why you're holding me prisoner and threatening my husband."

His eyes narrowed. "You know why, *bitch*."

She drew back as if he'd slapped her, abhorring the evil she saw in his gaze and heard in his voice. She tried to find something to say, but her throat had gone dry.

Diego entered the parlor just then, Orin's gun pointed at his back. Leona started to rise.

"Sit down." McCabe's warning resembled a snarl. "And don't move." He glanced at Diego. "Come on in, Salazar, and have a seat next to your wife."

Diego's expression was one of mild surprise, but he showed no fear. When he looked at her, she felt her confidence returning. Now that he was with her, she knew she would be all right.

"What's the meaning of this, McCabe?" Diego asked as he moved across the room.

"You tell me."

"I don't know. I got back from Monterey, and Dulce told me my wife had left with you. She said something about Ricardo being in trouble?" When he reached her, he took hold of her hand, squeezing her fingers between his. "I came to see what this trouble was all about. Beside, I didn't want Leona riding back to the ranch after dark."

"Very touching, but I'm not—"

"Boss!" Orin burst into the room. "We've got trouble!"

The words were hardly out of his mouth when a barrage of gunfire exploded outside. Orin ran over to the window and pushed the heavy draperies aside.

"They've stampeded the livestock!" he shouted. "Look! It's La Rosa!"

McCabe was on his feet. "It can't be!"

Leona glanced quickly at Diego, but his expression revealed nothing. Still, she knew who the woman had to be. Dulce! But Dulce wasn't equipped to fight McCabe's men. She could get hurt, maybe killed. She started to speak, but Diego's fingers tightened in silent admonition.

"Send the men after her," McCabe commanded. "Kill the rest of the bandits if you have to, but bring her back to me. Whatever you do, *don't* let her get away!"

Outside, pandemonium reigned. Leona heard the panicked cries of horses, the shouts of men, the thunder of galloping hooves on hard-packed ground, the firing of guns. The tension mounted in her chest. She wanted to be with them. She felt so helpless, held here at gunpoint while others did the fighting for her.

"It's over, McCabe," Diego said in a low voice. "Let us go."

There was an unnerving air of confidence in her enemy's green eyes when McCabe turned his gaze toward Leona, ignoring Diego. "It *isn't* over. I don't know who that woman is, but it isn't La Rosa. *You're* La Rosa. And when my men bring her back to me, she'll tell me the truth even if you won't." His grin mocked her. "Is it Miss Ramirez? If it is, I know how to make her tell me what I want to know. Several very pleasurable ways." He sat down again. "We'll just sit here and wait. It won't take my men too long, I'm sure."

"Bastard!" She rose quickly, shaking off Diego's hand as he tried to stop her. "You would sit there and brag of what you did to Mercedes? I would cut out your heart if you had one."

His grin vanished. His face twisted in hate. "That's not nearly as bad as what I mean to do to you, La Rosa." He turned the pistol on Diego. "Sit down or he dies now instead of later."

Leona seethed with impotent fury but could do little except obey him. She knew that she and Diego were alive now only to entertain McCabe. When he was no longer amused, he would kill them—unless they could escape first.

Increased gunfire sounded in the distance, drawing the lawyer's gaze toward the window.

Leona saw the nervous twitch pulling the corners of his mouth and the slight unsteadiness of his hand as he held the gun on his hostages. She sensed that Diego was judging the distance between them and McCabe, just as she had done a short time before.

The sounds of the battle between La Rosa's hombres and McCabe's men filled the room, growing almost imperceptibly louder. Leona felt her pulse quicken as she guessed what was happening. His men were being pushed back toward the house. Her hombres were winning.

McCabe thought so too. "Let's go," he ordered as he got to his feet. "Up the stairs."

Diego felt like a damned fool. He'd walked into this trap with his eyes wide open. His only thought had been to be by Leona's side when she needed him most. He should have plotted more carefully. He should have been prepared for this.

As he took hold of Leona's arm and drew her up from the chair, he decided to take the risk of speaking the truth. "You won't get away, McCabe. Even if you kill us, the federal marshall is going to be here tomorrow to arrest you. You've been charged with the murder of Lawrence Decker."

McCabe's complexion turned ashen, then reddened. His eyes narrowed. "Get going."

"If you give yourself up, they might go easy on you."

"Shut up, Salazar." McCabe's finger tightened on the trigger.

Leona's fingers pressed into his arm.

"Listen . . ." he tried again.

"I said, shut up! Shut up and let me think." McCabe waved the pistol. "Get up those stairs before I shoot you both right here."

The glint in the lawyer's eyes seemed slightly crazed. Diego knew he'd pushed him far enough. If he said more, Leona just might die in this parlor before Diego had a chance to stop McCabe.

They were half-way up the stairs when the front door opened, and the ranch foreman burst into the house.

"We'd better get outta here, boss!" Orin shouted. "Don't look like the men are gonna be able t'hold them off for long. We've lost six already."

Leona glanced at McCabe, sensing his frustration and surprise. Always La Rosa had told her hombres to shoot high, and if forced, to wound and not kill. It had made her enemy think the hombres were poor shots, that they were disorganized and weak opponents. Tonight, they were proving him wrong. Once again, she had shown him to be a fool.

Her satisfaction over his discomfiture was short-lived. Within moments, he had forced his captives up the stairs and into his bedroom. As soon as they were inside the door, McCabe pulled Leona away from Diego. He pressed the muzzle of the gun against her jaw, then ordered her husband to lie down on the bed. He had Orin bring a rope, which the foreman used to tie Diego's hands together. Then his wrists were secured to the headboard, his ankles to the footboard.

"Seem familiar?" McCabe whispered in her ear as his fingers dug into her upper arm. "If we had more time, I'd have done to him what you threatened to do to me."

Her eyes widened, but she said nothing as she stared toward the bed. Up until this moment, she'd held out hope for their escape. She'd still believed that they could overpower McCabe, that he would make a mistake and, together, they would break free. Now her hope was fading. Her mind seemed numb. If Diego died, she would have nothing left of any worth.

"What do you plan to do now?" Diego asked, the sound of his voice bringing her up short.

She looked into his eyes then. Really looked. He hadn't lost hope. He was still fighting. Fighting for the both of them. *Think*, he was telling her. *Listen and plan. We will do this together.*

"I'm going to get out of here," McCabe responded. "And I'm taking your wife with me."

"I'll follow you. The moment I'm free, I'll be hot on your trail. You won't stand a prayer of escaping me. I'll find you wherever you go."

The lawyer grinned. "No, you won't. They're going to find you here, and think you're me." He glanced toward his foreman. "Get my horse and the little lady's ready. Bring them around to the back of the house and wait for us there."

"Yessir, boss." Orin disappeared into the hall.

"Why would anybody think I'm you?" Diego asked, voicing the same question Leona had been thinking.

"Because it'll be damned hard to tell the difference."

She watched in stunned disbelief as McCabe kicked the nearby table. The lamp fell to the floor, shattering the glass. Kerosene spilled across the thick carpet, and greedy flames followed the trail. She took a quick step toward the bed but was jerked violently backward.

"I've got a few things to get from my office." McCabe shoved her out of the room.

She glanced over her shoulder. She caught a brief glimpse of Diego straining against the ropes before she was pushed toward the stairs.

Leona felt a momentary panic. Her mind was empty of anything except the vision of fire spreading across the floor and Diego tied to the bed. She didn't care what happened to her. She had to get to him. But what could she do? She was helpless. She was powerless. She was . . .

She was Leona Salazar, the wife of Diego. She was La Rosa! She would not let Rance McCabe win. The panic left her, and she watched for her first opportunity.

With the gun pressed against her spine, McCabe guided her into his office and over to his desk. He jerked open a drawer and began pulling papers and files from its depths. When he'd apparently found what he was looking for, he ordered her from the room, the sheaves of paper tucked beneath his left arm, the gun in his right hand. She wasn't surprised this time when he knocked over a second lamp, setting his office on fire.

Never do the expected, Gaspar had once told her. *Fight dirty if you must. It doesn't always pay to be a gentleman.*

Or a lady, either.

She whirled on him suddenly, bringing her fist up underneath his chin. Before he could react to her unexpected resistance, she bent forward and rammed her head into his stomach, knocking him against the wall, a whoosh of air forced from his lungs. His papers fell from his arm and scattered across the floor, some of them falling into the flames.

He swung his gun hand in her direction, but rather than backing away or trying to run, she lunged toward him. Her fingers closed on his right arm as she sank her teeth into his wrist.

He howled his fury as the gun discharged, then fell to the floor.

McCabe shoved her away from him, his superior strength bouncing her off the opposite wall. There was no time for her to grab the gun herself. The best she could do was make sure he didn't get it.

They went for the weapon at the same time, McCabe reaching for it with his hand, Leona kicking with her foot. Leona got there first. The gun was sent spinning across the wood floor of the office, disappearing amid the flames that had begun to climb the edge of McCabe's desk.

"Damn you!"

His backhand sent her to the floor. She tried to scramble to her feet but was knocked flat again, then flipped onto her back. Pushing with her hands and heels, she scooted across the floor until she was stopped by the wall at her back, her knees drawn up to her chest. He towered over her, sweat dripping from his face as he leaned down. She saw him draw back his hand to strike her again. She knew she hadn't the physical strength to beat him. So she did what he least expected.

She smiled.

"You are not man enough to stop me, *gringo*," she said in the husky voice of the bandida.

He froze, his expression twisting into a grotesque mask of fury and disbelief.

It was the chance she'd wanted. She knew he didn't see anything but her smile. He didn't see that her skirt was above her knees. He didn't see that her hand had closed around the knife hidden beneath her garter. He only saw her confident smile, heard her taunting words, and that was his greatest mistake of all.

Catching him totally by surprise, she grabbed hold of the front of his shirt and pulled herself to her feet. With the same agility she used to wield a sword, Leona brought the sharp, cold steel up to his Adam's apple. "Move and you are dead."

He made a strangled sound in his throat, cowardice replacing boldness in the expression on his face.

"Turn around." When he obeyed, she pressed the knife point against his back, centered between his shoulder blades, hard enough that he could feel it through his shirt. "Upstairs."

"There's no time. The fire—it's spreading too fast."

She knew he was telling the truth. From the corner of her eye, she could see that the office was completely ablaze. Even now, the hungry flames were inching their way out into the hall and beginning to climb the walls.

If you will threaten with your sword, Rafael had always told her, *then you must not hesitate to use it when the time comes.*

She pushed the knife just enough to cut him. "Up the stairs, *gringo*, or draw your last breath. La Rosa has no more patience."

Flames were licking at the foot of the bed by the time they reentered the bedroom. Her cool control slipped as her eyes found Diego. She heard his coughing, and she realized how little time remained.

She ordered the lawyer forward, the knife now pressed against his neck at the base of his skull. "Untie him."

It seemed an eternity to Leona before Diego was free. Relief swept through her as he rose to his feet beside her.

"Are you all right?" he asked as his glance briefly met hers.

"*Sí*, I am all right."

His fingers touched her cheek. "I knew you would be, La Rosa."

His use of the bandida's name said far more than anyone else would have known had they heard him. Later, she would tell him how much it meant to her. Now was not the time.

He held out his hand for the knife. She gave it to him without protest. It felt right to her now. She was willing to stand back and follow his lead.

"Where's Ricardo?" Diego shouted at McCabe above the rising noise of the fire.

"You'll never get to him in time."

"Where is he, McCabe?"

"Are you crazy? We've got to get out of here!"

"We'll all die if you don't tell me. Where is he?"

Coughing, McCabe covered his nose and mouth with his arm. "In the cellar."

"Let's go. You're going to show us where it is."

Leona's eyes were stinging, and she felt as if a giant hand was squeezing her chest. She could scarcely see through the smoke, and the heat in the room made her think of the padre's warnings about hell.

"Stay close," Diego told her.

The three of them started forward, but McCabe came to an abrupt halt as he stepped into the hall. Leona saw why when she leaned forward. The staircase and hallway were ablaze, blocking their escape.

"Get back!" Diego motioned with the knife. "We'll never make it through there. We'll have to find another way."

Before she could react, Leona felt a violent jerk on her head. She stumbled toward McCabe, pulled by his fingers tangled in her loose hair.

"Die, bitch!" he yelled as their eyes met.

The dense smoke choked her. The intense heat threatened to blister her skin. The noise was paralyzing, deafening. It was truly a scene from the depths of hell, and McCabe meant to push her into the inferno's center.

Diego struck without warning. His arm was a blur near her face as he plunged Leona's dagger into the lawyer's chest. She fell back, Diego's arms catching her. In horror, she watched McCabe stagger backward, his hands pressed against the bleeding wound. She saw his eyes widen as he teetered on the top of the staircase. She heard his shriek of terror as he lost his fight for balance. With arms flailing in the air, he tumbled into the conflagration.

He could never survive in that, she thought.

A chill shot up her spine as La Rosa's prophetic words flashed in her memory.

Roasted in a pit of his own making.

She shuddered.

Diego hauled her back into the bedroom, reminding her sharply of their own peril.

"The window!" he shouted. "We'll have to jump."

Together, they raced through a room ablaze. Diego tried to open the window, but the latch wouldn't budge. Without hesitation, he picked up a chair and sent it crashing through the glass.

It seemed to Leona as she climbed out onto the steep roof that the whole world was on fire. Hungry tongues in bright orange and red hues licked the sky from the roof behind her. Below, flames lashed out of broken windows on the ground floor, daring her to try to escape.

She heard voices shouting at her and squinted at the ground through the haze of black smoke. She saw men running, congregating beneath her. She heard someone shout her name, and then she saw a blanket stretched between them.

"Jump, *gatita*! We will break your fall."

She couldn't believe her eyes and ears. Ricardo was holding one corner of the blanket. His face was blackened with soot, but otherwise, he seemed all right. And then she realized that the two others holding the blanket were Johnny Parker and Paco.

"Diego, look!"

"I see them. Go on. I'll be right behind you."

"Diego . . ." She turned and looked at him. "I love you. With all my heart."

"And I you, *querida*."

After taking a deep breath, Leona closed her eyes and hurled herself toward the ground.

Epilogue

Moonlight spilled through the curtains, casting a gossamer weave of light and shadow across the bed. The *hoo, hoooo-hoo* of a great horned owl drifted on the night air.

Leona stirred in her sleep, then snuggled closer against Diego's side.

He smiled as he turned and kissed the top of her head. Contentment flowed through his body like warm honey. The night of their final confrontation with Rance McCabe seemed a lifetime ago rather than just a few days.

Thanks to Joseph McConnell, there was no danger of any charges being brought to bear against Leona or any of her men. McCabe's death had been ruled accidental. His body had been found in the ashes of his home, lying at the bottom of the stairs.

It was over now, and Diego and Leona could start building a life together. Not that it would be easy. He had lived long enough to know that life was never easy. But with Leona by his side, he knew he could tackle anything and win.

She stirred again. He stroked her arm, marveling at how soft her skin was to the touch. That there could be so much strength, so much spirit, so much passion in one so small continued to amaze him.

He supposed he should have been angry with her for going to McCabe's alone that night, but he was beginning to understand that he would never be able to keep Leona from doing what she felt was right or from doing what she thought she must. He supposed he would just have to learn to live with it.

Her hand slid across his chest, her fingers splayed. He thought at first that she had simply moved in her sleep. He thought so until her index finger drew a circle around his nipple. Then her head turned and lifted off his shoulder, allowing her to nibble the tender spot on his neck.

"Mmmm." The sound of contentment came from deep in his throat as he pulled her on top of him and stared up into her beautiful face. She was wearing a smile that was both seductive and mischievous, and he couldn't help smiling at her in return.

Joy, like a great symphony, rose to a crescendo in Leona's heart, exploding in a crash of cymbals.

To think she had been afraid to love him for fear he would make her less than she was. Instead, he had made her twice what she'd ever been.

"I love you, *mi corazón,*" she whispered.

She never tired of saying it.

"I love you, *mi pequeña leona,*" he replied.

She never tired of hearing it.

Her hair fell forward as she leaned down to kiss his lips, playing lightly across them with her own, teasing his tender flesh with the tip of her tongue.

He growled as his arms tightened. He moved so quickly, she scarcely knew how she'd come to be lying on her back, this time with him above her. She felt the hardness of his desire pressing against her, and her own passion flared, white hot and searing.

Some time later, they lay side by side, sated, their movements and voices languid.

"Remember the first time I saw you?" Diego asked, his breath warm upon her hair. "You nearly trampled me in my bedroll."

"Never. I saw you in plenty of time."

He laughed. "I opened my eyes to see Pesadilla's hooves over my head and a red cape flying in the wind."

"And I saw the most handsome man I had ever known. I was afraid I would never see you again."

"La Rosa . . ." He whispered the name. "She was an intriguing mystery to me."

"Do you know how jealous I was of your fascination with the *bandida*?"

"But it was you I loved, Leona. What made La Rosa fascinating is all a part of you." His arms tightened around her. "But that's all behind us now. With McCabe gone, there will be peace along the Salinas. We can build our own ranch and start our own family. There won't be any more need for you to carry a gun or a sword or to ride a black horse by night. There won't be any more reason for you to risk your life."

Diego trailed light kisses over her temple, the tip of her petite nose, her rosy lips, and her stubborn chin.

Peace. *Sí*, it would be good to live in peace with Leona. He would take her soon to meet his grandmother and the rest of his family, soon before the hours they spent making love left her with his child growing beneath her heart.

"We'll go to Texas before the end of summer," he said aloud, echoing a portion of his thoughts. "My grandmother will be very fond of you. The two of you are much alike, I think."

Peace. It would be good.

Leona sighed as she drew closer to him. "I'd like that. I'm eager to meet your family. But we can't go before Ricardo and Mercedes are married. That will be soon, I think. Then we can go to Texas." She yawned lazily, her voice growing weak. "Perhaps we should return by way of Los Angeles. My cousin has written to say that the *rancheros* there are in great trouble. He says the people talk of La Rosa. Perhaps . . ."

"*Caramba!*" he muttered—visions of peace evaporating—and silenced her with more kisses.

Author's Note

Dear Reader:

I remember watching those old Zorro films, hearing the swish of his sword as he left his mark, feeling the excitement of the chase as he raced his horse through the dead of night, and cheering as he outwitted the villains. I don't know if I would think so now, but at the time I thought Zorro was very handsome, and his accent was unbelievably sexy.

Then, of course, there was Robin Hood, taking from the rich to give to the poor. How many countless times did I watch Errol Flynn giving grief to the wicked Basil Rathbone and then later saving his beloved Olivia de Havilland from that slimy villain?

Ah, those adventures were grand, weren't they?

But when the idea for MIDNIGHT ROSE came to me, I knew I wanted it to be a woman who fought for the common people, and so the bandolera La Rosa was born. Thanks to her nine (!) brothers, Leona was well suited to take up the cause of justice as the masked bandida. However, finding the right man for her wasn't easy. I think Diego will do all right, don't you? I just hope he didn't have his heart too set on a life of peace and serenity.

I had a great time creating MIDNIGHT ROSE, both for myself and for you, my readers, and I hope our next adventure together is just as much fun. Coming in the spring of 1993, watch for my pirate novel, THE MAGIC.

Your letters are always welcome.

With fondest regards,

Robin Lee Hatcher
P.O. Box 4722
Boise, ID 83711–4722

GLOSSARY OF SPANISH WORDS AND PHRASES

abuela/abuelo	grandmother/grandfather
adiós	good-bye
amiga/amigo	friend
amor conquista todo	love conquers all
bandida/bandido	bandit/outlaw
bandolera/bandolero	bandit
buenas tardes	good afternoon
buenas noches	good night; good evening
buenos días	good morning; good day
caballos	horses
café con leche	white coffee; coffee with milk or cream
Caramba!	Well! Good grief!
casa	dwelling
cena	supper
corazón	heart
de nada	your welcome; it's nothing
dueña	chaperone
feliz cumpleaños	happy birthday
fiesta	festival, holiday, celebration
ganado	cattle
gatita	kitten
gracias	thank you
gracias a Dios	thank God
gringa/gringo	Anglo

Glossary

hacienda	a large estate; the main dwelling of a hacienda
hermana/hermano	sister/brother
hija/hijo	daughter/son
hombre	man
leona	lioness
Madre de Dios	Mother of God
mi	my
muchacha/muchacho	girl; maid/boy; young man; pal
niña	girl, child
nos vemos	I'll be seeing you
novia/novio	fiancée/fiancé
papá	daddy
pequeña	little
perdón	pardon
perdóneme	excuse me
pistola	gun; pistol
por favor	please
qué bien!	splendid!
querida/querido	love; dear; darling
rancho	ranch
reata	lariat; rope
señor	mister; Mr.
señora	lady; Mrs.
señorita	young lady; Miss
sí	yes
siéntese	sit down
tesoro	treasure
tía	aunt
un momento	a moment
Válgame Dios!	Good heavens!

Glossary

vaquera/vaquero	cowgirl/cowboy
Vaya con Dios	God Speed
Vive Dios!	By heaven!

WOMEN WEST

This sweeping saga of the American frontier, and the indomitable men and women who pushed ever westward in search of their dreams, follows the lives and destinies of the fiery Branigan family from 1865 to 1875.

Promised Sunrise by Robin Lee Hatcher. Together, Maggie Harris and Tucker Branigan face the hardships of the westward journey with a raw courage and passion for living that makes their unforgettable story a tribute to the human will and the power of love.
__3015-2 $4.50 US/$5.50 CAN

Promise Me Spring by Robin Lee Hatcher. From the moment he sets eyes on the beautiful and refined Rachel, Gavin Blake knows she will never make a frontier wife. But the warmth in her sky-blue eyes and the fire she sets in his blood soon convinces him that the new life he is struggling to build will be empty unless she is at his side.
__3160-4 $4.50 US/$5.50 CAN

LEISURE BOOKS
ATTN: Order Department
276 5th Avenue, New York, NY 10001

Please add $1.50 for shipping and handling for the first book and $.35 for each book thereafter. N.Y.S. and N.Y.C. residents, please add appropriate sales tax. No cash, stamps, or C.O.D.s. All orders shipped within 6 weeks via postal service book rate. Canadian orders require $2.00 extra postage. It must also be paid in U.S. dollars through a U.S. banking facility.

Name _____

Address _____

City _____•___ State _____ Zip _____

I have enclosed $_____in payment for the checked book(s).
Payment <u>must</u> accompany all orders.☐ Please send a free catalog.

DEVLIN'S PROMISE

WOMEN WEST

ROBIN LEE HATCHER

Winner of *Romantic Times*
Storyteller of the Year Award!

With a two-year-old son and no husband in sight, sultry Angelica is an object of scorn to the townspeople of her frontier home—and the target of Devlin Branigan's unabashed ardor. But Angelica needs more than a one-time lover. She needs a man who can give her respectability once she reaches her new homestead in Washington State. And after one earth-shattering kiss, Devlin is ready to prove he is all the man she'll ever desire.

__3272-4 $4.99 US/$5.99 CAN